Totally Bound Publishing books by Robin Gideon:

Ecstasy in Eden
Passion of Madeline

The Regency England
Satisfying Olympia

Wild West Passion
The Cheyenne Maiden
The Sioux Warrior

I0646147

Wild West Passion

THE SIOUX WARRIOR

ROBIN GIDEON

The Sioux Warrior
ISBN # 978-1-78430-127-9
©Copyright Robin Gideon 2014
Cover Art by Posh Gosh ©Copyright June 2014
Interior text design by Claire Siemaszkiewicz
Totally Bound Publishing

Published in 2014 by Totally Bound Publishing, Newland House, The Point, Weaver Road, Lincoln, LN6 3QN, United Kingdom.

THE SIOUX
WARRIOR

Dedication

This one is dedicated to Keith.

Chapter One

Amanda Wright looked at the three men, an overwhelming sense of relief sweeping over her. They were dead, thank God. They could no longer touch her, could no longer hurt her, could no longer force her to bend to their will.

The nightmare had lasted not much more than a minute. Amanda had been returning through the Badlands after looking at some prize horses her brother was considering buying, when three Indians had appeared out of nowhere. They'd said nothing when they'd blocked her path. Amanda had smiled, her internal warning signals not yet registering danger. Then the Indians had attacked, swiftly and silently, pulling her from her horse, tearing at her clothes — her familiar cotton man-cut shirt and new Levis. With the buttons of her shirt popping off when the men attacked, she'd fought and screamed, managing to kick one of her attackers in the groin so hard that he'd fallen to his knees and had abandoned his assault upon her.

But the other two hadn't. Grim-faced, as silent as death itself, they'd moved in relentlessly, separating Amanda from her horse, making sure she had no avenue of escape.

Suddenly her rescuers had ridden in, guns blazing. And though both cowboys had been badly in need of shaves, baths, and a clean change of clothes, they'd seemed heaven-sent to Amanda. They'd swiftly and surely cut her attackers down with a barrage of gunfire as deadly as it was quick.

"Thank y-you," Amanda stammered, getting to her feet. She pulled her shirt closed, covering her chemise, which had been badly torn during the assault.

If Amanda's warning signals had been slow initially, they intensified when her 'heroes' dismounted. The nearest one—the one who had wielded the shotgun with lethal efficiency and great pleasure against her Indian attackers—grinned wide to show stained, rotting, and missing teeth. He spat a long stream of tobacco juice onto the ground in the general direction of the corpses. Then, with his free hand, he rubbed his crotch as he walked slowly toward Amanda, his gaze devouring her as a wolf's gaze might devour a young fawn moments before he moved in for the kill.

"Killin' redskins is what I do second best in the whole world," the man said with a twisted glint in his eyes. "And 'cause I'm such a nice fella, I'm gonna show you what I do best."

Amanda stepped backward, nearly stumbling. Judging from the filthy appearance of these two white men, they were even worse than the men who had attacked her.

"D-don't do this," Amanda said, the breathy rush of words little more than a whisper. She hated the weakness her voice betrayed.

The man chuckled then spat another stream of tobacco juice onto the ground. "You're not being very social, 'specially after what me an' my partner here jus' saved you from."

Amanda turned her attention away from the leader. The other man grinned, hungrily assessing her as he moved to the side. All Amanda had to do was look into the man's eyes to know that he would obey any orders given to him. Amanda would find no sympathy in his heart.

"Make it easy on yerself," the leader said, slowly walking forward, still fondling himself. "It ain't a matter of *if* we're gonna do it, only on how mad you make me 'fore we start."

The sound of pounding hooves made all three turn to see a tall, lean Indian riding through the trees into the clearing. The Indian leaped from his horse at a gallop, lunging for the man closest to Amanda, moving with astonishing speed and precision, not giving the man time to raise his shotgun. Together they went spinning and tumbling to the ground.

The Indian reacted like an agile, powerful mountain lion. After knocking the white man to the ground he moved quickly to his knees. Amanda trembled, awestruck, as the Indian drew a revolver from the holster at his hip and fired with speed and deadly accuracy.

The shotgun-wielding white man, the first to demand Amanda's sexual favors, had recovered and was raising his weapon to cut the Indian down.

"Look out!" Amanda shouted, lunging at the shotgun and knocking it aside a second before it roared with a lethal charge of buckshot.

Amanda fell face down onto the grass at the crack of a firearm a moment after the shotgun blast. She heard the startled gasp of the white man but felt no sympathy for him at all as she saw him fall heavily to the ground.

"Was it just those two?" the Indian asked, the revolver still in his big right hand.

Amanda got quickly to her feet, clutching at her shirt to pull it even more tightly around her. She stared at the Indian suspiciously, unwilling to trust any man after what had happened to her during the past ten minutes.

"Was it just those two?" the Indian asked again, a hint of anger in his tone. He was obviously concerned that the danger was not over. He glanced first at the two white men whom he'd killed, then at the three Indians they'd shot. Finally, he holstered his weapon and approached Amanda slowly, his hands out in front of him, his palms pointed upward, as though to show he would not harm her. "It's over now. There's nothing more to fear."

Amanda backed away from the man. She would not trust him. She had trusted too many men already, and it had very nearly gotten her raped. She refused to trust this one, even if there was compassion and sympathy in his dark eyes instead of lust and savagery.

"Don't come any closer," Amanda said, biting the words off sharply, sounding considerably more forceful and in control of herself and her emotions than she really felt.

"I won't hurt you," the tall Indian said, the timbre of his voice resonating with Amanda's need to trust him. "I promise, I won't hurt you. And these men can't hurt you anymore."

Ten feet separated them. Amanda gazed straight into his eyes and he did not look away, as she'd expected him to. Her surprise made her remember that the eyes were the windows to the soul, and that a liar instinctively knew this. If he was lying to her, telling her the words she wanted to hear just so she would let down her guard, she would see the mendacity reflected in his eyes. But he wasn't trying to hide anything at all...or did it just seem that way?

"My name is Hawk Two Feather," he said. When he gave her a half smile, a dimple formed in his gaunt cheek. "I'm telling you the truth. I'm not going to hurt you."

Amanda was momentarily suspicious. "You speak English very well."

"And you'll hold that against me?" Hawk replied, cocking a brow over eyes that feigned offense.

"No, I guess not. My name's Amanda."

"Amanda?"

Instantly, all her protective walls went up once more, and she took a step away from Hawk. She wouldn't give her last name.

"Just Amanda," she said quietly.

For several seconds they stood there, eyeing each other, passing silent questions back and forth. Still, Amanda didn't speak. The Wright name was well known throughout the territory, and the Circle S horse ranch was famous for the quality of its riding stock. She did not want to tempt Hawk with the possibility of getting a ransom for her safe return. So far, he'd shown himself to be a gentleman, but she'd assumed the two grizzled men who'd killed her original attackers to be honorable men, too.

"Where are you from?" Amanda asked, breaking the silence with a question.

Hawk gave her the first truly honest smile. "I'm a Sioux," he said. "I was hunting elk near the creek fork and I heard your screams."

Amanda tucked her chemise into her Levis, then pulled her shirt tighter and tucked that in too. It was difficult maintaining modesty when the chemise had been rent in half, and all the buttons from her shirt were missing. Even though she was suitably covered, there was something in Hawk's eyes that made her feel just a little bit exposed, almost as though her breasts were naked to his gaze. But strangely, he wasn't leering at her, nor ogling her like the men who had attacked her. He was just watching her, nothing more than that, and yet there was an intensity to his dark, fathomless gaze that touched Amanda and made tiny shivers run up her spine.

As Hawk inspected the area where the fighting had occurred and paid a second look at the corpses that moments earlier had been would-be rapists, Amanda was given the chance to gaze at the enigmatic man more closely. He was tall, particularly for a Sioux, standing at least an inch or two over six feet. His shoulders were broad, swathed in a leather shirt that laced in the front. His waist narrowed nicely, and he had lean hips. His thighs were thickly muscled, telling Amanda that he was a man who'd spent his life on horseback, though she'd already guessed as much, having been witness to his riding skill.

"Are you going to bury them?" Amanda asked, though she didn't care if these contemptible men received a burial, or not.

"We'd better not take the time," Hawk replied, having finished his inspection. "This is Cheyenne territory. Or maybe it's Crow. Either way, I'm not welcome here, and neither will you be. We'd better just get our horses and…"

His expression went blank, as though he was listening to some mysterious voice in his head. Then, several seconds after Hawk had heard the approaching riders, Amanda did too.

"Come on," Hawk said, reaching out his hand for Amanda as he rushed toward her.

Amanda hesitated for only a moment before taking Hawk's hand. Hearing the approaching riders, she decided there was absolutely no telling whether the newcomers would be a greater or lesser threat to her than Hawk himself. Amanda had already been 'rescued' once, only to find herself needing to be saved from her rescuers.

Hawk's fingers were long and callused, Amanda noticed when she placed her small, pale hand in his much darker one. Yanking her hand, he took off like a shot, half-dragging her through the trees behind him. In the hilly, wooded area, Hawk moved with the instinctive grace of a natural-born hunter and, in just a few seconds, the forest had swallowed them up.

"Where are we going?" Amanda asked, almost breathless. Keeping up the pace Hawk had set had been difficult, especially since he was pulling her left arm and she was using her right hand to hold her shirt closed.

"Quiet!" Hawk snapped, looking over his shoulder at Amanda for just an instant.

As they ran in a wide circle, Amanda quickly discovered what the Sioux warrior had in mind. They again approached the clearing, only this time coming upon it from a different direction. Amanda was gasping from the exertion of the run, Hawk was hardly breathing faster than he had been when he'd first started running. Though she'd always considered herself physically fit, Amanda was nowhere near the athlete Hawk was.

He still held her hand as he crouched down on the balls of his moccasin-shod feet. Twisting, he faced Amanda and put a finger to his lips, indicating silence.

Who are we running from?

Behind a thick bush that concealed their presence, they looked at the clearing from a southerly angle. Amanda wanted to pull her hand from Hawk's grasp, but when she tugged he only tightened his fingers around hers. Studying his profile up close, Amanda was startled by the starkness of his features. His cheekbones were high and clearly defined, and his cheeks were slightly hollowed, in keeping with the gauntness of his physique. His hair was black, pushed away from his forehead to sweep almost straight back and coming down over the neck of his buckskin shirt. His nose was prominent and hawkish, rather slender, and his eyes moderately deep-set. He was, even upon close inspection, a strikingly handsome man.

Don't start thinking that way! This man has just killed two men in the blink of an eye.

Three riders approached the clearing, moving cautiously, speaking in a language she did not understand. They were Indians, though Amanda had no idea from which tribe. It was clear that they weren't Sioux—at least not from the band that Hawk belonged to—and they weren't from the same tribe as the three men who had originally attacked her, since they didn't show the slightest remorse over the deaths.

Amanda's heart beat faster. She'd already been witness to more violence and bloodshed than she cared to remember, and she didn't want to see any more.

She tugged at Hawk, wanting to draw his attention away from the clearing so that she could whisper to him. But, his attention fixed, he refused to look away. More forcefully, Amanda pulled at Hawk's hand, and when he turned the full force of his deep brown gaze upon her, she knew instantly that he was not pleased that she had broken his concentration.

"I don't want—" she began, only to be silenced by Hawk's broad palm over her mouth.

Angry, Amanda twisted her face, trying to get the hand off her mouth. Hawk pulled her against him, his strength like a steel band around her. Her struggling stopped, Amanda found herself eye-to-eye with Hawk, their foreheads nearly touching, his hand still clamped tightly over her mouth.

"Are you trying to get both of us killed?" he whispered, his dark gaze cutting into Amanda. "There are a dozen men out there who'd love to cut my throat. And what they'd do to you *before* they cut your throat is something you don't want to think about."

His arm loosened around her and his hand softened its grip over her mouth. Tentatively, Amanda looked into the clearing again. This time, after searching for the men she'd been told were there, she found them. A dozen or so were combing the brush on the far side of the clearing, apparently following the tracks left by the horses who'd run off in panic.

"Come on," Hawk said, backing away from the clearing.

For the first time Amanda experienced a fear that truly terrified her. When the three Indians had first attacked her, everything had happened so swiftly that she was hardly aware, even, of their intention. And when the unwashed white men had arrived on the scene, they, like the Indians, had attacked without provocation. Again, there hadn't been time to think or feel honest fear.

But now there was time, and she knew what it was she dreaded, knew the beast that lurked in the shadows of her consciousness. As she ran alongside Hawk, she prayed for the strength and stamina to keep up with him. She cursed her riding boots, perfect for stirrups but terrible for running. Hawk, with his long legs and his moccasins, ran with effortless ease. Amanda could see that he was not the cold, invincible warrior she had first thought him to be. He wanted no fight with a dozen enemies if he could avoid it. This realization surprised Amanda, and in some ways she rather appreciated knowing that Hawk was not immune to fear.

They ran for nearly a half-mile without stopping. Spotting a game trail that led through the woods, Hawk stopped to peer closely at the gasping Amanda.

"I'm sorry this happened to you," Hawk said quietly, as Amanda caught her breath. They were both leaning against the same tree at the edge of the game trail. "This shouldn't happen to anyone. I don't know exactly what happened back there in the clearing, but I can guess much of it from the signs and…"

She caught him looking at her exposed bosom, and he turned away quickly, guiltily, his lips pursing into a thin line of self-anger.

Amanda noticed all, however, even Hawk's anger at himself. She was pleased to discover that he was a man of desire and passion, like other men, but one who *governed* his passion, controlling it and himself. She now knew he was a man with high expectations of himself, apparently taking advantage of a young woman who'd already had a horrifying experience with men was not what he considered acceptable behavior.

In the distance to the south Amanda heard an Indian brave shouting in victory. In that direction lay a grassy valley, but it was also the direction in which the danger would be the greatest. Amanda peered at Hawk questioningly.

"We might as well," Amanda said after a moment. How eerie it was that she and Hawk could communicate so well without words! How could this be, when they came from two entirely different worlds and knew almost nothing about each other?

"Yes, we might as well," Hawk responded after a long, doubting pause.

Cautiously, Amanda moved to the edge of the tree line, to the point where the upper rim of the valley began. Looking down into the valley, she saw two braves doing a victory dance around the stallion Hawk had ridden into the clearing. Hawk cursed under his breath in a language that Amanda did not understand, with an unmistakably obscene and angry meaning.

"Now they know who they're after," Hawk whispered, shaking his head.

Amanda looked at him, wishing he wasn't so handsome. In her society, Hawk would never be considered one of *us*, only one of *them*, and that meant that if Amanda was to follow propriety, she would never think of Hawk as handsome. She'd never before wondered what it would be like to be kissed by one of *them*.

Hawk, no longer holding her hand, began to move away from the edge of the valley, once again heading deeper into the cover of the trees. When she did not immediately follow him he stopped, his dark eyes expressing annoyance, though only part of his ill-humor was directed at her.

"How will they know they're following you?" Amanda asked, pulling once again at her blouse to close it tightly around her, then tucking the tails into her Levis.

"From the markings on my horse. Every Sioux paints his own marking on the rump of his horse. It's as distinctive to the various tribes as the brand is to the white man."

"Are you somebody I should know?" Amanda asked, at last moving in step with Hawk.

He remained silent for several seconds. He finally replied, "The Sioux and the Cheyenne have been fighting for many years. The little wars go back generations. The Cheyenne warrior who kills me will gain favor with his tribe."

Amanda was shocked. How could anyone live with the knowledge that his death would bring status to the person who killed him? A little voice inside her warned her that she would be safer if she wasn't with Hawk, but what could she do? She was on foot, unarmed, and pursued by an enemy of at least a dozen men she knew nothing about. She needed someone to help her if she was to survive, and that someone had appeared in the form of Hawk Two Feather.

"You've done something to the Cheyenne, haven't you?" Amanda accused without meaning to.

Hawk glanced sideways at Amanda. A grin, at once boyish and devilish, pulled at the right side of his mouth, prompting the re-emergence of his dimple. He reached out to tuck a lock of hair behind Amanda's ear. Looking at him then, she would have sworn he was a young man in his teens who'd been caught being naughty.

"Let's just say that whenever there's a raid being organized by the Sioux to steal Cheyenne horses, it's safe to assume I'll be there."

"You're a horse thief?" Amanda exclaimed.

Hawk's smile broadened, his dazzling, straight white teeth on display. "The Cheyenne would call me a horse thief, the Sioux call me a warrior. Viewpoint, as you can see, is everything. Among the Sioux and the Cheyenne, stealing horses from each other's tribe is a rite of passage, something that must be done if a young man is to be considered a true warrior."

Amanda shook her head. She didn't understand the logic, but then, there was much about the Sioux that she found absolutely unfathomable. She was certain that she was in a great deal of danger, and that at least a dozen men were chasing her and the man she was with.

"Let's go," Hawk said, reaching out once again for Amanda's hand. "They're not going to give up easily."

Amanda cautiously placed her hand in Hawk's and muttered, "I know I'm going to regret this."

Chapter Two

"Do... Do you...?" Amanda gasped, finding speaking almost as impossible as breathing.

Hawk, his hands on his hips, looked at her. He, too, was breathing harder, though not nearly as hard as her.

"Catch your breath first, then ask me," Hawk suggested, placing his large hand comfortingly, upon Amanda's shoulder. "I'll keep an eye out behind us."

Amanda nodded. Bent over, her hands on her knees, she gulped in air. Seeing that Hawk was going to allow her a minute or two to rest, she crouched, then lay flat upon the ground on her back, her arms stretched high above her head.

How much time had passed since she'd first set eyes on Hawk? How many miles had she run since the Cheyenne had found Hawk's horse, as well as her own? Many times during her life Amanda had been forced to reach deep into her inner reserves of strength to face a challenge, but she could never remember needing to physically push herself so hard for so long.

She looked at the Dakota sky. It was a beautiful day, with thick white clouds drifting lazily by. A beautiful day for a picnic, or in which to train a new horse, or maybe even get into a race with her brother around the homestead. A perfect day for almost anything other than running for her life while relying on an Indian brave who spoke flawless English and provoked many more questions than he supplied answers.

Amanda closed her eyes and forced herself to calm her breathing. Every second counted, she knew, so it was critical that she regain as much strength and stamina as possible in what little time was allotted to her by Hawk.

Not far away, Hawk was down on one knee, studying the trail they'd been following for the past hour. He knew the Cheyenne were back there somewhere. Twice he'd lost them, using tricks he'd learned during his wars with the enemy of his people, but his evasive tactics couldn't succeed in completely stopping his enemies, only in fooling them momentarily. They were at least an hour behind, he figured, maybe even more than that. But they were still following. Like himself, they were tenacious.

Every time Hawk thought about his stallion being ridden by a Cheyenne warrior he gritted his teeth in rage. The value of a good horse to the Sioux was almost incalculable, and Hawk had trained that particular stallion from a colt. When he returned to his tribe, the elders would ask him what had happened to the stallion, and Hawk would have to tell the truth. He could already hear the laughter the other braves would try to hide. And some would *not* try to hide their derision. Hawk had been born a bastard, and there were those who would never let him forget it.

Hawk knew that he was not liked by the entire tribe. His mother's white blood flowed in his veins, and there were those among the Sioux who felt he could not be trusted because of it. Also, some braves resented Hawk's considerable charm with the women. More often than not, the women had thrown themselves at him and, though he tried to be temperate in his life where women were concerned, Hawk was a man with a prodigious sexual appetite that occasionally bordered on the unquenchable, even the insatiable.

Satisfied that the Cheyenne would not be upon them in the immediate future, Hawk turned away from the trail to see how Amanda was faring. He took one step toward her then froze in his tracks.

On her back with her arms flat on the ground above her head, Amanda was a vision of beauty. Since the attack, she had been struggling to maintain her modesty, fighting with her now buttonless cotton shirt and a chemise that had been torn very nearly in half. So far, Hawk had tried to keep his eyes averted, and to some extent, he had succeeded. But from this angle, with Amanda breathing deeply and slowly, he was given a stunning view of her cleavage, of pale skin that glistened with fresh perspiration, of firm flesh that was smooth and white and absolutely forbidden to him.

For an instant Hawk wondered whether Amanda had intentionally positioned herself to have just this effect on him. He immediately dismissed the notion. She was too frightened and exhausted to have seduction on her mind. Besides, something about her suggested that, though her life had been spent with men, her sexual experience with them was limited—if she had any experience at all.

"We'd better keep a move on, if you can," Hawk said quietly, his gaze gently caressing the inner swells of her undulating bosom. He needed to be on the run again if he was to get his mind off Amanda, and away from the attraction—the *forbidden* attraction—that she represented.

"Yes, of course," Amanda sighed.

He watched as she rolled over, curling her knees beneath her. He witnessed the heavy sway of her breasts when she moved, though her seductive display, he now believed, was completely accidental. No woman could appear *that* innocently seductive without being truly innocent. He looked away as she again pulled the shirt tightly around herself, causing the tails to overlap at her stomach as she tucked them into the waistband.

"Can you keep going?" Hawk asked, moving closer.

Amanda was sitting on the backs of her heels, still kneeling on the ground. Tendrils of honey blonde hair curled softly against her cheeks, having come loose from the ribbon. As Hawk extended a hand to help her to her feet, he tried to tell himself that she really wasn't as beautiful as she appeared, that her allure was as much powered by the fact that he had spent days searching for game, away from his tribe and consequently had been celibate for over a fortnight. Naturally, his separation from the tribe, and his quiet and discreet lovers, would account for Amanda's intoxicating beauty, he tried to tell himself.

I don't even come close to believing that, Hawk realized as he pulled Amanda to her feet.

"You don't have to worry about me," Amanda replied, sweeping grass from her knees. "I'm tougher than I look. Just ask my brother, if you don't believe me."

"When I get you home, perhaps I will," Hawk said, a smile again tickling his mouth.

Amanda straightened suddenly, looking up into Hawk's dark eyes. "Do you mean it?" she asked in a hushed whisper. "Will you really take me home?"

"Yes," he said. Hawk was pleased to see happiness shine in Amanda's blue eyes. Then, as the reality of the situation insinuated itself into his thoughts, he added, "Just as soon as I can."

He turned away, pretending to check the trail they had followed, though it was just that he couldn't bear to look into her eyes a moment longer. She trusted him in a way that made Hawk uncomfortable. Typically, women trusted him not to hurt them, they trusted him to be discreet about the passion they shared with him, they trusted him to see that they were satisfied in every way possible, but they did not see him as a man who could right whatever wrongs life had thrust upon them—and that was the way Amanda peered at him now.

"Come on," Hawk said. "We can talk more about getting you home as soon as we're sure you're not going to be the main reason for a Cheyenne victory dance."

* * * *

The water was cool and clean and felt exquisite to Amanda—just the elixir for rejuvenating her aching body. She glanced once more at Hawk, who was kneeling some distance away with his back to her. He had not once turned toward her, and for that she was thankful.

Her opinion of Hawk had gone from one extreme to the other, but now had settled somewhere in between. She had at first seen him as a devil, then as an angel. Now he was a man. Just a man. But, oh! What a man! His word, it seemed, was a contract that he did not violate, and that was something that she could not say with absolute certainty about any other man.

She had made him promise he would not try to look at her while she bathed in the cool artesian pond that bubbled up naturally from the ground. As she stripped out of her shirt and chemise, she kept her eyes upon him, expecting to catch him going back on his word. But he never did. Not once. Not during the entire time that she had been completely naked less than thirty feet from him.

But he did like her appearance, Amanda knew, because she'd seen the way he tried to keep his eyes from her bosom and couldn't. That was enough to let her know she was not without physical charms.

She thought of all the boys with whom she had danced at weddings and other celebrations, and how they had ogled her and how tightly they'd held her while they'd danced. Amanda had been disdainful of their interest in her, scornful of their boyish desires for her. To her, they were just boys — occasionally pleasant companions but nothing more than that.

She had yet to reconcile herself to what her feelings were at Hawk's interest, but she *did* know that she felt differently about him than she had about any other man ever to enter her life. The fact that he was an Indian didn't make this fact any easier to accept.

Sinking into the pool to rinse herself again, she considered his background. Though not as brown as most Indians she'd seen, he was certainly too dark to be considered a white man. He was, she realized, a mixture of the two races.

Would a Sioux brave kiss the same way as a cultured white man?

The thought brought a smile to Amanda's lips, immediately followed by a self-deprecating frown. That was *not* a line of thinking appropriate for a well-bred young woman, especially not when she was completely naked in the company of the man whose kisses she was pondering.

She rose uncertainly out of the pool, her eyes never leaving Hawk, expecting his gentlemanly behavior to end any second. It didn't. She was able to shake the water from her legs, then shimmy into her drawers. Within seconds she had her trousers on. Her chemise, torn as it was, was useless. After a moment of contemplation she used the remains of the undergarment to dry herself, then tossed it aside. She put her shirt on, pulling it tightly around herself, then tucked the tails into her trousers again, feeling vaguely scandalous for not wearing anything underneath. Still, she had no choice in the matter and should therefore be blameless.

"I'm done," Amanda said, sitting on the ground to pull on her thick white cotton stockings. "You can turn around now."

Hawk turned slowly, his expression unreadable, his eyes veiled. He would not let whatever pleasure he received in seeing Amanda show in his eyes.

Amanda felt refreshed and considerably more confident now that she had bathed in the cool pond. Even though her shirt was still damp from a wash and clinging to her skin, it was at least clean. For that she was grateful. She would no longer take clean clothes for granted.

"Now what?" Amanda asked, holding her boots in one hand as Hawk approached her. "Do we keep moving on?"

"It's going to get dark soon." Hawk came over and sat on the ground beside Amanda. His gaze looked distant, unfocused, Amanda decided. She waited for him to say more, not wanting to disturb his thoughts. "The Cheyenne will be making camp as well." Hawk nibbled on his lower lip for a moment. This unconscious gesture drew Amanda's attention to his mouth. She wished it hadn't. It looked to be a thoroughly kissable mouth. In fact, the most kissable mouth she'd ever seen. "That was a good stallion. He had the heart of a true warrior."

Amanda could sympathize with his loss. She'd been around high-quality horses her entire life. "What was his name?"

"Didn't have a name," Hawk said quietly, pulling absent-mindedly at the grass near his moccasins. "The Sioux don't give their horses names. Just respect."

Amanda thought about the way she'd seen horses treated by so-called civilized white men then replied, "More often than not, the opposite is the case where I come from." She watched as Hawk nibbled on his lip, and an idea came to her. At first she struggled against it, not wanting to put it into words, but finally she had to set the thought free. "If you didn't have me with you, what course of action would you take?"

Hawk grinned then, glancing at Amanda. For a moment he said nothing, just smiled with that devilish twinkle in his eyes. Then he shook his head and made a passing motion with his hand, as though to dismiss the question without comment.

"Please, I want to know," Amanda prodded. She placed her hand lightly on his arm. Even through the soft buckskin of his shirt she could feel that his biceps was as solid as iron. "Be honest with me."

"If I didn't have to worry about you, I'd be working to double back on the Cheyenne. That stallion's too valuable to walk away from so easily."

Amanda was visibly shocked. "You mean you'd attack them, even though they outnumber you?"

"Of course I would. They're the enemy. They've stolen my horse — and yours as well, I might add. Why shouldn't I try to take back what is rightly mine? Besides, they'd never expect me to do that, which is what would probably enable me to succeed."

"You are a bold man, Mr Hawk Two Feather," Amanda said softly, shaking her head in amazement.

He grinned. Amanda was just barely able to keep from asking him how he had learned to speak English so well. Several hours earlier she had alluded to his grasp of the language and she hadn't gotten another word out of him for a long time. Though asking personal questions was a mistake she didn't want to repeat, her curiosity was burning.

"It would be foolish of me to try it now, though. I will wait until later, then I will go on the attack again, and take back what is mine." He ran his fingers through his shoulder-length ebony hair. "You will find that we Sioux are a very patient people...with very long memories. We don't forget what is ours, or who our enemies are."

Amanda shook her head, as though fighting against ideas too forceful to be denied. "Let's do it," she heard herself say. The words tumbled from her lips. "Let's steal our horses back. They'd never expect it from us. You said so yourself."

"Not with you," Hawk replied, the smile fading from his lips. "It would be too dangerous."

"No, it wouldn't!" Amanda continued, rising swiftly to her feet. "We could do it. I know we could. And you don't have to worry about me. I've been playing these sorts of games with my brother my whole life. I've kept up with you today, haven't I?"

Hawk watched her moving, pacing nervously like a young colt. The scissoring motion of her legs as she walked, and the way the Levis molded to her behind. Her legs were strong, and she was nimble on her feet. He'd been witness to that many times during their flight from the Cheyenne. When she turned to pace past him again, the rise and fall of her full breasts beneath the cotton shirt drew his attention. With the tattered chemise gone now, her breasts moved even more freely, and their swaying motion brought an immediate and entirely unwelcome awakening in Hawk's lower regions. His body, always ready for feminine adventure, began to respond to Amanda.

"The difference is that when this particular game is over men will probably be dead," Hawk said in an icy voice, trying to turn his thoughts away from the direction they were headed. This was not, he reminded himself, the time to let his balls do his thinking for him.

Besides, he'd fought too many battles, been in too many full-on fights and skirmishes, to have any romantic notion of warfare.

His words brought Amanda to a standstill.

"You're right, of course," she said softly, "but I still think it's what we should do. How long do you think we can elude them? They're on horseback — *our* horses, as frustrating as that is to admit — and we're on foot."

Hawk had to turn away from Amanda. Her frantic pacing had caused her shirt to open again, showing the inner swells of her pale, extravagant breasts. The vitality and energy she exuded forced Hawk to wonder if she would be as energetic on a warrior's buffalo mat. Thinking such thoughts heightened his anger even further, and added to the length and thickness of the growing erection he had trapped inside his buckskins. He began doing mental calculations of how far from his tribe's encampment they currently were, and how long it would take him to return on horseback. He didn't like the answers he came to.

"Where do you live?" he asked.

"I live on a ranch outside of Deadwood."

Hawk's reply was softly spoken. "You're a long way from home," he said, with a trace of annoyance. Her presence in his life wasn't something he had been counting on. Her presence in it now wasn't something he was happy about. "What do your parents think of a girl traveling so far from home all alone?"

Amanda shot Hawk an angry glare. "My parents are dead. And before you make any snide comments about my brother and sister not raising me right, let me put that thought completely out of your head. I'll have you know that I was raised to be independent, to be able to look after myself."

She would have liked to explain to Hawk that her family counted on her judgment of horseflesh, which was the reason she was so far from home. Amanda indisputably had the best eye for foals of any of the Wright children, a skill she'd developed from a very early age, and her siblings knew it.

"And I'm a woman, not a girl, I'll have you know," she concluded, immediately wishing she hadn't finished her diatribe against Hawk that way. It was difficult enough being taken seriously without sounding petty and childish.

With sarcasm not even thinly disguised, Hawk replied, "I would not dream of impugning your family name in any way...even if I knew what it was."

Amanda tried to keep a smile from her face but just couldn't. Not while observing Hawk's battle to keep from smiling, too. All right, she had to admit that she'd been less than forthcoming with a man who'd put himself in considerable jeopardy to help her.

"My name is Amanda Anne, and I absolutely hate being called a girl," she said, putting her hands on her hips, conveniently omitting her last name.

Unfortunately, the movement of her arms caused her shirt to open another inch. Luckily, Hawk turned his gaze away in time, hiding his unruly thoughts of her, trying to ignore his very nearly thoroughly awakened cock. She was most enticing when she wasn't trying to be in the least bit erotic, Hawk was learning.

With his back to her, he thought about the options he could take. Deadwood was days away. His own encampment was a full day away, maybe more...and all in terms of travel on horseback. On foot it would take twice the time, especially if the Cheyenne continued to follow them. Avoiding them would take time.

"Do you think you're up to it?" Hawk asked.

Amanda dropped down to her knees beside Hawk, her light blue eyes shimmering brilliantly. The sudden move caused her heavy, round breasts to sway and tremble. A smile played on her moist, glistening lips that made Hawk want to taste them. Though her shirt had opened with her movements, she was oblivious to it, and Hawk kept his eyes trained upon her face, though his cock throbbed with hunger.

"I've trusted you, now you've got to trust me," Amanda said, confidence ringing in every word she spoke.

* * * *

The moon was a crescent overhead, so eerily close that Amanda believed she could reach out and touch it. She stood with her back against a tree that had died from a lightning strike years earlier. Only a twisted, charred trunk remained, its silhouette distinctive on the midnight horizon.

Hawk had been gone for at least an hour. Amanda tried to remind herself that he'd warned her it might take that long, or even longer, for him to gather the information he needed. While alone, Amanda took time to truly ponder the events that the day had brought her. Oddly, no matter how she looked at it, she couldn't tell if it was the most exciting day of her life or the most hideous one. The attack still made her shiver whenever she thought about it. Amanda had no doubt at all that it would be a long, long time before the nightmares would stop altogether.

But there was Hawk to consider. He had behaved as a cultured gentleman of honor, even if he did wear buckskin trousers and shirt. Not only had he treated her with every possible respect, but when she'd wanted to be a part of the two-person raiding party to steal back their horses, he eventually had relented. Though it was clear he didn't think much of a woman participating in such matters, Amanda considered it a good sign that he was capable of changing his mind, of listening to reason.

"It's me."

The voice made Amanda jump, her heart racing. Hawk slipped out of the shadows, moving as silently as his namesake. Amanda at last saw his tall, broad-shouldered silhouette as she slumped against the tree trunk, a hand over her heart.

"You about scared the very life out of me."

"Sorry. I didn't mean to."

Amanda watched as he approached, stepping with his typical long-legged, athletic gait. There was no trepidation in his step despite the darkness.

"My heart's pounding," Amanda said, giving Hawk a cross look as he moved even closer. "I can hardly catch my breath."

His stark facial features became even more pronounced in the moonlight. He was, she decided then, much more beautiful than he had any right to be.

Hawk stood close, raising his hands to rest lightly on Amanda's shoulders. "Scaring a beautiful woman seems an entirely inappropriate way of making her heart race and leaving her breathless."

At that very moment, looking up into Hawk's face, Amanda couldn't say whether her heart was racing, or if it had stopped altogether. All she knew was that in her life she had been kissed four times by two different men—or boys, more precisely. In each instance, Amanda had found the first kiss distasteful, but had been willing to receive a second, in hopes that somehow the second wouldn't be as bad as the first. But, after two bad kisses, she'd decided that men, kissing, and everything else kissing led up to, simply weren't worth the effort.

Hawk raised his right hand to lightly cup Amanda's face in his huge palm. Tenderly, he passed the pad of his thumb back and forth over her lips.

"Have you ever been…breathless before, Amanda?" Hawk asked, his eyes dark as midnight, shiny as diamonds boring into hers. "I'm inclined to think not, though I couldn't really say with any certainty. At least, not until I've kissed you. Then I'd know if you've ever been breathless."

As he began to bend down, his face coming closer and closer to Amanda's, he asked, "Are your lips really as delicious as they look?"

Chapter Three

Amanda, watching his face coming closer, moved away, feeling herself spinning from between the tree trunk and Hawk. Unconsciously moistening her lips in preparation warned her that she was about to make a mistake. Hadn't her better judgment warned her from the very beginning that Hawk was a dangerous man, and that she would regret following him?

"W-what did you find out?" Amanda asked, continuing to retreat from Hawk.

Her heart hammered against her ribs, and when she tried to smooth the tangle of her hair into place she noticed that her hands were shaking. Was this the kind of reaction from her that Hawk had wanted? To her irritation, Hawk appeared composed and not at all angry that she'd successfully avoided his kiss.

She wanted to be angry with him for wanting to kiss her, but how could she be angry when she'd *wanted* him to kiss her—and still wanted him to? For reasons even she herself did not fully understand, she could not let herself enjoy the pleasure that his lips promised.

"The Cheyenne are closer to us than I'd thought," Hawk continued, his face devoid of expression.

Amanda still had no clue how he felt about the fact that she had eluded his kiss.

Hawk continued, "I found the place where they made camp. It's not really that far from here."

Amanda was brought back to reality. "Did you see the horses? Do they have Daisy?"

"Daisy? You named your horse Daisy?" Hawk smiled.

"Why not? It's a perfectly fine name."

"Daisy is the name of a flower."

"And Hawk is the name of a bird."

Hawk studied Amanda for a moment, then his grin spread across his face. "Touché," he said.

"Where did you learn to speak like that?"

The words were out of Amanda's mouth before she had thought them through. When she heard them she winced, not wanting Hawk to freeze up on her again. He looked straight at her, clearly weighing the importance of her question, then shrugged his broad shoulders.

"From many places, I suppose. I didn't want to be at any of them, but then, nobody was asking what I wanted."

"You've learned well," Amanda said, aware that she had been given a glimpse into Hawk that he usually kept hidden.

"I've learned many things," Hawk replied, his gaze once more taking on a distant quality. "Some of them a man is better off not knowing, some things a man must know if he is to be any kind of man at all. Either way, I've learned many, many lessons in my life, Amanda, and I've learned most of them the hard way." His gaze quite suddenly became as sharp and precise as the blade of a straight razor as he said, "If we're going to get our horses back, we'll need to hurry. I've got a plan, but the only way it will work is if you help me."

His abrupt switch from man of seduction to deadly warrior left Amanda feeling disoriented.

* * * *

The more Hawk thought about it, the more amazed he was that he was allowing Amanda to go with him on the Cheyenne raid. This lack of solid judgment on his part, he decided, was simply due to lust, infuriating lust. Amanda, the beautiful young woman who'd tempted him, had successfully avoided his kiss. It was for this reason, he tried to tell himself, that he had allowed her to come with him.

For a man who'd prided himself on clear thinking under all circumstances, taking Amanda on the raid was damning proof that he wasn't immune to stupidity. He'd counted thirteen Cheyenne in the raiding party. That was as many as Hawk had seen moving about the camp, anyway. Their defenses were up. They were alert for danger. They had camped in a copse of trees in a hilly area, keeping themselves well hidden, and this rather surprised Hawk.

Were these men renegades? That could be a reason they were behaving so cautiously. They wouldn't be the first group of young warriors who had decided to split off from their tribe and try their luck on their own.

Renegades, Hawk knew, were always dangerous. They tended to make raids on the white man's wealth. And the white man, rather than blaming the individual Indian or Indians responsible for thefts or murders, invariably blamed all Indians. Many people suffered because of events set into motion by renegades.

"What's wrong?" Amanda asked, kneeling beside Hawk in the darkness.

Together they'd been watching the activity near the campfire in the distance. She placed her fingertips lightly on his shoulder.

Hawk temporarily ignored Amanda's question. Now he understood his original plan for stealing the horses would not work. The Cheyenne were not as content with their victory as he had at first thought. It wouldn't work to have him divert their attention while Amanda stole the horses.

"Tell me," Amanda prodded, whispering just a little louder. Her fingers kneaded the solid muscles of Hawk's shoulder. Hawk wondered whether or not she was aware of touching him more often.

Hawk shook his head. He was angry that the Cheyenne were too alert for him to retrieve his prized stallion, angry that Amanda had gone with him on the raid, angry that the only way he could prevent Amanda from being on the raid with him was to break his word, something no true Sioux warrior would ever do lightly.

He looked at her. In the thin moonlight filtering through the trees, she was almost supernaturally beautiful. The shimmering luxury of her blonde hair, still pulled back and tied loosely at the back of her neck with a ribbon, reflected a golden hue. Her lips, full and moist, glistened invitingly.

He thought it might be possible to convince her not to follow him on the raid. If she *agreed* not to be a part of it, then it wouldn't really be quite as if he had broken his word.

"What's wrong?" Amanda whispered, her face very close to Hawk's. "Please, we're in this together. I want to know."

What's wrong is that you're much too beautiful. He said, "I'll explain it later. We can't go for the horses tonight. They're expecting trouble. We'd never get away with it."

* * * *

"Keep your voice down," Hawk warned. "We're not that far from their camp."

Amanda was doing everything she could to keep from pacing. She simply couldn't understand why Hawk wouldn't at least *try* to steal their horses back, especially after all the trouble they'd gone through to find the Cheyenne camp. At one time they'd been within thirty feet of the Cheyenne sentries.

"Why not at least *try*?" Amanda pressed.

She sensed that she was getting into dangerous territory with Hawk, but she didn't care if he did get angry with her. Amanda had discovered within herself a surprisingly strong desire for revenge. The Cheyenne had stolen her horse and she wanted Daisy back. It was as simple as that.

"Because to try now would—"

The words stopped so quickly that it frightened Amanda. He raised his hand palm outward to her, indicating the need for silence. Then, a second later, he bolted to his feet, grabbing Amanda's hand in the process, and pulled her away from the small, grassy clearing that they had intended to use as their camp for the night.

The experiences of the past hours had taught Amanda that sometimes it was better to keep all her questions to herself and just do whatever Hawk indicated he wanted. So she followed him, ducking her head beneath a low-hanging tree limb, moving swiftly without actually breaking into a noisy run through the underbrush. Hawk moved in a semicircle, as he had before, so that he could see back into the camp. Only this time, near the edge of the clearing, he leaped high to catch a tree limb, pulled himself up with startling swiftness, then reached down for Amanda.

She looked first up at him then at the hand he reached down for her. It had been years since she'd climbed a tree and, though she did not quite understand why it was so necessary now, she leaped to catch Hawk's hand. Instantly, he curled his fingers around her wrist, and easily hoisted her up to where she could kick her booted foot around the tree limb. As she did this, her shirt pulled from her trousers once more. A warm flush of embarrassment colored her cheeks as she hauled herself onto the thick, horizontal limb, gaining a secure position before her cotton shirt came completely free.

Quietly, Hawk led the way higher in the tree, all his movements quick, silent and economical, indicating a menace in the shadows that Amanda could not see. She followed him, having difficulty seeing in the near total darkness as she worked her way higher into the thick foliage.

When they were far up the tree, Hawk sat on a substantial limb and pulled Amanda to sit between him and the trunk. They were, she now realized, safely ensconced between two different limbs of almost the same thickness, and a third one behind her that she could reach to use as a support.

She looked at Hawk, who sat so close beside her that she could feel his strength and heat emanating into herself. Smiling, he gave her a quick wink, which rather worried Amanda because it was a jaunty gesture meant to buck up her confidence. Amanda knew it meant they were in greater danger than Hawk wanted her to realize. It was, ironically, the kind of thing her brother would do when a situation was looking bleak.

Hawk took her hand and squeezed it, then placed the tip of his finger against Amanda's lips. Silence, he was indicating without words, was absolutely necessary.

Amanda soon found that she was reasonably well balanced, with the trunk of the tree against her shoulder, a limb in front of her to put a foot on, and a branch behind her on which to place a steadying hand. Just when she started to relax, since it appeared the wait might take a while, she heard voices directly below her, and the meaning of all that Hawk had done now became evident.

Below were at least three Cheyenne braves, as far as Amanda could tell, though she was afraid to move much for fear of drawing attention to herself. Hearing a whistle of some sort, sounding like something an owl would make, she guessed that there were more Cheyenne communicating in the shadows.

Hawk looked at Amanda again, reaching out to touch his fingertips lightly to her chin to raise it, so that she was forced to gaze at him rather than at the threat below. He smiled at her, as though to say, 'The danger is all down there. We're safe up here. There's nothing to fear as long as I'm with you'.

With all her courage, Amanda forced herself to smile back at Hawk, though it was a tight, strained smile.

He was trying to ease her fears, and even though his efforts were only marginally successful, she was thankful for his concern, and her estimation of him as a man rose because of the effort.

Amanda waited, making the supreme effort to remain silent. Below, the braves moved about, inspecting the area where she and Hawk had been sitting, taking note of the cushion of grass they'd gathered and constructed for sleeping. Gratefully, she knew that if Hawk had not heard the Cheyenne's approach, she most assuredly would now be a captive of the men below. A shiver ran up her spine.

As time passed, Amanda heard other sounds, other voices, then it was clear to her why Hawk had climbed the tree rather than run. The Cheyenne were all around them and would certainly discover anyone on foot.

Hawk leaned over, and Amanda angled her head to the side, offering her ear to him. "It won't take long," he said so softly that Amanda had to strain to hear him. "They'll look around, find nothing, then leave."

When Amanda shifted so that she could speak into Hawk's ear the tips of her breasts brushed against the thickly muscled surface of his biceps, and warm, unintended tingles went through her. The force of the feeling was so shocking that Amanda could not at first speak, so she sucked in her breath and held it until the feeling passed and she was once more in control of her emotions.

"How did they know about us? Where to look?"

Her lips brushed against Hawk's ear as she spoke, and she wondered what it would be like to explore the shell-like circumference of his ear with the tip of her tongue. It was a naughty thought, she knew, but she dismissed it as an irrational response to Hawk's beauty and the other circumstances that were entirely beyond her control.

Additional conversation was difficult, since both Hawk and Amanda had to shift positions slightly to speak directly into the other's ear. When Amanda moved once more to offer her ear to Hawk, her breasts again brushed against his arm.

Was he aware of the contact? Was he just as aware of it as she? To Amanda, though she wore a shirt of cotton and Hawk one of buckskin, the contact was such that it felt as though it had been skin to skin.

"You stepped on a twig that broke when we were walking away from their camp," Hawk explained. "I thought one of them might have heard it. They probably found your boot-prints."

A chill went through Amanda as she realized she was dealing with men who lived in a world so vastly different from her own that she could not truly conceive of it. Though she had always been a tomboy, and thought that she was aware of the world around her, she had been completely oblivious of the twig. But Hawk hadn't.

Amanda wanted to ask Hawk more questions, but she did not because she knew that moving again would cause her breasts to brush against him. That, in its own and tempting way, could be more dangerous than facing the Cheyenne who were searching for her on the ground below.

Her body felt sensitized in a way that it never had before, as though in Hawk's presence she was heightened to the possibilities of touch. Amanda wondered if the nearness of danger made her skin tingle, her flesh feel alive, and what it would be like if she allowed Hawk to *intentionally* touch her.

Hawk looked down, but he could not see any of the Cheyenne who had trailed them to this spot. The leaves and branches were too thick, and the only way that they'd be spotted at all was if one of the Cheyenne stood at the base of the tree and gazed straight up. The possibility of that happening didn't seem likely.

At last Hawk felt that he could relax, at least slightly, and he breathed a soft sigh of relief. When he'd heard the approaching footsteps he hadn't at first been sure that it was the Cheyenne. The sound could have come from one of the many night creatures that walk and stalk these grounds. But he had been cautious, which had proven to be a lifesaver.

And now Hawk Two Feather was enormously pleased with the spirits, feeling that they were guiding him. Never before had he ever climbed up a tree to avoid an enemy, or even thought of doing such a thing. The advice had come from the spirits. It was their wisdom that he had to thank, not his own intelligence, Hawk suspected.

He heard the Cheyenne speaking in hushed tones and, though he could not hear all that was said, the topic and tone were clear to him. Where had Hawk and the white woman gone? The Cheyenne wanted to know. How could they have disappeared into the night like shadows?

Hawk smiled. His legend might grow because of the events of this night. And though a flattering notion to him, it also meant that among the Cheyenne, his death would provide great rewards and coups for the warrior who killed him.

He studied Amanda's profile. She had impressed him enormously in the little time they had spent together, especially with her actions of the past half hour. Following his direction without comment or protest, they'd managed to baffle the Cheyenne, with not a drop of bloodshed by anyone.

He would have liked to speak more words of reassurance, but he didn't dare. Each time she swiveled her shoulders to whisper into his ear, he felt the soft fullness of her breasts slide lightly across his arm and, though there was danger everywhere, his body was once more responding in a most disquieting way to Amanda's lush sensuality.

Hawk heard the Cheyenne slowly expanding the circle of their search on the ground below. They were completely at a loss as to where the Sioux and the woman had gone. Hawk thanked the spirit guides that climbing a tree had never occurred to them. Now all Hawk had to do was wait quietly until the danger finally walked away.

He began thinking of Amanda, of the tender flesh that he'd seen when he pulled her up onto the lowest of the tree limbs, the gentle curve of pale bosom so near to him yet so untouchable.

Stop thinking that way! He felt a tightening beneath his trousers as his cock continued its slow but steady expansion.

He fought against the impulses of his burgeoning erection. This was *not* what he needed at a time like this. He did not need to embarrass himself with an unwanted and unwarranted response to a woman who had refused to even kiss him, much less allow him a caress. But the problem was that logic held no sway over his passions. And now the buckskin was restricting his cock, which wasn't at all comfortable. Hawk tried to concentrate on the Cheyenne, tried to consider the threat that they represented, so that his body would not react to Amanda. Surprisingly, the danger of the Cheyenne was nothing compared to the allure of the young woman beside him.

For a man who could go days without eating, ignoring his own hunger when necessary, a warrior who could withstand the cold in the winter and the heat in the summer without complaint, a Sioux whose code of honor and greatest personal pride was derived from his willpower being stronger than the weaknesses of his physical self...being drawn in by Amanda's allure was a form of slow torture.

His unruly manhood continued expanding, responding to the young woman's nearness, and there was nothing Hawk could do to stop it. Though he was uncomfortable, the tenting of his buckskins was an embarrassingly blatant testimony to the direction of his thoughts.

Careful to remain silent, Hawk leaned forward, placing his foot on the branch in front of them. Then, cautiously, he stood and twisted so that he was standing on the branch beneath the one Amanda was sitting on. He swiveled his hips and surreptitiously adjusted his irrational penis to a more comfortable position, then fidgeted with his holster, hoping that Amanda would be unaware of the real reason he'd needed to change positions.

His back was to her when he felt Amanda's small, soft hand upon his shoulder. Hoping that she would remain oblivious to his condition, he turned toward her, carefully repositioning his moccasined foot on the thick branch to remain balanced, then dipped his head down so that she could whisper into his ear.

"What's wrong?" Amanda breathed.

She curled her right hand lightly around Hawk's neck, her fingers touching beneath his hair. The anxiety she tried hard to conceal could be heard in the softness of her voice. She was putting on a courageous front for Hawk, and he felt a pang of guilt for his libidinous thoughts when her primary emotion was fear.

"Nothing," Hawk lied. Absolutely everything was wrong because he wasn't in control of his own thoughts and emotions, which left him feeling set adrift and starkly vulnerable.

He tried to stand upright once more, to put some distance in between himself and Amanda. He turned to Amanda, and this was his undoing. Stunningly beautiful to him then, her face glowed pale and flawless in the shadows. Her honey blonde hair was radiant with vitality and, in the back of his mind, Hawk wondered whether he was enthralled with Amanda because she looked so different from the women he usually pleasured himself with, or whether in some mysterious way she had bewitched him with tricks an evil shaman might use.

I should stay far from her, Hawk considered, feeling himself being irrepressibly drawn in by Amanda's gentle strength, by her beauty, and by the mystery surrounding her.

With Hawk now standing, Amanda did not dare to speak, afraid that the Cheyenne below might hear her, so she simply mouthed the words, 'What's wrong?'

Hawk shook his head, as though he did not understand, so Amanda reached up for him with her right hand, indicating that she wanted him to bend down toward her. When he did she slid her fingers beneath his thick, ebony hair and pulled him so close to her that her lips brushed against his ear when she spoke.

"What's wrong?" she repeated. "You look...I don't know what the word for it is. You seem..."

She pulled back just enough so that she could see into his eyes, and when she did it was as though for a moment she could glimpse into his unguarded soul. Now she saw his anxiety was not caused by the danger the Cheyenne represented, but caused by her...

Should I feel proud or ashamed of the reaction I've drawn from the powerful Sioux warrior?

As he'd done before, Hawk bent his head toward Amanda, only this time she could not escape. There was no chance to spin away from him. She closed her eyes and waited for the touch of his lips against her own, her heart rate rapidly accelerating.

Chapter Four

He kissed her, his lips warm and moist, just barely touching her mouth. Amanda heard a throaty sigh that shocked her as she realized that the sound had come from her. This sound, she thought, should have come from someone else, some woman far more experienced in the glories of passion than she.

Her heart was beating strong and fast, pounding against her ribs. Amanda was confused about what was expected of her, of what exactly she should do, though this fear was short-lived because a little voice inside her head whispered confidently that whatever she needed to know, Hawk could teach her.

From one side of her mouth to the other, Hawk kissed her lightly, occasionally trailing his tongue along the sensitive surface to moisten her lips. Amanda trembled, simultaneously confused and enthralled at what was happening, shocked at the pleasure coursing through her.

In a distant corner of her mind a single, logical thought whispered that it really shouldn't feel so good to be kissing Hawk. The kisses were light, and their impact upon her senses couldn't possibly be as powerful as it seemed, she reasoned.

Amanda quickly concluded that logic held no sway over her body when she was kissing Hawk. Her head was spinning, and she worried about falling off the limb. She leaned just a little more firmly against the trunk of the tree for support, and twisted her arm a bit more securely around Hawk's neck.

Hawk was confused at his need to taste her sweet lips. He was no stranger to passion, to kisses from a beautiful and willing woman. He was also well aware of the danger that the Cheyenne represented. So why, he wondered, considering his experience with women and the Cheyenne, was he feeling the blood need to kiss the frightened, young blonde woman until she trembled with desire and begged for more? Why did it please him so to kiss her when, as she kissed him back, he could tell that she had not kissed often in her life?

Hawk, still standing on a limb beneath Amanda's, moved to the right, nudging her knee to the side. Then he leaned forward fractionally, sliding his leather-clad hips between Amanda's knees. He felt her try to close her legs, the pressure of her knees on either side of his hips, and a powerful rush of delicious images made him sigh softly into Amanda's mouth as he kissed her. What would it feel like to have her knees parting for him, to feel the strength and velvety softness of her thighs surrounding him as he plunged his cock deeply inside her?

He felt her hand at the nape of his neck, slowly winding his long hair around her fingers. Then she slid her hand once more across his shoulders, touching him through his buckskin shirt, holding on to him tightly as they kissed. Hawk kissed her more firmly then, wanting the tension between them to heighten and deepen the sensuality they shared. But Amanda only tilted backward upon the tree limb to lessen the pressure, and the instant she did, she lost her balance and her feet shot out. Her legs now surrounded Hawk's lean waist. He instantly whipped his one free arm around her waist to pull her toward him, once again securely positioning her.

"W-wait...Hawk," Amanda stammered.

When Hawk moved to kiss her again she turned her face to the side, avoiding the warrior's lips. Hawk kissed Amanda's cheek, then bent lower to kiss her jaw, her throat. The sensations that seeped into Amanda's body when she felt his warm, tantalizing lips touching her neck were much different than when he had been kissing her mouth, though no less stimulating.

"I c-can't breathe," she whispered, wanting Hawk to stop his passionate assault upon her better judgment but lacking the conviction to push him away.

A stern denial of her own passion and an insistence that Hawk no longer kiss her would put an end to it all, Amanda knew. Hawk had the ability to control himself, even if she did not. She'd seen him exercise his self-control earlier in the day. But now she needed him to stop of his own accord because she could not insist upon it herself with anything other than a half-hearted plea, spoken through a breathy sigh of pleasure that whispered its own honesty.

She angled her head to the side, tilting her chin slightly upward to allow Hawk easier access to her sensitive throat. His teeth were sharp against her flesh, nipping at the skin, drawing a short, high gasp of surprise.

The dizzying kisses continued, much to Amanda's mixed feelings of ecstasy and dismay. To steady herself, she lightly hooked her heels around the backs of Hawk's knees. Her heart continued to pound faster and faster. She felt the lips of her pussy becoming creamy, her femininity responding to Hawk's blatant virility.

"That's right," Hawk whispered, the timbre of his voice richly sensual. He edged just a little closer to Amanda, forcing her legs wider apart, his lean hips tight between her thighs, the straining front of his buckskins so close to Amanda now that she could feel his cock's strength and heat.

The words rang in Amanda's ears. *No!* she wanted to scream, *I didn't do it to make you happy! I was afraid of losing my balance again!*

She squirmed as she sat on the tree limb, trying to move so that she no longer had Hawk's hips between her thighs. But her perch was not terribly solid, and when she once again nearly fell backward, her booted feet hooked more firmly around Hawk's legs to hold on to him tightly, almost as though they were making love.

She felt his mouth against her collar of her shirt, and another soft cry of desire escaped her parted lips. Every place his lips touched her, every time he kissed her, a new part of her body blazed in passionate reception to pleasure.

Amanda had not dreamed that she could feel anything so intensely. Every sensation passing through her was unprecedented, mysterious in its scope. She wondered how she had failed to realize how capable she was of feeling passion until this moment, until Hawk had entered her life and saved her from the evil men who'd meant her harm.

"Kiss me," Hawk whispered, standing straight, his ebony hair framing his starkly masculine face. The command in his voice suggested he had made similar demands before and was accustomed to feminine compliance.

Amanda looked at Hawk for a moment, wanting to resist him, her natural feistiness coming to the fore. She did not accept orders from *anyone*, and most certainly not an order of *that* nature, especially not under these circumstances.

"I shouldn't," she whispered. It wasn't much of a refusal, but it was all she could manage.

Amanda looked at Hawk's mouth. How had she drawn so much pleasure, her body become so heated, so impassioned, just from his kisses? He was so completely different from any other man who'd ever shared any part of her life that there was no possible correlation between him and anyone else. But why couldn't she resist his kisses when she'd adamantly resisted, refused, and hotly denied nearly all the other men a taste of her lips?

"You're wrong," Hawk replied, bending low. Virile and alluring, his masculine presence hovering about him, ready to engulf and surround Amanda.

She closed her eyes, tilted her face up to him, and slid her arm more tightly around his powerful shoulders. And as she began to taste Hawk's lips pressed against her own, she feared she'd never again resist the temptation of his kisses.

As the kiss grew deeper, more commanding and forceful, Amanda shivered, melting into Hawk. Amanda nearly swooned, kissing Hawk passionately.

Was it possible to be completely consumed with passion? Was this Hawk's own way of kissing, or did everyone, except the two boys she'd previously kissed, kiss like this? She didn't care. All that mattered was that Hawk was kissing her and, with each passing second, the heat within her intensified. She could feel a soft but insistent pulsing in her clitoris, and in a corner of her consciousness was aware that this was something unprecedented. Her body simply didn't respond this powerfully, this libidinously, to a man's heated kisses.

Or so she'd thought.

She felt Hawk's hand against her hip, sliding slowly up her side, his broad palm warming her skin through the denim of her trousers. His warmth now touched her shirt.

He's going to touch my breast. Amanda flinched, though she did not stop kissing Hawk. She'd never allowed anyone to touch her so intimately.

Then, as Hawk caught her lower lip between his teeth and bit softly, she breathed surprise into his mouth. In near total darkness she felt him smile, and wondered what she could have done that he found amusing. Was it that he could make her body feel on fire? Or did he find her passionate confusion a source of humor?

Hawk leaned back then, pulling partially away from her and into a space of moonlight. She looked up into his shadowed face, into those dark, fathomless eyes that glowed with vitality. He smiled again, a soft, wry half smile that tugged at the corner of his mouth, making his dimple appear in his cheek. Despite her confusion, she smiled back.

"This is madness," Amanda heard herself whisper.

Her lips tingled. So did her scalp. She felt all jittery inside. Though she'd led an active, athletic life, her balance now was so poor that, without the tree or Hawk to hold on to, she would not have been able to remain sitting on the thick limb.

Suddenly Hawk's mouth was an inch from Amanda, whispering, "Divine madness, perhaps."

He seemed to know exactly how long to kiss her, and when to pull away so that she could breathe again. He was, she realized instinctively and a bit peevishly, truly experienced in these matters.

Don't be competitive. Amanda recalled the refrain her older sister had used so many times. It isn't ladylike.

From the branch below, Hawk stood upright again, looking down into the pale face of the young woman he'd saved hours earlier. By allowing her to accompany him on the raid, he'd gotten her into this situation with the Cheyenne. She was his weakness, and it was an unsettling revelation for him, since he was not a man who accepted weaknesses in others, or tolerated them in himself.

Slowly, he raised his hand to her face, needing to touch her, to see his fingers against the smoothness of her cheek. Could this beautiful weakness be merely some illusion created within the confines of his own mind?

"Lovely," he whispered, his fingertips brushing lightly over Amanda's cheek.

She said nothing in reply. Rather, she simply stared up at him, her clear blue eyes reflecting the moonlight and showing the confusion she felt.

Hawk brushed the pad of his thumb lightly across the moist fullness of her lips, watching as she made only the slightest move to kiss his thumb. Her gesture was a sign of passionate acceptance that his masculine senses—honed to precision to such responses from women—picked up on instantly. The blood surged through his veins, and only superior self-restraint kept Hawk from pulling her into his arms.

"The Chey-Cheyenne..." Amanda whispered.

She tried to concentrate on the Cheyenne warriors walking in darkness beneath her, to think about the danger that those men represented to her, but she couldn't dwell on such a subject when Hawk's fingertips were trailing slowly, tantalizingly down her throat. Unconsciously, she tilted her chin upward, making her throat taut and available to Hawk's caresses. Though Amanda suspected she shouldn't make this seduction easier for him—her surrender appeared too easily won as it was—she couldn't force herself away from those fingertips.

"The Cheyenne are my enemy," Hawk whispered, his voice a breathy sigh.

As his fingertips trailed back and forth along the line of her collarbone, Amanda saw him watch the rise and fall of her breasts, rapid and uneven. It was visual proof, she knew, of her sensual agitation. When his gaze at last moved up to her face, she closed her eyes. It was impossible to look at Hawk and not feel chaotic inside.

"You shouldn't be thinking of my enemy now."

Amanda tried to say something in response, but she could not. This madness had to come to an end. But how could she protest when her throat felt tight and breathing was nearly impossible with Hawk using a strong, long-fingered hand to casually brush the lapels of her shirt aside, opening it even further, exposing more of her breasts?

Open your eyes, glare hatefully at him, and slap his hand away! She recalled how successfully that had worked on another night with another man.

But knowing what should be done and doing it were two entirely different things. Hawk's kisses had intoxicated her, had stripped away her good judgment. No wonder she couldn't tear Hawk apart with a glare and a few sharply chosen words, as she'd done with any man who dared taunt her in any way. Her body had become a traitor, hungrily accepting what she knew she should resist.

Now he slid his fingers down the front of her body, brushing lightly against the inner swells of her breasts to push the cotton shirt open even more. Amanda's nipples, erect and aching, throbbed with tension. They felt so tight and erect the sensation was almost painful. When she opened her eyes she watched as the long, bronze fingers moved tantalizingly, brushing right and left to very nearly touch the tips of her breasts.

Why isn't he going further? She didn't want him to touch her. At least that's what she tried to tell herself. But as long as he was going to touch her anyway, he might just as well caress her nipples.

It was that thought, that acceptance of a passion she'd never before considered, let alone desired, that warned Amanda she was going too far.

With a trembling hand, Amanda took Hawk by the wrist and pulled his hand from her body. She looked up at him, gaining some semblance of control at last. Several weighty seconds passed as Amanda stared up into Hawk's shadowed face. During those intervening moments she was able to calm her racing heart and recover the sound common sense she'd always felt she possessed.

About to speak, to whisper that Hawk must never again kiss her, she heard the sudden sharp, high cry of a Cheyenne warrior, standing almost directly beneath her. The warrior's scream rumbled through the trees, luckily masking Amanda's own startled gasp. The tree bark's rough texture was harsh against her shoulder. Did Hawk know what to do? Amanda felt on the verge of panic.

Hawk was almost thankful for the diversion, allowing him time to think about his foolish behavior of late, and to remember exactly who and what he was...and, perhaps even more importantly, who and what *Amanda* was.

Below them, a Cheyenne was talking. One of the party had taken Amanda's discarded chemise, tied it around himself, and was cavorting about in a lewd pantomime. But the Cheyenne hadn't discovered anything of importance, hadn't a clue that the quarry they pursued was so close at hand.

Realizing he wasn't in any immediate danger of being discovered gave Hawk time to think about Amanda, and precisely what it was he had been doing with her. She was forbidden, of course. Hawk knew there were many braves in his tribe who coveted white women, who lusted after them even more than after Sioux maidens. Hawk's own mother was white. He'd seen the tribe's subtle bigotry against him because of the white blood running through his veins, just as he'd experienced raw hatred in the white man's villages he'd visited with his mother.

Who hated half-breeds more? The white man or the Sioux?

It didn't really matter. Hatred was hatred, pure and simple. Hawk wasn't going to get caught up in it. He was going to find a lovely Sioux maiden when the time was right, and take her to his tepee. His child would have only a trace of white blood flowing in its veins. His child would not know the confusion, the sense of eternal dislocation, that Hawk had known as a child, that he had struggled with when he was young, and on occasion still fought to this day.

So a romantic entanglement with Amanda was out of the question. Definitely out of the question, he told himself, with her long blonde hair and her pale white skin. She was undoubtedly a fantasy woman for other men, but not for Hawk.

Added to her race was the fact that she'd already had enough trouble with men, hadn't she? She'd tossed away her chemise because it had been destroyed by callused hands, and her shirt was missing its buttons because of other vicious men. Did Hawk really want to put himself in league with such men?

"What's wrong?" Amanda whispered.

Hawk had angled himself away from Amanda. He gazed over at her, startled. How deeply he had sunk into himself and his thoughts. With the laughter of the Cheyenne moving away now, the danger was receding. He realized then, as he watched her pull the shirt more tightly around herself, that he had to remove her from here. He had to put her some place safe where she would be out of danger from the Cheyenne and, perhaps more importantly, no longer be a lure to his senses.

But first he needed to steal back their horses. Once that was accomplished he could ride with her until she was again in a white man's village, where *she* belonged, and he could ride away, back to his own Sioux camp, where *he* belonged.

"Nothing is wrong," Hawk said gruffly. "I'll help you down. We can't stay here all night."

* * * *

"Brandy?" Sonny Wright asked.

Vanessa Wright nodded, then accepted a snifter from her brother. Her thoughts, even as she sipped the fine Napoleon brandy, were on her sister Amanda. Another day had passed without a telegram. Sonny, the eldest child in the family, had wanted to take charge of the situation, sending a telegram of concern and hiring men to ride to Fort Keogh to investigate the matter. That was Sonny's way—to take charge, take immediate action. It was left to Vanessa to be the voice of moderation, to be the one to let reason and logic prevail.

"She can be damned annoying," Sonny said, throwing himself onto the library sofa.

"Amanda can be more than just annoying," Vanessa replied, "and we both know it. We also know this is neither the first, nor the second, nor even the third time that we've sent her off to look at horses and she's gotten so involved in her work that she has forgotten to telegram us on how she's progressing."

"I ought to put her over my knee," Sonny mumbled.

"I know you're angry with her," Vanessa continued. "I'm angry, too. But if we take a moment to think about it, we'll realize that Amanda is not like other women her age. She can take care of herself. She's an independent woman."

"Woman?" Sonny made a sound of derision in his throat. "She's just a girl!"

"A mere child, you'll say next, right?" Vanessa smiled to herself. "If that's so, then why do several of the girls she grew up with now have husbands and children?"

Vanessa smiled again when Sonny shot her a fierce look. Vanessa was not intimidated. As a lawyer, her skills in debating issues such as this one were greater than her brother's. He knew it, though she knew he didn't like it.

"Are you intentionally trying to get on my nerves?" he asked.

"No, I'm trying to tell the truth. It's the truth that's getting on your nerves, not me."

She smiled more broadly at Sonny, raising her brandy snifter in a silent toast and, even though he was angry, he smiled back. His tension evaporated. Sonny shook his head, mumbling about how much easier his life would be if he'd been blessed with younger brothers instead of sisters. Vanessa heard the love behind the criticism and let her brother calm down at his own pace.

"When will you be leaving for Fargo?" Sonny asked.

"I'm not certain, actually," Vanessa replied, pleased at the change in subject. Though she was, in fact, a little worried about Amanda's welfare herself, her sister had neglected to inform them about her activities or whereabouts more times than she could remember.

Vanessa turned her thoughts to the right-of-way water dispute that required her to go to Fargo to file the necessary legal documents at territorial court.

"I'd guess in a day or two," she answered at last. "I can't wait too long, but there's no great hurry. These cases tend to move at a snail's pace."

Sonny huffed, shaking his head in disgust. He had no patience for such slow-moving problem-solving, though he was eternally grateful that his sister did.

She was his eyes and ears in the courts, and he counted on her to fight the legal battles that he could not fight himself.

"Don't worry so much," Vanessa said as she finished her brandy, rising to her feet to go to bed. "I'm certain Amanda's sleeping like a baby, having worked herself to exhaustion for days now. And when we finally do get word from her she'll be asking for much more money to be sent to her, claiming it is the only way we'll get the bloodlines the Circle S needs."

* * * *

Amanda wondered what time it was. Typical of people in the ranching business, she was accustomed to going to bed early and rising at dawn. It had to be close to three in the morning by now, she decided.

Sitting on the ground with her back to a tree trunk, she watched Hawk complete his circuit of the area. He'd already told her that there were no Cheyenne around, but he'd gone to check anyway.

Hawk moved like some giant cat stalking an unseen prey. Though a big man, he was silent, light, and quick on his feet. The loose-limbed grace of his body when he walked, climbed a tree, did almost anything physical, reminded Amanda again of a lazy cat. Except there didn't seem to be anything at all lazy about Hawk. He almost quivered with energy and vitality even when he was perfectly motionless.

Such a man, Amanda thought with amazement as he approached her, at last finished with his investigation of the surrounding area. When he knelt beside her in the grass her heart fluttered a bit.

"Try to get some sleep," he said, keeping his voice low. "A couple of hours will do wonders for recovering your energy."

"I *am* exhausted," Amanda admitted. "Are you going to sleep, too?"

Hawk shook his head, his raven black hair swirling about his shoulders. "I'll stay awake for a while. Someone has to keep an eye out. Maybe I'll sleep some later."

"You can't go on forever without sleeping," Amanda reminded him. She reached out to lightly touch the buckskin sleeve of Hawk's shirt. "Even *you* have your limits."

Hawk grinned and took his distance from her. Then he motioned for Amanda to lie down, which she did, rolling onto her stomach and cradling her head in her arms. She liked it when Hawk smiled. He didn't do it often enough, she decided, not nearly often enough.

Amanda looked at Hawk one last time, then closed her eyes and was asleep before she knew it.

Chapter Five

Amanda watched Hawk kneeling at the stream, splashing cool water on his face. He hadn't gotten much sleep, but at least he'd gotten some, she had awakened to notice. With four hours' sleep, not her usual seven, Amanda felt fine, though a little stiff from sleeping on the ground.

Arching her spine, she then threw her head back and raised her arms skyward, stretching out all the stiffness.

Hawk pivoted on his knees to watch Amanda. With her face tilted upward, her arms raised high, and her eyes closed to the morning sun, she looked as if she was worshiping the sun. A wry smile curled Hawk's lips. No, Amanda wouldn't worship the sun, but a Sioux maiden would. And though he wasn't sure what Amanda's spiritual life was like, he was certain it wasn't at all like his.

As she turned and stretched, working the muscles in her back, her shirt loosened slightly, and once again he was given a glimpse of generous breasts that trembled tautly. He turned away immediately. He didn't need to torment himself with such ostentatious femininity.

The allure that Amanda represented was much too great to be toyed with. He'd demonstrated his weakness the previous night. He didn't need to prove he was a weak man once again.

He would have given Amanda something to eat but all the provisions he'd brought with him on the hunt were in his pack, with his stallion.

At the thought of his horse, Hawk gritted his teeth. The Cheyenne had his stallion, and they were probably still gloating over their victory. It galled him to realize that enemy warriors would be speaking of Hawk Two Feather with derision, telling exaggerated stories of the way they'd stolen his stallion.

He turned his attention back to Amanda, who was tucking the tails of her shirt back into her denims. Why did she wear trousers like a man? Hawk wondered. It didn't particularly bother him, though he did find it curious.

"How do you feel?" he asked quietly.

Smiling, Amanda rose and walked over to kneel beside Hawk. "Fine. I'm ready to go after the Cheyenne just as soon as you are."

"I'm afraid not. Last night proved to me that it's going to be much too dangerous to have you along."

"According to you," Amanda replied, her eyes promising anger.

"Yes, according to me."

"But not according to me. But my opinion doesn't count, right?"

"That isn't what I said."

Amanda bolted to her feet. For an instant she had a height advantage to Hawk, which she wanted. "You didn't have to."

Hawk rose, then, edging closer, he looked down at Amanda from his much greater height. "Do you always attack men when they disagree with you?"

Amanda refused to be intimidated by Hawk's size and strength. "No, only when they're wrong. Most times, it's men who attack me."

The words were out of Amanda's mouth before the full significance of them hit her. She turned sharply away from Hawk. The pleasure of kissing Hawk, and the frustration of dealing with his stubbornness, had made her forget — at least momentarily — the horror of the multiple attacks she'd suffered, along with the trauma of seeing the violence Hawk had dealt to her attackers.

Amanda wasn't sorry that the men who had attacked her had died. Not at all. But just the same, the ugliness of violence was something she would not soon forget, no matter how desperately she wanted to.

She took several steps, needing to put some distance between herself and Hawk, if only for a moment. Then, slowly, she turned toward him again, and squared her shoulders.

"Do what you want to," she said. "*I'm* going to get my horse back."

"Alone?"

"If necessary."

"You're crazy."

"Quite likely, but I'm still going to get my horse back. At least I'm going to try."

Amanda waited for Hawk to continue to resist her or to relent and at last accept that she had a legitimate right to fight the Cheyenne. Instead, he simply stood there, tall and imposing, impressive in his fringed buckskins, an uncomprehending expression in his ebony eyes.

"Fine. Be stubborn then," Amanda said, stomping her booted foot on the ground.

She turned and started walking strong and fast, without the slightest knowledge of exactly where she was headed. A moment later, just as she had hoped, she felt Hawk's strong fingers encircling her elbow, stopping her and spinning her around so that she faced him.

"You can't be serious."

"You don't know me very well, Mr Two Feather," Amanda replied. Saying his last name formally sounded strange in her ears, so different from his first name, which fell wonderfully upon her tongue...almost as wonderful as his kisses had, though that was something she was trying hard to forget.

Several seconds passed. Amanda looked at Hawk. She was angry but knew that without him there was the very real possibility that she'd be dead by now.

"You're a little fool," Hawk whispered, but Amanda could hardly take offense at the remark.

She nodded, feeling a smile spread slowly across her lips.

"A little fool, indeed," she said proudly, "but this little fool isn't going to have her horse stolen from her without making at least a very serious attempt at getting that horse back. Besides, Daisy would be heartbroken if I didn't try to rescue her."

"I'm risking my neck for a horse named after a flower," he muttered softly, sarcastically.

"You don't have to."

"Yes, I do."

Amanda's heart clenched at Hawk's iron-hard declaration.

* * * *

They'd gotten close enough to hear the Cheyenne talking. Amanda was certain her heart was pounding so hard that she would alert the enemy braves. She glanced over at Hawk. He made a brief motion with his hand that she was to remain in place.

Calm down. You've done everything right so far. Don't make a stupid mistake now, when the Cheyenne are so close.

The day had been difficult. After convincing Hawk to take her along on the raid, Amanda had run endless miles, pushing herself to the limit of her endurance. The Cheyenne braves, on horseback, were moving in no particular hurry, but being on horseback gave them an enormous advantage.

"Don't worry," Hawk had said at least a dozen times that day already. "We'll get them. They're moving without a set destination and, if my guess is correct, they're no longer worried about being followed. Remember how in the morning they checked to see if they were being followed? Now they're checking to see if they are riding into a trap. That tells me—I mean, us—where they think the next danger will come from."

Once this had been explained to her, Amanda paid a different type of attention to the Cheyenne warriors as they rode along, leading the stolen horses. Again and again, it was clear that everything Hawk had said was correct.

A Sioux warrior like Hawk Two Feather was never to be destined for her, Amanda thought. Despite this, she questioned whether he might be the only one man enough to interest her where the other men traipsing through her life had not. And there had been many men. By the time she was sixteen, the men had begun lining up, all of them wanting to go on a private walk with her, to hold her hand, to impress her with the things they owned, the things they had done, the things they could say.

A quirky smile tugged at the corner of Amanda's mouth. She had never once been impressed with the tales she'd heard. She recognized bragging when she heard it, and it didn't matter to Amanda if a man had more money than her family, or less. What mattered most was that *he* thought she would be impressed, when in fact Amanda's reaction to hyperbolic tales of business acumen simply bored her. And when she wasn't bored, she was disgusted.

As she knelt in the grass, assuring herself again that the Cheyenne could not see her, Amanda closed her eyes and tried to see inside herself. Perhaps the truth was there, hidden deep within her own heart, the answer to the questions that tormented her.

She turned her eyes toward Hawk at precisely the same moment that he looked at her. He offered her a confident smile and extended his hand toward her, palm upward. Though she couldn't possibly reach his hand, Amanda understood the gesture. He was letting her know that there was nothing to fear, that as long as he was there, she needn't worry. Even though logic dictated that this couldn't possibly be true, Amanda felt her heart constricting, Hawk had done what he could to ease her fears and comfort her, silently and without moving from his sentry position.

She closed her eyes, shutting out everything in order to recall their kisses of the night before, high up in the tree. Was there any other man who could kiss like

Hawk? Any 'civilized' white man who could make her ache for his caresses? Her breasts had felt so tight and full from the desultory, almost casual way Hawk had touched them. He'd teased her by coming so very close to caressing her nipples without ever quite touching them, making her long to beg him to palm the risen crests. But she'd controlled herself, as a 'civilized' woman should.

She opened her eyes then and saw Hawk, standing there more beautiful than any man had a right to be. More charming and intelligent as well.

Feeling guilty, Amanda turned her face away. Hawk shouldn't see the way she was looking at him, shouldn't look into her blue eyes and see the passion she felt rising warmly within her.

Really, what is the harm in flirting with Hawk? He was a man who would not act the barbarian—he'd already proven that many times over. So where was the harm in some innocent fun?

Amanda moistened her lips with the tip of her tongue. Would it be so naughty to taste his kisses just once more? Once more, before she returned to her life at the Circle S, and again was required on most Saturday nights to sit on the porch swing with this rancher's son or that banker's son, pretending to find the conversation entertaining?

Hawk had returned to Amanda and was kneeling beside her. He'd moved so silently that he'd startled her at first, seeming to appearing right before her eyes.

"We'll wait until dark, and when they're asleep we'll take the horses," Hawk said. "They're not a bit worried that they're being followed, and that's going to make all the difference. I hope you don't mind waiting another night before going home."

"My pleasure," Amanda replied cryptically, only a part of her thoughts on getting Daisy back.

* * * *

Only one man—a sleepy Cheyenne brave with the lowest rank of the band—had been assigned to watch over the horses. During the day, the Cheyenne had stolen four more horses.

Hawk moved like smoke through the shadows, and though his natural inclination was to take permanent measures to incapacitate his enemy, for Amanda's benefit he only struck the sentry hard on the back of the head with his gun, knocking him unconscious. The sentry, who had been sitting cross-legged on the ground, slumped to the side without uttering so much as a gasp.

Hawk motioned for Amanda to circle around the horses. They would each locate their horse.

The horses weren't hobbled, though two long ropes had been fastened around a group of trees to form a makeshift corral. Most of the horses had bridles on them. Some had brands, others had Cheyenne paint marks. It didn't take long for Hawk to find his powerful stallion, who nuzzled his chest in greeting.

After leaping on the stallion's back, Hawk took the reins in his left hand, keeping his revolver in his right. The horses were making more noise now, and he knew that soon someone from the sleeping camp would come to investigate.

He looked for Amanda. She still wasn't astride her mare. Hawk clenched his teeth. What was taking her so long?

Hawk heard a male voice from the camp call out but he couldn't make out the words. Certain that the first stages of a band-wide warning had sounded, Hawk hissed through clenched teeth. "Hurry!"

The moon, obscured by clouds, allowed him little light. Where was Amanda? The horses were spreading out, no longer restricted by the rope, which he had cut.

Amanda found Daisy and leaped on her, allowing Hawk to finally see her, and a Cheyenne warrior spotted a horse walking nervously through the camp. The Cheyenne, realizing the corral had been breached, let out a high warning cry. The horses, already spooked, turned in a single, chaotic unit, then ran off into the night.

Hawk kicked his heels to his stallion's flanks and the powerful animal took off in a gallop. Futile gunshots rang out in the night. Hawk was smiling. He knew the bullets had been fired blindly and that he and Amanda had accomplished all they'd set out to do.

They pushed the horses through the trees and onto the grassland, where they could keep them moving more quickly as a herd. Three times Hawk had counted the stolen band, counting twenty-three horses each time. Not including Amanda's Daisy, he'd be able to return to his tribe with a veritable fortune in horses.

For her part, Amanda had needed time to get her heart to settle down. Even though she'd been riding Daisy at an easy canter for almost an hour, she continued to look over her shoulder, convinced that somehow the Cheyenne were still following them. Logic told her they couldn't possibly keep to such a pace on foot, but the gunshots she'd heard had put a fear to her that went to the marrow of her bones.

When they reached a small stream, Hawk pulled his stallion to a halt. "Let's let them drink," he said. His teeth gleamed brilliantly in the moonlight. "We're safe now." He tossed a long buckskin-clad leg over his stallion and jumped to the ground. He closed the distance separating them and reached out to assist Amanda to the ground. "I don't suppose you're used to riding bareback."

Amanda twisted on Daisy and kicked a foot over the mare's head. As she slipped off the mare's back, Hawk caught her by the waist, his powerful hands warm and strong around her, slowing her descent. In all the activity and riding, Amanda's shirt had once again pulled free of her Levis, this time revealing the entire front of her body to the stomach, as well as the pale swells of her breasts. As she felt the ground against her feet, she gazed up into Hawk's face and saw that he was looking at her open shirtfront.

"That was," Amanda said in a whisper, "the second most exciting thing I've ever done in my life."

The quirky half smile so characteristic of Hawk's charming ways brought the dimple to his cheek. "Would you like to enlighten me on your most exciting experience?"

His hands were still at her waist, warming her skin through the fabric of her shirt. Amanda knew she should step away from him, take his hands from her so that she could turn her back, tuck her shirt once more into her pants, then talk to him in a civilized manner. She knew what she *should* do. What she was less certain of was exactly what she *wanted* to do.

"Are you going to tell me?" Hawk asked, inching just a little closer to Amanda and looming over her. "Or is guessing part of the game?"

"You're a very dangerous man, Hawk," Amanda whispered a moment before his mouth slanted down over hers. She felt him claiming her lips in a breathtaking kiss that demanded a response.

Amanda couldn't help leaning into Hawk. Her head was still spinning from the dizzying excitement of stealing horses from murderous men. She had loved the whirlwind ride through the night, and from being so near a man as courageous, seductive and unmistakably dangerous as Hawk Two Feather. When his mouth covered hers, Amanda could do nothing but give in to the carnal cravings that had tugged at her consciousness since that first kiss.

Hawk wound his arms around her, pulling her in tight. Amanda moaned at the soft, pleasing tingles emanating from her peaked nipples and spreading slowly throughout her body. She felt a soft but insistent throbbing in her clitoris, but tried to ignore it because, she believed, her body simply didn't respond that way to Hawk.

I'm only kissing. But she was creating an illusion, and she knew it. She enjoyed the warmth of Hawk's magnificent body against her breasts, and she could not deny this because she had done nothing to pull her shirt more modestly around herself. Even now, as she angled her head a bit to the side to silently invite Hawk to pleasure her throat with his tantalizing kisses and those wicked little bites with his teeth, she wondered if she'd ever be able to deny herself Hawk's more intimate caresses. She wanted them, but what would she think of herself afterward? Could she control Hawk's passion after she'd let him go too far?

His teeth at her throat, nipped against her neck, the sensation at the brink of pain. Amanda issued a startled gasp and her knees trembled even more. When she wrapped her arms around Hawk's middle, the texture of his buckskin shirt against her fingertips pleased her.

Bent backward, Amanda allowed Hawk to kiss her throat. Without his secure hold on her she would have fallen. Feeling disoriented, she opened her eyes to see the crescent moon and a few stars overhead.

"Hawk," she whispered, for no other reason than that she liked the sound of his name. Just saying it tasted like a kiss on her lips.

He kissed her neck, teasing her with his tongue. Amanda turned in his arms, directing his kisses across her collar and the front of her throat to the other side. Suddenly he was down on one knee before her, and she placed her hands lightly on his shoulders.

Where was her resistance? she wondered. Amanda had behaved as bravely as she could, facing dangers that evening that no woman she'd ever known had encountered. And now, kissing Hawk, feeling his powerful body so close to hers, was just one more excursion into new, exotic and perilous territory.

He kissed Amanda's collarbone and slowly began working his way down the front of her body. When she pushed her fingers into his long, dark hair he tilted his head back to look up at her.

For several seconds Amanda didn't speak, uncertain of what would happen next. Then, giving in to curiosity and burgeoning passion, Amanda simply closed her eyes and tilted her head back. Turning her face up to the stars, she decided to let whatever would happen next happen of its own accord.

Then Hawk pressed his lips against her stomach, kissing her, his strong teeth nipping at her. Amanda's heart raced, pounding against her ribs. How could she remain standing motionless? Not with the giddy feel of his shoulder-length hair against her fingers! Not with his moist lips kissing her stomach!

Where has my sanity gone?

She nearly fainted at the slick, darting delight of Hawk's tongue against her navel. She trembled at the surprising sensation but made no effort to move away. And when she felt his large hands reach around her hips to cup her ass she still didn't try to get away, despite all the whispered warnings that had sounded in her brain, which were now panicked screams to escape while it was still possible.

"Hawk...oh, Hawk!" Amanda whispered, weaving slightly as he kissed her stomach, his tongue circling her navel before dipping inside. She felt his hands against her ass, kneading taut flesh through the denim trousers. Hawk's caresses had ignited a fire down low, her body responding instinctively. She felt herself creaming, and it seemed as though her insides were melting. Her clitoris was, by this time, fiercely erect, semi-hidden between the lips of her slit.

His kisses ended, and for a moment Amanda stood waiting impatiently for them to continue. Then she opened her eyes and looked down to see that he was once again gazing up at her.

"Have I done something wrong?" she asked.

Hawk shook his head, and Amanda entwined her fingers a bit more securely into his ebony hair. She loved the silken feel of it as much as she enjoyed the sensation that his hands on her body elicited.

He smiled at her lazily, and as he kissed her stomach, he nudged her shirt open with his chin. How intoxicating it was to have such a large and powerful man kneeling before her! Could this be an act of supplication from a man as forceful as Hawk, who never would have to beg for anything, certainly not for attention from a woman? Not with his abundance of seductive charm and devastating looks.

"I've never..." Amanda began but didn't know what to say. She'd never felt more lost. Hawk, she had noticed, was infinitely more knowledgeable in these matters. Could he give her some hint of what was expected of her? "Hawk, I don't know..."

He turned his fiery, magnetic gaze on her, straightening his spine so that his face was level with her bosom. His hands never left her bottom. Slowly, seductively, he kissed the tip of her left breast, the warmth of his mouth passing through her cotton shirt to make her nipple throb so much it was almost painful.

The sensation of heated moisture against the sensitive tip of her breast startled Amanda with its intensity. A gasp caught in her throat and her entire body quivered in responsive, though she neither tried to get away from Hawk nor did she prevent his deliriously passionate quest.

For a moment Amanda concentrated on what she was feeling, on the sensations charging through her body.

She looked at him, confused and shaken. Then she looked down at her bosom, concealed by her shirt, and saw the round, darkened area that had been moistened by his kiss. Her nipples were erect, making prominent dents in the fabric, an undeniable indication of the excitement her body was experiencing.

Then Amanda reached up with her left hand, sliding her palm along her side and across her body so that she very nearly cupped her own breast. She twisted her right hand a bit more securely into the hair at the back of Hawk's neck. Trembling, not at all sure she was doing what she should—but absolutely convinced she was doing what she was compelled to do by desires unprecedented and irrepressible—she pulled her shirt aside. Her breast was full and round, the areola surrounding the peaked nipple a soft pink.

When she heard Hawk's sudden, sharp intake of breath, a hint of a smile, softly confident in its nature, curled the fullness of Amanda's mouth. She knew Hawk enjoyed looking at her and, searching his eyes, Amanda realized that he wasn't nearly as aloof and casual as he had seemed.

"Kiss me," Amanda whispered, pulling Hawk to her exposed bosom. Her face flamed with embarrassment when she added, "Suck."

The intensity of the feeling was infinitely stronger without a barrier between Hawk's lips and tongue and the sensitive crest. A cry of ecstasy was ripped from her throat, and her knees sagged when she had been pleasured on by such a handsome man.

"K-Kiss me," Amanda begged. "Suck. Hard."

The initial pleasure of being sucked on had been transformed from a searing heat spreading through her flesh to a warmth of passion going deeper into her bones. The warmth passed—through her fingertips, her toes, and even the top of her head. Urgently, she exposed her other breast, and Hawk showered it with kisses, opening his mouth wide to engulf as much of her between his lips as possible.

Time stood still as she guided Hawk, turning her shoulders, her body throbbing as the warrior's experienced lips tantalized her nipples. Hawk's great, bronzed hands were caressing her—from the backs of her knees to the cheeks of her ass, sliding his fingers around her thighs, pressing upward to feel the heat of her sex through her trousers and drawers.

Amanda trembled, her hips slowly undulating from side to side. Hawk's hands had ignited a fire within her, quickly burning away the last vestiges of the untouchable tomboy who loved horses more than men. His powerful fingers were at once both commanding and gentle. Amanda moaned incoherently, her eyes pinched shut as a strange pressure began to build inside her, as though a mainspring in her pelvis was being wound tighter and tighter inside her.

A little voice in the back of Amanda's mind whispered a warning that at first she did not recognize and then, when she did, would not heed.

Too far, too fast, the tiny voice repeated.

Amanda didn't want to believe that she was out of control, that the passion now erupting within her was beyond her comprehension or influence.

Hawk's reached between her legs and touched her cunt with strength and forcefulness, demanding that she respond to his caresses even through two layers of clothing.

It's wrong, Amanda's brain warned again. *Don't let him touch you there!*

Yet she found herself spreading her feet a little wider, further availing her sex to the enigmatic warrior's powerful caresses, shivering as he kissed her breast and used his teeth against the aroused nipple, trembling while he worked with increasing urgency between her thighs to turn her sex into a cauldron of fire.

The pressure within her pelvis was growing on itself, making it difficult for her to breathe evenly. She gulped air, trying to relax, feeling the muscles in her stomach tighten with each revolution of Hawk's hand as he caressed her cunt, with each devilish swipe of his tongue against her nipple.

An inner voice warned, *Stop it! Stop it now before you can't stop him at all!*

The pressure within her was almost painful, and this helped Amanda regain control. She opened her eyes and watched as Hawk kissed along the slopes of her breasts, moving from one crest to the other. Her fingers still entwined in his ebony hair, she suddenly pushed him backward, using such force that Hawk was knocked off balance. She twisted sharply, and turned her back to him, disentangling herself from his arm, which was still wrapped tightly around her hips.

Amanda took three steps, staggering slightly, then took another three. Distance from Hawk would help her regain her composure. She was certain of it.

"D-Don't!"

The single word warbled in the night air. She stopped, her back toward Hawk, gathering her shirttails and tucking them into the waistband of her Levis. Her breath came in deep, uneven gulps. Amanda believed that she'd just experienced something close to intoxication, or else some temporary madness that no one ever spoke of. All she knew was that her behavior had not been characteristic of the young woman she'd always thought herself to be. And even now, even after Hawk's kisses and caresses had ended, her body still tingled, her heart still pounded, her breasts and pussy remained even more desirous of his touch.

"What's wrong?" Hawk demanded, getting to his feet to follow Amanda. He was clearly angry with her abrupt change of mood.

"Everything! Everything! Please, just leave me alone! Please...at least for a little while! I need to think!"

Chapter Six

Red Wolf sat in front of the campfire, his belly full and his spirits at ease. Several tribal elders had joined him, as well as Buttercup, Hawk Two Feather's younger sister.

Red Wolf prepared to say the well-rehearsed words, pretending that they were spontaneous. Speaking to the distinguished and powerful Sioux elders, Red Wolf would not actually have to present his 'suspicions' to them formally.

"I do not understand why Hawk Two Feather is not here." Red Wolf shrugged his naked shoulders, as though the matter really did not mean much to him. "After all, is not Hawk the one who says we must plan for the next season today? He is the one who says we must all work together if we are to do the most good for the tribe. And where is he now? He is off hunting on his own. He said he would be gone for two days, maybe three. He has been gone five days now."

Buttercup said, "Maybe he is busy. You do not know him as I do. Maybe he has been hurt. What if he needs your help instead of your insults?"

"Needs my help? Been hurt?" Red Wolf asked, leaning away from Buttercup, as though shocked by the questions. "More likely he has found a squaw, and he will not return to us until he has had his fill of her. For that he does not need my help."

Red Wolf laughed then and, though Hawk was respected by the elders, many of them laughed as well, knowing Hawk's weakness was his fondness for women.

Buttercup quickly rose to her feet and stomped off, her teeth clenched in obvious rage.

Watching her retreat into the darkness, Red Wolf managed to keep the smile of victory from his lips. Buttercup was furious with him and he knew it, just as he knew that some of the tribal elders did not appreciate his talking about Hawk when he wasn't there to defend himself. But Red Wolf also knew that he had planted the seed of doubt in every mind—even in the minds of the men who did not approve of what he said. Red Wolf could have said more regarding Hawk, but he did not. To be too negative might jeopardize the victory he had gained, and he'd lived too long with the dream of destroying Hawk Two Feather to let impatience get in his way now.

* * * *

Wishing she could sleep longer, Amanda awoke slowly, blinking her eyes. Her body, so recently pushed long and hard, had needed the rest.

Suddenly she remembered that she wasn't at home, recovering from a hard day in the breaking corral, but was sleeping outside. She sat bolt upright and was completely awake in an instant. She looked around the small campsite, sensing that something was wrong.

The horses they'd taken from the Cheyenne were still grazing on the thick grass near the bank of the stream, a little more than twenty-five yards to her left. They seemed at ease, and that was a good sign. If the Cheyenne were approaching, the horses might be spooked.

Hawk. Where was Hawk?

Amanda whipped her head to the right and left, looking for the tall warrior with the bold smile. Until that very instant she hadn't realized how completely she counted on him to keep her safe.

"Hawk?" She spoke in a conversational tone. She wanted Hawk with her. Only then would she feel safe. "Hawk, where are you?" she repeated, louder this time. "Hawk! Hawk, where are you?"

Rising to her feet, Amanda searched the thick trees, hoping to see the Sioux warrior leaning nonchalantly against a pine. He'd be there, a smile on his wide, sensual mouth, his arms crossed over his broad chest, taking naughty delight in Amanda's anxiety. She began looking up into the trees, hoping to find him sitting on a limb, perhaps looking into the distance for the Cheyenne.

Hawk was nowhere to be found.

"He wouldn't leave me," Amanda said aloud, trying to reassure herself as she combed her fingers through her hair. She hoped that the sound of her own voice would give her confidence, but it didn't. She could detect in her tone the rising panic she was pretending didn't exist.

She glanced at the horses again. Some were studying her, picking up on her fear, watching her as she moved around the campsite.

Memories flooded through Amanda as she adjusted her shirt, tucking the tails into the waistband of her

Levis. In her mind's eye she saw herself in Hawk's arms, kissing him passionately, her heart racing with excitement as his practiced sensuality melted her resistance. She recalled that *she* had been the one to pull open her shirt to expose her breasts, that *she* had guided Hawk's kisses to receive them wherever she most wanted them.

Amanda shuddered, recalling the way she had pushed Hawk away, staggering from him on legs weakened with passion. Frightened of her own ecstasy, she'd walked into the shadows, where she'd remained, alone, until her hands had finally stopped trembling and good judgment was once more guiding her actions.

A tentative truce had been called between Hawk and Amanda, so that when he'd suggested they get some sleep she'd been only too happy to find a grassy place—at least ten yards from Hawk—to stretch out and close her eyes. Amanda had expected a sleepless night, with her mind spinning in circles, but exhaustion had overtaken her and, before she'd known it, she'd been sleeping soundly under the stars.

Soundly...until she'd woke to find she was alone. The Sioux warrior who was her protector had abandoned her.

Amanda went to the roped-off area where the stolen horses grazed. Daisy was walking forward, munching on grass, when she tossed her head up and down in greeting.

"Hey, girl," Amanda whispered, rubbing the horse's powerful neck. "At least you didn't leave me, did you?"

Hawk's big stallion wasn't there, which didn't surprise Amanda. If he was going to abandon her while she slept, he'd certainly take the stallion he'd risked his neck to retrieve from the Cheyenne.

Amanda shook her head in disgust. Men were such idiots. She knew that Hawk had left her because she had turned him away—stopping his seduction before she'd lost her honor and dignity. And virginity. Fool. Amanda realized now that it didn't matter if a man's heritage was European or Indian. In the end, the common factor was that they were all stupid, simpleminded, stubborn, lusty simpletons, every one of them.

"At least he left you here to take me home," Amanda said aloud, still rubbing Daisy's neck. "He could have left me on foot, I suppose."

Amanda's shivered at a troubling thought. Why would Hawk leave behind the horses he'd risked his life to steal?

Amanda could understand him leaving her, even if it was for a very stupid reason. What made no sense at all, no matter how angry Hawk was with her, was his abandonment of the stolen horses. He'd been overjoyed when they'd recaptured them the previous night, calling it a personal victory over his enemy, the Cheyenne. The exuberance and triumph she'd witnessed in his eyes had led to that first kiss, which had led immediately to the second kiss, which had led to a near-complete seduction.

Turning away from Daisy, Amanda closed her eyes and rubbed her temples lightly with her fingertips. Where was Hawk? Was he searching for food?

She began to inspect the grass around the horses, hoping to find a clue to Hawk's disappearance. Though she'd been around horses her entire life, she'd never developed tracking skills. Why should she? The Wright family had never needed to track their stock.

"Now what do I do?" Amanda mumbled, looking at the ground and trying to decipher what the stallion's hoof prints meant.

Should she wait around for Hawk to return, or should she get on Daisy and ride away? Though she wasn't certain of her location, it wouldn't be long before she would find some tree, some valley, some geographical marker that would help her find her way back through the Dakota territory. And it would just be a matter of time before she was home again.

Was she safer with Hawk, or without him? Safer? What were the real dangers? The Cheyenne, or Hawk himself?

When she was with him she certainly behaved in ways diametrically opposed to the way she behaved without him. But what about the Cheyenne? She had no idea where they were now. If they had traveled throughout the night, the Cheyenne could be stalking her, perhaps even—

Stop thinking that way! Amanda was angry with herself for letting in fear.

But stopping the questions from going through her thoughts was not as easy as she had hoped. She *did* know why Hawk frightened her so. He'd made her feel things she had dreamed of on so many nights. For several years she'd had passionate dreams had that made her toss and turn in her bed as she slept, tormented by the dream-caresses of a faceless stranger who made her tremble with desire. In the morning when she would awaken from her restless sleep, she would recall fragments of her dreams and feel embarrassed and frightened by her own mind.

It hadn't mattered to Amanda that the dreams were just that—dreams she could not direct or guide in any way. She was still embarrassed by their ungovernable passion, especially because in her dreams she'd been ecstatically happy, erotically aroused to a point where she'd tingled from head to toe and her pussy had throbbed with an aching need.

She had cautiously asked several friends whether they'd ever had such dreams. 'Never! Have you?' came a typical response, with eyes large and round with shock. Amanda knew then that she had to keep the nature of her dreams a secret from everyone. Otherwise she would surely suffer social censure the likes of which would make the scorn she received for being a tomboy appear as nothing more than the mildest teasing.

She was on her feet an instant later, walking purposefully toward Daisy. How much better, she thought, to take control of her own life, even at the risk of making a mistake, than to wait, doing nothing, hoping that someone else would show up to make all her troubles disappear.

"Girl, we're getting out of here," Amanda said to Daisy, just about to step over the rope surrounding the horses.

"Without me?"

Amanda wheeled around, her heart in her throat, to find Hawk standing directly behind her, his great stallion at his side. The smirking half smile on his face that Amanda had hoped to see had appeared, but now she was furious. There could be no doubt that Hawk had intentionally snuck up behind her to scare her.

"Someday somebody's going to punch you in the nose," Amanda warned, thinking that her brother Sonny probably wouldn't mind doing it. "And if you ever scare me like that again, I'm going to be that somebody." She hit his steely arm with her fist.

Hawk laughed softly, not at all put off by Amanda's attack.

"Did you think I'd left you?" he asked.

Amanda scowled, wishing there was something she could do to wipe the smile from his lips. "Of course I thought that. What else could I possibly think when I wake up to find you gone?"

"Only temporarily," Hawk replied, the timbre of his voice suggesting added meaning that sent a shiver up Amanda's spine. "There were things that I had to do, and I didn't want to put you in danger. Also, you needed your sleep."

Finally Amanda noticed the packhorse Hawk had been leading. Piled high on the horse were the possessions he'd taken from the Cheyenne—and Amanda's saddle.

"You got my saddle back!" she exclaimed, rushing to examine the saddle she'd used for six years. It had been a gift from Sonny, so she was emotionally attached to it, as well as being appreciative for its quality and craftsmanship. "How did you get it?"

Hawk's dark eyes met Amanda's, but he didn't answer, he simply stared at her. For Amanda the message that, in Hawk's world, a woman did not ask such questions of a man came through loud and clear. The battles were fought by the men, and though they might brag of their exploits, they did not care to be questioned about them.

After a moment Amanda nodded. Perhaps she shouldn't know what had transpired during the retrieval of her saddle, she decided. It could well be a bloody, violent tale, one she wouldn't want to hear.

"I have food." Hawk began to unstrapped Amanda's saddle from the packhorse. "I hope you don't mind eating while we ride. The Cheyenne were angry before, when we stole their horses. Now they're murderously mad that I've stolen most of their belongings." A smile crossed his lips as he ran the tips of his fingers down a hickory bow. "And I've got my bow and arrows back." He spoke of his weapon as one might speak of a loved one.

"Let's not spend time standing around talking," Amanda said, much more nervous about the Cheyenne than Hawk was. "I'd rather not have to explain to the Cheyenne that I wasn't the one who decided to steal their horses."

* * * *

Hawk was settled in his saddle, letting his stallion pick an easy pace. The Cheyenne had to be miles behind them at this point, and it was highly unlikely that they would have followed Hawk's tracks very far. They'd lost their horses then had been thoroughly disgraced when he'd returned to get the saddles. The Cheyenne wouldn't forget their enemy, Hawk Two Feather, but they wouldn't be foolish enough to jeopardize themselves by following him on foot.

With the Cheyenne now far behind him, Hawk could again dwell on more entertaining questions...like why Amanda wore trousers like a man, instead of dresses, like a woman? What would she look like in a Sioux maiden's dress? The thought made him smile, and he glanced over at Amanda. Out of the corner of his eye he saw her twist in the saddle to check for the thousandth time to see whether they were being followed. Noticing that her shirt had opened slightly, she pulled it tight again.

It'll make it easier for me when she wears something besides that shirt. Her breasts could tempt those Jesuit priests who were so strict with me as a child.

He didn't like being so continuously lured by her. It didn't matter to him that, in many ways, she was one of the bravest people he'd ever met, and certainly the bravest woman. It didn't matter that she had a hidden, passionate nature that, he suspected, would be thrilling to help her set free. What mattered — and Hawk had to always keep this in mind — was that as a white woman, Amanda could never be the woman for him.

He wasn't going to make the same mistake his mother had. His children wouldn't know the same humiliation he'd so often encountered as a child.

"What's wrong?" Amanda asked.

He looked at her, his eyes as sharp as flint. "Nothing," he answered. "I was thinking, that's all."

"Oh?"

"We'll go to my camp first," Hawk said quietly. He would not tell her of the horror he had known as a child, once he'd been able to truly see his mother for what she really was. "That will give us the chance to leave the horses there, rest a while, and get plenty to eat. After that I'll escort you home."

"That sounds fine," Amanda replied. She doubted this plan was what he had been thinking of with that scowl on his face, but she wasn't going to say so. "It won't cause any problems bringing me to your tribe?"

"No," Hawk said, though his tone was ambiguous. "The Sioux are gracious hosts. You'll be welcome."

They continued to ride, and Amanda now welcomed the silence, which gave her some uninterrupted time to put in order her feelings for Hawk.

Should she tell him that she was wealthy? Hawk Two Feather deserved a reward of some sort for rescuing her from the rapists, and for protecting her afterward. If she talked about money, would she offend him? Could the reward money help purchase items needed by the tribe?

Hawk had a fine Colt revolver and a gun belt strapped around his lean hips, so he clearly had used the white man's currency before, and understood the value of money. But would he look at her differently — more importantly, would he behave differently — if he knew her family was one of the wealthiest in the territory?

After long and hard consideration Amanda decided to reward Hawk for saving her life — but *after* she'd been safely returned to her home. Only then would he discover her last name was Wright, that her share of the family fortune was considerable, and that the combined strength of the Wright name and finances made a force to be reckoned with.

She looked up at the sky. The sun sat on the horizon. They could ride for perhaps another hour before making camp. After spending a long day in the saddle, Amanda's feelings about Hawk and her own behavior had mellowed. She hadn't gone too far, had she? Was allowing a kiss and a caress such an unforgivable thing?

If she allowed Hawk to kiss her again, who would ever know about it?

Amanda pushed the thought away, but not before she felt heat rising slowly upward, coloring her neck and cheeks. *That* line of thinking *had* to be avoided like the plague.

Realizing she needed a diversion to get her mind off the ecstasy of Hawk's skilled caresses, she twisted in the saddle and asked him, "Will you show me how to shoot your bow? I've never shot one before, and I want to learn."

"No. Never," Hawk replied sharply.

Amanda was shocked. But the vehemence of the response served to remind her once again how little she actually knew about Hawk and the world he called his own.

"I'm sorry for asking," she muttered, wondering why he could be so generous with both his time and his possessions at one moment, and selfishly aloof in the next.

In the silence that ensued, Hawk had to remind himself that Amanda's foolish questions were driven by ignorance of the Sioux culture, not a callous disregard for it. She simply didn't understand that, to a warrior, his weapons were sacred objects, and that no one else was allowed to use them, to even touch them.

Even now, though he was thankful that he'd been able to recover his bow, quiver and arrows, he needed to purify them because they'd been touched by his enemy, the Cheyenne. When he had time he would perform the purification ceremony privately so that his bow and arrows would again be unsullied, and would protect him from harm, feed himself and his family, and not allow himself or his name to be dishonored.

But since his bow, quiver, and arrows *already* needed to be purified...

"We'll make camp early," Hawk said quietly. "Then I'll show you how to use the bow."

Amanda's face broke into an enormous smile as she almost shouted, "You will?" Several horses flinched at the exuberance of her response.

"Only on the condition that you never tell anyone about it," Hawk said.

Chapter Seven

The horses had been taken care of, the campfire was crackling to life, at least thirty minutes of acceptable sunlight remained...and Hawk was shaking his head in amazement at the things he agreed to when Amanda was near.

"It can't be that bad," Amanda teased.

"What I am about to do goes against many time-honored laws my people believe in," Hawk said. "Women are not to touch that which is made for war."

Unable to find the right words to express his feelings, Hawk was astonished that, for all his discomfort, he couldn't insist that Amanda wasn't allowed to use his bow. He didn't want to see the disappointment in her eyes, eyes that had been so beautifully bright and blue when he had first agreed to teach her.

Amanda herself nearly confessed to Hawk that the things she'd done with him—in his arms as she feasted on his breath-taking kisses—were against the beliefs of *her* people. Though she bit her lip to silence the words, a smile still tugged at the corners of her mouth. The

Cheyenne now seemed far, far away, and Amanda felt truly safe for the first time since she'd first been attacked.

"There are two ways to grip the arrow," Hawk explained. "One way is like this." He notched an arrow on the string. Then he curled his right index finger tightly and pinched the notched end of the arrow between his finger and his thumb. He pulled the taut string back slightly. "The other way is like this," he continued. He shifted his grip so that the arrow was between his first and second fingers. Then, with just the tips of his fingers around the string, he pulled the arrow back a bit. "See how that works?"

Amanda was eager to try. When Hawk handed her the bow, with the arrow already notched on the string, she couldn't hide the smile that blossomed on her lips. Even though she suspected that he had shared his passion with many women, she knew that this was something Hawk had never done with or for another woman. It added a special dimension to the experience for her.

At first she pinched the end of the arrow, but when she tried to draw the arrow back, to bend the bow tightly as Hawk had done, she could hardly move it more than a few inches before the end of the arrow slipped from her grasp. The arrow shot weakly from the bow, missing the tree by four feet.

"Oops. I didn't mean to shoot that," Amanda said with a sheepish grin.

"Don't be embarrassed. This is difficult. A warrior starts by learning to make his own bow and arrows when he is very young. By the time he is ready to hunt he has had a bow in his hands for years." Hawk handed Amanda another arrow, standing beside her and to the back. "Try the other grip that I showed you."

Amanda notched the arrow, then turned her hand so that her fingertips were around the string. Instead of just using two or three fingers to grip the string, she used all four. Amanda sensed that Hawk had made the bow for himself, not for a woman half his size.

Amanda's jaw was clenched as she strained against the bow, pulling back on the string. Her left arm quivered as her right pulled the line more and more taut, drawing back the arrow. She squinted her left eye closed and tried to sight down the arrow at the tree stump. The strain made it impossible for her to keep her left arm steady, and her biceps were beginning to burn with fatigue, even though she'd only been tugging at the bow for a few seconds.

"Release, Amanda," Hawk commanded.

She relaxed her fingers just a fraction and in an instant the arrow shot away. The burn of the line sliding across the sensitive tips of her fingers caused Amanda to grimace, but the stone arrowhead hit the tree with a resounding *thunk!* and Amanda let out a shout of joy.

"I hit it! Did you see that?"

"Maybe you've got Sioux blood in you," Hawk said through a smile.

Amanda laughed at the absurdity of such an idea, considering her ivory skin, her blue eyes and her honey blonde hair.

But once the initial burst of enthusiasm for her small victory subsided, she felt the stinging in her fingertips once again.

"Let me see," Hawk said.

When she pretended she wasn't in pain, he took her by the wrist, pulling her hand toward him and turning it palm up so he could inspect her fingertips. They were pink from the bowstring, but wouldn't blister unless she continued shooting the bow in that manner.

"There's something we can do to help prevent this," Hawk offered, quickly releasing Amanda's hand.

Touching her hand had conjured up memories of him touching her elsewhere, and seeing her pink fingertips made her want to kiss him.

Amanda sensed a change in Hawk, though she was not entirely certain what had caused it. As he went to his pack of belongings, she quickly adjusted her shirt, which had pulled open more than she'd liked during the archery practice. Most troubling of all was that she'd been wearing the nearly ruined shirt for so long that she'd almost grown oblivious to its condition—no longer always aware when it had opened.

Hawk returned with a small, flat piece of leather, cut in an odd shape. Amanda quickly discovered the shape was designed so that she could pull back on the bow with the leather cushioning her fingertips from the string.

Amanda then shot four more arrows, some hitting the tree stump and others missing. During the next set of shots, Hawk taught her how to keep both eyes open as she aimed, and Amanda was able to hit the tree the next five times.

"This bow is too much for me, though," Amanda said, when the arrows had been retrieved. "I can't get the line all the way back."

"Perhaps…" Hawk said, then stopped.

"Will you help me?" Amanda asked, notching up another arrow, turning her back to Hawk to face the target tree once more.

Hawk stepped close behind Amanda and extended his arms, wrapping his left hand around her left wrist so he could help her steady the bow, sliding his right hand around to grip the bowstring just above her hand. She felt his chest against her back.

"Keep both eyes open and, instead of thinking about the arrow, think about the target," Hawk instructed, helping Amanda to pull back the bowstring.

Amanda's request for help had been issued innocently enough, but now her thoughts had nothing to do with the target. Even though he wore buckskin, she felt his heart pounding fast. Or was that just her heart hammering? Why did her heart do that whenever Hawk was so near she could catch the scent of him, so subtle and indefinably masculine?

"Aim, then release," Hawk said, trying to concentrate on the task at hand.

Hawk loosened his grip on the bowstring, and the force it exerted against Amanda's fingers was much greater than she could withstand. The bowstring snapped from her fingertips, and the arrow sailed off, shooting high and well off the mark, disappearing into the distance.

"You missed," Hawk said.

There was a huskiness in his voice that she didn't quite understand.

Amanda lowered the bow and turned slowly, never completely easing the contact of her body against Hawk's until she faced him. She tilted her head far back to look directly into his dark eyes and saw his gaze go from her own eyes down to her breasts then quickly back up again.

He doesn't want to look at me, Amanda guessed. At first she felt inadequate in the face of this suggestion that perhaps she wasn't beautiful enough, not feminine enough, to hold his interest. But this fear was short-lived, in her heart she knew he found her attractive. He wasn't like the white men of Deadwood who thought her Levis and cotton shirt would be best left for men to wear.

Hawk likes to look at me, but he doesn't like to like it.

"Want to try again?" Hawk asked.

Her mouth dry, Amanda felt the heated sexual tension between them. She wanted very much to tell Hawk, in plain, simple language, that what she really wanted was to have his kisses begin once again. His kisses had awakened in her a passion that she'd believed existed only in her dream world, a passion she had been afraid to experiment with in real life.

Do it, Amanda! Tell him to kiss you!

Though the inner voice of her passionate self cried out, Amanda could not make her lips form the words that needed to be spoken.

"It's getting late," Hawk said then, stepping backward, pulling his gaze away from Amanda and obviously having a difficult time doing it. "We should make camp."

"Yes, of course. Camp."

The words sounded wooden in Amanda's mouth. She felt eerily disoriented as she watched him walking away to retrieve the arrows. Make camp? They'd already made camp. Amanda realized, with some amount of relief, that Hawk was as confused by the chaotic emotions that ricocheted back and forth between them as she was.

Why can't he allow himself the pleasure of looking at me? In Deadwood the men usually made no effort to hide their comments and their ogling. But Hawk was resisting that which other men had sought. Why?

A shiver ran through Amanda, working its way from her toes all the way up her spine. She felt jittery inside, knowing with absolute certainty that she wanted Hawk, wanted him with every fiber in her body. She needed him in ways that she did not entirely understand. She knew at that moment that she had wanted him from the first instant they had kissed. At least her *body* had wanted him, had known this instinctively, and had heeded the unconscious whispers that had been directing so many of her actions recently. Her mind, and all the inhibitions foisted on her by others, as well as the self-imposed guilt she felt because of the erotic nature of her dreams, had made her think that she was wrong to accept the pleasures of the deeply arousing kisses that the powerful Sioux warrior had bestowed on her.

Amanda turned her back to Hawk and quickly tucked the tails of her damnably buttonless shirt into her Levis once more.

Clearly, the next time she kissed Hawk, the next time she wound her arms around his neck and held him close, her body would not be satisfied with just his kisses. The next time in his arms, she would take the next step, and Amanda knew exactly what the next step was. The step she couldn't allow herself to take. Her body was intemperate, she realized, and accordingly could not moderate the passion she shared with Hawk. It was all or nothing, and since she could not allow herself to have all, she would have to have nothing.

She walked to her bedroll and hoped to get some sleep, though she doubted she would.

* * * *

A gaiety passed between Amanda and Hawk throughout the morning. Amanda was delighted to be with Hawk. When he was happy he was infinitely more enjoyable to be near than when he was quiet and brooding. She didn't understand the change in him, though she suspected that his high spirits were a facade to hide an even more troubling frame of mind.

"There isn't really anything you have to know when we get there," Hawk told her. "I think you'll like my sister. She'll talk your ear off and ask you a hundred questions."

"You have a sister?" Amanda asked.

"You make it sound so unusual," Hawk replied.

"I just didn't picture you with a brother or sister, that's all. No disrespect intended."

Amanda almost added that if Hawk were more open about himself and his life, she wouldn't be so surprised when she discovered something as mundane as a sister. However, Hawk was not a man she could tease about such issues.

"Actually, she and I share only our mother. We had different fathers," Hawk explained, though his tone changed considerably. Amanda could tell that he didn't want to talk about his family, that there were secrets he wanted to keep. "Buttercup—that's my sister's name—is the most spirited woman I've ever known."

"Even more spirited than I am?" Amanda asked, her coquettish tone surprising her. Hawk's easy smiles were working seductive magic on her senses, even though she was doing all she could to inure herself against them.

Hawk looked at her. "That's a difficult question to answer so quickly. I'm confident in saying that Buttercup has probably made as many men furious with her as you have, but in regard to pure spirit—"

"Are you saying I'm difficult to get along with?" Amanda shot back, turning Daisy to the side so that she rode so close to Hawk that their knees nearly touched. "Be honest, now, am I really difficult to get along with?"

Hawk shrugged, then shook his head slowly, his smile boyish. Amanda wanted to kiss him. She wanted to leap right out of her saddle and tackle him to the ground, and shower his face with kisses. Then she intended to kiss him on the mouth—a long, slow, unending kiss that would bring little tremors of satisfaction to the surface of her skin.

Amanda was almost thankful for her apprehension about riding into the Sioux camp. It provided a diversion to the romantic thoughts running through her mind.

"You're sure they won't mind?" Amanda asked softly.

"How many times have I told you that you'll be welcome?" Hawk asked.

"A few."

"A few dozen is more like it."

Amanda had heard stories of Indian massacres, of unspeakable atrocities too horrifying for a woman's ears. But the women were always told eventually, and the men who spread the stories were always there to put comforting arms around the frightened ladies, and to offer promises to protect them from the redskin savages. Amanda knew that most of the stories she'd heard were lies, but she also knew that some of the stories—stories of rape and murder—were probably true. She'd been attacked by Indians herself only a few days earlier.

And saved by an Indian as well, she reminded herself.

They rode slowly over the crest of a hill, driving the horses they had taken from the Cheyenne. Then in front of them in the valley unfolded the Sioux camp, nearly eighty tepees grouped in the valley. Children ran excitedly everywhere.

"They know we're coming?" Amanda asked, shocked that though a considerable distance separated them from the outskirts of the camp, everyone apparently had been forewarned of their arrival.

"They've known for at least the last mile," Hawk answered. "We Sioux don't like surprises. We like to know who's approaching our camp."

Children ran forward to greet them, their faces open and guileless. Many of them shouted out Hawk's name. Amanda was pleased to see the children's smiling faces, but along with them came a handful of braves on horseback, armed with bows and a few rifles. These men looked on Amanda with open scorn.

A dangerous-looking brave rode alongside Hawk, speaking to him in a short, clipped fashion. Amanda didn't have to be told that there was no love lost between the man and Hawk.

"I captured the horses from the Cheyenne," Hawk said, speaking English, "but you can see that for yourself, Red Wolf. Speak the truth now. Are you angry that I have returned late, that I have returned with such a bounty, or just angry that I have returned at all?"

Red Wolf didn't reply. He kicked his horse into a gallop and returned to the camp quickly and, in his haste, frightened two of the horses. Hawk had to retrieve them, chasing them back to the small herd before he and Amanda could ride into camp.

* * * *

After two hours in the Sioux camp Amanda finally relaxed enough so that she didn't jump at every sound. As Hawk had predicted, Buttercup had instantly stepped to the fore and volunteered to stay with Amanda while Hawk spoke to the tribal elders and chiefs.

Amanda sat cross-legged on the buffalo mat as Buttercup had indicated, while the younger woman rummaged in a cavernous canvas bag. Amanda guessed her age to be sixteen, but perhaps a little younger. She had all the energy Hawk had indicated, but none of the wary seriousness of her older brother. From the time they'd met, Buttercup had stopped talking only long enough for Amanda to answer a few questions.

"Here it is," Buttercup said, her constant smile growing wider as she pulled a deerskin dress from the canvas bag. "Why don't you try this on?"

Amanda almost refused the offer. She didn't want to make herself a burden to anyone, but the look on Buttercup's face — the look of someone who wanted nothing more than to be of assistance to another young woman far from home — convinced her that to refuse would be a mistake.

"You're sure?" Amanda asked.

Buttercup dropped down to kneel beside Amanda, then thrust the dress into her lap. "Please. It would make me happy."

Amanda undressed quickly, leaving on only her drawers, which Buttercup found fascinating. She asked, "What is that?"

"They're called drawers."

"Why?"

"I guess because you draw them on."

Buttercup frowned. "Why do you draw them on?" She shrugged. "There is much about the yellow eyes I do not understand."

Amanda pulled the deerskin garment over her head and smoothed it down over her body. Sleeveless and unintentionally snug-fitting, the dress came down to her knees in a straight line. The garment was practically shapeless without a belt. Tight across the bosom and at the hips, Amanda could tell that it was made for Buttercup's more youthful, less curvaceous figure.

"Try these on," Buttercup said excitedly, extracting moccasins from the canvas bag. She practically forced them into Amanda's hands.

Amanda glanced at her boots. Reluctant to give up this loving gift from her brother, she worried how the boots would look with a dress. The question brought a smile to her lips as she began putting on the moccasins. What difference could it possibly make how she looked? In a day or two she would be leaving the Sioux camp, and once she did she would never again see any of these people. She could paint herself red and green if she wanted to, and nobody back in Deadwood would ever know about it.

The moccasins fit perfectly, lacing up to just above her ankles for a pleasantly snug fit. Amanda stood up and took a few tentative steps inside the tepee. She decided she liked the feel of the moccasins. They reminded her of the kidskin slippers she'd worn in the past, the dancing slippers fashionable young ladies wore—the ones Amanda had almost never been seen in and hadn't worn in over a year.

"Do you like them?" Buttercup asked. Buttercup rose to her feet and began pacing with Amanda.

"Yes, the moccasins feel wonderful," Amanda answered. Then, seeing the unhappiness flash across Buttercup's face, she added quickly, "And so does the dress. It's beautiful."

Buttercup laughed. "It is not beautiful. It is just a common dress a Sioux maiden would wear every day. But I thank you for not telling the entire truth. Come now," Buttercup said, taking Amanda's hand to tug her toward the flap of the tepee. "Hawk has to see how you look in this dress."

Chapter Eight

Not all of the elders were as happy with Hawk's success in capturing the horses from the hostile Northern Cheyenne as Hawk had hoped. He sensed immediately that Red Wolf had been speaking badly of him to the elders, and even if Red Wolf's claims bore only a grain of truth, that would be enough to plant a seed of doubt in the minds of some of the men.

"We are all thankful for the horses that Hawk Two Feather has brought to us," Red Wolf said, turning slowly to address the collection of elderly men who represented the governance of the tribe. "But I think we must also remember that Hawk was not here when we needed him during our last hunt. Where was he then? Threatening the peace by attacking the Cheyenne? Who knows? Who can say?"

Hawk clenched his teeth, but that was the only outward sign of anger he displayed. He wouldn't be able to fight Red Wolf's accusations and win without shedding a little blood of his own. The way Red Wolf had framed his accusations, Hawk was guilty of either inciting the Cheyenne or neglecting the tribe. Either way, at least some of the council elders — whether they were more or less inclined to military action — would be unhappy with Hawk's absence from the tribe.

"And he has brought an outsider to us," Red Wolf continued. "I understand she has yellow hair and eyes the color of the sky. Some might say she is beautiful, and I have nothing against beauty. What I do question is why Hawk should have involved himself in this woman's battle with the Cheyenne. The fight is hers, not ours. From what Hawk has told us, white men were killed as well in his rescue of this young woman. Hawk, it seems, has made many enemies who might now be searching for him...and he's made them without gain for the tribe. That makes me wonder whether he has brought his enemies, and the enemies of this woman, to us. Are they massing now, just beyond our vision, waiting for the best time to attack? Do we need the white men to hate us more than they already do? Do we need to give them another reason to hunt us?"

It took all of Hawk's discipline to keep from interrupting Red Wolf's diatribe. But to interrupt Red Wolf would only make himself look bad, so he held his tongue, waiting for his turn to speak.

After pulling his gaze away from Red Wolf, he studied the stony, unreadable expressions of the council elders. Some of them, he guessed, would be impressed with Red Wolf's fiery speech, with his defiant rhetoric, with the subtle way he reminded everyone of Hawk's half-breed status within the tribe. But there were others among the elders who would be put off by Red Wolf's attack, who would see that it had been motivated by hatred for Hawk, and not a desire to assure what was best for the tribe. Surely, none of the elders could be ignorant of the hatred that had blossomed between Hawk and Red Wolf from the time they were young men.

At last, after nearly forty minutes of innuendo and rhetoric, Red Wolf sat down. The council of elders, saying nothing, turned in unison toward Hawk, awaiting his response.

"Red Wolf talks a great deal," Hawk began, "but, unfortunately, even when he has nothing to say, he insists on saying it."

A snicker passed among the elders. Hawk did not look in Red Wolf's direction, but he felt he'd scored a telling blow. Then, with a calm confidence that belied the anger he'd been hiding, he gave his version, once again, of what he'd done since riding away from camp. The elders listened to Hawk's words. Success couldn't be argued with, and there was almost nothing that was more highly prized among the Sioux than healthy, well-trained horses. Though Hawk had not returned with a bounty of food, the horses he'd taken—and, better still, taken from the Northern Cheyenne—would benefit all in the tribe by making it easier for them to hunt.

"And as for the woman with the yellow hair," Hawk continued, "she is a maiden, and will remain a maiden until she leaves our camp. A fight with the white man because of what I have done? I killed white men who were trying to rape her. Do the white men value their white rapists? I think not. So you see, the words that Red Wolf speaks are filled with zeal, filled with emotion...but they are not filled with knowledge or wisdom, and they certainly are not filled with the truth."

Hawk sat down after that, keeping his face thoroughly impassive. He did not want any of the elders to see into his heart, but he believed that his defense had not only been articulate but had also successfully beaten down the challenge to his reputation. Now Red Wolf looked like the warrior who would irresponsibly cast aspersions against another warrior, and do so for the unacceptable motive of trying to make himself appear superior.

* * * *

"Hawk, before you go very far, can I talk with you?"

Hawk had just stepped out of the tepee in which he'd explained his actions to the tribal elders when the deep voice stopped him in his tracks. He turned sharply to his left and smiled broadly, as he did at the sight of only one man.

"Crow!" he shouted.

The two men embraced excitedly, drawing the attention of other braves standing nearby. Such open displays of affection between men were not common, though Hawk didn't care about the attention they attracted.

Hawk and Crow walked toward the outskirts of the camp, discussing inconsequential matters. Hawk knew many people were listening to them. Once they were alone, Crow stopped walking and turned to face Hawk.

"I think we're going to have some trouble," he said, shaking his head slowly. He fished into the pocket of his cotton jacket for his tobacco pouch and cigarette papers. His attire consisted of a bizarre mixture of leather loincloth, leggings, moccasins, and a blue cotton jacket. He wore no shirt. "I've been going through some documents in Fargo."

Crow finished rolling the second cigarette. He handed one to Hawk, then they both lit up. Hawk inhaled the first cigarette he'd had in more than a month. It tasted wonderful. Tobacco held magical and religious implications for the Sioux.

"What do you want to do?" Hawk asked.

"That's why I needed to talk to you. I'd like to go to Fargo and sit in on the trial, maybe get involved if I can. This silly young fool in court doesn't have the slightest idea of how much trouble he's really in, and I'd like to sit in to make sure he gets as fair a trial as possible."

Crow took a second puff from the cigarette then tossed it aside.

"When would you like to leave?"

"As soon as possible, but I've just returned from there."

"Ah, now I'm beginning to see," Hawk replied with a grin.

The tribal elders had profound suspicions of Crow at Dawn, even though the attorney had, on more than one occasion, protected the tribe by forcing the territorial government—and one time even the federal government—to make good on treaties made with the Sioux, insisting that they be fulfilled. He had also successfully defended a young brave on charges of theft, proving beyond any doubt that the charges were false. His arguments for the defense were so compelling that the all-white jury even criticized the town marshal of Kanton for bringing forward such a preposterous charge.

Crow spent considerable time in the white man's cities, wearing the white man's clothing, speaking the white man's English, which Hawk had heard made the elders fearful that he would *become* a white man, and turn against his own tribe unless they were ever-vigilant. Crow needed to go to Fargo, but if he asked for permission from the elders, they'd want to discuss the issue at length, and consider the matter for several days. Hawk understood his friend was much too impatient for that kind of delay.

"Can you help?" Crow asked.

"Leave during the night," Hawk responded. "I'll explain it to the elders. They'll be angry, and they'll be suspicious, but they'll get over it. They always do."

"Thanks. And now can I give you a little free advice?"

Hawk felt his heart sink. Crow had never truly approved of Hawk's romantic adventures with the women of the camp, though before he'd always pretty much kept his opinion to himself. Hawk wasn't in the mood for a lecture about Amanda.

"Just say the word," Crow added, when Hawk didn't answer, "and I'll keep my mouth shut. A good attorney knows when to stay quiet."

Hawk grinned. If he couldn't take advice from his best friend, from whom could he take advice? "Go ahead, tell me what's on your mind."

"Get the girl away from here as quickly as possible, and make sure she makes it home safely," Crow said, the tone of his voice somber. "I had the chance to see her walking through the camp with Buttercup. Red Wolf was following her—discreetly, of course, from a distance. But he was following her nevertheless. *Stalking her* would probably be more accurate. We both know what Red Wolf is like. If that girl leaves here without an escort, Red Wolf will devour her. And nobody will ever find the body."

"Yes, I know all too well what he's like," Hawk replied quietly.

"And can I ask you something else? Again, you have the right not to answer if you don't want to."

Hawk looked at his old friend and tried to smile but couldn't. He'd been close to Crow for too long to cheapen the friendship with half-truths or outright lies.

"Have you taken her as a lover?" Crow asked.

"How like an attorney of you to ask the difficult questions so bluntly," Hawk replied. He wanted to be annoyed at Crow for being so bold, but he wasn't. In his heart he knew that Crow had only his best interests in mind, was concerned only with what was best for the tribe. If Crow caused a few tempers to wear thin now and then, it seemed a small price to pay for all the good he did.

"Someone has to," Crow commented. "Now answer the question. Are you and the white girl lovers?"

"No. Not really."

"What exactly does that mean?"

"I'm sure you can guess," Hawk snapped, not wanting to get into the specifics of his transgressions with Amanda. He didn't want to appear to be one of those repellent men who seduced women, and then bragged about it afterward to his friends.

"Yes, I can guess, but I'm a lawyer, and that means I like the facts more than speculation. What's happened between you two?"

In stumbling sentences, Hawk told of their time together, his and Amanda's. He did not leave out anything, but neither did he embellish the essential facts.

"Do you want to be her lover?" Crow asked when Hawk had concluded what he felt was a rather damning confession.

"What? Of course I do," Hawk exclaimed. "But I can't. You've got to see that. I can't. I don't want to be like…"

"Like what?"

Hawk shot him a fierce look, and this time there was no need to feign annoyance. The anger in Hawk's heart was real enough.

"I'd rather not get into that," Hawk said quietly, his words frozen by emotions he did not wish to explore.

Crow sensed his friend's unease, but he also knew that until Hawk confronted the questions of his past he could never go on to a peaceful future. "Is it that you don't want to be like Red Wolf? Or is it that you don't want to be like your mother?"

Crow watched Hawk's pent-up rage escalate. Only their lifelong friendship could protect him against Hawk's pride and temper. Crow alone, among all the Sioux, dared to force Hawk to confront his own hidden enemies.

"I...I really don't know," Hawk answered at last. "Amanda is beautiful. All you have to do is look at her to see that. But she's much more than that. I can't begin to tell you how much more."

"Then why aren't you lovers?" Crow could not imagine a situation where Hawk would want to sleep with a woman and not eventually succeed. In such pursuits, Hawk appeared invincible, seduction inevitable.

"I don't want to be another Red Wolf. He sleeps with our women only when he can't find a white woman to spread her legs for him." Hawk spat on the ground, as though the truth of his words left a foul taste in his mouth. "I don't want her just because she has pale skin, blue eyes and blonde hair."

"Then want her for more than that."

"Are you trying to annoy me?"

"No, I'm trying to make you see that you're as much white as you are Sioux. Sleeping with a white woman doesn't mean you'll end up like your mother." Crow put a hand on Hawk's shoulder. "Do whatever you must. I know you as well as any man—better than any man, I'd say—and yet there are times when I'm convinced I hardly know you at all. I only want to see you happy."

"And what about you? Are you happy?"

"I'm an Indian and a lawyer. I'm quite certain it's against the law for me to be happy."

* * * *

Amanda tried to keep her eyes and attention focused solely on Buttercup, but she couldn't. No matter how hard she tried, she found herself searching the camp, looking for Hawk. She hadn't seen him since the previous afternoon, when he'd left her to speak to others in the tribe.

"It's a beautiful day," Amanda murmured absently, sitting on a blanket. "So peaceful."

Buttercup smiled as she continued working to soften an elk hide.

"When will you be going back to your home?" Buttercup asked. Her hands worked the elk hide. It was clear to Amanda that she'd been doing this kind of work since she was a very young girl.

"I don't know," Amanda answered after several seconds of silence. She kicked her feet in front of herself, crossing them at the ankle. She tugged at the hem of the deerskin dress. She found it ironic that earlier she had worn a shirt she was forever fumbling with, and now she'd been given a dress that exposed more of herself than she liked. She leaned back with her hands behind her in the grass. "Hawk said there were things he had to do, and then he would take me back."

"How far from here do you live?"

"Outside of Deadwood. On a ranch."

Amanda thought of saying more, but she stopped herself. She genuinely liked Buttercup, enjoying the Sioux girl's enthusiasm for life, but she did not want to put all her faith and trust in the girl. Money had a way of turning decent people into cretins, transforming honest people into criminals. So far, the Sioux had treated her graciously, but Amanda saw no particular reason to inform them of her wealth. Later, when she was home once again, she would buy gifts for everyone, and something special for the entire tribe to thank them for all they'd done to assist her.

A grin tickled Amanda's lips as she began thinking about what gift Buttercup would enjoy receiving most, and what would give Hawk the greatest pleasure.

"What was Hawk like when he was younger?" Amanda asked, trying to make the question sound innocuous.

"Hawk was never young," Buttercup said with a laugh. "There was always a streak in him, something that made him run. Always so serious. It is part of the reason he hunts alone, I suppose."

"Part of the reason?"

"Hawk and I...our mother...she came from a very wealthy family," Buttercup began. She stopped kneading the elk hide, and her eyes took on an unfocused, distant quality. "She wasn't very particular with whom she shared her body, so long as it was an Indian brave. It wasn't that she loved the Sioux so much—quite the opposite, actually. I think she hated us. But she hated her own family more, and she figured she could hurt her father most by sleeping with Indians. Hawk and I don't have the same father. In fact, I don't even know who my father is."

"Sometimes there are those within the tribe who think less of Hawk and me because of who our mother was," Buttercup continued. "I think that's why he's always been so serious when it comes to providing meat for the tribe." Buttercup removed her headband, smoothed her long, straight black hair, then returned the headband. "Hawk and I have each other, though, and that's enough of a family, I think."

Amanda could not imagine her life without her family. Even when they infuriated her, all the Wrights—brothers and sisters, aunts, uncles and cousins—made up a family, and they stuck together. An attack upon one of them was an attack upon them all, and this knowledge provided the underpinning which had given her the confidence to follow the guidance of her heart, rather than being just another pampered debutante, giving teas and attending socials.

As Buttercup looked at Amanda, a mischievous glow lit her eyes. "I wonder what you'd see in a vision quest," she said, her voice lowering, as though in discussion of something dangerous or naughty.

"A vision quest? What's that?"

"Maybe I'll be able to show you," Buttercup said, leaning closer, her voice dropping to a whisper, even though Amanda saw no one near enough to hear. "Father Lefevre, the priest who taught Hawk, Crow and I to read—along with Mother, of course—said that the vision quest is the work of the devil, but we never believed him. They're exhausting, but once you've had one—once you've really seen the vision— you'll never think of yourself in quite the same way again. Hmmm. I wonder if it is even possible for a woman with no Sioux blood in her at all to have a vision."

"I'm sure I can!" Amanda said quickly, not wanting to be left out just because of the color of her skin. It sounded like an adventure, and Amanda was ready for one. "Let's do try."

"All right, but you mustn't tell anyone."

* * * *

"Crow at Dawn shows his disrespect," Red Wolf said, shaking his head slowly, as though amazed that any Sioux brave would even dream of doing such a thing. "To leave just like that, without a word of explanation?"

Hawk, who had been busy inspecting arrows that some of the very young braves had made, turned to face Red Wolf. "I explained to the elders why he had to leave, Red Wolf, and you know that."

"I know that you have spoken for him," Red Wolf replied, "but that is not the same as saying he actually had a reason, is it?"

"What kind of accusation are you making?" Hawk's voice was low, threatening. He was in no mood to listen to a man like Red Wolf slander the name of his best friend.

"I make no accusation," Red Wolf said.

Hawk was aware that many men and women, and the elders themselves, were moving closer, listening more carefully to what Red Wolf was saying.

"I only speak the truth when I say that Crow was here and now he is gone, leaving without permission or explanation. He has not spent much time with his people lately, has he? Instead, he wears the clothes of the white man, speaks the tongue of the white man. He probably thinks like the white man."

For a second Hawk closed his eyes, forcing himself to remain calm. If he lost his temper, he would be playing right into Red Wolf's hands. It was bad enough to allow a man like Red Wolf to make him angry, it would be doubly bad if he actually let others in the tribe see his anger, witness his lack of self-control against a man he held in such low esteem.

"You are hardly one to talk of respect," Hawk said. "Is there anything you respect? Anyone? The way you behave sometimes, it is clear you have no respect for yourself."

"I have plenty of respect for myself," Red Wolf replied softly, venomously. "But respect for you? Why haven't you taken a wife to your tepee yet, Hawk? You talk so much about what is and is not good for the tribe, but do I see you with even a single wife? No. Unless it is not a Sioux wife you want, but a woman with yellow hair and pale skin, like the one you brought to us to feed and clothe. Why did you put yourself in jeopardy, risking your life for a white stranger? What possible good can that be to us?"

"You would not understand," Hawk said, turning, about to walk away. Red Wolf was looking for a fight, and Hawk wasn't going to give him one. "It has to do with understanding what a Sioux brave really is."

"And holding another brave as if he is a woman? Is that what you think a brave should be?"

Hawk turned to face Red Wolf, at first confused by what he'd said. There was an insult there, but it made no sense to him. And then it dawned on him that Red Wolf was accusing him and Crow of inappropriate affection.

"You maggot." Hawk hissed through teeth clenched in rage. He took a step toward Red Wolf, but then a highly respected elder, Dull Knife, stepped between them.

"We have so many enemies," the old man said in his characteristic, slow manner of speaking, "why must two young men make war among themselves? Is it death you want? There are many outside our camp who will be thought heroes if they kill you. So why help your enemies by hating yourselves? Do you not see that we cannot fight among ourselves and survive?"

Hawk, instantly contrite, replied, "Yes, you are right."

Red Wolf apologized for letting his 'sense of pride in the tribe' get the best of him, but the undercurrent of scorn he felt for Hawk never completely left his voice. Dull Knife walked away slowly, and Hawk turned his back on Red Wolf, promising himself that he would never again allow himself to be taken in like that again. He had behaved exactly as Red Wolf had wanted him to, and he'd lost some of Dull Knife's respect in the process. Hawk was furious with himself.

Chapter Nine

The heat seeped into Amanda's pores. It squeezed her body as though it was a physical thing. Sometimes, when she tried to relax, she would breathe in deeply, and when she did she felt the moist heat of the sweat lodge go down her lungs. It only made her feel all that much hotter.

"You're fighting it," Buttercup noted softly, her voice barely rising above the hissing of the steam coming off the rocks. She'd just poured a fresh cup of water onto the heated rocks, and the steam and heat was once again swirling with renewed energy in the small, confined tepee. "The whole point of this preparation is to release. Release everything that is within you so that you're empty inside. Only by releasing everything will you be able to receive your vision."

"You make it sound so easy," Amanda murmured.

Stretching out her legs, she then leaned back onto her elbows. It was too hot to have any part of her body touching any other part. Perspiration ran down her naked body, and even though she occasionally wiped it away, an instant later she was wet again.

"I never said it was easy," Buttercup replied. "But it's worth the effort. If you—" She stopped herself, then began again. "*When* you receive your vision, you'll know that any sacrifice needed will have been worth it. A vision will change your life, change the way you look at yourself and your world."

"Let's hope so," Amanda replied, lying on her back and placing her hands lightly on the soft buffalo hide beneath her.

Let it go, don't think about the heat. Don't think about anything at all. That's the trick.

When the image of Hawk, smiling devilishly, entered her mind, she pushed it away quickly. If she let him into her thoughts now, she knew she'd never get him out, and she would never be receptive enough to receive her vision.

Time passed, and another awareness entered Amanda's consciousness. This one concerned only her awareness that she had, for several minutes, thought of nothing at all. Now, whenever errant ideas came to her, she could push them away more easily than she had in the past.

Amanda kept her eyes closed and was soon deeper within herself than she'd ever been before.

* * * *

Hawk's rage had not yet cooled when he was told that Buttercup had taken the white woman to the sweat lodge. Hawk jumped on his stallion and rode hard out of camp, needing to feel the wind against his face, in his hair, to feel the comforting rhythm of the horse beneath him. He needed action.

His tribe held higher expectations of him—more than for any other Sioux warrior—and he knew it.

Hawk had always been tested harder. He needed to prove that his white blood had not made him soft, had not made his loyalties malleable. He was *expected*— much more than any other brave, with the possible exception of Crow—to take a Sioux wife, and to have children. Only then would the white blood that ran in his own veins be diluted sufficiently for him to be considered a true Sioux.

With this destiny continually taunting him, to have his sister bring a blonde-haired vixen to the sweat lodge was infuriating. Was Buttercup trying to turn Amanda into a Sioux? Of course, the idea could have come from Amanda, Hawk mused. It could have been her idea from the very beginning, to tempt him even more as a Dakota maiden…

No, it couldn't have been her idea, he decided a moment later. Amanda didn't know enough about his world to have suggested it on her own. She would have followed Buttercup's offer willingly, though.

Women!

Hawk reined in his stallion. It wouldn't do to push the animal into a protracted gallop just to get away from for a while.

He looked back at the camp and shook his head slowly. Perhaps Red Wolf had been correct when he'd accused Hawk of carelessly becoming involved in a battle with whites and the Northern Cheyenne. Perhaps Hawk simply should have ridden in the other direction when he'd heard Amanda's frightened screams.

No, that wouldn't have been right. No matter what Red Wolf or anyone else in the tribe thought, leaving Amanda to defend herself would not have been proper. Just as it wasn't proper now for Hawk to recall with absolute clarity the sweetness of her kisses, the warmth of her smooth skin, the trembling touch of her hands as passion burned hotter and hotter within them both.

Under his breath, Hawk uttered a single foul word in English. He was angry with himself for always thinking about Amanda and disappointed with himself for not having resisted the temptation that she represented. Even if he had to take Amanda kicking and screaming by the hair, he was going to get her back to her family as soon as possible. It was the only way he'd ever regain the peace in his mind and soul that had been his before she'd entered his life.

* * * *

Amanda felt weak. Very weak. Her legs had so little strength that it was difficult to ascend the sloping hill, not far from camp. The sweat lodge had sapped more of her strength than she knew existed. Buttercup had warned her that weakness might occur, so Amanda wasn't worried. Just the same, she hoped that her efforts so far would result in a successful vision quest.

"Later, after the vision quest, we will know what your natural name is," Buttercup said as they reached the tree line. "Perhaps it will come to you instantly, but it is more likely that we will need to interpret your name."

"Natural name?"

"And we must find your *Wotawe*. That is important."

"*Wotawe?*" Amanda was struggling with the Sioux language, though in the time she'd spent with Buttercup, she'd learned a number of words.

Buttercup smiled at Amanda. Buttercup seemed pleased with how quickly she was learning the ways of her people. "A *Wotawe* is your personal charm. It's a personal stone. It helps to keep and contain your power and to remind you always of who and what you are."

"There's so much to learn." Amanda looked over her shoulder. The camp could no longer be seen in the valley. She wondered how far up the hills into the trees Buttercup intended to take her. "What was that about a name?"

"A natural name. There are names that we give ourselves, and names that the spirit world gives us. When my brother went on his vision quest the spirits returned him with a hawk's feather in each hand. That is why he is Hawk Two Feather."

"I see," Amanda replied, though she wasn't entirely certain she did.

Spirits returned Hawk? Where had they taken him? The skeptical part of Amanda's nature wormed its way into her thoughts, but she quickly banished it. One could not be open to new experiences and cynical at the same time.

They followed a deer trail farther up the hill, where it eventually led to a small clearing. To Amanda, this was an idyllic place, secluded and confined by all the trees. The clearing could have been made by man, but Amanda suspected it had occurred naturally.

"This is where I had my first vision quest," Buttercup explained. She walked to the center of the clearing then turned around slowly, a faint smile on her lips and in her eyes. Her memories of this place and the vision quest were obviously happy ones. "Hawk had his here also. There are good spirits here. *Ida Maka* treats us kindly here." She smiled at Amanda. "*Ida Maka* means Mother Earth."

"There's just so much to learn about your ways," Amanda said, disheartened.

"Don't think about what you don't know, think about what you do know. Only then can you keep going forward and not dwell in the past." Buttercup spread out the small square of elk hide on the grass in the center of the clearing. "Give me your dress and moccasins. I'll return for you tomorrow afternoon."

A heated flush instantly went through Amanda. "You're going to leave me here naked?"

Buttercup's eyes narrowed in confusion. "You don't need to hide yourself before the spirits, and *Ida Maka* loves you as you are."

Buttercup made it sound so natural to be naked outdoors, but Amanda could not blithely dismiss the teachings of a lifetime. "What difference could it make?" Amanda conceded softly, after some hesitation. "Only Mother Earth will see me here, right?"

She pulled the dress over her head and handed it to Buttercup, then removed her moccasins. She had removed her drawers earlier, under Buttercup's insistence, who'd said it wasn't a Sioux garment. Buttercup took the three items and placed them in the grass some yards away, as though to ensure that the garments would not interfere with the ceremony. Amanda was relieved to discover that she would not be left without any clothes.

"Now empty your mind and heart and wait for the voice of the spirits to whisper. Shortly after they do a vision will appear," Buttercup instructed. "Become comfortable however you choose. To see the vision, you must look within yourself."

Amanda felt uneasy, being outdoors without any clothes on, but she did as Buttercup suggested. As she sat on the elk hide blanket, she found it at first impossible to get comfortable, especially with

Buttercup still there. Then, after a murmured, "I'll be back for you tomorrow," Buttercup left without another sound.

The minutes ticked by, and finally Amanda was able to relax enough to allow herself to stop feeling so self-conscious.

I am alone with Ida Maka on a sacred vision quest. Amanda was finally regaining the self-confidence that was so much a part of her personality. *Nothing bad can happen to me when I am with Mother Earth.*

Amanda stretched out on the elk hide, slowly spreading her arms and legs, as though to catch the afternoon sunlight with as much of herself as possible, as a spring flower does the sunshine with its petals.

I was not born Sioux, but I can learn to think like one, feel like one.

Within moments she felt the tension leaving her body, gently slipping away, without regret, and she knew it was best this way. Without a care or any concern for time, or even of the world around her, Amanda moved slowly deeper and deeper into herself.

* * * *

Hawk was distinctly aware of the fact that he probably should not be doing what he was. He was also aware that he probably would regret his actions, and that the fight that would surely ensue between himself, his sister, and Amanda would be a most regrettable one.

Even though he knew all of this, Hawk was determined to go forward. The women of the tribe were buzzing with the gossip that Buttercup had taken the yellow-haired woman to the sweat lodge then, from the lodge, Buttercup had escorted her out of camp. Immediately Hawk concluded that Buttercup was instructing Amanda on a vision quest. And if she was doing that, then more likely than not they were up on the hillside, in the small clearing in the trees Hawk had discovered so many years earlier.

The only person he had ever told of his *Hocoka* was Buttercup, and it rather perplexed him that his sister had chosen to break that silence with Amanda. Why her? Buttercup's easygoing, loving nature had made her many friends in the tribe, in spite of her embarrassing parentage. She had many friends to confide in, yet she had chosen Amanda over all them.

Why?

"I'll go crazy trying to understand women," Hawk muttered.

Though several summers had passed since Hawk had visited the clearing, he knew it wasn't far ahead. His first vision quest had changed the way he looked at himself and his life. Even blindfolded, he would have been able to find his way back to such a momentous place in his life.

Unconsciously, he began paying more attention to his footsteps, reducing what little sound his moccasins made against the ground to virtual silence. The Sioux were trained to hunt on foot as well as on horseback, and from a very early age young braves developed the habit of silent stealth.

When he reached the clearing he broke his silence. In fact, the sound of his own breath suddenly sucked in and held would have drawn Amanda's attention had she not been so focused on her vision quest.

She was stretched out on an elk hide blanket with her eyes closed against the last of the sunlight making its way through the trees. Naked, her body caught in light and shadow, she was even more beautiful than Hawk had dreamed she could be.

This is wrong.

The reality of the impropriety of his conduct struck Hawk hard. He was a man who lived by hard rules, not malleable notions abandoned the instant they became inconvenient. Hawk *believed* in his self-made laws for living.

So why was he rooted in one place, unable to tear his eyes from the stunning young woman not thirty feet away when he knew—both emotionally and logically—that looking at her during her vision quest, when she didn't know he was there, was wrong? Why couldn't he turn his back to her and walk away?

Her beauty gripped him like an invisible hand. Her curvaceous body, splendidly naked, was displayed to him in almost perfect profile, so that he might see the slow rise and fall of her pink-tipped breasts, the line of her rib cage, and the curve of her hips. But it was also something more than that. There was an added thrill of looking illicitly at Amanda when she was unaware of his presence that heightened the eroticism of the moment. Had Amanda looked him in the eye and simply cast aside her clothes, he would have been struck by the splendor of her form. Struck, yes, but not dumbfounded, frozen in place as though he'd never before seen a woman's body, or understood the pleasures of the flesh.

Ida Maka would not approve of his behavior, Hawk knew.

The invocation of the all-seeing eye of Mother Earth forced Hawk to behave as he knew he should. He turned slowly away from the clearing, then headed back for camp. The things that needed to be said he would say to Amanda there, where her compelling allure would be muted by clothes, by the nearness of members of the tribe, by Hawk's own belief that the only acceptable females for him were Sioux-born.

* * * *

For Amanda, the world did not exist—at least not the physical world that she could see with her eyes and touch with her fingertips. Inside her mind a new world had suddenly and miraculously been revealed to her, and she was utterly fascinated with it.

It's so beautiful, she kept thinking, *this world of Ida Maka.*

The animals nearby seemed to have no fear of her. Several rabbits munching on clover not ten yards away, ever-vigilant yet not in the least bit concerned with her presence, had caught her attention.

Deep within her mind, Amanda could not actually *see* the rabbits eating the sweet clover. Yet somehow this discrepancy—this distinction between what she knew to be true with her heart with what she knew could not be true—didn't bother her in the least. Such mundane matters of whether her eyes were open or closed should bear little significance, she realized, on whether she could see.

A doe stepped into the clearing, light-footed, with its tail twitching nervously. Seeing Amanda, the doe gave no outward sign of alarm.

I won't hurt you. You needn't be afraid of me.

"*I know you won't,*" the young doe replied. "*But there are many others who are not like you.*"

The sound of a slender tree limb snapping caused Amanda to, in her mind's eye, look sharply to her left. She could not see what had caused the sound, but she sensed that danger—not for her so much as for the doe—was present, lurking in the brush, hidden from her view.

Amanda turned back to the place where the doe had been, but there was no need to warn the gentle creature. The animal had already disappeared, and though Amanda was saddened at losing the company of the doe, she felt blessed for the short time they'd spent together.

* * * *

Sonny Wright was frowning, trying to convince himself that there was no reason to worry. There was still no word from Amanda, and she hadn't picked up his telegram to her. To complicate matters, he couldn't go chasing after Amanda because Vanessa had left for Fargo, and Sonny thought he might need to get the boys together to protect her. If ever there was a woman more adept than Amanda at finding trouble and embroiling herself in it, that woman had to be Vanessa.

Sisters! They'll drive me to drink.

Sitting in the leather swivel chair in the ranch house office, Sonny decided to send one of his men after Amanda. She'd be furious with him for it, but he didn't have a moment's doubt about his action. At least then he'd know she was safe.

Sonny pushed himself out of the chair and took a last sip of coffee. The sun was just coming up in the valley, and it looked like it was going to be another beautiful day.

* * * *

Amanda sat upright on the elk hide rug. She blinked several times to clear her vision, then ran her fingers through her long blonde hair to put it into some semblance of order. She rolled her head back on her shoulders and winced as muscles that had not been used in hours protested.

Overhead, the sun was high in the sky, though dropping toward the western horizon. By Amanda's calculations, it had to be several hours past noon. She'd been at the clearing more than twenty-four hours now.

As full consciousness returned to Amanda, she was aware of her nudity. She crossed her arms over her bosom and looked around the clearing guiltily. Then a soft smile pulled at her mouth, and she relaxed. She was alone with Mother Earth, and hadn't Buttercup explained that there was no reason for her to hide?

Amanda rose to her feet, stretching her arms and legs, twisting her back and neck until her body once more felt supple and limber. Her clothes—the soft leather dress and moccasins provided by Buttercup—were nearby, and though Amanda's first instincts were to go to them, she resisted the impulse.

Another smile pulled at her mouth, this one hinting at a self-satisfaction that had never been there before.

She was beginning to think like a Sioux. Amanda realized that she was only in the initial stages of the transformation, but she'd begun the journey. Of this there could be no denying, and when the awareness filled her senses she started to skip and dance naked in the clearing, unashamed of the present and unfettered by the past.

When Buttercup arrived an hour later, Amanda was anxious to tell her friend all that she'd seen and discovered during her vision quest, but Buttercup put a hand up to silence the avalanche of words.

"Tell me tomorrow," Buttercup instructed, handing Amanda her dress, indicating that it was time to return to the camp. "Let the memories of your vision quest stay within you. If you speak of them now, while they are still so fresh within you, they may escape, and then you will lose them forever."

Keeping the experience to herself, not speaking of the wondrous new sensations, was very nearly the most difficult thing Amanda had ever done, but as she walked slowly back to camp, she began to fully grasp the wisdom of Buttercup's advice. By not speaking of her experiences, her memories of them remained clearer, more precise and defined. Suddenly Amanda understood that her memories of the vision quest would be as accurate and unchanging in twenty years as they were at this moment.

* * * *

Hawk had heard that his sister and Amanda had returned to the camp, but he couldn't see them immediately. He was much too busy talking with Dull Knife, defending Crow's honor, integrity, and loyalty to the tribe.

"The white man trained Crow," Hawk explained for the third time. "Crow understands the laws of the white man, and that is why he is not with us now. He is needed in the white man's courts. Crow's knowledge can protect us even better than a rifle."

"If Crow knows the law so well," Dull Knife said quietly, "then why must you be here now, giving me excuses for what he has done? He knows that he must receive permission from the council before he is allowed to leave the tribe."

Because time is critical, and the old men of the council make their decisions very slowly. Judiciously, he said, "It was necessary. Hasn't Crow worked hard to protect us from the white man, to make the white man live up to his agreements with us? I cannot tell you why it was necessary for Crow to leave so suddenly. I only know that he said it was so, and because Crow is a man of his word I believe him."

Dull Knife looked away, and Hawk knew that it was going to take a while longer to mollify the proud, stubborn elder whose wisdom had helped guide the tribe for so long.

Chapter Ten

Hawk was furious, but Amanda couldn't focus on his anger. Not when he was wearing only a deerskin loincloth, and when his bronzed chest was naked, all the raw power he possessed there on display. Hawk was arguing quietly with Buttercup at the entrance to her tepee, angry that she had helped Amanda experience some of the more spiritual elements of Sioux life. Though they kept their voices low, Amanda noticed more than a few women and braves keeping a surreptitious eye on Hawk and Buttercup.

I don't care if Hawk thinks it was wrong of me to have a vision quest. It opened my eyes to a new world, to a new way of thinking, and that's what's really important.

But even as she thought this, she knew it wasn't entirely true. She *did* care what Hawk thought, because more than ever before she didn't want him to be angry and brooding. She wanted him to help her celebrate her vision quest.

She noticed Hawk glance in her direction, then quickly back at his sister. He turned, and now she saw him in profile. Amanda's mouth went dry. From the side, the loincloth covered very little of his legs, so she was able to see his thighs and the tautness of his buttocks. He possessed such power! All bronzed and beautiful, sculpted like a statue.

Amanda forced herself to turn away, concerned with the sinful pleasure of gazing at the body of a man. But, oh. What a man he was!

She couldn't help herself. She had to look at him, her eyes drinking in the beauty of his arms and chest, his broad shoulders, the thick muscles in his calves and thighs...and, most of all, his deliciously curved bottom. His ass, she decided, was a thing of beauty, and the revelation made a shiver go through her.

She wondered how the young women could control themselves and their emotions when the braves wore only loincloths. Amanda decided that it was possible other women weren't as susceptible to masculine beauty as she was. Perhaps the sensuality of looking at a gorgeous man was something that only she experienced. She'd never before heard her friends say anything about wanting to look at a man's naked body, though she'd always known that men enjoyed looking at women.

Amanda went into Buttercup's tepee, sat down, and tried to relax. Suddenly she rose to her feet again. Too restless to remain seated, she paced the cramped confines of the tepee, trying to force the image of Hawk's tempting body from her thoughts.

Amanda soon realized that nothing made her think of Hawk more than attempting not to think of him at all.

At that moment the tepee flap was thrown open and Hawk, bending low, entered. His expression was intimidating. His features were granite hard, his lips tightly pursed, his eyes glittering with angry fire.

Crossing his arms over his chest, he stared down at Amanda, and she knew he was intentionally trying to frighten her. But rather than making her afraid, his stance heightened the definition of the muscles in his arms and chest, and Amanda desired him even more.

"You're leaving for home," he said, his tone brooking no rebuttal. "If not immediately, then tomorrow morning at the latest."

"No."

"Yes." Hawk moved closer, forcing Amanda to look straight up into his eyes. "That's final. There's to be no argument."

"Because you have so decreed," Amanda replied.

"If that's the way you want to look at it, I suppose your conclusion isn't all that far from correct."

Amanda's mouth quirked into a half smile, mimicking Hawk's. Her refusal to follow his order never quite came. Instead of putting her nose close to his and screaming, Amanda moved several steps back and appraised him coolly, her gaze appreciatively roaming up and down over the length and breadth of him. Making no effort to hide the direction or intention of her gaze, neither did she attempt to conceal her deep interest in what stood before her.

"If I must leave," Amanda countered, enunciating the words carefully, "then the least you can do is kiss me goodbye."

Amanda saw a different fire ignite in Hawk's eyes, but she didn't have a clue whether she'd incited his fury, or his passion, or elements of both. When he moved toward her Amanda wanted to run away, but her mind couldn't make her feet obey.

"You just try to make me angry, don't you?" Hawk said as he pulled Amanda into his arms, crushing her trembling body against the hard surface of his chest.

The instant Amanda moistened her lips to speak he slanted his mouth down hard over hers, forcing her lips apart with his tongue to explore deeply.

Shocked at the force Hawk used, Amanda felt her breasts, already confined within the deerskin dress, crushed to his lower chest. She was pleasantly aware of how her nipples had peaked with excitement, becoming tight and sensitive as they were forced to rub hard against the soft inner surface of the dress. Amanda hesitated only a moment before she wrapped her arms around Hawk's neck and leaned into him as he devoured her.

"Why must you always fight me," Hawk asked, his lips moist from Amanda's, still touching hers even as he spoke, "in everything I try to do?"

"I'm not fighting you now," Amanda said between kisses, with guileless honesty. She could feel the fury bubbling within Hawk, but she accurately sensed that his anger was only partially directed at her refusal to follow his commands.

Amanda raised herself up on her tiptoes, reducing the height difference between them, and opened her mouth wider. She felt his hands slide from the small of her back down to the cheeks of her ass, forcing her pelvis to press tighter against the rising column of the erection trapped beneath leather. She loved the heat of his powerful thighs against her own legs.

"Oh, Hawk," she whispered, turning her face away, struggling to catch her breath, hoping to contain the wildfire emotions racing through her.

She raised her knee, sliding it up Hawk's leg. She was not at all surprised to feel the heat of his naked skin, nor the strength of his body, though she was shocked by the reaction of her own body. With his body pressed to hers, Amanda felt Hawk's vitality, his fiery outlook on life, passing right through his pores and into hers. An instant later she was shocked when he pulled her dress higher and cupped her naked ass in his large, strong hands, pinning her even more tightly against him, forcing her to feel the rapidly burgeoning cock.

All the warnings Amanda had heard earlier were very insistent now, clamoring for her to run, to escape from the seductive influence of this Sioux warrior whose kisses tasted like nectar and whose caresses were pure carnal indulgence. Would she listen to the warnings?

Not this time.

Hawk, powerful and commanding, squeezed her tightly, touched her intimately, forced her sex to rub against a thigh that was solid as stone from countless hours on horseback.

"I haven't been able to stop thinking about you," Hawk whispered. He kissed Amanda again as he pulled her hips toward him. She had no choice but to feel the length, breadth and heat of his desire for her.

Amanda couldn't help herself. Though she'd dealt with the sin of letting Hawk touch her, it had to be even more wrong for her to touch him. She was aware of this, yet she could not resist the temptation to bring her hands down Hawk's body, then slide them beneath his loincloth to cup the contours of his ass. When he sighed, his hips moving slowly, Amanda, shocking herself, pulled him toward her so the hard column of his cock was pressed tightly against her stomach. The front flap of Hawk's loincloth and her deerskin dress remained the only barriers between them.

Still on her tiptoes while Hawk kissed her, Amanda knew the intensity of Hawk's emotions were escalating rapidly. Suddenly, Amanda felt herself tumbling backward, with Hawk following her onto the buffalo mat. Then Hawk pulled Amanda by the ankle, forcing her to sit the way he wanted her to, with her legs extended in front of her instead of tucked beneath her. But when he kissed her again she tumbled onto her back and pulled Hawk with her, his weight crushing down on her.

Nothing had ever felt quite so right, quite so satisfying, as the weight of Hawk's powerful, warrior's body pressing on hers. Amanda wrapped her arms tightly around Hawk's middle, sliding her palms over his naked flesh.

When he stopped kissing her Amanda raised her head, her soft sigh protesting the interruption. Then Hawk kissed her again, his lips firm, stealing her breath and heightening her passion.

Unconsciously, she raised her knees, her thighs forming a valley for Hawk's lean hips. When he moved, his hips sliding from side to side as they kissed, she realized that the leather dress had ridden up high, bunching at her waist, and she could finally feel the naked heat of Hawk's cock against her abdomen, just above the rapidly moistening lips of her cunt.

The honeyed essence of her excitement flowed freely, and only an inner whisper of warning said she mustn't be so bold. But passivity had never been a part of Amanda's nature, neither in Hawk's arms nor out of them. She placed her hands on his chest and pushed hard until he raised himself, breaking their kiss.

"Love me," she whispered hotly. Looking up at Hawk, she was astonished once again at his handsome, chiseled features, framed by his long, raven-black hair. "I'm scared...but love me."

"You mustn't be scared," Hawk said, easing his upper body down once again on the cushion of her breasts.

"Kiss me, and I won't be," Amanda replied.

He kissed her mouth, running the tip of his tongue along her lower lip. Then he kissed her cheek, and her neck, and Amanda trembled. He moved his hips from side to side. Amanda shivered, feeling her naked thighs trembling as they squeezed him.

Amanda was scared. She couldn't help it. Now she'd spoken words that she could never deny, igniting a fire within the lusty warrior who'd kissed her so sweetly. How that fire burned her now, his rigid erection against her stomach, throbbing with a desire so powerful she could feel it.

Hawk slipped his left arm under her neck so that her head rested on his forearm. Then, with his right hand, he reached between their bodies, and a moment later removed the leather loincloth. Amanda felt him move between her legs, the heated length of his arousal tight against the moist entrance to her virgin sex. She gasped, arching her spine.

Hawk kissed her, recognizing her trepidation as well as her excitement. He'd waited so long for this moment, this final capitulation to passion. Now that Amanda was his for the taking, he wanted this moment to be special for her. He wanted to take his time so that she felt all the pleasure of which she was capable of experiencing, and this meant he must control the clamorous desire, primal and urgent, urging him to thrust himself primitively into

Amanda's sweet depths, experiencing immediately that which had been denied him for so long.

He reached again between their bodies to cup her breast, squeezing the firm mound through the tight leather dress. Though Amanda moaned, Hawk knew that if her responsive body was to reach the heights, the dress had to be removed. He tried moving away from her, but Amanda wound her arms more tightly around him, and he felt her fingernails against his shoulders.

"Don't!" She gasped, pulling at Hawk, her lips moist and parted as she sought yet another kiss.

"Your dress," Hawk said, reaching down to grab the bottom of it, wanting to pull it up and over Amanda's head. "I want you naked."

"Hurry," she replied, understanding what he wanted but not wanting the delay.

He saw fear in her blue eyes, and finally understood precisely why the young woman was so urgent. True, passion spurred on her haste, but fear also played a part in Amanda's fervent demand. Clearly, she did not know how long her courage would hold and, if Hawk did not act immediately, her passion would evaporate, replaced with the apprehension and inhibition that had plagued all their previous romantic moments.

Hawk, his heart pumping red-hot blood through his veins, raised his hips and reached between their bodies. He touched her softly with the plump head of his arousal, feeling the heated moisture of her readiness, hearing her breath get sucked in…and held.

So passionate, and yet so frightened, he thought, finding her twin emotions simultaneously baffling and exciting.

Amanda squirmed beneath him, arching her back once more. He wanted to remind her to breathe, but he didn't. If he hadn't known her so well, if this had, instead, been the first time he'd ever felt her responding to his seduction, he would have thought that she was responding falsely, giving a theatrical performance for some reason.

"Are you all right?" Hawk asked, raising himself, pulling away from Amanda. He'd felt a sudden change in her and, however much he hungered to feel his cock sinking deeply into her, he would not force himself on her.

Amanda's eyes flew open and she reached up, cupping Hawk's gaunt, handsome face in her hands. "There are so many people nearby. It frightens me. Don't stop. Hurry. Hurry, my darling."

Hawk guided his cock to her entrance, then bore down, slowly and with controlled force. He felt the lips of Amanda's sex opening to him, felt the slick nectar of her excitement, her sex tight and stimulating, surrounding him. A low groan of ecstasy rumbled from his chest as he pressed deeper and deeper — withdrawing then advancing once again. Discovering the barrier of her inexperience, he paused, then pressed on, and only the soft, short exclamation of sound that Amanda emitted warned him that she'd felt temporary pain, and that her virgin barrier was no more.

Then, blissfully, at long last, he was completely engulfed within Amanda, their bodies joined intimately. Hawk rested in the valley of her thighs, giving Amanda time to adjust to the intrusion of his hard cock, to relax if possible. He kissed her and was surprised when Amanda thrust her tongue between his lips, not at all the kiss of a woman who moments earlier had been frightened by the prospect of making love for the first time.

He began to move, slowly and with a steady rhythm, sliding his shaft between her delicate lips, and Amanda's worry about what the tribe would say about her vanished. Every idea disappeared from her mind except those pertaining to the pleasure she was feeling now, the strange sensation of having Hawk filling her to overflowing, then leaving her nearly empty before filling her once again. Nothing could have prepared her for the sensuous reality of having Hawk inside her, moving, a slick friction from each measured stroke of his hips staggering to her senses. She felt like her bones were melting. She held him close, digging her fingernails into his solid back muscles, and she never wanted the kiss to end...at least not while they were joined so intimately, so deliciously.

Even without previous experience, Amanda felt that Hawk was keeping himself in check, reining in his passion so he would not hurt her. With his big, powerful body tensed, the muscles were coiled like a mountain lion's before an attack.

Was this just sex, or was she making love? Amanda wasn't sure, and she didn't want to think about it. Not now, anyway. There would be plenty of time later, when she was back at the Circle S ranch and Hawk was still with his tribe, for her to dwell on regrets and wallow in self-recrimination and doubt.

She kicked a leg around Hawk's and discovered that by doing so she'd shifted her hips, changing the angle at which his thrusting sex entered her. Amanda kicked her other leg around him, gripping him now, their legs entwined as Hawk moved slowly and steadily, and Amanda was able at last to feel the full weight of him on her. Her clitoris pulsed so furiously it was almost painful.

"Does it...?" she began, keeping her eyes closed as she spoke. Passion cut the sentence off short, but she was determined to get her answer, so she moistened her lips and began again. "Does it always feel this wonderful?"

"No," Hawk replied. "I promise you, I'll make sure it always gets better."

That can't possibly be true. Nothing could be better than this.

Hardly able to think of anything but the feelings shivering through her, the intoxicating sense of oneness with Hawk, she felt his great heart pounding feverishly close to hers, feel him filling her, stripping away the doubts and turmoil that had troubled her for so much of her young life.

Harder and faster, Hawk thrust deep into Amanda. Each time he impaled her, the breath was forced from her lungs, and she clung a little more tightly to him.

He groaned without changing his tempo. Amanda held him close. Then, with a deep growl of desire, Hawk thrust himself hard and fast into her. An instant later, he withdrew completely and released a torrent of thick semen.

"Yes," Amanda whispered, stroking Hawk's ebony hair. "You are magnificent."

When Hawk started to move away Amanda tightened her hold on him, squeezing her eyes shut again, afraid—for one of the very few times in her life—that the tears would begin to flow, and Hawk would see them.

"Don't move," she whispered. "Not yet. Just give me a minute...then I promise I'll be brave."

"Don't worry," Hawk replied huskily. "Whatever you want is yours."

Buttercup's voice, just moments later, shattered whatever tenderness Amanda had hoped for. "Amanda, are you all right in there? Dull Knife is looking for Hawk."

Hawk hissed something through his teeth, and Amanda was thankful that she could not understand the single word. He rolled away, reaching for his loincloth, apparently practiced at the art of a quick escape after a romantic interlude.

"Don't worry," Hawk said again, on his knees beside Amanda as she smoothed down the leather dress over her thighs. The essence of Hawk's passion matted the soft curls of her pubic hair. "Everything will be all right. I'll see you as soon as I can."

Then he was gone from the tepee, leaving Amanda alone with her thoughts, alone with her doubts and worries. She knelt without a single distraction from the recriminations ricocheting in her mind, echoing like church bells through the streets of a deserted city.

She reached down and lightly touched herself, thankful that Hawk had not climaxed inside her. In the fog and blur of passion, she had forgotten to insist that he withdraw before climaxing, and her opinion of him escalated significantly because he had shown the good sense that she'd forgotten.

* * * *

Three hours later, Hawk finally freed himself from his other obligations and returned to Amanda. When he at last found her she was on the outskirts of the encampment, carrying a basket made of woven reeds.

"Where are you going?" Hawk asked, though it was apparent that she was going into the mountains to pick berries.

He got off his stallion, wanting very much to take Amanda into his arms to stroke her hair softly soothingly. Having to leave her so quickly after the culmination of their passion was, he felt, a barbaric thing to do, even though in his heart he had known he had no choice in the matter.

"I'm helping Buttercup," Amanda replied. There was a sleepy smile on her lips as she looked at Hawk. "She needed to pick berries, and she also needed to work on a piece of elk hide, or was it buffalo hide? Either way, I thought I'd help out where I could. I don't know how to cure leather."

Hawk stepped closer. He didn't particularly care for Amanda's behavior. Was she simply hiding more turbulent emotions? He suspected so. And though he knew it wasn't very flattering to him, he preferred Amanda hiding any tumultuous emotions to not having them at all. Though not an egotistical man, Hawk could not bear the thought of being the first man to make love to a woman as beautiful and unique as Amanda, and not have her thinking about it afterward. Whether for good or bad, Hawk wanted to be on her mind, in her thoughts.

"Do you need some help?" he asked. Quite suddenly he felt very young, as he had when his experience with young women was just beginning and he was learning that his smile, his looks, the way he walked and moved, affected women in a powerful way.

"I would appreciate that very much," Amanda replied, hardly speaking above a whisper. She looked to the western hills. "How much light do you think we have left?"

Hawk looked at the sun, calculating the time in measurements that Amanda would understand. "Two hours. Maybe three, if the clouds stay away."

Amanda's smile grew fractionally broader, and an unmistakable light came into her blue eyes. "That should give us enough time, I suppose." She hesitated a telling moment. "But then, you know more about these things than I do."

Hawk felt a tiny release of pressure within his heart. He still couldn't guess what her feelings were, but she wasn't overwrought, and that was a good sign. The twinkle in her eyes freed Hawk from the worries plaguing him since he had left Amanda alone in Buttercup's tepee that afternoon.

Chapter Eleven

Billy didn't like the look of it at all, not even a little bit. When his boss, Sonny Wright, had asked him to do him a 'personal favor', Billy had been overjoyed. The chance to go to the city and kick up his heels was something he just couldn't turn down. Especially when he found out that all that was expected of him was to track down Amanda and shoo her behind back to the ranch.

Billy had known Amanda for years, and when he had been told that she hadn't been sending the telegrams she'd promised, he wasn't terribly concerned. As far as Billy could tell, Amanda not doing what her older brother had specifically instructed her to do was pretty much the way it always went with her. Billy figured he'd find her at some out-of-the-way ranch, looking at horses that everyone else had either given up on, or had judged to be of inferior quality. Nobody had an eye for horseflesh like Amanda. She could spot traits, such as intelligence and temperament, better than anyone Billy had ever known. She had a knack for buying a lot of horse for a little money.

Billy had ridden off thinking he had nothing to worry about and would have a paid vacation, to boot, since Sonny had given him fifty dollars in folding money to spend however he wanted.

When the clerk at the hotel said that Amanda had been gone for several days Billy got an empty feeling in his stomach. He had better saddle up and ride off, but first Billy checked around town, talking to the various horse traders, which naturally would have drawn Amanda's attention.

Everywhere he went, he was told that she had been there, but not in several days. Amanda, it seemed, had been everywhere. But not recently. That worried Billy right down to his boots. And what would Sonny Wright do if Amanda wasn't found? Would he hold Billy responsible?

With rapidly escalating unease, Billy rode to the telegraph office and sent:

Amanda has been everywhere stop still trying to track her down stop will report tomorrow stop Billy end.

He hoped it would buy him enough time to find Amanda. Otherwise, Billy wasn't entirely certain what he would do, though he had no desire at all to find out just exactly how protective Sonny Wright was of his kid sister.

* * * *

It had been difficult for Amanda in the immediate period following Hawk's abrupt departure from the tepee. Buttercup had entered shortly thereafter, preventing Amanda from having a quiet time for reflection. Buttercup, spirited as ever, wanted to know just exactly how angry Hawk had been, and when he planned to take Amanda back to her home in Deadwood. Though Amanda had felt guilty about her lies, she told one after another, concocting a story of the 'argument' she and Hawk had had.

When finally Amanda saw the chance to spend some time by herself—by picking berries for Buttercup—she leaped at the opportunity. She had intended to spend the time alone, to sort out her feelings about Hawk's lovemaking, and of her partially successful vision quest.

But the moment she saw Hawk astride his stallion, broad-shouldered and regally commanding, with his head held high, Amanda knew that she did not really want to be alone. There would be plenty of time later, after she returned to Deadwood, to reminisce about her brief journey into Sioux spirituality, and remember the dark-skinned, mysterious man who'd taught her that sensuality wasn't just in dreams and fantasies.

Now, she sat behind Hawk on his stallion as the big animal easily carried them both higher into the hillside, where the berries grew thick and sweet on the vines. The soft leather dress she'd borrowed from Buttercup, Amanda discovered, was not made for riding—at least, not for riding astride a horse, which was the only way Amanda knew how to ride, the side saddle having been noticeably absent from her education. The dress was forced high and tight across her thighs and Hawk's hand was resting lightly on her bare knee.

"How was your day after...after I left?" Hawk asked.

"I like your sister, but she talks an awful lot," Amanda said. She held the basket in one hand, the other resting lightly on Hawk's stomach. "Sometimes it's hard to believe the two of you are related, you can be so different."

Hawk laughed. "I talk," he said. "At least occasionally."

"You talk only as long as you can guide the conversation, and make sure that it doesn't go anywhere you don't want it to," Amanda replied, playfully slapping Hawk. "But the moment someone else starts asking questions—"

"—someone like you," Hawk cut in teasingly.

"Yes, someone like me!" She slapped him again, harder this time. "The moment I start asking questions, you conveniently have to ride off to tend to something vitally important, or get so cold a woman could freeze her fingers to the bone just by touching you."

Taking his hand from her knee, Hawk pointed to bushes thick with dark red berries. "Even *Ida Maka* is on my side. There's the patch we're looking for."

Amanda made a huffing sound of indignation. He had made his usual evasive reply. This time she decided to let the issue pass, having no desire to provoke a fight while they were alone together for a little while.

"Let me help you down," Hawk said, kicking his right leg over the stallion's head and sliding gracefully to the ground.

Hawk placed his hands on Amanda's narrow waist. When she slid out of the saddle he held her suspended for a moment before setting her slowly to the ground. Amanda turned until she faced him, feeling the familiar quickening of her pulse. For a moment their eyes met, but Amanda broke the contact, twisting away from Hawk then walking toward the berry bush.

"It's been quite a day," Amanda observed, not looking at Hawk. A cool, gentle breeze played across her bare arms and legs and fluffed her hair. "First a vision quest, then...then you. That's quite a day by any standards."

She sensed his presence close behind her, though he said nothing. When she walked she was suddenly aware of the gentle scissoring of her thighs, of being naked beneath the deerskin dress, and of a slight tenderness from the loving they'd shared earlier. She was a little sore, but this kind of discomfort did not bother Amanda. In fact, it brought back passionate memories only hours' old that made her shiver just to think of them.

The fact that there was dried semen on her, from her neck and breasts, over her stomach, and all the way down to her the sparse pubic hair, was an itchy sensation that reminded her of Hawk's discipline and her own intemperance. Fortunately, Hawk had been sensible enough to withdraw completely at the last moment.

"Are you cold?" Hawk asked.

A creeping smile tugged at the corners of Amanda's mouth. *No, Hawk, I'm not cold. In fact, my skin feels so hot, I might just take off my dress.* She realized some response was required of her, but she couldn't think of a thing to say. She thought about making love to Hawk again and was aware of her limited understanding about such matters. Was he even able to try so soon again?

What a sign of wantonness to even *think* about making love a second time in one day! But hadn't she already lost her virginity — or given it away, Amanda realized — to Hawk? Was it a greater or lesser offense, she wondered, to commit the same transgression with the same man a second time? And hadn't Hawk promised that the next time would be even better than the first?

It was a promise, she suspected, that he was infinitely capable of fulfilling.

She was about to turn to confront Hawk, to demand answers about the normalcy of the feelings going through her. Hawk Two Feather knew the answers. All this—the lush sensuality, the wanton surrender to pleasures of the flesh—was well within his realm of experience. He could tell her if all women responded to him this powerfully, or if she'd been weak, the erotic dreams that had plagued her sleep finally intruding into her waking world.

Before she could ask him, his hands were on her shoulders. Her eyes closed instinctively. He slid his thumbs beneath her hair, then began moving in a circular motion at the base of her skull. Her scalp began to tingle, and it was only with a conscious effort that she was able to keep from moaning.

"Amanda, sweet Amanda," Hawk whispered, standing directly behind her.

Slowly and gently, he pulled her hair so that the left side of her neck bare. He bent low and kissed her ear, then followed the outline of it with the tip of his tongue.

She felt his hands move over her shoulders and down her arms, and his touch elicited another moan that Amanda did not try to silence this time. His hands on her gave her pleasure, so why pretend otherwise?

When she felt his sharp teeth at her earlobe, biting her with enough pressure to hint at pain, Amanda cried out in surprise, leaning toward Hawk so that her back was against his chest.

"You're all I've been able to think about," Hawk said, the timbre of his voice already showing the hoarseness of sexual tension. "I couldn't wait to get back to you, to see you again, to kiss you again, to touch you again."

Amanda turned her face away from Hawk, offering her neck for his kisses. He nipped her tender flesh with his teeth, caressing her breasts through the deerskin dress.

Taking Amanda by the shoulders, Hawk then turned her to face him.

My God, he's gorgeous.

She tried to say the words, but her throat wouldn't form them.

Slowly, he untied the slender leather cord at the neck of her dress, loosening it so that the garment could be pulled over her head. Amanda stood motionless, neither helping nor hindering Hawk. She was shivering, then shuddering as she looked up at him. He placed his hands firmly on her shoulders, then bent to kiss her mouth. His kiss was firm and commanding, displaying strength and a dominating confidence. Even as they kissed, Hawk found the hem of the dress and raised it. As Amanda brought her arms over her head, Hawk removed the dress completely and tossed it aside.

When Hawk turned toward her, Amanda crossed her arms over her body. She felt she was being scrutinized, and it wasn't a feeling she cared for. And, damningly, there were several flakes, pale but visible, of dried semen on her stomach and breasts, a taunting reminder of previous illicit behavior.

"You always do that, but you shouldn't." Hawk's voice was husky, seductive. "You are so beautiful,

Amanda. Don't deprive me of the pleasure of looking at you."

Amanda wanted to say that she doubted Hawk had ever been deprived of much in his life—especially by women—but she remained silent.

Taking Amanda's hands by the wrists and uncrossing her arms, Hawk revealed her breasts with their soft pink areolas and bud-hard nipples.

"Too beautiful," Hawk whispered, bending his knees. "I cannot resist you, even when I try."

"Then don't try." Amanda sighed, pushing her fingers into the satiny abundance of Hawk's hair, guiding his hot, moist mouth to her breast. When she felt him capture her nipple between his lips she tossed her head back on her shoulders, giving herself over to the feeling.

"I must have you," Amanda whispered. "Oh, Hawk, I don't care if it's wrong, I must have you again!"

Amanda hugged Hawk's face to her breast, reveling in the heat and moisture of his mouth against her sensitive nipple. Her eyes were shut, her legs trembling. She had no intention of going anywhere, of doing anything other than experiencing the magnificence of Hawk's intimate kisses.

She ran a hand down his back and over his leather vest. The feel of the elk hide disappointed her. While continuing to twine his raven-black hair around her fingers to hold his head securely, she used her other hand to push his vest off his shoulders. The breadth of his shoulders, and the flawlessness of his bronzed flesh, must not be denied her, Amanda decided in the entirely selfish manner of a young woman aware that her lover was not merely an extraordinary man but a unique one, one desired by many. And Amanda, whether she realized it fully or not, had no intention of sharing Hawk with anyone.

Now, this man's hands were upon her, touching her legs, her thighs, adding to the incredible sensations aroused by his moist kisses. And when he touched the moist lips of her sex, Amanda made a soft, purring sound. The throbbing in her clitoris became more insistent, more demanding of attention.

"Lie back," Hawk instructed, kneeling in the grass before Amanda.

She complied, too aroused, too needy, to do anything else. Hawk moved toward her, about to kiss her on the mouth, when she put a hand to his chest to stop him. "No," she said firmly. "I want you to stand now. Stand so that I can look at you."

A slow half smile made the dimple form in Hawk's gaunt cheek. He rose swiftly, bronzed and beautiful in the sunlight, and looked down at Amanda.

"I've never really looked at you. Not *really* looked," Amanda whispered, though there was no need to keep her voice down, they were far from anyone but *Ida Maka*. Impatient to once again receive Hawk's experienced attentions, she felt bold, daring, and infinitely curious. "Let me see, Hawk. Let me look at you the way you've looked at me."

She had expected Hawk to remove his loincloth first, but instead he balanced on one foot and removed first one moccasin then the other. The muscles in his forearms and biceps bulged with suppressed power as he removed his footwear.

When he finally stood erect again, Amanda drank in the beauty of his naked chest with her eyes. His pectorals in particular drew her attention—hard, smooth muscles that were clearly defined beneath cinnamon skin. Then her gaze slid lower, to the rippled surface of his stomach, which led, inevitably, down to his loincloth.

"Hurry," Amanda urged in a husky voice. As she leaned back on one elbow, she realized the little game she had started was taking more time than her impatience could tolerate.

But Hawk didn't hurry. Amanda realized he knew the value of delay, of heightened anticipation, to increase the pleasure of the final moment of satisfaction, and she felt a vague resentment of his greater awareness. Rather than removing his loincloth, he took his time in taking off his leggings, first one then the other, until at last he stood over her wearing only the bulging, overfull loincloth.

"This, too?" he teased, touching just the corner of the loincloth with his fingertip.

Amanda nodded. Her heart was pounding, yet she'd seen him before, in all his glory. She nibbled on her lower lip in nervous anticipation.

The loincloth was tied at the hip. Hawk pulled loose the knotted leather cord, but the material did not fall completely free of him. It was caught on the prominence of his erection.

"Hawk," Amanda whispered.

Hawk slowly stepped forward, his eyes burrowing into Amanda's. Without a word he moved closer, his sex on prominent display beneath the loincloth. Amanda tore her gaze away from Hawk's to examine his body. With a hand that trembled, she reached out and took the edge of the loincloth in her fingertips and slowly pulled it until Hawk's extravagance was exposed to her greedy senses.

The awesome sight of him, fully aroused, took Amanda's breath away. She'd never really looked at him before. Now she saw he was intimidating in size, and a shiver worked its way up her spine. She found it vaguely hard to believe that this particular part of his insatiable body had given her such pleasure when it was buried inside her. He seemed very large, perhaps even too large, but she knew this wasn't the truth because it had given her such bliss.

When she reached for him she saw that her hand was shaking. It stopped short of its mark.

"Touch me," Hawk said softly.

I shouldn't.

There were many good reasons for her not to, not the least of which was that she did not like following anyone's command—and certainly not the commands of a lusty savage like Hawk.

But in her heart Amanda knew that there was a secret part of herself who *did* like following his commands. She was only a little surprised when, a moment later, she saw her hand come into view, her slender, pale fingers reaching out to curl slowly and sensually around Hawk's solid shaft. She squeezed the manly flesh, and a single, pearl-white drop of fluid formed at the slitted tip.

She felt him throb against her palm and the heat of his blood made him even larger and more rigid. As Amanda touched him, she stared at her hand as though it belonged to someone else. Could this person be Amanda Wright, an heiress to the largest cattle empire in the Dakota Territory, caressing a Sioux warrior's so intimately—and loving every moment of it?

Hawk's throaty groan of pleasure drew Amanda's attention. She looked up at his face. Seeing the pleasure reflected in his eyes, she felt more powerful than ever before in her life. Hawk moved his hips, forcing his flesh through the firm encirclement of her fingers. Then it was Amanda's turn to sigh.

"I don't really know what you want—expect—of me," Amanda said softly. The instant the words were out, she regretted having said anything.

"I'll want everything from you, expect everything of you," Hawk said. He reached down and captured Amanda's free hand by the wrist. Bending, he raised her hand to his mouth, kissed the palm wetly, then brought her hand to his erection. "Better," he murmured when she'd taken him tightly in her grip. "Much better."

"Did I do something wrong?" she asked.

"Nothing you do could be wrong, Little Flower," Hawk said with a roguish smile, the endearment spoken casually. "Just the opposite." He knelt beside her and, still holding on to her wrist, kissed her palm slowly, then paid attention to each finger. "Everything about you fascinates me." He began kissing Amanda's wrist, then her forearm, his tongue leaving a thin, moist trail where his kisses had traveled. "I could kiss you for a thousand seasons and never tire of it."

They were the words Amanda most wanted to hear, though she couldn't consider anything so permanent as *forever* with him. Amanda closed her eyes and leaned back on her elbows as Hawk, kneeling near her hip, nipped teasingly at her shoulder and neck.

Her eyes closed, Amanda sighed with pleasure as Hawk closed his lips over her tingling breast at the exact moment he brushed his fingertips lightly against her. She felt him search briefly to find her most sensitive place, that tiny nub of pure sensation from which, it seemed, all other sexual feelings emanated.

A choked cry of ecstasy sounded in Amanda's throat, and she arched upward, raising her hips so that only her hands and feet were still on the ground. When she felt the pressure of Hawk's hands guiding her, followed by the prickly sensation of the grass against her bottom, she realized he had coaxed her into sitting once more.

"I can't believe how you make me feel." Amanda's face tilted toward the sun as Hawk flicked his tongue over her left nipple. Down low, her cunt felt slippery, empty, neglected. Then, at last, Hawk eased a single finger between the lips of her sex, and she emitted a long, low, warbling sigh.

"There is much more," Hawk whispered. "So much more. And I will be your teacher."

Once again, Amanda wasn't entirely certain she approved of the possessiveness in Hawk's tone. He sometimes sounded as if there were no justifiable opinions that differed from his own. How had Hawk, who in so many ways was an outsider among the Sioux, developed such an aura of superiority? Amanda intended to pose this question to Hawk later…when her skin didn't feel as if it was going to burn in all the delightful places that she was being touched by Hawk, and when her muscles and bones weren't melting from pleasure.

"Lie back, Amanda," Hawk instructed, kneeling between her legs, leaning over her with one hand on her shoulder, pushing down. "Just lie back, relax, and let yourself feel."

For Amanda, relaxing was, quite simply, out of the question. Even *thinking* about relaxing was a bit ludicrous with Hawk touching and kissing her so intimately, probing her intimately with his fingers in just such a way to make her feel as though she was expanding endlessly, opening for him. But whether she wanted to or not, Hawk was infinitely stronger and decidedly more persistent, and when he put more pressure against Amanda's shoulder she had no choice but to topple backward until she was stretched out in the fresh green grass.

Curious about Hawk's latest lesson, Amanda raised her head and shoulders enough to peer through the valley of her breasts at the warrior who was occupied in the task of leisurely kissing the inside of her left knee. When he caught her looking at him, he smiled, then dragged the tip of his tongue along her inner thigh, moving slowly upward, his gaze never once leaving Amanda's.

He's going to kiss me. She felt dizzy. *There?*

This singular, inchoate thought was something even Amanda's erotic fantasies had not concocted. She'd thought her inner, hidden self — the one that created the sinfully pleasing dreams of passion while she slept — had in one dream or another run through all the possibilities of passion, yet this wasn't one she'd envisioned.

I shouldn't let him.

Amanda had no idea whatsoever why she should deny Hawk anything when clearly his competence in these matters was without parallel.

Then he kissed her. He kissed her deeply, darting his tongue out to probe and caress. The sensation it drew from Amanda was nothing she could ever have expected. Once again she flinched as her body reacted to this newly discovered ecstasy, thrusting her hips upward. Amanda sensed that Hawk was willing to resort to his greater strength to get what he wanted. Despite Amanda's rather frantic maneuverings, this time her legs ended up tossed over Hawk's broad shoulders, her heels thumping against his back as the tantalizing kisses to her cunt and the button above continued.

Amanda's breathing grew labored, especially when she felt strands of hair against her lips and in her mouth, eventually realizing that she was rolling her head from side to side, her own hair in wild disarray. Frantically, she pushed the hair away from her face, gulping in air, trying to keep herself from becoming more excited, still having no notion at all of why she should hide what she was really feeling. When Hawk sucked her sensitive bud between his lips, then flicked his tongue against the erect nub, she said a single word in English that she'd never before spoken aloud, and only on the rarest of occasions even thought.

But nothing had ever felt like this. Nothing. Hawk was introducing her to a whole new world, and she couldn't see the outer boundaries.

A woman was whispering then, and it took a second or two before Amanda recognized that she was the woman speaking the impassioned words. What embarrassing words—words of instruction to Hawk, asking, demanding, and sometimes even begging that the kisses continue unabated because she sensed that she was close...close to what, exactly, she wasn't at all certain, but whatever it was, it was awfully powerful. And close. Very close.

Slow down, a tiny voice whispered inside her head, just loud enough to be heard above the ringing in her ears.

Amanda felt Hawk release one leg from his powerful grasp, and for a moment she worried that he would stop kissing her. Had she done something wrong in her uninhibited response to his wicked, wanton kisses? Then his hand was on her again, this time crushing her bosom against her ribs, his long, forceful fingers grasping the firm, tender flesh. The power he used danced on the borderline between intense pleasure and pain.

Though she hadn't known it, this caress to her breast was exactly what she had wanted. Hawk had known, and her body had known, though *she* had not. With the pressure building tighter and tighter within her as she was pushed closer to the chasm by pleasure, what Amanda needed wasn't gentle, subtle caresses, but strong, forceful ones.

It took a moment before Amanda was able to calm herself enough to notice what Hawk was doing now, and how it made her feel. She opened her eyes for briefly, but the sun was blinding and she closed them again quickly.

The world didn't matter to her. Nothing external mattered. The only thing that was important was what she felt, what was going on within her own body.

"It's...so..." Amanda whispered.

She had tried to tell Hawk how magnificent he made her feel, but words failed her. However, she suspected he didn't have to be told to know. With her eyes still closed and her face warmed by the sun, Amanda moistened her lips with the tip of her tongue and tried briefly to slow her ragged breathing. It was impossible. She might as well have been on a runaway train. Nothing she could've done would've prevented the train from racing faster and faster until eventually, inevitably, it ran out of track.

The tightening within her intensified, and suddenly Amanda's breath stopped altogether. It hurt now. She felt tension inside. Her stomach knotted and she curled inward, doubling forward, the pressure too great to withstand.

Stop! Stop, stop, stop! She could not speak, though she desperately wanted Hawk to cease his pleasure-giving, which was now eliciting such intense emotions and sensations that they were painful.

Then, when Amanda was certain she would die of happiness, that she simply could not withstand such ecstasy even a second longer, she shuddered through a series of contractions that were like emotional explosions inside, one nearly violent convulsion after another. Three powerful spasms, then three lesser ones before the climax was complete.

Trembling and weak, her body had been turned inside out and her breath came in quick, uneven gulps. As a gentle breeze played over her nudity, she suddenly felt cool. But rather than search for something to cover herself for warmth or modesty, her most overwhelming urge was to laugh.

"What was that?" she asked softly when her breathing had returned to nearly normal.

Hawk kissed her thigh, then her stomach, moving slowly upward, pushing Amanda's legs off his shoulders. He eased his middle two fingers out of her. There was a pleased smile on his lips, which glistened with her cream.

"You want to know what that was?" Hawk teased, kissing Amanda's chin then the tip of her nose. "That was just the beginning."

Amanda laughed, joyously, amazed at what she had felt and the way her body had responded to everything Hawk had done.

"I don't think I could live through anything like that again," she whispered, feeling the heat of Hawk's erection burning her inner thigh, solid and pulsing with virility.

"Trust me." Hawk's lips brushed Amanda's as he spoke. "You won't die. In fact, you'll never be quite so alive."

"You *are* an arrogant man," Amanda said.

Some part of her needed to respond to Hawk's insolence. He was so confident about everything, so absolutely certain that he would always be triumphant, no matter what. But she kissed him, and when she did she could taste the nectar of her own passion upon his lips. Perhaps another time she would stand her ground. It was enough now to just enjoy his extraordinary skill and learn what it was he could teach her.

As they kissed, Hawk raised his hips sufficiently to guide the inflamed crown of his cock to Amanda's entrance. With insistent pressure, he entered her slowly, only a little at a time, pressing deeper and deeper into her slick sheath with each smooth, measured thrust.

Amanda had thought herself incapable of feeling ecstasy again, but, as had been the case so often on matters regarding the limits of sensual pleasure, Hawk was right and she was wrong. Each sweet thrust of his hips, each impaling charge of his tireless body, pushed Amanda back toward the edge of an orgasmic chasm that was both frightening and beguiling.

She wrapped her arms around Hawk's neck, holding him, kissing him continuously until at last she was certain that she'd taken the full length of him into her. Only then did she break the kiss, and whisper "Hawk" softly, the name delicious on her tongue.

Making love to Hawk was different this time. She felt his great power thrusting deep into her, joining her to him. There was nothing but pleasure, not even the residual pain that had afflicted her earlier remained to dampen even the most subtle sensations. The slide of his rigid sex, moving between the lips of her femininity, was long, smooth and measured.

He explored her with his hands, touching her everywhere, knowing exactly where he should, toying with her breasts, tugging and rolling her nipples lightly. He kissed her mouth, cheeks, neck, and ears. He ran his hands up the backs of her thighs, squeezing her bottom, thumbing her clitoris occasionally pulling her up so that she met his downward thrusts.

For Amanda, the accumulation of stimulations, each one unique in its own way, added to the mixture of feelings sending her careening toward another powerful orgasm.

Her climax was approaching again—that great, cataclysmic eruption of sensation. Closing her eyes against the pressure, she concentrated on what she felt, what her body was going through, and how astonishing it was that the most unlikely man in the world had set her body free to experience all that was sexually possible.

He was not gentle with her, and she didn't want him to be. Harder and faster he drove into the depths of her sex, and the second orgasm to shudder through her was nearly as powerful as the first.

Amanda was just coming down from the heights of her climax when Hawk groaned with passion, withdrew completely, then released his seed, his sperm leaving white lines of cream from her breasts to her cleft.

When he slumped down upon her after climaxing, Amanda once more felt a sense of oneness with Hawk, of being joined with him spiritually this time, as well as physically.

Chapter Twelve

Returning to camp was about the last thing in the world Amanda wanted to do. Actually, it was the second to the last thing Amanda wanted—what she really dreaded was returning to the ranch outside Deadwood.

Don't think about that now, was the ceaseless refrain going through Amanda's mind. There were so many things to worry about later, when she and Hawk were no longer together, when there was no longer the pleasure of reaching out and touching him, when there was no longer the happiness of looking into his rich, brown eyes and seeing the humor there.

Hawk *did* have a wonderful sense of humor, Amanda was discovering. Usually hidden, he kept it buried beneath him self-imposed discipline and duty. Amanda was discovering all sorts of wonderful things about Hawk, and that was why she felt the poignant loss of time so acutely.

Soon—either today or tomorrow at the latest—the alarm would sound at the Circle S Ranch. Her return would be too late to be on schedule, and Sonny would cause one hell of a commotion, as Amanda well knew, because he'd done it once before when she'd dallied too long without letting anyone know where she was.

How long would it take Hawk and her to reach the Circle S? At least a day and a half, she figured, provided they rode hard. Maybe two days. If the latter was the case, then there would surely be hell to pay by the time she rode through the ranch gates.

Hawk was standing by his stallion, waiting for Amanda, motioning for her to get up into the saddle. He would ride behind her, with his arms around her.

"No, you get on," Amanda countered with a hint of sadness in her voice. "I'll ride behind you."

Agreeably, Hawk swung up into the saddle, then reached down for Amanda and helped her onto the rump of the stallion. Slipping her arms around Hawk's middle, she then laced her fingers together at his stomach and leaned forward to place her cheek lightly against his back. When she sighed he patted her hands, then he tapped his heels against the stallion's ribs to get the animal started down into the valley.

The descent would be slow. Neither Hawk nor Amanda was in any hurry to return to the camp. The sun had fallen and now almost total darkness covered the hillside, making the ride a more cautious one.

"How do you feel?" Hawk asked. They'd gone some distance from the clearing, leaving the memories of their hours of loving behind them.

"Wonderful. And sad," Amanda replied. She hadn't intended to be entirely honest, but now it seemed the best approach. Why hide her feelings from Hawk now? "You're right about me having to leave. I do. My brother's going to be furious with me, and I wouldn't be at all surprised if he doesn't...well, let's just say that I have to get back home."

"Yes," Hawk replied softly.

Amanda kept her eyes closed. It bothered her more hearing Hawk say she had to leave, than hearing herself say it. She wished there was something she could do to make time stand still.

She and Hawk couldn't stay together always—for many reasons. They were too much alike in too many ways, both stubborn, each wanting to lead and neither willing to follow. They couldn't stay together forever, and Amanda accepted this. She just didn't want their time together to end *now*.

I'm not going to cry, Amanda decided when she felt hot tears burning at the backs of her eyes.

And she didn't cry, but the ache she felt inside was terrible. She probably would feel better if she did cry—if she'd just let loose all the emotions pent up within her—but Amanda had spent too long fighting such 'womanly' emotions and responses to allow the tears to flow now.

"We'll leave at sunrise," Hawk announced.

Amanda nodded, her head against his shoulder and her arms around his waist, but she didn't speak as the big stallion carried them slowly back to the tribe.

* * * *

The bile rose in his throat, and Red Wolf had to close his eyes for a moment to compose his thoughts.

She was beautiful beyond words or measure, and when she looked at him the revulsion she felt showed in her expression, in the blue light that shined in her eyes.

Red Wolf hated with all his heart and soul the golden-haired woman who had arrived in the camp with Hawk. He loathed her because she saw him instantly for what he was. And for that she had to be punished. She was like the other women who felt themselves superior to a warrior like Red Wolf, though not too superior for Hawk.

But was his first impression accurate? In the past Red Wolf had held similar thoughts about other women, only to discover that they were not repulsed by him at all. During his sojourns to Fairmont, where he had gone alone three times, he'd felt that the white prostitutes had looked on him scornfully, though he'd discovered later that their passion could be purchased easily. Perhaps the golden-haired woman with Hawk would be no different from the others. How much gold would it take to buy her passion, he wondered.

Red Wolf thought about this for several minutes. Was the woman with Hawk truly scornful of him, or was that just her way of getting his attention? Her skin was flawless, Red Wolf had noted, pale and smooth, and her figure was curved despite her youth. Such beauty was wasted on a man like Hawk Two Feather. Hawk had known the pleasures of too many willing women for him to appreciate any one woman in particular.

The anger boiled once more in Red Wolf's stomach, this time because of Hawk and everything the half-breed warrior represented. The married women and maidens flocked to Hawk, while only a few would give Red Wolf the passion he required. Surely the injustice of this was a sign of some evil power that Hawk exerted to keep Red Wolf from ever truly being happy.

What else could explain the way women reacted to Red Wolf, and the way they responded to Hawk?

What if the young woman's apparent disgust was just a ruse, a trick to get Red Wolf interested in her?

She wouldn't be the first maiden to use such a trick on him, he believed. Twice before Red Wolf had needed to use force to get what he wanted from women, and though they cried, he knew that he hadn't done anything wrong.

A smile settled on Red Wolf's face as he realized why the beautiful golden-haired woman had dismissed him so quickly from her attention—because she had wanted him to pursue her with the cunning and determination of a mighty Sioux warrior.

* * * *

They'd been unable to leave the camp as quickly as Amanda and Hawk had planned. Red Wolf had tossed out some accusations about their trip that Hawk needed to address, and even though almost everyone knew that Hawk was a proud warrior who would never abandon his tribe, he still needed to explain to the elders why it was necessary for him to ride with Amanda back to Deadwood.

Once on their way, as luck would have it, they nearly rode into a small band of Northern Cheyenne braves. Hawk couldn't be sure, but he thought they might be renegades, like those who had attacked Amanda. They avoided the braves, but it had cost them several hours, forcing Hawk and Amanda to make camp for the night.

Amanda had slept in Hawk's arms that night, but they hadn't made love. She'd expected him to want to, and if his desires had moved in that direction, she would have submitted to him. There was an underlying and painful realization that if she made love with him again she would be doing so for the last time.

The next morning they rose early and, without much talk, saddled Daisy and Hawk's enormous stallion, and headed off for Deadwood.

As they approached town, Amanda began to grow nervous. For all the things she had shared about herself, she'd never told Hawk her last name. Had he assumed she was some impoverished tomboy? Would he feel betrayed if she told him now that she came from one of the wealthiest families in the territory?

"Can we stop a minute?" Amanda asked. "There's an artesian well just west of here. We can let the horses drink there."

Hawk nodded, pushing a strand of ebony hair off his forehead. Once more wearing his buckskin trousers, cotton shirt, and leather vest and jacket, he appeared as handsome to Amanda as he had the first time she'd set eyes on him.

"How far are we from Deadwood?" Hawk asked.

"About three hours." Amanda felt a strange tingling sensation in her stomach. She didn't like concealing the truth from Hawk. Withholding information carried with it an undercurrent of treachery.

"And your home is in Deadwood?"

"It's outside of town a ways. We'll be there in a little over three hours, I guess."

Hawk narrowed his eyes as he looked at Amanda. He could tell that there was something she wasn't telling him, though he couldn't guess exactly what it was. Was she ashamed to be seen with a half-breed Sioux? That wouldn't surprise him in the least.

"When we get close to your home, I'll turn back," Hawk offered. He saw immediately the disappointment in Amanda's eyes, but he raised his hand to stop her protests before they started. "It'll be best. I know the way some people think. You and I traveling together...some in my tribe didn't like it, and your people won't either. It's just the way things are."

"It doesn't have to be that way," Amanda said softly.

"But it is."

Amanda squared her shoulders, taking a step closer to Hawk. "No," she said firmly. "After all we've been through, after all we've shared, after all the miles we've ridden together, you can't abandon me now. Not when we're so close to my ranch."

"But Amanda—"

"The least you can let me do is introduce you to my family, and show you a little of my hospitality. Can't you grant me that much?"

Hawk gave her a naughty grin, prompting a blush from Amanda that made him want to kiss her, though he resisted the urge.

Almost everything she did made him want to kiss her. She was, to that extent, entirely unprecedented in his life. He seemed to find *everything* about her captivating. This was a fact that both fascinated Hawk, and somewhat peevishly disconcerted him.

"There are other types of hospitality." Amanda felt her cheeks turning pink and warm. Whenever Hawk looked at her that way the memories of the thrilling moments she'd known in his embrace came flooding back.

Hawk smiled, and it made something inside Amanda soften, made her want to take him into her arms, made her want to lead him someplace where the differences between them wouldn't matter. As it was—with the Sioux and her own people—more energy was spent making sure people of different cultures and races *weren't* happy together.

Now she wanted to kiss him, or in the very least hold him close, but if she did, she would also want to make love to him, and that part of their life together was over. With a sigh of resignation, and wondering, then, if perhaps Hawk's cynicism wasn't closer to reality than her own optimism, she fitted her boot into Daisy's stirrup and got up into the saddle.

It would be good to be home again, to have the creature comforts that had been denied her for so long. She would have to calm the fires of anger that were no doubt flaming within Sonny first, but then she would be able to relax.

Amanda smiled at Hawk as they headed into the final stretch toward her ranch. She hadn't said a word about herself, about the vast fortune that was hers. She hadn't said much about anything that really mattered.

He has to come to the ranch to get his reward for saving my life. And if he thinks that I've deceived him by not telling him who I am, that's something I'll just have to live with.

* * * *

Sonny's first thought on seeing Hawk was that this was a dangerous man.

Not only was Hawk a Sioux warrior, but he carried himself with his head a little too high, and he dared to look straight into a man's eyes, instantly sizing him up.

Sonny had made his fair share of enemies in his day. No truly successful man could ever accomplish lofty goals without leaving lesser individuals feeling cheated. Sonny Wright didn't back down from fights, though he chose his battles carefully...so what bothered him most was that Hawk was very much like himself.

"Now, Sonny, don't you dare be angry," Amanda warned him, stepping close so that she stood between her brother and her lover. "It wasn't my fault I was late, and it wasn't Hawk's fault, either. If Hawk hadn't come to my rescue"—she stabbed a finger into her brother's chest to emphasize her next words—"at considerable risk to himself, then I'd be dead right now."

Her voice dropped low as she shamelessly played on her brother's protective instincts. "Dead," she said very quietly, "or worse."

Amanda watched as Sonny looked over her head at Hawk. Sonny was more heavily muscled, but Hawk stood a bit taller. In hand-to-hand combat, the violence between them would be horrific.

She could tell that her brother didn't want to hate this handsome stranger who had brought her home, but he couldn't forget that she should have been home at least three or four days earlier. She knew her brother well enough to know that he was wondering what they had done together during those days. She knew she couldn't possibly tell him the truth.

"Sonny, please," Amanda whispered, begging for understanding.

Sonny looked down into his little sister's face and smiled for the first time. "I never could stay angry with you."

Amanda threw her arms around Sonny, hugging him tightly. Then, at last certain that violence had been avoided, she turned toward Hawk, her face animated, alive with joyous emotions.

"Come on, I want to show you the house," Amanda said, as she took Hawk's hand. She tried to pull him across the threshold, but Hawk resisted. She couldn't budge him. "Please, Hawk? You showed me where you live, and I just want to do the same."

"No," Hawk said quietly but firmly.

Amanda felt a nervous flush go through her. Just a few moments earlier she'd been overjoyed because her brother had put his anger aside. Now she was being confronted with an equally stubborn man who, for reasons Amanda couldn't even guess, had suddenly decided to rob her of her happiness.

Amanda glanced at Sonny. After a brief communication with their eyes only, Sonny said, "I'll go into the library and have a good stiff shot of rye. You coming home to roost seems a good enough reason to celebrate with a drink, I'd say." He took a step, stopped, and then said, "If you need anything, just holler and I'll come running." Then he walked away, leaving Amanda alone in the great archway of the huge ranch house.

Alone with Hawk, Amanda frowned, her hands on her hips. "You can't leave," she declared, quietly and forcefully. "Your camp is much too far away, and it makes no sense at all to sleep outside on your bedroll when we have a dozen perfectly comfortable rooms here for you to choose from."

"A dozen bedrooms unused?" Hawk cocked an eyebrow, mocking her.

"I'm sorry if I wasn't completely honest with you before. It wasn't that I didn't want to be. I was afraid at first that if you knew of my family's status, you'd hold me for ransom." Amanda flinched inwardly at the look Hawk gave her. She'd hurt him with her comment, and she felt guilty about it. "It was my own suspicions, Hawk. Foolish, unfounded suspicions. It had nothing to do with you at all."

Amanda looked into the entry way and, beyond that, into the foyer. The library, with its gleaming, polished double doors, was to the left. She had noticed from the very beginning that Sonny had left the library doors open several inches. He might not be able to overhear a whispered conversation, but should she raise her voice, Sonny could reappear in the hallway in an instant, probably with a blazing six-shooter in each hand.

"No, I can't go in there," Hawk said sternly.

"What's wrong, Hawk? It's obviously something more than just my not telling you I'm a Wright."

Hawk looked at her and smiled.

"You can't leave," Amanda said again, encouraged by Hawk's smile. "There's something my brother and I have to give you. A small reward for saving my life."

Hawk shook his head quickly. "I didn't do it for money Amanda. You know that."

"Yes, I know. That's exactly why I'm going to be so stubborn about this now. If you'd done it for money, I'd have paid you, but you wouldn't have had my respect. By being such a gentleman" — Amanda was stopped dead for a moment as she wondered whether a Sioux warrior could ever, in fact, be considered a gentleman, or would even want to be thought of as such — "you have earned my respect and my reward, and I will not allow you to deprive me of the privilege of being kind in return for all that you have done for me."

Amanda saw that Hawk was determined to hold his ground, but she had spent plenty of time horse-trading with men much older and more experienced than herself. She wasn't easily mollified, and she wasn't above arguing on a purely emotional basis to get what she wanted.

"If you won't take the money for yourself, at least take it for your people. They'll think you're a hero for it."

"I don't want to be a hero."

"It's too late, you already are," Amanda replied, her voice dipping as images of Hawk's extraordinary courage, intelligence, and resourcefulness flashed through her mind. "You can't change what and who you are any more than I can," Amanda continued softly. "Please, Hawk, take the money. You can buy many things with it, things that will make life easier for the women and children of the tribe. Think of them. You don't have to spend a single cent of it on yourself if you don't want to."

She had him there, and she knew it. Amanda had skillfully maneuvered Hawk until his position of refusal appeared as proud, foolish, and, in a bizarre way, selfish and cruel to the women and children he was supposed to protect.

"You can be a very persuasive woman," Hawk said quietly. Absolute respect filled his eyes. "But there's got to be room for compromise."

Amanda smiled with unalloyed delight. "Compromise is my middle name," she said, remembering all the times she'd said that to horse-traders and eventually ended up getting pretty much everything she wanted without taking so much as a single step backward from her original position. "However, I see no reason in the world that we should..." She paused, searching for the right word before deciding upon "...*negotiate* the terms of our agreement out here. There are some very comfortable rooms inside, and I'd love a cool drink." She looked him in the eyes and said in a voice just above a whisper, "If there's anything you'd like, I'd be only too happy to oblige."

She could see in his eyes that he'd caught her double entendre, and that he was affected by it. She suspected he stubbornly didn't want to enter her house, but he did want to enter...her.

"I plan to ride into town tonight, and tomorrow we can discuss what needs to be done," Hawk said. "It's been quite a while since I've been in Deadwood. Perhaps it won't be as bad as I remember."

"Why ride all the way to Deadwood and pay for a room?" Amanda glanced over her shoulder toward the library doors. She didn't want Sonny to hear her. There was no mistaking that she wanted to be with Hawk, that she wanted to hold him in her arms and taste his breathtaking kisses once again.

"I just have to," Hawk replied without embellishment. "Can we leave it at that?"

For once, Hawk had requested that a subject be dropped rather than simply clamming up and shutting Amanda out, and for that she was grateful. Not quite grateful enough to give up easily, but grateful just the same.

"Why spend your money?" she persisted with a coquettish lilt to her voice. "Do you have enough to get a suite?"

"No, I don't have enough for a suite," Hawk replied, an edge to his voice, "but then, I don't need a suite. My needs are very simple."

Amanda smiled, not at all put off by the sharpness in Hawk's voice. "Your needs may be simple but they can be...*voracious*" —she drawled the word sensually— "nevertheless. And don't try to deny it, because I know you, Hawk Two Feather. I know you better than you think."

Though stunned at Amanda's words, Hawk never allowed it to show in his face. Yes, Amanda did know him better, to be sure, than any of the other women who had traipsed lightly and quickly through the romantic and sensual quarters of his life.

"Tomorrow," he said, smiling now with some difficulty. Alone tonight, he could think about Amanda and figure out why he had allowed her, and no one else, into the previously unreachable regions of his heart and soul.

He turned then and headed for his stallion, not wanting to allow Amanda to say more. She was more intelligent than he had initially thought, and that would cause him problems. Rather than blithely assuming that he could convince her of the lightness of his needs, he was discovering that she could, in all likelihood, convince him that her position was the correct one.

"But, Hawk…" she whispered.

"Tomorrow," he said over his shoulder, using his long-legged stride to make his way to the stallion that had carried him through countless battles.

* * * *

"I'd like a room for the night," Hawk said, using a tone of voice that was neither aggressive nor insulting. He looked straight into the hotel manager's eyes, sensing the animosity lurking behind the man's oily smile. "I'd appreciate it if you'd hurry. I've been riding a long time, and I'd like to get some sleep."

The manager seemed taken aback by Hawk's forceful and confident request.

"There's no room here for you," the manager said steadily, hatefully. His expression said without words that he resented the fact that he even had to speak to an Indian, much less actually have to explain to him what his true place in society was. "I'm sorry. You'll have to go somewhere else."

Hawk looked past the hotel manager at the wall, where a row of small, square boxes holding room keys was attached. Messages for the guests were also saved there. Even at a glance from a man who'd spent few nights in hotels, it was clear to Hawk that there were rooms to be had.

"I have money," Hawk said, resenting the fact that such a statement had to be spoken.

"Yes, I'm sure you do, but the fact remains that there are no rooms for you. Now if you'll please leave immediately, everyone will be happier for it."

The last little dig set Hawk off, making it impossible for him to walk away from this one. He was, after all, just as much white as he was Indian, why couldn't he rent a room for the night, providing he had the money to pay for it?

"No, I will not leave. If you need your money for the room in advance, I can do that."

Hawk watched as the man made a little move with his hand. In other circumstances it wouldn't have been a threatening gesture, but Hawk realized from the very beginning that trouble was on the way.

"Problems, sir?" a big, bearded man asked, his eyes cold and steady on Hawk. He'd stepped out from a back room. "I can get rid of this trash any time you want."

Hawk looked at the man who had entered the scene. Though he had bathed recently and was wearing reasonably new, fashionable clothes, Hawk pegged him instantly for hired muscle, several steps below a hired gun. The man was as big as an ox and powerful, though at least fifty pounds heavier than Hawk.

"I'm sure he'll leave now," the hotel manager said, a vicious, satisfied smile curling his lips as he looked at Hawk.

"That's where you're wrong," Hawk replied, his voice hinting at the violence and hatred that had been brewing for decades within him. "You see, I'm going to be treated just the same as anyone who comes here looking for a room and has the money to pay for it."

The hired muscle just couldn't resist opening his mouth. "You'll get treated just the same as all the other two-legged manure that walks in here, thinking they's just as good as white folk."

That was his first mistake. He hadn't been content with merely insulting Hawk, he had insisted on touching him as well.

Precisely one second after the man's hand touched Hawk's shoulder, Hawk decided that he'd been pushed around as far as he was going to allow. He lashed out with his right hand, aiming not for the nose or chin but for the forehead. The heel of his right palm made solid contact, snapping the big man's head back on his neck in the blink of an eye. The large man fell to his knees, a stunned expression on his face, his eyes unable to focus. The entire force of the blow had been absorbed by the man's brain. Shortly after he dropped to his knees, Hawk swung far back and delivered a roundhouse punch to the man's chin, which sent him flat onto his back and into unconsciousness.

After checking to see that the heavy-set man would eventually recover from his injuries, Hawk wheeled on the hotel manager, his hands clenched into fists. Hawk wanted, at this point, to beat the man to a pulp. He reached over the counter and grabbed the lapel of the manager's coat.

"There are no rooms for you," the hotel manager repeated. Though he was maintaining his self-righteous indignation, the undercurrent of fear, the unspoken awareness that he wasn't in control and hadn't been for some time, could be seen.

Hawk shook the manager, feeling the lapel tear in his hand. "Do I get the room or not?" Hawk asked.

"Y-y-yes, sir," the hotel manager finally stammered. "Any room you want is yours for the asking. If there's someone in there now, I'll have him thrown in the street before you know it."

Hawk smiled. He sensed the hotel manager believed in nothing other than strength. Like a spear of wheat, he stood straight and true only so long as there wasn't a wind blowing.

There weren't any lavish suites at the hotel, despite the man's words, but Hawk was happy with the simple, clean room. He tested the mattress and was pleased with its newness and quality. It would feel good to sleep in a bed again. How long had it been since he'd felt a mattress beneath him?

Chapter Thirteen

Amanda looked at the array of nightgowns in her closet and decided on the high-necked, simple white one. It had been a gift from Sonny, for either her birthday or Christmas. Amanda couldn't remember the occasion because her brother was absurdly generous with her and Vanessa, always buying them gifts, trying to do little things to make their lives easier, happier.

With slippers on her feet and clad in a nightgown and robe, Amanda went downstairs to the library, where Sonny was waiting for her.

"Now tell me everything, from the very beginning," Sonny said, sitting on one side of the couch with a whiskey glass in his hand. Amanda held a small glass of white wine. "If I'm going to pay this Hawk fellow a king's ransom for your return, at least I should get the details of his heroism."

Amanda smiled, took a sip of wine, then began relaying the events immediately following her departure from the horse auctions at Fort Keough. She had been mentally rehearsing what she would tell

Sonny since she'd returned home, and the facts now rolled effortlessly off her tongue. The deletion of certain details—like the way her body felt all jittery inside whenever Hawk was near, and the way she couldn't catch her breath whenever he kissed her—was an easy matter, though she'd never before had any reason not to tell her brother everything.

This time was different. This time there was a special man in her life, and even though he would soon be riding away, never to be seen again, Amanda knew that she'd keep memories of him in her heart forever. She wouldn't share them with anyone. Not ever. By keeping the memories to herself, by never speaking of them to anyone, she would keep them fresh and alive and infinitely precious.

"What was the vision quest like?" Sonny asked quietly, his eyes narrowing with concern.

"It's wasn't very successful, I'm afraid, though I did see a doe briefly. Buttercup says the doe is my spirit guide, but that might not be the case. She said that in a vision quest the visions should last longer than mine did. I might have just made it up because I wanted to see something."

Amanda sipped her wine, knowing she couldn't tell Sonny that she very much wanted to go on another vision quest. Sonny was much too provincial in his outlook on life to view kindly such activities.

They spoke then of Hawk, and Sonny was polite enough not to ask directly if the alleged hero was also a gentleman. Through omission, Amanda let Sonny believe nothing romantic had transpired between them. Then she busied herself with discussing the inferior quality of the horses she'd seen at Fort Keough, and that none of the mares or stallions had bloodlines worthy of the Wright herd.

By ten o'clock Amanda had pretty much told her brother everything she'd done. After a second glass of wine, fatigue came over Amanda, and she excused herself. Sliding between the sheets of her bed, she sighed, closed her eyes, and within seconds was asleep…and dreaming of Hawk.

* * * *

A few minutes after ten o'clock, Hawk heard angry male voices coming from the dusty street. They could have been discussing anything, but Hawk had been an outsider long enough to assume he could well be the target of such aggressive language. Sitting on the edge of the bed, he picked up his revolver and holster and quickly strapped the belt around his lean waist. The moment his moccasins were back on, he heard the same angry male voices in the hallway.

Under his breath, Hawk cursed himself. Why had he ever assumed he could come to the white man's town and not suffer the consequences?

He stepped out just as the men—four of them, led by the bruised security guard—approached his room. Spotting Hawk, they spread out shoulder-to-shoulder, completely blocking his path. All were armed and angry that an Indian had gotten the best of one of their own. They were looking for swift vigilante justice.

"Are you going to let me pass?" Hawk asked, surprising the men by speaking first. He stood in the center of the hallway, his feet spread to shoulder's width and, his hands loose at his sides but ready to go for his gun in an instant. By Hawk's calculation, he could shoot one, maybe two of them, before they got him.

"Maybe," the hired muscle said. There was an ugly purple mark on his forehead, matched by an ugly look in his eyes. "Maybe we'll just stomp on you right here."

The men were clearly vicious and violent. Hawk knew their type. He didn't respect it, but he knew it.

Hawk stood his ground. He couldn't get past the men if they didn't want him to, and trying to walk between them to get to the stairway would be suicidal. The moment they had their hands on him, Hawk knew he was as good as dead, though these men probably wouldn't be in any hurry to actually kill him. He recognized the type who would prolong the agony before the inevitable murder.

Three doors in the hallway opened, then quickly closed. Nobody wanted to get involved. Hawk didn't blame the terrified people one bit.

"Walk away from this one," Hawk said quietly, his voice even and measured. "I'll leave town on my own tonight. Just walk away from this one."

The smallest of the four men grinned broadly. "The redskin's yellow. He's just a yellow bastard."

Hawk gritted his teeth against the insult, bothered more than he cared to admit at being called a redskin, and a coward. What hurt the most was being called a bastard and knowing that, in truth, he was.

"Hey, redskin, what you got to say about that? Are you a coward, or ain't you?" the little man taunted. He jeered at Hawk from behind the big security guard, confident in the protection of his three friends. "Cat got yer tongue, redskin?"

"If you were man-sized," Hawk said slowly, "I'd take offense to such words. When you grow to be a man, we'll talk."

The little man made up for his lack of size with sheer savagery. Hawk could tell that he had killed before when insulted, and that he intended to kill again. He went for his revolver.

Hawk drew and fired. In the enclosed hallway, the revolver's report was a deafening explosion. He struck the little man in the thigh, dropping him to the floor as the fellow's gun sent a bullet into the floor between Hawk's moccasins. Hawk thumbed back the hammer quickly, seeing that his other three foes were drawing their weapons.

"Kill him!" the little man screamed in agony.

The big security guard was slow, so Hawk dismissed him as a pressing threat. But the man to his left wasn't. He was just raising his revolver from its holster when Hawk fired, his aim deadly accurate this time. The man fell onto his back and didn't move again.

The huge hired muscle was in a hurry to kill. Firing too quickly, his bullet struck the wounded man squarely between the shoulder blades. The guard was still staring in shock, when Hawk's bullet found its mark, sending him toppling backward like a gigantic redwood.

The one remaining man apparently wanted no part of the fight with Hawk now. Three of his friends had been killed in seconds. He tossed his gun to the floor and raised his hands over his head.

"Don't shoot! Don't shoot me!" he shrieked, his eyes wild with fear.

Hawk wanted to pull the trigger but he didn't. He wouldn't be a cold-blooded killer, it wasn't in him.

"Get the hell out of here," Hawk said through clenched teeth.

The last man ran as though he'd been granted a reprieve from God himself. Hawk holstered his weapon, wrinkling his nose at the smell of burned gunpowder and the stench of instant death.

What had made him think he could come into Deadwood and not find trouble?

"Don't move, Injin!"

Hawk looked first into the twin barrels of the shotgun, then into the face of the man who'd spoken—Sheriff Darren Richards. There on his vest was pinned the silver badge of authority in the courts of the white man.

"You're under arrest, Injin, for the murder of these men here," the sheriff said, keeping his shotgun trained on Hawk's chest. "Real careful and slow, you jus' drop that gun belt and lay down on the floor. You so much as breathe funny an' I'll cut you clean in half with this scattergun."

Hawk knew the sheriff was looking for an excuse to kill him, so he did as he was ordered, then felt the cold steel manacles being locked around his wrists.

"Do I get a trial before you lynch me?" Hawk asked when he'd been hoisted to his feet and pushed toward the stairway. He had to step over the corpses.

"We do things legal in Deadwood," Sheriff Richards replied. "We're going to give you a trial, then hang you, all nice and legal."

Hawk was escorted out of the hotel and down the dusty street to the jail. Sheriff Richards opened the jail cell door wide and turned to Hawk with a smile on his face.

"Injin, you killed men who ain't much better than coyotes," the sheriff said. "Just the same, they was white men, an' it always looks bad havin' an Injin do something like that. If I don't do somethin' about it, the townsfolk would have no respect for me at all."

With his hands manacled behind his back, Hawk was defenseless against the barrage of fists that followed. The sheriff began to beat his ribs and stomach, and when Hawk finally fell to the floor he kicked him several times. Only then, with Hawk writhing on the jail floor, his breath beaten from his lungs, did the sheriff grab him by an ankle, drag him into the cell, and lock the heavy iron door behind him.

"You sleep good now, you hear?" The sheriff smiled as he walked away.

* * * *

Sheriff Darren Richards headed for the nearest saloon. He could hardly wait to taste the whiskey the men would buy him in congratulations for the beating he'd given Hawk. This was the kind of evening that had made Darren want to become sheriff in the first place.

He wondered if one of the ladies of the evening would give him some pleasure without charging him. Sometimes they were impressed with the kind of things he'd just done, but most of the time they just wanted the money.

The sheriff smiled. Even if he had to pay for it, he was going to get some. And soon.

* * * *

Amanda rode into town wearing new Levis and a new blue cotton shirt beneath a jacket of lightweight brown wool. She'd had the staff polish her boots that morning so that they shined as though they were fresh from the cobbler.

This was the fourth outfit she'd tried on that morning. Her first three attempts had been dresses, which she'd rejected after looking at her reflection in the mirror. Though she wanted to look nice for Hawk, she didn't want him to guess the trouble she'd gone through for him.

She went to the bank first to withdraw two thousand dollars. The bank president, always alert when such large sums of money were withdrawn, smiled at Amanda and suggested that it must be a very beautiful horse the Wrights were planning to buy. Not wanting to explain that the money would soon be in the possession of the most handsome Sioux warrior in the world, Amanda merely returned the smile, letting the banker think what he wanted.

There were only two hotels in town. Since the clerk at the first one Amanda tried hadn't seen Hawk, she was confident, on reaching the second, that she'd find him. Would she stir gossip if she went to Hawk's room without an escort? And once there, would she be able to control her romantic urges? Just thinking about Hawk's embrace brought a smile to her lips.

The morning clerk at the Deadwood Hotel, a Mr Jamison, developed a troubled expression when Amanda began asking him questions. Though it was early—just a few minutes past nine—Mr Jamison appeared to have been awake for many hours, and to have had insufficient sleep.

"These are not really difficult questions." Amanda was finding it impossible to remain polite to this evasive man. "Is Hawk Two Feather staying at this hotel?"

"He was." Mr Jamison finally replied.

"Then he's checked out?" Amanda was just about ready to vault over the counter, take Mr Jamison by the throat, and choke straight answers out of him.

"Not exactly. You see, there was a disturbance last night, and I'm afraid Mr Feather was in the middle of it." Mr Jamison shook his head and sighed. "I still can't believe my night manager was foolish enough to rent a room to an Indian. Everyone knows they cause nothing but trouble."

Amanda had never been one to use the weight of her name carelessly. Nevertheless, she looked Mr Jamison straight in the eye and warned, "Unless you tell me everything that happened last night, everything from the very beginning, I'm going to buy this hotel, and then I'll be your boss. Imagine what your life will be like with me telling you what to do every minute of the day."

Mr Jamison quickly summoned the night manager from his room, making him suffer the indignity of answering Amanda's endless, piercing questions.

By the time the night manager had explained his version of what had happened, Amanda was mad enough to burn every building in Deadwood to the ground, then chase every person in the city out of the territory. When she left the hotel, headed for the jail, she was already making plans to destroy the careers — and maybe even the lives, if her temper held — of certain people in town, most notably Sheriff Darren Richards.

Amanda burst into the jail and found the sheriff was nursing a wicked hangover. Darren Richards was sitting on the cot in the office, holding his head in his hands.

Amanda pointed a finger in the sheriff's face and spat, "You pathetic dog! You let Hawk out of jail or so help me God I'll destroy you!"

"You watch your tongue, little lady, or I'll arrest you, too!" the sheriff shot back.

"Go ahead and try it, but you'd better think about your own long stretch in prison if you do, because if you put one finger on me, that's where you'll go."

Although Amanda was furious, she was very aware that Vanessa had left Deadwood. If Vanessa's services were needed, it would take a couple of days for her to return. Unfortunately, Darren Richards represented legal authority in Deadwood, and even the territorial judge would consider his word as credible.

Deputy Foster Samuelson came walking into the office. "Now hold your horses for a minute, Amanda," the deputy said, placing his hands lightly on her shoulders. Amanda knew him to be an honest and dedicated man, and one who believed in making Deadwood a decent place for everyone to live. "I know what you're thinking, but we just can't let that fellow out of jail. There are three dead men over at the undertaker's, and that's something we can't pretend isn't so."

"It was self-defense, Deputy, and you know it." Amanda pushed the deputy's hands from her shoulders. She knew he meant well, but she wouldn't be mollified by words or gestures—no matter how reasonable they were—unless they were followed up with the immediate action of freeing Hawk from his jail cell.

"Go talk to some of the hotel guests," Amanda suddenly ordered the deputy. "If you say you can't let Hawk out of jail without evidence of his innocence, get busy and find some."

Looking somewhat irritated and holding back a retort, the deputy left, issuing a quiet suggestion—which sounded more like a warning—to Sheriff Richards that he was to stay in the office and out of trouble until the deputy returned. Amanda's demand that she be allowed to see Hawk was rejected, and she suspected the sheriff refused only because she'd already made him so angry.

Two hours later the deputy returned. In that time, Amanda had devised no less than a dozen can't-fail plans to make Sheriff Darren Richards wish he'd never heard the name Amanda Wright. With luck, he might even wish he'd never been born.

"Several people heard what was said in the hallway before the shooting started," Deputy Samuelson informed Amanda as he went to the large ring of keys that hung from a peg in the wall behind his desk. "It seems the Indian was trying to walk away from the fight."

"His name is Hawk," Amanda said testily, following close at the deputy's heels.

"What is he to you, anyway? You seem awful worked up about an Indian."

Now Amanda realized gossip would flow, but she didn't care a whit what anyone thought of her. Just the same she flirted with the truth when she replied, "He's a friend of the family."

When she saw Hawk sitting on the small bed in the jail cell, she wanted to rush to him and take him into her arms. She wanted to apologize not only for all of the citizens of Deadwood, but for everything the whites had ever done to the Indians. With Deputy Samuelson there, already highly inquisitive about the relationship between her and Hawk, Amanda kept her feelings to herself.

The instant Amanda saw Hawk move off the bed she knew that he'd been beaten. He tried to keep the pain from showing, but Amanda remembered too well his usual effortless grace, like that of a mountain lion. As he bent over slightly and approached the cell door, the light shining in his eyes was fueled by pain and hatred.

"We're setting you free," Deputy Samuelson said, fitting the long, heavy key into the iron lock. "If any family members of the boys you killed cause a fuss, you may have to tell your story to the judge."

Hawk didn't reply, merely looking on the deputy with undisguised loathing. The door finally opened and Hawk stepped out, holding his head high.

"I'm going to make everything right," Amanda said to Hawk, her tone and concern informing the deputy that she was motivated by something more than mere friendship. A lifetime of wealth made Amanda's declaration a credible one, though a testimony to her youth as much as to her financial power. "We'll get back to the ranch and send for the doctor."

"No," Hawk said, limping to the office of the jail.

"But Hawk…" Amanda began, then stopped herself. She wouldn't say anything else in front of the deputy. He sensed too much about her and Hawk as it was.

Standing on the boardwalk outside the jail, Deputy Samuelson turned to Hawk and said, "I know them boys didn't give you a choice in the fighting, and I know what the sheriff did to you was wrong, but I'm going to give you some free advice right now, and if you're a smart man, you'll listen up. You just ride straight out of town and don't look back. Don't go looking for revenge, because that won't change any of the wrongs that have been done to you. Just ride out and put it all behind you. Deadwood isn't any place for you, I'm sorry to say."

"I'll *bet* you're sorry," Amanda shot back sarcastically. "But you're not nearly as sorry as some other people in Deadwood are going to be. I can promise you that."

"Just in case you haven't figured it out by yourself," Samuelson retorted, "I'm not your enemy. You'll have plenty of enemies—trust me on this—but I'm not one of them, so don't talk to me as if I am."

As difficult as it was for Amanda to admit when she was wrong, she looked directly at the man and said, "I'm sorry, Deputy. This whole affair has got me confused. It makes me say things I shouldn't. I get stupid."

Foster Samuelson replied, "Already forgotten. And of all the things I've thought about, the word 'stupid' has never once crossed my mind. Now get out of town, both of you. And don't worry about the sheriff. I'll keep him in line."

* * * *

Though Hawk was able to pull himself into the saddle, he couldn't hide the pain that ripped through his body like a lightning bolt. The cracked ribs caused him incredible agony. He could still feel where each boot tip had connected with his body, where each of the sheriff's well-placed kicks had hit him as he writhed, manacled and defenseless, on the ground.

Once in the saddle, his stallion ready to run, Hawk instead kept the great beast in check. His sides hurt too much for him even to think about riding out of Deadwood at a gallop. After a moment he swung down from the saddle. The stallion was more inclined to maintain an easy walk without Hawk sitting on his back.

"Are you all right?" Amanda asked softly, standing beside the horse and watching Hawk try to hide his pain.

"I'm fine."

"You don't look it."

"I never asked you for your opinion."

"No, you didn't," Amanda replied, too concerned for Hawk's welfare to allow his moodiness and prideful temper to deter her. "You seldom ask for my opinion, though I give it to you often enough."

"I've noticed," Hawk said, turning the stallion around and walking out of the corral of the livery stable.

Amanda, on foot, moved to block the stallion's path. The animal, highly trained and attuned to his master's wants, was skittish.

"Don't be a fool," Amanda spat, disgusted with Hawk's display of stubbornness. "You can hardly walk. You couldn't ride fast if your life depended on it—and it just might, if I'm any judge of the vindictiveness of some of the folks in this town. What would you do if you got in a fight on your way back to your tribe? Will dying prove just how independent you are?"

Amanda, not to be put off, maneuvered around so that she was once more blocking his path.

"You can't get away from me that easily." Amanda reached out, intent on pushing Hawk so that he couldn't walk onto the street.

The instant she got close to his ribs Hawk grabbed her by the wrists, his hands flashing out so quickly that she'd hardly seen them move. Even though he wore buckskins and not the traditional leggings and loincloth of a Sioux warrior, and even though anything more than a cursory glance at his gaunt, handsome features established that he had as much Caucasian blood in him as Sioux, Amanda knew the townspeople considered him an outsider, an Indian brave through and through.

Now the townspeople will never stop talking about me. Amanda followed Hawk to the livery.

* * * *

Hawk checked his harness. The livery owner had saddled the stallion for him, and he didn't trust the man's work. He groaned slightly when he had to tighten the rear saddle surcingle.

"Just look at you," Amanda said, very quietly this time, more sympathy than anger in her tone. "You can hardly saddle your own horse, and you think you're healthy enough to ride out of Deadwood as though you hadn't made any enemies while you were here?"

Hawk kept his back to Amanda as she spoke. He didn't want to believe that he was incapable of defending himself against his enemies. He'd lived by his strength and cunning for too many years to think that he was anything other than a capable warrior. But even pride and courage couldn't mend ribs bruised and broken by the toes of the sheriff's boots. When Hawk pulled himself up into the saddle again, the pain seemed to shoot straight up from his ribs, exploding inside his skull like dynamite. He'd known discomfort before, but this was reaching a whole new level.

"The least you can do is take me to my horse," Amanda said, making it sound as though she was giving up the argument, though she had no intention of doing that. "I've got something in my saddlebag for you." She'd left a small fortune in cash in her saddlebag, completely unprotected, and was only now thinking about it.

"I'll walk," Amanda said, though she very much wanted to get onto the stallion behind Hawk. She also wanted to be wearing the deerskin dress that rode up to her hips when she was stride a horse, and her cheeks turned warm when she became aware of the errant, libidinous thought.

She wanted to touch him, to hold him in her arms, not in a sexual way, but to give him comfort. She wanted to soothe his pain and ease his troubled mind. It infuriated her to know that he'd never allow her to do that because it would offend his preposterous notions of manly behavior. Most frustrating of all, Amanda had never before experienced such tenderness in her soul. She wanted to give Hawk comfort, protect and nurture him. Now that she was finally experiencing these feelings—feelings that were so *feminine*—she was denied the chance to express them.

Making their way back down the street, Hawk was fully aware of Amanda's compromised position. Walking beside an Indian brave on horseback simply had to make her look subservient, and yet she was voluntarily doing just that, with many of the townspeople of Deadwood looking on.

Though Hawk didn't want to look into the men's faces, it was in their eyes that he would discover his enemies. Expecting to see one or two men with enough hatred in their hearts to want to kill him, he instead saw half a dozen or more. Word of how he had killed several men in the hotel and then been released from jail obviously had spread quickly through Deadwood.

A grizzled man spat a stream of tobacco juice into the street, wiped his mouth with the back of his hand, then muttered, "Somebody oughta string that redskin up."

Hawk looked at the man with the foolish tongue. The urge to put an end to his life was strong, but he resisted it. Insults meant nothing to him. Certainly not the idiotic talk of a man who had the appearance of being continually intoxicated.

Although Amanda wanted to scream at the disheveled drunk, she kept on walking. Telling the man who'd threatened Hawk what she thought of him would only make a spectacle of her, and the source of her wrath would likely remain immune to her insults. As much as his words pained her, her words couldn't hurt a man like that.

Before she reached the hitching post where Daisy was waiting patiently for her to return, Amanda lost any respect that might have remained in her heart for Deadwood.

After untying the reins, she climbed into Daisy's saddle. It was easier talking to Hawk when she didn't have to look up so far.

"I've got two thousand dollars in twenty dollar coins in my saddlebag for you," she said. "Don't even think about trying to refuse it because I'm not going to let you."

Three men had stepped into the street, fanning out just enough to obstruct Hawk and Amanda's exit from town. Amanda shook her head slowly in disgust.

"They'll be waiting for you sooner or later. You know that."

"Yes, I know that."

"Come back to the ranch with me," Amanda said. She was actually pleased that the three toughs had decided to be intimidating, validating her concerns. "Give yourself a day or two to recover. Then, when you return to your tribe, you'll be stronger, and you can leave without all of Deadwood knowing about it."

"You know something, Amanda? You're about the smartest woman I've ever met."

Amanda couldn't tell whether he was being mildly sarcastic or purely complimentary. She smiled and replied, "That's what I've been trying to tell you for some time, only you wouldn't listen."

Chapter Fourteen

Hawk's present environment made him uneasy. Surrounded by books, their smell filling his nostrils, he truly regretted not getting the education that he had wanted.

"The knowledge of the whole world is in this room," Hawk said quietly, a brandy snifter in his hand.

On his second brandy he noticed that the pain in his ribs was considerably duller. The doctor had examined him, and once he'd bandaged the ribs tightly, Hawk had begun to feel better. The doctor had left a packet of powder behind, should sleep prove impossible, but Hawk was leery of using it, having heard stories of permanent imprisonment by white men's medicine.

"Not quite," Sonny replied, relaxing on the long leather sofa. "But we're trying. My sisters and I spend a lot of time here. I like being surrounded by books."

"So do I," Hawk said, "though I confess it makes me feel unlearned."

"Pick out whatever you want and consider it yours," Sonny said.

Hawk ran his fingertip along the spines of some handsome leather bound volumes. He'd always been thankful that the missionary priest, Father Lafevre, and his mother, had insisted he learn to read. He selected a translation of Balzac.

"Thank you," he said, "but just for tonight. I'll leave the book here when I go."

"You don't have to. Please, I want you to have it." Sonny smiled sheepishly. "I'm feeling a bit guilty for my rude treatment of you earlier. Let me make up for it."

When Hawk finished his second brandy he excused himself and went to the guest bedroom on the second floor of the ranch house. Amanda had gone to bed an hour earlier, leaving the men alone in the library to talk.

The bed was huge and unimaginably comfortable, the sheets brilliantly white, crisply laundered, the entire room casually and comfortably appointed. But Hawk couldn't envision himself staying here. Not for very long, anyway. He had the strange sense of being a thief, half-expecting someone to rush into the bedroom, exclaiming that there had been a terrible mistake, and that this Indian didn't belong here and would have to leave immediately or the sheriff would be summoned.

Hawk stripped out of his clothes and tried on the nightshirt that had been provided for him but decided against wearing it. The nightshirt seemed to bind beneath his arms. Besides, he'd never worn clothes to bed before, and saw no reason to start now.

He stretched out on the bed, his head and shoulders propped up by several pillows. After angling the reflecting mirror on the lantern so that it slanted light down across his book, Hawk waited a moment for the pain from his ribs to diminish, then he opened the book and began to read. Balzac was the French writer the priest who'd taught Hawk to read had insisted was nothing more than a pornographer. From that time on Hawk, naturally, hadn't been able to get enough of Balzac, though it had been several years since he'd read one of the French writer's bawdy tales.

* * * *

In her bedroom, Amanda considered the nightgowns she owned. Four of them were displayed on her bed, three more still hung in the closet. Choosing one was difficult since she'd never before paid much attention to what she wore to bed. Previously, her considerations centered on winter warmth and summer coolness. Some nights, when it was terribly hot, Amanda would sleep in the nude, though she seldom felt entirely comfortable doing so. Even though no one, not even her brother or sister, knew she'd slept naked, *she* knew, and she felt positively wicked doing it.

She was naked now, though, her weight shifting from one foot to the other as she tried to decide which gown she would wear. And should she even bother? She highly doubted that her courage would last long enough to get her to the guest bedroom where Hawk was probably sleeping right now. Most likely he didn't want to be disturbed, needing his rest so that he could recover his strength.

Amanda picked up two of the nightgowns from the bed and brought them back to hang them in the closet. Winter-weight gowns of flannel, warm and cozy, were not right for this occasion. That left Amanda with two to choose from.

One, cream-colored, had a neckline that was positively scandalous, plunging deeply in a V, with lace along the bodice. High-waisted in the Empire fashion, the loose skirt molded to her legs when she walked.

The other gown was also a gift—from Vanessa. Exactly the kind of nightgown an older sister would give, it was plain, simple, and comfortable as can be, and about as wholesome as anyone could ask for. Amanda brought that one to the closet also. Wholesome wasn't what she was after tonight.

She picked up her friend's gown, took a deep breath for courage, and pulled it over her head. She'd never even tried it on before, having been somewhat embarrassed by any clothing blatantly intended to attract a man's eye. After making some adjustments with the bodice—she had looked down at herself, shocked at the fullness of her breasts in the décolletage—she was ready to study her appearance in the full-length mirror in the corner of her bedroom.

The sight took her breath away. Was this what a man wanted a woman to look like?

The cream-colored silk was probably not the right color for her pale complexion. Perhaps a dark green or navy blue would have gone better with her honey-blonde hair and her pale skin. But the gown itself—its fine fabric defining the curves of her hips and breasts, the décolletage with its edge of delicate lace presenting an abundant amount of the inner swells of her breasts—all combined to give her an appearance of extravagant femininity. And that, she knew, was what men wanted. There wasn't a woman in the world who didn't know that.

Looking at her reflection in the mirror, Amanda could scarcely picture herself in her usual attire of Levis and man-cut shirt.

She turned right, then left, to look at her reflection in profile, and as she did so, she realized how fast her heart was beating. When she held out her hands, she saw they were trembling. Not with fear. At least, not entirely. Anticipation and sensual tension also played havoc with her peace of mind.

What if he didn't want her in his room? Hawk was so angry with the people of Deadwood that she wouldn't blame him if he didn't want anything to do with her. And even worse than being rejected by Hawk, what if she was discovered by Sonny? That thought sent a cool shiver racing down Amanda's spine. She looked at the reflection of her eyes in the mirror. Was there really a passionate woman lurking there, ready to visit Hawk's bedroom wearing this unbelievable gown?

Yes. Yes, there *was* a passionate woman behind those eyes, and she was feeling the desire to touch once more the man who'd taught her what sensual excitement was all about, what heights of ecstasy were possible with a skilled and considerate lover.

Amanda adjusted the bodice of her nightgown once more, trying to conceal more of her bosom than the material would allow, then walked slowly on bare feet to the bedroom door, opened it.

Her brother's room was right next to her own. The guest bedroom assigned to Hawk was down the hall and to the left. Taking a half step into the hallway, Amanda saw a thin beam of light beneath Hawk's door. At least he was awake.

She moved slowly, pleased that Sonny's door was closed, and that no light emanated from within. She decided he was either in bed and fast asleep, as she hoped, or he hadn't gone to bed yet. Amanda wasn't dressed to search the quiet house for her brother and wouldn't know what to say should she come upon him. Rooted in place, she knew that if she thought too long on her fears, they would paralyze her.

Go on, Amanda! If you don't see Hawk now, you'll regret it for the rest of your life! Where has all your courage gone?

She went to the far side of the hallway, as far away from Sonny's bedroom as possible as she went past it, her bare feet soundless against the carpets on the floor. When she reached Hawk's room she heard a sound from inside, and her heart nearly seized up. Waiting a moment, she realized it was just Hawk inside, yawning. Very, very lightly, she rapped her knuckles against the door, not even sure the sound would carry inside.

Amanda heard movement inside.

"Yes?"

Rather than doing the polite thing—waiting for him to open the door for her—she opened it and stepped inside quickly. Hawk was sitting up in bed, a white sheet tossed across his lap, his bandaged chest and ribs a reminder of the brutality that had been visited on him.

"I just thought I'd stop in to see if there was anything you needed," Amanda improvised in a whisper. She didn't know where to hold her hands. The urge to cross them over her breasts to hide the revealing décolletage was strong, but that would defeat her intention in wearing the nightgown in the first place. She left her hands at her sides and tried to appear more at ease than she felt. "Can I get you anything?"

He patted the bed, and Amanda crossed the room to sit on the edge of the mattress. Turning slightly away from Hawk, she nervously twirled with her forefinger a long strand of hair that had fallen free from the loose coiffure she'd fixed for the occasion.

"I have *almost* everything I need to make me comfortable," Hawk said quietly, the timbre of his voice deep. "Everything...now that you're here."

Amanda blushed. She was being terribly forward and she knew it. Sonny would never forgive her if he discovered her in Hawk's bed. But she couldn't think about that now, not when every second she had with Hawk was fleeting.

Amanda's felt the heat of Hawk's gaze on her, warming her, touching her with invisible caresses.

"I'm sorry for what happened to you in town," Amanda apologized quietly. "You should have stayed here. Then it wouldn't have happened."

"It wasn't your fault," Hawk offered after a moment. "And thank you for getting me out of jail. I'd still be in there now, if not for you. In jail, or dangling from a rope outside of town."

Amanda turned to look at Hawk, intentionally showing herself in profile. "Let's not think about that now. You're here, and you're going to stay here until you get better." Amanda was painfully aware that her brother was nearby. "I'd like you to stay. Please?" She was willing to beg, if necessary. "I won't ask for anything."

"I don't know how long I can stay, but it can't be very long," Hawk said.

Amanda turned toward him and slid over on the mattress. She placed her hand lightly on his thigh, covered with the white cotton sheet. His words reinforced her fear that time, more than ever, was all too fleeting.

"How badly do you hurt?"

Amanda looked into the ebony darkness of Hawk's eyes and saw there that he *wanted* to make love to her but doubted that he could. His expression shocked Amanda with his vulnerability. She'd been the one to see him as invincible, a man who would be victorious under any circumstances and against any adversary. He was a man, ultimately, the same as any other man, and Amanda felt guilty for concerning herself with her own needs when he was in such pain.

"I'm sorry, Hawk," Amanda said suddenly, starting to rise from the bed. How selfish and foolish she had been! Why had she let herself even think about doing anything as silly as sneaking into Hawk's bedroom?

"Don't leave," Hawk replied, quickly reaching out, wrapping his large hand securely around her wrist. "I want you here with me."

Amanda instinctively tried to get out of his grasp. She'd already made one mistake by coming to his bedroom. She didn't intend to make another one by forcing him to do something that would tax his battered body beyond what it could withstand.

"No, Hawk, don't," Amanda whispered, still attempting to free her wrist.

Injured or not, he was incredibly strong, and she didn't have a chance of getting away until he decided to release her. He drew her closer, looping his other arm around her waist.

"You didn't come here just to talk," Hawk said.

Amanda flinched. Somehow hearing him say that— even though it was patently true—seemed a little insulting, as though she were no different than the soiled doves who worked in the saloons in Deadwood.

"You're right, I didn't come here to talk," Amanda said, struggling a little as Hawk pulled her even closer to him. "But I also didn't come in here to hurt you. I've made a mistake."

She tried to escape, and when she did she inadvertently pushed against his abdomen. He clenched his teeth, and Amanda promised herself that she would rather walk across burning coals than ever hurt him like that again.

"I'm sorry! I'm so sorry!"

Hawk's smile was strained. He released his hold on Amanda.

"Remember the night I asked you to hold me?" Amanda inquired softly. When Hawk nodded she said, "I can't stay the whole night with you, though you know I'd love to. But for just a little while, perhaps I could hold you instead. There wouldn't be anything wrong with that, would there?"

But Hawk, still set in his ways despite his injuries, insisted on holding Amanda. Placing her head lightly on his shoulder, he then curled his right arm around her.

"Closer," he urged, aware that Amanda was doing everything she could to keep her weight off him.

Though she didn't move any closer, she did toss her leg over his, transmitting the warmth of her body through the silk nightgown and the sheet.

"There, that's better."

But Amanda still regretted having hurt Hawk. She wished now that she'd stayed in her own bedroom, where she belonged. How painful it must have been for Hawk to accept that he was incapable of making love. Because of her impetuosity, she'd forced him to do just that.

"Maybe I'd better go," Amanda whispered.

"In a minute," Hawk replied.

He kissed the top of her head. She heard him inhaling deeply. Idly, he stroked her shoulders and back.

Amanda's eyes were closed, her cheek against Hawk's shoulder, her hand resting very lightly on his stomach. As nice as this was, it wasn't what she wanted, and she knew that if she stayed in the room with Hawk much longer, it would only fuel the frustration now gripping her.

"I should leave," she whispered again, rolling away from Hawk.

She felt his hand on her back and wanted very much to feel him touching her elsewhere, with the consummate skill she'd learned to appreciate. But she also knew that this wasn't the night for such activities. Hawk was in no condition to satisfy desires he'd taught her to crave. She kicked her legs over the edge of the bed, then looked over her shoulder at Hawk, about to apologize once more before leaving.

She realized pain wasn't the only sensation going through the Sioux warrior. The sheet was tented prominently, and there was a vaguely guilty, slightly impish expression in Hawk's eyes.

"I can't help it," he said softly, though there wasn't an ounce of regret in his tone. "You were so close, and that nightgown is so beautiful on you and…well…I'm incapable of being near you without, um, rising to the occasion."

For the twentieth time that evening, Amanda saw herself as a very passionate, very wicked woman. Rather than leaving Hawk, she curled her knees beneath her on the bed and leaned down to kiss him lightly on the mouth.

"Hawk, you must stay very quiet," she whispered, looking into his eyes even as her right hand slipped beneath the sheet. Her fingertips trailed over the crisp, curly hair that grew down low, then she gripped the throbbing shaft of his cock tightly in her fist.

When Hawk groaned Amanda purred with contentment. He might not be able to give her satisfaction, but that didn't mean she couldn't satisfy him without endangering his battered body.

Hawk's groan of pure carnality was one that Amanda had heard before. At least, she'd heard the female equivalent of it, coming from herself whenever Hawk touched her, caressed her with his libertine hands that drew such quick and satisfying responses. His eyes were closed now, and Amanda could study his face, his subtly changing expression, as she moved her hand over the entire length of him, from base to the tip. She rubbed the pad of her thumb against his slit, and he flinched.

"Do you like that?" she asked, only half-facetiously.

She was too inexperienced in her sensuality to have confidence ingrained in her personality. A smile tugged at the right corner of Hawk's mouth as he nodded his head, not opening his eyes.

Amanda leaned back. She sat on her folded legs, then pulled the sheet down, needing to see the rigid cock she was caressing. Hawk, now leaning back against the headboard, was clearly at ease with his nudity. He neither flaunted nor tried to hide himself.

"It must surely be a sin to commit violence to a body as beautiful as this," Amanda whispered.

The sheet had been moved down to Hawk's calves, where he kicked it off completely so that his bronzed body was displayed for Amanda's benefit. With the exception of the area from just beneath his pectorals to down just above his hips, which was concealed by the tightly wrapped bandage protecting his ribs, Hawk was gorgeously naked, his erection magnificently formed and beautiful.

Amanda placed her right hand on Hawk's thigh. Even at rest, the strength in his muscled legs was incredible. She ran her upward slowly until she encircled his shaft with her fingers once again. Hawk moaned softly in approval. This time she suspected the moan was for her benefit. In so many ways, he seemed to understand exactly when her confidence needed bolstering, and was ready to give it to her.

Amanda moved a little closer to him, still keeping her legs curled beneath her. She bent over to kiss his mouth lightly, quickly. "Lie down," she whispered, her face very close to Hawk's.

He slipped his arm around her, his broad-palmed hand cupping her ass. "Only if you lie with me." He smiled.

Amanda shook her head and kissed him again, slowly this time, letting the tip of her tongue touch his lips. When his mouth opened she languorously explored his mouth with her tongue, kissing him deeply.

She felt the simmering sensuality of her awakening body go through her, a feeling both heated and tantalizing, making her feel moist and quivery inside. Still kneeling, she pressed her knees together tightly, trying to stop the sensation from spreading. But the action merely increased the slowly building sense of emptiness in her pussy, and heightened the smoldering passion that had taken flame within her. Her clitoris, erect between the delicate lips, itched and throbbed for attention.

He's wounded, Amanda reminded herself. *He can't satisfy you.*

This was a disquieting thought, and she wished the real world, the world of cruel men and deadly guns, would stop intruding on the happiness she sought to share with Hawk.

She experienced so much at that moment, with such crystal clarity, that she wondered how she could have been unaware of all the separate feelings before. She tasted brandy on his mouth, and, when she kissed his neck, the unmistakable flavor of Hawk himself. She nipped lightly at his flesh and caught the fresh scent of soap from the sponge bath he'd taken after arriving at the ranch. She was aware of the intense heat of his passion. But most intensely of all, she was aware of the solid arousal that signified his great need for her. The feel of his warm, powerful hand touching her bottom through the silk nightgown made Amanda writhe as she kissed him on the mouth again, as deeply and passionately as before.

Amanda sat back suddenly, looking carefully into Hawk's face. Again, she'd almost forgotten that he was a wounded man who only minutes earlier she'd promised to leave so he could get the rest he needed to recover. But there was little pain in his dark eyes now.

A sense of relief washed over Amanda. She looked away from Hawk, out the window at the starry sky, her hands now folded in her lap.

Stop now, before you go too far, she told herself.

She wished Hawk hadn't taught her to crave the feelings he could provoke.

"Come here," Hawk whispered. He hooked his arm lightly around the back of Amanda's neck.

She knew what that tone of voice meant, and she would have none of it. Careful to keep her hands on his chest, well above his damaged ribs, she prevented Hawk from pulling her into his intimate embrace.

"Don't." Her hands, still resisting, felt his smooth flesh beneath her fingertips, the sensation of suppressed strength and power just beneath the skin. "You're a wounded man, and I'm a wicked woman for coming here. Tomorrow, when you're better, we'll sneak off together. I promise."

Hawk shook his head slowly, his ebony hair stark against the white pillows behind his head and shoulders. His face, always gaunt, appeared stark in the light of the lantern on the bedside table.

"I'm not *that* wounded," he whispered. He took Amanda's right hand from his shoulder, kissed the palm briefly, let the tip of his tongue moisten her fingertips. Lastly, he brought her hand down to his cock. Amanda held him gently, and Hawk moaned his approval. "As you can see, I'm not too wounded for you."

Such tempting words for Amanda to hear, particularly in her state of heightened passion! He *did* seem hale and hearty.

Don't be selfish. You're only thinking of yourself.

Why was leaving Hawk such an impossibility?

"Later, my darling," Amanda whispered, her tone tight and strained, her needs escalating at an alarming rate. "I promise you…later."

Hawk didn't say anything. Instead, he brought his right hand to Amanda's bodice and gently cupped her breast. He brushed his thumb over the rigid tip, bringing Amanda's nipple even more prominently on display.

"Don't leave," Hawk said, his words as much a command as a request.

He used his forefinger and thumb to tug at the crest of Amanda's breast through the silk, destroying her willpower.

Amanda closed her eyes, allowing herself to concentrate on what she felt and to forget for a few seconds what she thought. She loved it all. The strength and skill of Hawk's powerful hand touching her through the sheer silk added a new and tantalizing aspect to the delicious moment.

Only when she heard Hawk sigh did she realize that she had reached for him again, her fingers curled around the pulsing shaft, moving slowly, unconsciously, over his entire length. She opened her eyes and looked first into Hawk's dark eyes and then down to his erection.

"Didn't you get a nightshirt?" Amanda asked, knowing it to be a silly question to ask a man whose throbbing flesh filled her hand.

"Yes. I tried to sleep in it, but it was too uncomfortable, so I took it off. I guess I'm not very civilized."

"No," Amanda replied, her breath coming in tiny, rapid gulps. "You're not a civilized man at all. In fact, you're the most uncivilized man I've ever met." She let her eyes caress Hawk's body, for once making no effort to hide her appreciation. His sex was a living, rather dangerous animal filling her hand. It both fascinated and frightened her. "There's nothing about you that's in the least bit civilized," she said appreciatively.

With her free hand, Amanda took Hawk's wrist and pushed his hand from her breast. She couldn't think clearly when he touched her so provocatively.

"Stop it now," Amanda said, as sternly as she could manage. "You've got to preserve your strength." She took her hand from him, as though at last realizing her words had to be followed with appropriate action. "I promise you, tomorrow night we'll go somewhere together, and then I'll be the lover you want me to be."

She saw him looking at her, and the raw, virile hunger was evident in his eyes.

"Be patient," Amanda whispered, speaking as much to herself as to Hawk. "Besides, my brother is nearby."

I'll kiss him, then I'll leave. I've left him before when he's aroused, and he forgave me. He'll forgive me again.

She leaned down, fully intent on giving Hawk a light kiss on the lips—one that whispered of passion delayed and the promise of later fulfilment. But the instant her mouth touched his, she parted her lips to receive his tongue. The passion that Amanda had fought so hard to deny—Hawk's desires, as well as her own—flared up like a volatile substance. She kissed him fiercely, forcing her mouth even more tightly against his, mindful of his damaged ribs as she reached once more for that ardent symbol of his passion for her.

"You mustn't make a sound," Amanda whispered when the kiss had finally ended. She wouldn't disappoint Hawk again.

But Hawk couldn't remember a time in his life when he'd felt more frustrated. Blessed by nature with an extraordinary physique, strengthened daily by the physical demands he placed on himself, and nightly by passionate pursuits, he found it intolerable to be at less than his best.

"My brother...he's very close," Amanda warned, her face near Hawk's.

For the first time, Hawk gave serious consideration to asking Amanda to leave his room. Perhaps she had been right from the beginning about waiting until tomorrow, allowing his ribs a day to heal and his strength a day to recover. It would be frustrating to have her leave…but what could be worse than having her so near when he couldn't move or even inhale deeply without discomfort? Even the slightest exertion brought teeth-clenching pain.

"Listen, Amanda—" Hawk said, but before he could say more she silenced him with a kiss.

When she finally pulled her face away from his there was a mysterious light in her blue eyes. "I've always hated sentences that start with 'listen'. Whatever comes next is always something I don't want to hear."

Hawk placed his hand lightly upon her cheek, and Amanda turned her face to kiss his palm.

"I don't know if you're an enchantress or a devil," Hawk said. "But whatever you are, I'm helpless against you. You've bewitched me. I can't imagine anyone but you."

Was there another man quite like Hawk in the whole world? Could there possibly be another man so strong and yet so gentle?

She moved her knees more securely beneath her, turning to rest on her hip near Hawk's waist. Her hair spilled over her shoulders and onto his stomach. Half leaning over him, ever mindful of his bandaged midsection, she looked at his legs, the thighs thick with muscle. A tremor went through her, an instinctive, primal response to the raw force of his beauty.

Slowly, with more determination than ever, she took his cock in her hand, squeezing and stroking, feeling his body tense as she pleasured this one incredible part of him.

Is he watching me? Suddenly self-conscious of what she was doing. She didn't dare look to see whether there was passionate happiness shining in his eyes. She shifted her position, turning so that all Hawk would see was her back and shoulders.

Slowly, tentatively, Amanda leaned down, and lightly kissed the flaring head.

Is this what he wants me to do? Is this what other women have done for him?

The thought of another woman amusing herself with Hawk's cock, determined to give him pleasure, caused a sunburst of jealousy to flare in her bosom.

Putting her questions aside, she kissed the crown with greater ardor. No longer was she concerned whether what she was doing was right or wrong, or if other women had more experience in such matters. She was simply determined to please him until he could take no more pleasure. She decided, impetuously, that whatever she didn't know, either she could learn on her own, or Hawk could give her instructions. Either way, she was determined that she would not, under any circumstances, leave the bedroom until Hawk had been thoroughly and completely satisfied.

Hawk felt it all—the quick, wet, darting tongue, the soft, moist lips, the warm breath passing over sensitive flesh. He placed his hand lightly on Amanda's shoulder, his eyelashes tapping against his cheeks before he finally simply closed his eyes and gave himself over to pleasure.

He caught strands of her silken hair and wound them slowly around his forefinger. When she sucked him between her lips and deep into her mouth, it seemed as though all his senses were heightened, all his perceptions infinitely sharper than ever before. He felt his excitement escalating at an alarming pace. No pain caused by any demented sheriff's beating could diminish the ecstasy that Amanda was providing.

"Amanda…" Hawk whispered, leaning back against the pillows piled at the headboard. Could he gently coax Amanda from her passionate task? She resisted him, and it wasn't until he grabbed her shoulder and forced her to sit up that she finally acceded to his unspoken wishes. "There are no words to describe how you make me feel."

Amanda's initial reaction was fear. Had she done something wrong? But all it took was a single look into Hawk's dark eyes to know that she hadn't been stopped for that reason. In fact, just the opposite was true. She quickly sensed that the only thing bothering Hawk was that, for once in all their time together, he wasn't in control.

"Don't you try to stop me, Hawk," she whispered, her glistening lips curled into a confident smile. At that moment, seeing Hawk's unwilling and yet total surrender to her charms, Amanda felt like the most confident, sensual woman in the world. "No matter what you say, I know you don't want me to stop." She rose up onto her knees to kiss Hawk's mouth, then smiled at him as she casually tucked his long, ebony hair behind his ear. Then, with her confidence soaring, Amanda set out to please Hawk more thoroughly.

She sucked his cock to the opening of her throat, then rotated her face around the pulsing flesh. Hawk's soft, low groan told her she was doing what he wanted, even if he couldn't admit it. She bobbed slowly, nibbling gently with her lips on both the down and up strokes, paying careful attention to all of her lover's reactions. When she worked her tongue against the underside of his crown, she felt Hawk's entire body flex, his muscles tightening.

He's sensitive there. Her confidence escalated.

She was in no hurry to bring this to fruition, even if her brother was in a nearby room. Amanda was determined to draw out the pleasure, to make it last and last the same way that Hawk teased her before he finally brought her to climax.

"That feels *sooo* good," Hawk whispered. "But turn a little, my darling. You're so beautiful. I want to watch you."

Amanda felt a sudden flush of embarrassment go through her. To wantonly suck him was one thing, but to do as a visual performance seemed entirely wicked. She hesitated, her mouth filled to overflowing with his virile flesh, her thoughts whirling dizzily.

In a soft yet dominating tone, Hawk said, "I want to watch you." He paused a moment, then added, "Keep sucking."

It was a blunt, rather crude declaration, but Amanda was quite certain she'd never heard anything so erotic in her life.

She shifted on the bed, turning so that Hawk could see her profile. She looked into his eyes very briefly, then turned her gaze away, feeling very much scrutinized, on display.

You can't stop now. If it excites him to watch, then let him watch.

She stroked the saliva-moistened shaft and trembled as a pearl of fluid formed at the slit. Slowly, knowing she was being watched, she bent down and ran her tongue over the crown's slit. The fluid was salty and not particular pleasant, but the reaction Amanda received—Hawk flinched from head to toe when she licked the head of his erection—was precisely what she had hoped to accomplish.

Feeling emboldened, Amanda licked down the cock's shaft until she reached twin orbs nestled between his powerful thighs. She tucked them, one at a time, between her lips and sucked lightly. Hawk uttered something in Sioux which Amanda couldn't understand. She didn't need to understand the word, all she needed to understand was the emotion behind it. Hawk was pleased with what she was doing. As she sucked a little harder on the testicle, Amanda purred softly, kittenishly.

By the time she'd finally abandoned his balls and had begun licking up to the throbbing crest once again, Hawk's breathing was labored, and despite her inexperience, Amanda could tell that he couldn't take much more of the pleasure she was so willing to dispense. More quickly than before, Amanda bobbed, taking the conical knob until it pressed against the opening of her throat, then pulling up to whip the tip with her tongue. She used both hands on the shaft, pumping them up and down and twisting them in opposite direction as she feasted on the bounty that was her lover.

He made a sound in his throat. It was a short, strangled sound, but it was enough of a warning to let Amanda know he was going to come. An instant later, thick, salty sperm splashed against her tongue. The flavor was sharp, rather bitter, causing Amanda to shiver on her knees even as she continued to suck on his erupting flesh. She swallowed once, squeezed his balls in the palm of her hand, and swallowed a second time.

Hawk's entire body almost instant went slack with satiation.

Amanda couldn't have been happier with her performance. Even after she'd sated him thoroughly, she continued sucking, not stopping until Hawk entwined his fingers in her hair and pulled her head up enough that she had no choice but to release him.

Chapter Fifteen

"There's enough food here for three people," Hawk observed, looking at the tray that Amanda had brought him.

"You need it to get back your strength," Amanda replied. A telling glance from her blue eyes informed Hawk of precisely why she wanted him to return to his former physical perfection.

"I'm feeling fine," Hawk said. To prove his point, he patted his bandaged midsection to show he was in no pain. The gesture was a bit of a bluff, however, since his ribs did hurt when he touched them. The sheriff's boots wouldn't be easily forgotten by Hawk's mind or body.

"That's good, but you're still staying in bed until at least after the noon meal." Amanda unfolded a large white napkin and spread it out on Hawk's lap. "Even Sonny insisted on that. Apparently you made quite a favorable impression on him last night." She gave him a puzzled look. "Truth is, my brother doesn't really like most people."

Hawk was only half listening to Amanda. Though concerned with Sonny Wright's opinion of him, Hawk was more interested in the food under the covered plates on the tray on his lap. He sat upright in the bed, then removed the silver covers. One plate held scrambled eggs, covering the plate in a golden mound, with crisp strips of thick bacon piled on top. Another plate held nothing but toast, liberally slathered with fresh butter. A small bowl contained slices of dried apple mixed with nuts of a variety he was unfamiliar with. Finally, there was a large mug of steaming coffee, next to a glass of cow's milk.

When Amanda picked up a spoon Hawk quickly snatched it from her. "I appreciate everything you've done," he said a bit sternly, thankful for the abundance, but uncomfortable with being doted over by a woman. "However, I absolutely refuse to be spoon-fed like a child."

"You never let me have any fun," Amanda pouted, looking pretty as she sat at the foot of the bed, her feet tucked beneath her.

As usual, she was dressed in Levis and a cotton shirt, appropriate for her early-morning task of supervising the new foals' feedings in the barn, then watching over the cooking of Hawk's breakfast. Now she watched him intently as he devoured the bacon, eggs, and toast with gusto. She plucked the pottery coffee mug from the tray and took a sip.

Hawk felt uneasy at first, eating under Amanda's watchful gaze. It was still strange for him to be in a large, comfortable bed, between clean sheets, and it was especially odd to be in bed when others had been up and about, doing their work for hours. Having worked virtually every day of his life, the habit of industriousness was deeply ingrained in Hawk, and he felt more than guilty that Amanda had been working that morning while he had slept on.

The food was delicious, especially the eggs. Hawk hadn't had chicken eggs in a year or two, so he chewed them slowly, savoring the taste and texture. Wasn't this the decadence Father Lafevre had warned against when Hawk, Buttercup, and Crow were young? Hawk didn't really care. If this was decadence, he wanted more of it.

"I figured you'd eat and nap a little, and then you might be interested in seeing the Circle S," Amanda said cheerfully, pleased that the breakfast she had supervised was disappearing rapidly.

Hawk glanced up at Amanda, his gaunt cheek bulging slightly as he chewed. There was mischief in his eyes.

"I know what you're thinking," Amanda said quickly, her tone hushed. "But that absolutely *must* wait until later, after the sun has gone down and the ranch hands have settled in the bunkhouse for the night. Last night was dangerous enough." She patted his leg through the blanket as embarrassing, though pleasing, memories of the previous evening's conduct returned to her. "Just keep those thoughts to yourself until tonight. I'm proud of the Circle S, and I want to show it off. That's not so bad, is it?"

Amanda was adamant that Hawk finish all the food she'd brought him. He couldn't, but she didn't protest for long, choosing instead to let Hawk rest, even though he wanted to get out of bed.

"Even if you don't sleep the rest will do you good," Amanda said, taking the tray with her as she left the room. "Read your Balzac. He's always entertaining."

* * * *

Suspicious looks from the white ranch hands notwithstanding, Hawk was enormously impressed with the Circle S ranch. He could only imagine the wealth such a ranch could generate. And though some of the men narrowed their eyes when they saw the buckskin-clad half-breed Sioux inspecting the grounds at Amanda's side, others had heard that it was Hawk who had come to Amanda's rescue on her recent adventure. Those men, who didn't care whether Hawk was half or all-Indian or not-at-all Indian, only that he had been there for Amanda when she needed help, came forward with a smile and an extended hand.

"I'd say you've won over my brother and about half the ranch hands," Amanda said. She and Hawk had paused to look into a corral where undersized calves were kept with their mothers to give them a better chance to grow. "By this evening you'll have three-quarters of the men." Amanda sighed. "Of course, some of the men will never accept you because of your Indian blood. There's nothing you could do to make them like you."

Hawk couldn't take that personally. He'd faced bigotry virtually every day of his life, in one form or another. Long ago he figured he had two choices: either live his life, perpetually furious at the way he was treated because of his mixed-blood heritage and because he was born a bastard, or do all he could not to think too long or hard about the people to whom those things meant so much.

Hawk chose the latter.

"And where did you say your other sister was?" Hawk asked, paying minor interest to the small pen where yearling calves were kept.

Would it ever be possible for the Sioux to raise their food as the white man did? Hawk asked himself, studying the pen. It seemed unlikely, but Hawk realized that something had to change. The Sioux couldn't go on the way they had in the past.

"Vanessa's in Fargo right now," Amanda answered.

"Really?" Hawk asked, honestly curious.

"She's often there in court." Amanda smiled up at him. "I'm glad you're here. I'm not pleased with the circumstances, but I'm glad you're here."

"So am I," Hawk replied, but it was only a half-truth.

Actually, he didn't feel comfortable at the Circle S. He couldn't feel at ease as Amanda's lover while her brother was so nearby. Hawk knew that though he had earned some of Sonny's respect, he wouldn't be able to keep it if the elder Wright ever discovered how passionate Amanda had become because of an Indian.

Outside the building the sound of two men talking interrupted Amanda's reply, and she quickly dropped Hawk's hand.

"There's something else I want to show you," Amanda said, her blue eyes bright and alive as she quickly stepped out of the building. Hawk followed her, wishing they were somewhere else, not surrounded by people. "It's our new colts. They're the pride and joy of the Circle S."

In a small barn which was clean and orderly, Amanda showed Hawk the six young colts, each in its own pen.

"They're the future of the Circle S," Amanda said as she reached into a small pail for a carrot. She gave the carrot to a foal, which munched contentedly as she stroked its neck and mane. "This is Mamie," she explained. "Her mother was the fastest, her father the strongest…Mamie will race for a couple of years, then we'll put her together with just the right stallion, and she'll have magnificent babies."

Hawk, a capable judge of horseflesh, needed only a cursory glance at Mamie to see that the animal did, indeed, have all the markings of a horse of distinction. But it wasn't the young horse that kept keeping Hawk's attention, it was Amanda. The love she had for her horses seemed to vibrate an enthusiasm for life out of her pores, and its energy touched Hawk.

"This is your favorite place in all the Circle S, isn't it?" he asked. He didn't need to ask the question to know the answer.

Amanda nodded, smiling, still petting Mamie. "It shows, I suppose, but I'm proud of this barn."

Overhead was the hayloft, and as romantic notions began filtering through Hawk's mind, he felt a sudden surge of hunger. He needed Amanda. He needed her here, now, in this place that was so special to her.

"Up here," he said, beginning to climb the ladder leading up to the loft. He was careful of his ribs, though they weren't as tender as they had been the previous evening, they still gave him pain, especially when he moved too quickly.

"That's just the hayloft up there," Amanda said.

Hawk paused halfway up the ladder. He looked at Amanda, a half smile of sensuality tugging at the right corner of his mouth. "I know," he replied, then continued the climb.

Amanda watched him disappear up the ladder. She stood frozen in place, knowing full well what Hawk's smile had meant, and knowing with just as much certainty that she shouldn't follow him up. To do that was pure foolishness. Passionate foolishness, to be sure, but still damned foolishness just the same. And it was dangerous. She could do irreparable damage to her reputation should the ranch hands ever discover.

But thinking about Hawk's kisses, his sweet, stimulating touch, put a fire in Amanda's blood, and she started for the ladder.

I'm weak. When it comes to Hawk, I'm the weakest woman in the world.

By the time Amanda got up to the loft, Hawk had already spread out a new horse blanket over a mound of hay.

"How fortunate to have new blankets up here," she said quietly, a bit nervously.

"If I didn't know better, I'd wonder if you'd planned it," Hawk teased as he sat down on the blanket and began unlacing his moccasins.

Amanda looked at him, then looked away. Hawk Two Feather was too bold, she decided, much too bold and daring and fearless for her own good. Though part of her wanted to rush over to him, there was another reaction—the one that said her brother would never forgive her if she was caught making love with Hawk in the loft in the middle of the afternoon—that kept her from going to him immediately.

She went to the large bay doors on the south side of the loft and opened one of them just an inch. She peered out cautiously. Outside, ranch hands were doing their chores. None of the men seemed to be paying any attention to the foal barn. Were any of the men aware that she was in the barn with Hawk? His presence on the ranch certainly wasn't a secret.

"You're wasting our precious time," Hawk said softly, his voice deep, melodic, rich with expectation that touched Amanda like a caress.

Amanda's back was to Hawk when he spoke. She paused for a moment, wondering if this was really what she wanted to do.

If I only have three days, then I'm going to make the most of every minute. She decided with angry determination.

Amanda turned slowly to look at Hawk. He had removed his moccasins and his buckskin shirt. He was stretched out, wearing only his leather trousers, bare-footed and bare-chested, the bandage still wrapped tightly around his midsection. With his fingers he combed back his long, ebony hair off his forehead. He was effortlessly casual, confident, sensual.

Twenty feet separated them, and Amanda took her time walking to him through the carpet of hay, wanting to remember him always as he was at that moment.

"It's really not fair of you to be so sure of yourself," Amanda teased, approaching the blanket.

Hawk was on his side, propped up on his elbow. He was gorgeous and he knew it, she decided. He understood all too well what happened to a woman's resolve when she looked at him. Amanda couldn't resent that aspect of Hawk's personality, even if she wanted to.

"You should be more confident," Hawk replied ironically, his tone cool. Amanda had started to kneel on the edge of the blanket, but Hawk stopped her with a hand. "Not yet," he said in a whisper. "There's something I want you to do for me."

Amanda's eyebrows furrowed in confusion. Only moments earlier he had been complaining that she was dallying, when time was precious, and now he was suggesting just the opposite. She looked down at him, saying nothing, her eyes asking the questions her lips were afraid to speak.

"Take off your clothes for me." Hawk gazed straight into Amanda's eyes as he spoke, daring her to look away, to defy him. "I want to see you...all of you. It's risky, I know, with your hired men all about...but that's part of the excitement, isn't it? Everything off. I don't want you holding back."

Several thoughts came to Amanda, but she bit her tongue to keep from speaking. This wasn't the first time she had felt the heat of Hawk's seduction, and she knew that passion could explode without any clothes being removed. How well he had taught her that!

"Your boots first, I think," Hawk said quietly, a glittering quality in his dark eyes.

Amanda noticed that Hawk wasn't nearly as nonchalant as he was trying to appear. His buckskin trousers were tented, struggling to contain his erection. His mouth appeared strained, but his eyes glittered — a pleasing reaction to her beauty.

"I don't know if I should follow your commands," she said softly, standing with her feet spread, her hands on her hips. "I've never been very good at taking orders."

"Not even from me?" He raised an eyebrow.

"*Especially* not from you."

"How do I rate special consideration?"

"Because you've had too many women following your orders already, that's why," Amanda answered. How she wished it didn't bother her!

"They don't matter. You're the only woman who counts."

Amanda would have resisted Hawk...but she was certain that, if she went along with him once again, allowing him to once again write all the rules of their passionate games, she wouldn't be sorry.

Amanda balanced on one foot, tugging off first one boot then the other. Next, she removed her thick white cotton socks. Beneath her feet, the wooden floor was strewn with prickly hay, and she wished that she could stand on the blanket on which Hawk lay. But that proximity would spoil her presentation, and Amanda was determined to make her disrobing a performance that would leave Hawk gasping for breath.

She waited a moment for Hawk's next instruction. When it didn't come she unbuckled her belt, then slowly unfastened the brass buttons of her Levis. Despite Hawk's calm demeanor Amanda saw a telltale glint in his midnight black eyes.

She hooked her thumbs into the waistband of her denims, pulling them down past the curve of her hips and wiggling her bottom slightly to assist in the descent. She was well aware of Hawk's greedy gaze devouring her every move. She bent forward to remove her trousers, and when she did, she took her time, allowing Hawk to look down the front of her shirt, giving him a view of cleavage she knew he appreciated.

He's seen me from head to toe. Amanda straightened again. *But this time is different somehow. It's like we've never even touched.*

Amanda paused for a moment, putting her hands back on her hips, covered by her new drawers and topped with a new matching chemise. All for Hawk. She had planned on stealing away with Hawk after supper, perhaps to the guesthouse north of the snow fence. But Hawk, as usual, had plans of his own...and now she'd decided to follow them.

"Continue," Hawk ordered after several seconds.

The tightness in his voice was unmistakable. His anxiousness pleased Amanda, enormously fueling her confidence and sexual courage.

Slowly, teasingly, Amanda unbuttoned her shirt, then, with a shrug, she let it slide down her arms. Standing only in her chemise and drawers, she waited for Hawk's next command. Her eyes enjoyed the naked expanse of his chest, exposed above the bandage, and letting her gaze trail lower, the long and bulging line of his rigid cock, still trapped inside his buckskin trousers.

"More? Or do you want to remove the rest yourself?" Amanda challenged, her fingertips toying with the silk shoulder strap of her chemise.

"Continue, if you please," Hawk said.

Amanda grinned. "I please." She pulled the chemise quickly over her head and dropped it onto the pile of clothes discarded in the hay.

Standing there with her breasts bare, Amanda was distinctly aware of feeling on display. She battled momentarily against the negative sensation, telling herself not to feel embarrassed about her body, but this attitude was easier thought than wholeheartedly embraced. Without waiting for instruction, Amanda pulled free the knotted drawstring of her drawers and shimmied them down her legs, stepping out of them to at last stand completely naked before her lover.

"Come to me, Amanda," Hawk whispered tensely. "Come to me now."

Amanda walked forward until she stood at the edge of the blanket near Hawk's feet. He reached for her, he curled his long fingers around her ankle. Though at first Amanda began to sink to the blanket and the welcoming embrace of his arms, she suddenly resisted Hawk.

"No," she said firmly.

Hawk still held on to Amanda's ankle, looking almost straight up at her. Her hands, folded one over the other at the juncture of her thighs, covered her vagina in the last vestiges of modesty. But then she removed her hands, placing them defiantly on her hips.

"No," she said again, even more firmly than before.

"Why not?" Hawk frowned, reaching for Amanda once more.

"Because it isn't what I want" — she hesitated several seconds, and the air seemed to leave the hayloft — "yet."

Amanda positioned herself on the blanket, looking down to see Hawk stretched from head to toe. Even from there she felt the heat of his passion, sensed the excitement sizzling through his veins. Suddenly all embarrassment she'd felt vanished. Her pussy felt wet, heated, needful, but she was determined to suppress these cravings for at least a few more moments.

"This isn't fair," Amanda said in a stern, commanding voice that pleased her because of its authoritative quality. "You see all that I am, but you're covered where you are, um, most interesting." Not wanting to conjure up unpleasant memories, Amanda conveniently neglected to mention the long, heavy bandage wrapped around Hawk's ribs.

"Then take them off for me," Hawk suggested, reaching up for Amanda's hand.

Amanda shook her head slowly. Her hair cascaded down her body, partially obscuring her breasts. Teasingly, she pushed the strands aside to expose her left breast, its areola pink with passion, surrounding a nipple that was hard and tight with excitement. She pinched her nipple lightly, and felt fresh honey moisten the lips of her sex.

He reached for Amanda, and again she nimbly slipped out of his reach, which meant stepping off the blanket and onto the hay-strewn floor.

"You do it for me," Amanda said, easing forward so she was once more on the blanket, near Hawk's feet. "But not all the way off. I want them just low enough for me to see how interested you are in me."

Hawk pulled loose the thong closing the front of his buckskins, then pushed the leather down to his thighs, just far enough to allow his erection to spring free. Amanda gasped and realized her passion was burning as hotly as his.

Amanda moved deftly to straddle Hawk's body, her feet stationed on either side of his hips. Her gaze locked with his, knowing he wanted her to put an end to the teasing just as much as she wanted him to.

"My..." Amanda said in a breathy whisper, looking at his bounty. "My, my, my!" After a moment, with absolute possessiveness, she whispered, "Mine."

Slowly, drawing out the first touch as long as possible, Amanda bent her knees until, finally, their bodies touched. With her sex already slick and heated and passionately ready for Hawk, she dropped onto him, impaling herself. The consummation, unexpected in its haste and force, ripped through her in a torrent of emotion that left her shuddering and shaken.

Her entrance had hardly reached the base of Hawk's erection when her climax started, powerful contractions squeezing that part of him which stretched tender tissue and filled her completely.

Amanda was breathing deeply, blinking her eyes to clear her vision. The climax had hit her harder and faster than she had expected. She was lying on Hawk, her knees curled up near but not touching his injured ribs, her breasts pressed against his chest, her cheek touching his as she gulped in air.

Amanda sighed when Hawk pushed his fingers through her hair, smoothing the strands away from her face. Then she pulled away from him, far enough to look into his eyes, seeking confirmation there that what she'd done wasn't wrong. She'd never before responded so quickly to Hawk's eroticism.

"Remember me?" he asked.

Amanda cradled his face in her hands as her breathing slowly returned to some degree of normality. She could feel him inside her, solid as stone, throbbing with wanton virility. His sexual self-control, she thought, was Herculean. In a distant corner of her brain, she wondered whether Hawk could teach her to have such astonishing discipline.

"Remember you?" she asked, still breathing somewhat deeply. "Not in ten thousand years could I ever forget you."

After the words were out of her mouth, Amanda realized there might be a second meaning to Hawk's inquiry. Did he feel forgotten, left out somehow?"

"My darling Hawk," Amanda said, putting her hands on his shoulders, high enough so that she was in no danger of damaging his painful ribs, "you've been occupying a majority of my thoughts from the first moment I saw you."

Amanda got her knees solidly beneath her, keeping them away from Hawk's ribs, and began to raise and lower her hips, gliding from the base of the erection all the way up to the pulsing crown, then traveling slowly downward again. She smiled at Hawk. When she took all Hawk had to give her into her slick sheath, she felt entirely and completely filled with the man, and connected to him in a way that, prior to him, she hadn't imagined possible.

"Trust me, my darling, I'm always thinking of you," she whispered, dropping down on him and giving her hips a forward-and-back shake to add emphasis to her words. "And now I'm going to do everything I can think of to show you exactly *what* I think of you."

And that was precisely what Amanda did. Faster and faster she bounced on him, and when she felt his hands tighten around her waist, then lift her completely off his arousal, she stroked his shaft as erupted.

* * * *

A hot bath was a luxury not afforded to any Sioux. Hawk was settled into the deep tub, having twice washed himself from head to toe with soap that quickly developed a thick lather. Now he was contemplating just exactly how guilty he would feel if he lathered himself up once more, for good measure. There was no telling when he would have this luxury again. A large tub, plenty of hot water, and expensive soap, simply weren't available at his tribe's encampment.

The tub, in particular, struck him as almost absurdly extravagant. Who had commissioned the blacksmith to make it? Amanda? Or more likely Vanessa? The sides were twice as high as any tub Hawk had ever seen, and the back sloped gently to enable even a large man like himself to recline comfortably in the warm water. Maybe Sonny was responsible, which would account for its incredible size. It had taken four strong men carrying buckets of steaming water to fill it.

He really did wonder if it was something Amanda would insist on having. She had seemed to enjoy herself while she was with the Sioux, but she was a wealthy woman who, he suspected, would sooner or later begin to miss all the comforts of her life here at the Circle S. How could she manage very long living with Hawk's tribe without feeling terribly deprived of the comforts she had grown up with?

Hawk took the enormous sponge that had been provided for him, filled it with water, and then squeezed it over his head so the soapy water cascaded down. Hot baths with wonderful soap were dangerously addictive, Hawk decided.

He heard the door to his bedroom open and was mildly surprised to think that Cookie, the cook and all-around helper at the Circle S, who had supervised the filling of the bath and brought the soap and towels to Hawk, hadn't knocked before entering. Hawk's initial thought was that if he had been a white guest instead of a half-breed Sioux brave, Cookie wouldn't have entered until being asked, but he quickly pushed these angry thoughts away. They would do him no good anyway, and nothing he thought would change the way Cookie felt.

"How is it?"

At the sound of Amanda's voice, Hawk grinned and shook his head slowly, wiping water out of his eyes. His long ebony hair was plastered to his skull.

"I thought Cookie had come in. You're not supposed to be in here," Hawk said softly, mindful of the fact that the bedroom door had been opened but never closed. "And your brother would want blood revenge if he caught you here."

Amanda grinned as she slowly strolled across the room, a slightly exaggerated sway to her hips. She was mildly disappointed that she couldn't see through the soapy water and the thick white blanket of bubbles that floated on the surface. All that was visible of Hawk was his head, shoulders, and knees. She sat on the edge of the steel tub, making no effort to hide the sensual appreciation she felt as she looked at Hawk.

"Amanda, I don't know if this is such a good idea," Hawk said. He knew full well what the light in Amanda's blue eyes signified.

Amanda just grinned. "For an intelligent man, you make some really silly mistakes. You see, I think this is an absolutely magnificent idea." She swirled the water around with her hand, working the lather up.

"But, Amanda..."

Hawk was passionate, yes, but not suicidal. He wanted Amanda, but he didn't want to die because only that afternoon she'd discovered she could experience ecstasy repeatedly. No matter how skilled a warrior Hawk knew himself to be, he couldn't fight his way out of a ranch where he was outnumbered more than thirty to one.

"By now," Amanda said, speaking slowly, the tips of her fingers trailing in the warm, soapy water near Hawk's thigh, "my protective brother Sonny is nearly to Deadwood, where he's going to meet a woman. I don't know who she is, though I could make several guesses. Either way, I don't really care, so long as she keeps my brother happy. But you see, my brother is gone, and so is Vanessa."

"What about that bearded fellow?"

"Cookie?" Amanda smiled wickedly. "Cookie was just given, not ten minutes ago, a twenty-dollar gold piece, and the night off. Cookie is headed for the bunkhouse, where there is always a card game going among the men. Cookie is going to stay there until he recovers from his excesses of gambling and drinking."

"Twenty dollars of gambling is excessive?"

"They play for pennies, nickels, and dimes. Cookie's a conservative card player but an unrestrained drinker. We pay him once a month, and he's broke three days after he's paid, but he has a good time in those three days, and the rest of the time he's sober."

"You think of everything, don't you?"

"Not true," Amanda said as she began to disrobe. "I've learned to count on your imagination. It's one of the things I love about you."

The instant the word 'love' was out of her mouth, Amanda wished she'd chosen her words more carefully. It wasn't that she *didn't* love Hawk's imagination—she did, with all her heart and soul. It was just that she didn't want to use the word, with all the emotions that went with it.

She was quickly naked, her clothes strewn carelessly around the room. "I've always thought this tub was large enough for two," she said, getting into the water. "I never dreamed I'd find out."

Hawk smiled and replied, "I like to be of service."

Amanda chuckled as she considered how best to get in the tub. Should she face Hawk, or enter the other way, so that her back was against his chest?

"I love it," she said, getting into the tub slowly, her bottom at face level to Hawk, "when you're amenable to suggestion."

The water was still quite warm as she slowly lowered herself. Hawk moved his hand to her waist to assist, but when she settled into the warm water and her hips were between his thighs, he slid his hands up her sides until he cupped the mounds of her breasts.

"I love your touch," she said breathily, leaning back against his chest, resting her head on his shoulder.

"I love your breasts," Hawk replied, warm, pinching nipples that had already become erect. "And your hair...and nose...and lips..."

Amanda closed her eyes, considered her use of language for a moment, then asked, "What about my...?"

"Especially that," Hawk replied, "goes without saying."

In a faintly petulant tone, she replied, "It shouldn't." Amanda chuckled softly, her eyes closed. "I almost said the word 'cunt'." She chuckled again. "That's the first time in my life I've ever used that word." She shifted her hips slightly, and felt Hawk's erection growing. "Does it excite you to hear me say a word like 'cunt'?"

Hawk's arousal grew to full, impression dimensions within seconds, pressing ominously against Amanda's back. Again she chuckled. It was a rich, throaty, confident sound.

"You didn't answer my question, but another part of you replied."

Hawk's long, bent legs surrounded her. To feel him, solid and perfectly formed, pressing against her lower back, was an aphrodisiac Amanda couldn't ignore. She wiggled against his erection, loving how it felt rubbing against her, personal experience having taught her the pleasure it gave.

"I could get addicted to you. Well, at least a certain part of you. Does it have a name? Is it always this hard?" The coarse language tasted delicious on her tongue. "Or am I your cock's inspiration?"

Hawk released her breast, then slid his hand down her stomach into the water. He pressed against the lips of her femininity. He used the pads of his middle three fingers against her clitoris, moving them in a slow circling motion.

"Oh, yesss," she whispered as worked his fingers skillfully, using his outer two fingertips to ease the lips apart to more completely expose the pearl for the middle fingertip beneath the soapy surface of the water. "I instantly get aroused when you touch me." She felt his teeth nip lightly at her throat. She angled her head aside to give him more room. "How do you want me? You can have me any way you want." His tongue slithered inside her ear, and she purred again. "I can deny you nothing. Even if you want my ass, I'll give it to you."

She heard him grunt with surprise.

Softly, he asked, "You know about that?"

"Betsy Hoffman told Julie van Durben that her first beau taught her to do it that way so she wouldn't get pregnant." She put her hand over Hawk's then forced his long fingers to press more deeply into her breast. "Betsy also said that her beau's you-know-what wasn't anything more than the size of a man's finger." She spread her knees a little wider as the tip of Hawk's finger slipped inside. "You'd be too big for me." Her voice was a whisper. "You'd rip me in two...but I'd let you, if that's what you wanted."

"Not necessary."

She reached into the soapy water, grabbed Hawk by the hand, and forced his palm to press against her.

"No more delays, Hawk." Though the bed was only a few feet away, they couldn't even make it that far. She stopped in the middle of the room, her dripping body bent at the waist with her hands white-knuckled and clutching her legs just above the knees. She looked down and watched as her breasts, full and heavy under any circumstances but seemingly supernaturally by gravity, swayed beneath her. Hawk grabbed her by the hips and he guided the flaring crown of his sex to her entrance, the breath caught in her throat. An instant later, with much for force than finesse, Amanda gasped as her tender body opened wide—both voluntarily and by the force Hawk exerted—to accept the thick, deep thrust of Hawk's seemingly indefatigable desire.

The slap of a wet torso striking the trembling cheeks of a wet ass echoed off the walls. It sounded naughty music to Amanda's ears. He buried his entire length into her on the first plunge, stretching her, forcing her to yield in the sweetest and yet most barbarian of all possible ways.

Amanda realized there was nothing tender in what they were doing together. Not like earlier, when they were joined face to face, when they had tenderly made love, sharing soft kisses, eking out the most minute sensations. But the desires that consumed them now were far too fiery to all for controlled emotions.

In the end, when she felt him splash against her back and shoulders, she was slightly amazed that she had been able to remain standing.

Chapter Sixteen

A smile spread across Amanda's lips as she sat in the rocking chair, watching Hawk nibbling at slices of cheese. He had, she now realized, a voracious appetite. Or at least he had the ability for voraciousness when the opportunity and abundance were there for him. She'd also seen him go for a long time without eating and not complain about it.

"In some ways you're like a wild animal," Amanda observed in the darkened guest bedroom. When Hawk looked up at her she laughed softly, realizing how her words could be misconstrued. "I don't mean that as an insult. It's just that you're like the mountain lion who can eat a great deal when there's plenty of food, then fast if there's nothing to be had. I suspect you're that way when it comes to making love, too. I wonder why that is?"

As though to remind herself of her excesses of late, she felt a twinge of discomfort between her legs. Her vagina was a little sore, but she was not in the least bit unhappy about her own voraciousness of late.

Resting on his side, a sheet tossed across his waist as he picked at the plate of cheese and sliced venison sausage, Hawk gave Amanda's a questioning look before answering.

"It's because I come from a world where nothing is guaranteed, nothing is certain. In your world, you know that there will be plenty to eat for breakfast, and when you're done with breakfast you know you'll be eating another meal in just a few hours. And another one just after the sun goes down, and maybe even a little something more if you decide to get up in the middle of the night. This allows you to eat only as much as you want, whenever you want. The Sioux developed the ability for 'voraciousness', as you put it, because we've had to. Our next meal is often in doubt. We eat what we can, when we can."

Though Hawk had spoken the words without any rancor, Amanda wondered if he was hiding his bitterness. Did he blame white people for the difficult life of his people? Did he blame *her*? She could hardly imagine a life of such uncertainty, even thinking about it filled her with dread.

"You don't have to go back, you know." Amanda spoke the words impulsively, without considering the full extent of their meaning. She was speaking from the heart, as she so often did, not knowing where her emotions would take her.

"Yes, I do," Hawk replied wearily, dismissing Amanda's comment with a simple shrug of his naked shoulders. He continued nibbling on cheese. "The tribe counts on me. I have to hunt to provide food."

"No you don't. I mean, the tribe could survive just fine without you, especially if you gave them the reward I'm giving you." Amanda smiled a bit sheepishly, aware that she was asking quite a lot of

Hawk but feeling bold because they had shared so much in the time they'd spent together. "Money will buy anything the tribe needs."

Hawk tilted his head slightly at Amanda. This unconscious gesture surfaced whenever he was uncertain of what was happening. Amanda, having single-handedly confused Hawk enough times to be acquainted with the look, pushed on happily — though a bit nervously — with her proposition.

"I'm serious, Hawk. There's no reason for you to live in such desperation when there's more than enough at the Circle S. You know how many rooms we have here. More than enough. Would that be so bad?"

Amanda couldn't have known that she spoke the same words Hawk's mother had. She couldn't know that her proposal was everything Hawk found repellent in the world of the wealthy whites. Buy whatever and whomever you want, the message went, and if that means abdicating responsibility to one's family and friends, so be it. Toss around enough gold to assuage the guilt feelings produced by whatever action was expedient, then forget everyone else and simply have a good time.

"Yes, Amanda, it *would* be that bad," Hawk explained quietly, doing his best to control his temper. He told himself that Amanda was very young, and that she was prone to saying things she'd not entirely thought through. "I'm not like you. I can't simply buy my way out of whatever trouble I get myself into. My responsibilities can't just be cast aside the moment they're inconvenient. It doesn't work that way with the Sioux."

He watched Amanda reacting to his words. He had hurt her and he knew it, but he couldn't leave his people, no matter how easy a life Amanda promised him. He gave her a smile, hoping it would soften the impact of his words.

"There might be another way," he said.

"Another way?" Her tone held a skeptical hopefulness.

Even though Hawk had believed earlier that Amanda wouldn't give up her wealthy life, he tried anyway. "You could come to the tribe." He touched his bandaged ribs and grinned. "Since it's clear that I can't live with your people without paying a terrible price for the effort, maybe you could come to the Sioux. You've got to admit that you were treated much better by my people than I was by yours."

"I...I just couldn't," Amanda replied. She ran her fingers through her disheveled blonde hair, still mussed from the energetic lovemaking she'd just experienced. "I've got too much to do here. My sister and brother count too much on my managing the horses for me to just leave the Circle S. Besides, this is my home, my inheritance. There's a lot of money tied up in this ranch. It's been in the family for generations."

Hawk, a practical man by both nature and necessity, sighed. As was so often the case, he'd known the answer before asking the question. He said, "Then there is a third option. One that, under the circumstances, might be the only one we can agree upon."

Amanda wasn't certain she liked Hawk's tone of voice. She asked softly, "And what might that option be?"

"Since you can't leave your home and your people, and I can't leave my home and my people, and since it is obvious that we are *so* good together, why not come to me? I'm not saying all the time. I know you have a life here that you can't leave behind. But once in a while. Just for a few days, if that's all you can spare from the ranch."

Amanda balled her hand into a fist and pressed it against her stomach. She could hardly breathe. He wanted her to come to his tepee and be his whore whenever she could no longer do without his kisses and his sweet lovemaking. Though it sounded possible at first consideration, the underlying message was that Hawk thought of Amanda as a whore. Perhaps a valued and desired whore, but a whore nevertheless. A part-time lover to be shown kindness, consideration, and endless passion, but only so long as it was convenient and didn't interfere with other, more important obligations to his tribe and himself.

"I can't," Emotion choked off Amanda's words momentarily. "I can't believe you'd actually ask that of me, Hawk. It makes what we have together sound so tawdry. It makes me sound so cheap."

"I didn't mean for it to," Hawk protested. "I'm not trying to be insulting. I'm just looking at what choices are available to us, and they seem limited."

Amanda had feared she might have been asking a great deal from Hawk, but his response, she felt, was entirely unwarranted. More than that, it was vicious in its own way, and she couldn't tolerate viciousness from Hawk when her body was still warm and tingling with the afterglow of the lovemaking they had shared.

"What are you saying?" she asked. Then, "What *exactly* are you saying? Because if it's what I think it is, then I don't think you know me at all. Not even a little bit, Hawk."

Hawk's face remained expressionless as he looked at Amanda. "I'm saying that I cannot just leave my people. I do not give my loyalty lightly, and once given, I do not abandon it. Not under any circumstances, or for any reason. I don't expect you to understand that. I'm just trying to explain to you the type of man I am."

Amanda felt the warm flush moving up from her chest to color her neck and cheeks. Each time Hawk spoke, even if he was only trying to be conciliatory, he heightened Amanda's sense of indignation.

"I know what kind of man you are," Amanda said softly, leaning toward him, her body suddenly becoming tense. "At least I *thought* I knew the kind of man you are." She spoke the words in such a way that they couldn't help but convey a sense of distrust, an aura of profound disappointment. "But now that I listen to what you've offered me, I'm not so sure anymore. Exactly what is it you think of me?"

Amanda watched the invisible walls coming up to surround Hawk. She saw them as clearly as if they were made out of brick and mortar. How she hated them with everything that she held dear, knowing that from that point forward she would not get another substantive response out of him.

"Damn you," she whispered, rocking agitatedly in the chair, furious that Hawk could sit so calmly. "Don't you try to pretend that you're not angry."

But a change finally came over him, the spontaneous dropping of the veil of implacable logic. "You think your money can buy you everything," Hawk accused. "Perhaps it can buy studs for your mares, but..."

He said no more, leaving the sentence unfinished. But by not finishing the sentence, he allowed Amanda to finish it herself, and she didn't do herself any favors.

"Damn you straight to hell, Hawk Two Feather," she whispered. "You're not my stud for hire. Damn you!" In an instant the faces of too many men who had looked at her with lust in their eyes flashed through her mind. And because Amanda had been insulted and wasn't above seeking revenge, she spat, "I buy all the studs for the Circle S, Hawk. If you knew me as well as you think you do, you'd know that I'm a *careful* buyer. If I'd put more thought in it, do you really think I'd chosen you?"

They were vicious words and Amanda knew it, though they were no worse than those Hawk had spoken, and she was still angry enough to lash out, to want to inflict pain on the person who had *caused* her pain. She waited to see Hawk's pain. But he didn't react by being outwardly furious with her, as she'd expected. He simply looked at her as though she'd said nothing at all. And that aloofness, that calm detachment from the reality of the moment, made Amanda hate him in some ways.

"To hell with you, Hawk!" She shook her head slowly, not entirely sure of the appropriate response for the feelings going through her. She was now uncomfortably naked, when only moments earlier she'd luxuriated in her nudity in Hawk's presence. "You think you're strong when you act this way, when you square your shoulders and pretend that nothing I or anyone else can say or do can hurt you. But all you're proving is that you are as vulnerable as the rest of us."

Hawk didn't speak for a moment. "I am at least as vulnerable as other Sioux. When the sheriff's boots struck me I felt pain. I simply saw no value in complaining about it during the time I shared with you." He, too, shook his head. "You turn strength into weakness, virtue into vice. Is it any wonder your people—the wealthiest among you—never have *enough*, while the poorest of your kind have *nothing* to eat?"

Amanda felt her face growing hot. "Are you saying that I treat the hired hands badly?"

Hawk looked around the guest bedroom. "Do they live like this?"

"You go straight to hell!"

Amanda bolted to her feet and, in the darkness and confusion, tried to find her clothes. Tears of rage burned her eyes, but she wouldn't give Hawk the satisfaction of seeing her cry. Undoubtedly he was mean enough to *want* to see her cry.

How could a man who only minutes earlier had been making love to her suddenly turn so vicious? Even if she had suggested something he couldn't agree with, why had he made her feel as though she'd purchased his passion? Should she assume that everything he'd said and done to her was simply a response to money well spent?

* * * *

Hawk was angry enough to kill. But whom could he kill? He'd left the Circle S ranch at sun-up and he hadn't seen a soul since. It was now nearing noon, and if he kept up this pace, he figured he'd reach his tribe by early the following morning.

Damn Amanda.

Hawk had tried to keep the thought of her from entering his head, but his anger was greater than his self-discipline. She had said things to him that were unforgivable. And after she'd said everything that had come into her head, she'd left without giving him even the chance for rebuttal.

In the morning, as he was getting ready to leave, he'd expected a teary apology, and perhaps a sentimental and romantic goodbye. He'd received neither. In fact, when Amanda finally showed up, she seemed distracted, as though the time she was spending with him would be better spent dealing with matters concerning the ranch.

She was just doing that to get even with me. Hawk enjoyed this thought because it absolved him of any responsibility for the rancor that now existed between himself and Amanda. *Stop thinking about her. She's in your past.*

Once he was able to clear his mind, he sensed that something was wrong. Dangerously wrong.

Hawk twisted in the saddle to look through the trees to the east and west on the sloping hill he was descending. He couldn't see anyone, but he felt a presence. Someone out there somewhere.

His stallion, now sensing his unease, sidestepped. Hawk patted the animal's neck, turning the horse for a better view of the territory he'd just crossed.

Allowing himself a minute to search for his followers, he finally turned the stallion and continued on his way. Though he appeared at ease, he mentally cursed himself for allowing his thoughts to dwell on Amanda. Daydreaming was a luxury only old men who had long ago given up their warrior ways could afford, Hawk believed.

An hour passed, and though Hawk pushed his stallion into a fast walk, he continued to pretend that he wasn't at all anxious, that he had no suspicions there was a man — or men — trailing him.

He ran through a list of the enemies he'd made in the recent past, then throughout his life. The first list was fairly short, the latter much longer. He could think of many people who would like to hear of his demise. All in all, there were many men, red and white, who would gladly pull the trigger or let fly arrows to see him die.

But who was it *this* time?

He very casually eased the safety thong from the hammer of his revolver. The thong, attached to his holster, prevented the weapon from bouncing out of the holster during a hard gallop, but it also prevented him from drawing the revolver quickly in a time of crisis.

"Our lazy days are over, boy," Hawk said quietly to his stallion, patting the animal's neck fondly.

He felt the transformation to becoming once again the Sioux warrior, the fighter. The days and nights with Amanda at the Circle S—eating well, relaxing often, making loving regularly—were all behind him now. An attack could happen at any time.

A tight half smile pulled up the right corner of Hawk's mouth. He'd been docile long enough. His instincts, the whispered voice of warning that had sounded, had saved him once again. His time at the Circle S hadn't made him soft after all, it seemed.

* * * *

Deputy Foster Samuelson could smell death, and he believed that the big Indian who'd been railroaded out of town was behind it. He didn't have so much as a shred of evidence to link Hawk Two Feather to the missing men, but Deputy Samuelson was certain he was involved.

Four horses had meandered into Deadwood, their saddles intact, their weapons still in the scabbards. They straggled into town at different times, searching for food and water, domesticated animals uncertain of their fate now that they were without riders.

Where were the riders?

Nothing pointed to the Sioux warrior Hawk Two Feather until the deputy learned that one of the missing men was Sheriff Darren Richards's brother.

The sheriff, on learning that his brother's horse had walked into town, immediately began arranging a posse to "Kill that bastard!" When the deputy asked him who 'that bastard' was, the sheriff tried unsuccessfully to pretend he didn't know. Though Deputy Samuelson never got a name from the sheriff, he suspected that the four men had ridden out of Deadwood intending to waylay Hawk on his way home from the Circle S ranch.

Sheriff Richards, his brother, and all their friends, were essentially a rotten crowd, the deputy believed. Poorly educated, hard-drinking, unnecessarily violent, these men thought nothing of hurting others, yet felt themselves to be unjustly put upon whenever they were shown anything less than full courtesy from everyone crossing their path.

More deaths in Deadwood. Even worse, unanswered-for deaths. Though the deputy had no facts or clues to indicate the men from Deadwood had been left dead, he believed they had. He also believed that Sheriff Richards knew who had caused the deaths and intended to get his revenge.

The deputy felt a dull, empty ache in the pit of his stomach. From the first moment Hawk Two Feather had ridden into town, trouble had followed him. And now, even though he was gone, the cloud of conflict still surrounded his invisible presence.

Sighing heavily, and not liking the violence undoubtedly headed his way, Deputy Foster Samuelson walked slowly back to his office. This would be a good time to clean and oil his double-barrel shotgun. He'd been deputy long enough to know that very soon he'd need all his weapons to be in working order.

* * * *

Hawk sensed a change in the mood of the camp even before he had reached it. Were the children looking strangely at him? He couldn't say. Twisting just a little in the saddle, he tested his ribs. They still bothered him, but the serious pain, the kind that had made him clench his teeth when he moved, was gone now. He was thankful for that. He sensed a fight ahead and wanted to be at his best. Though the battered ribs could prevent him from being the warrior he was capable of being, he was confident there were few men, if any, who could challenge him and survive.

He'd gotten off his horse near his tepee and was tending to his stallion when a young boy approached with the message that Dull Knife wished to see him. It wasn't an unusual request. Any brave who was away from the tribe for more than a day or two would be expected to speak with the elderly Sioux chieftain. The difference this time was that it had been more than a request. Never before had Hawk been *summoned* to the tribal elders, and he didn't care for it now.

He took the leather saddlebag filled with two thousand dollars in paper currency. Hawk preferred gold coin, but since he had received the money as a gift, and not a payment, he hadn't felt he could complain.

Dull Knife was seated in the large tepee, his face devoid of expression. As he looked at Hawk, his eyes were unreadable. Behind the elderly Sioux leader sat two lesser chiefs, silent and unmoving. Hawk felt instantly on the defensive and knew in his heart that, during his absence, the men had been discussing him and his way of life.

"Sit." Dull Knife nodded toward a folded blanket on the ground.

Hawk noticed that there was no bowl of berries or other Sioux treats to welcome him home from his journey. He folded his legs beneath him, wishing that he'd taken the time to change out of the buckskin trousers, which were so much like the white man's clothes, and into his loincloth and leggings.

He was enough of an outsider without dressing differently.

"Your journey went well?" Dull Knife asked.

Hawk nodded, not liking the old man's comment, suspecting there was something more behind it. Though he reminded himself that Dull Knife was a good and decent man, an honorable man and one whose judgment the tribe counted on, Hawk's sense of unease did not abate.

"Yes," Hawk answered. "But it is good to be here. It is always good to be back with my people."

"The yellow-haired girl was returned to her family safely?"

"Yes."

For several seconds Dull Knife simply looked at Hawk. He made no move, nor did he make any expression suggesting doubt about Hawk's answer, yet in his eyes *something* indefinable whispered to Hawk that Dull Knife didn't believe what he had heard.

What else might the elderly chieftain not believe? Hawk didn't want to think of that now, though it was all but impossible to keep his mind from drifting in such directions. He felt as though he was fighting an enemy now, one just as dangerous as the sheriff in Deadwood, or the men who'd so foolishly set the ambush for him as he'd ridden away from the Circle S ranch.

No, Hawk thought next, the enemy here is much more dangerous. *The enemy here pretends to be something other than an enemy.*

"Then you are back with us now?" This time there was no mistaking Dull Knife's implication that Hawk had been away from his people too long and some of them weren't at all pleased with his absence.

"Yes, Dull Knife, I am back." Hawk looked the old man directly in the eye. "And I have brought back with me a bounty. The family of the yellow-haired girl has given me something for protecting her." Hawk was pleased when he saw the glint in the elder's eyes. Dull Knife might not want to show his emotions, but when it came to money for the tribe he couldn't contain his enthusiasm. "Her family was grateful to the Sioux for saving her life." Hawk was careful to credit all the Sioux, not just himself, for saving Amanda. He handed Dull Knife the thick stack of paper money, fresh from the bank in Deadwood. "There is two thousand dollars here."

Dull Knife took the money in his hands and stared at it for several seconds, as though he wasn't at all certain it was real. Then his face clouded over as he pulled the veil over his emotions once again. When he again regarded Hawk, no thoughts or feelings could be discerned in the depths of his dark eyes.

"It is good that you have brought to your people such bounty," Dull Knife acknowledged quietly. "But you should know that there are many among us who have questioned your loyalty. They say that you ride away from your people, and when you return you have precious things that you have not hunted for. That makes many of us curious. You go hunting to faraway lands, searching for game, and what do you return with? Cheyenne horses. We are always thankful for Cheyenne horses, but we wonder how you came on them when you were searching for elk and buffalo. And then you ride away to bring the yellow-haired girl back to her people, and when you return you have a bounty that can hardly be believed. Is that not strange, Hawk Two Feather?"

Hawk wondered which answer he could give to maintain the slender thread of modesty he'd kept with his people. He'd actually shown himself to be an extraordinary hunter, often bringing game back to the tribe when the other hunters had failed. And though Hawk wanted greatly to point this out to Dull Knife, he knew he couldn't without sounding arrogant and disrespectful.

He looked at Dull Knife. He decided not to speak, suspecting that any answer he might give would likely become twisted somehow. Quite suddenly, Hawk felt as though he was a stranger to his own people, an outsider who might just as well be an enemy.

"But we must not speak too long on what might be," Dull Knife said then. "You have brought food to your people in the past, and I know you will in the future. You are back with us now, and you shall stay with us."

"Yes, Dull Knife, I am pleased to hear you say that, because staying with my people is what I want to do now," Hawk said, sensing that these were the sentiments that the old man most wanted to hear expressed, hoping they would assuage whatever fears and doubts were still in the elder's heart. "I have traveled far, and now I can once again know the peace of sleeping in my own tepee."

Dull Knife actually smiled at the comment, and even nodded slightly in Hawk's direction. Hawk didn't need to be told that he had chosen the right words to say, or that his time with Dull Knife was now over. He rose and left the tepee, a growing sense of being at war with himself and his people slowly and inexorably getting stronger within his breast.

Chapter Seventeen

I mustn't seek out Red Wolf.

The words rang out like a spirit's warning in Hawk's head. Stories had been told of him—lies, all of them!— and they'd put his name, his reputation, his loyalty to the tribe, in doubt. And there was only one man whom Hawk felt was capable of spreading such lies, and doing it in such a way as to make himself appear concerned only with the welfare of the tribe. That man simply had to be Red Wolf. Only Red Wolf's hatred burned hot enough, went deep enough, to do such a thing to him.

With some effort, Hawk forced himself to think logically, objectively, to see himself and his situation dispassionately. Wasn't it possible that he was blaming Red Wolf when, in fact, the person he was really angry with was Amanda Wright? Wasn't it possible that he was blaming Red Wolf for being conniving and deceitful when it was Amanda who had been conniving and deceitful, who had, through her charms and her seductive ways, besmirched Hawk's reputation and put his name and loyalty in doubt among the chieftains of the Sioux tribe?

That was possible, Hawk consented, but it was unlikely. Her deception didn't make her responsible for his tattered reputation here among his own people.

Hawk knew he needed time alone, time to withdraw within himself, time to look into his own heart to discover the truth waiting there for him. Only then would he truly have the wisdom he needed to make the necessary decisions. At this moment his mind was too muddied, too chaotic and distracted, to have full command of his abilities.

The sweat lodge would strip his body of impurities, Hawk decided, and after that a vision quest was in order. Many moons had passed since he'd sought a vision, since he'd searched so deeply within and outside himself.

But there was always Red Wolf to think about—

Don't think of him now!

Leaving camp, Hawk walked quickly, purposefully, toward what he hoped would be the return of the serenity he'd lost the moment Amanda had entered his life.

He was almost out of camp when Red Wolf approached him, riding one of the Cheyenne horses Hawk had brought to the tribe.

"You are back," Red Wolf said with a sneer on his lips. "I am surprised. I had thought the yellow-haired woman would keep you away longer than this."

"Not every warrior thinks with what is between his legs," Hawk replied, painfully aware of the hypocrisy of his statement. All too often in his life he had responded to the demands of his lusty instincts.

"True. True," Red Wolf replied. "But you are not one of those warriors with a dead spear between his legs, are you? Not you, Hawk. There is not a warrior nor a maiden in this tribe who has not heard of your prowess."

Red Wolf spit out the words hatefully, viciously.

Hawk turned on his enemy, understanding with knowledge acquired through his instincts and his spirit guides that listening to Red Wolf was a mistake. Allowing Red Wolf's words to create anger was folly, yet he couldn't help himself. He managed to stifle the urge to take Red Wolf by the throat, but only because out of the corner of his eye he saw a gathering of women and children. It wouldn't do to make the entire tribe aware of his inability to maintain his self-control and temper.

"You lowest of maggots." Hawk hissed, using the vilest insult in the Sioux culture to describe his enemy. "Every word you utter is a defilement."

In response, Red Wolf smiled, his smile suggesting that he would be pleased should Hawk attack him when others in the tribe could see.

But Hawk turned and walked away, determined to put as much distance between himself and his people as possible.

I must have a vision quest. Only there will I find the answers to the questions that plague me.

* * * *

In the sweat lodge Hawk felt perspiration running down his naked body and, as time passed, he sweated out the impurities and defilement of the past weeks. Soon, very soon, he would be whole and complete again, free of the influences of a culture that wasn't his own, free of a woman he could never call his own.

He was punishing himself. The heat of the sweat lodge was greater than it should be, Hawk realized, but still he stoked the fire, heating the rocks on which he poured the cool water from the hollowed-out gourd, creating the steam. Moment by moment, fresh rivers of perspiration ran down Hawk's naked chest and back.

Amanda Wright simply wasn't worth the torture that he was putting himself through. And he was doing everything he possibly could to make himself believe that.

The trouble was, no matter how often he told himself a lie, he was aware of it. And lying was something that Hawk had disliked no matter what the circumstances, and had avoided with all he held sacred.

Stretching out on the buffalo mat, Hawk closed his eyes and tried to imagine what wonders would be his to experience during his vision quest. It had been quite some time since last he'd dared look so deeply within himself, and he was frankly curious about what treasures would be his to experience...and what horrors would be revealed. True knowledge was a two-edged sword.

Hawk wasn't a man who frightened easily, but at this moment he felt anxious. Would he even be capable of having a vision, after all the time he had spent living in the white man's world, speaking the white man's language, eating the white man's food?

The white man is not my enemy.

Had being so closely involved with the Caucasian culture infected his soul?

What most disturbed Hawk, sweat pouring from his body, was that he continued to think about Amanda, even when he was doing everything he could to forget her. In the past, women who occupied his time and shared his passion had only been on his mind and in his thoughts when they were physically with him. With astonishing speed, Hawk had forgotten virtually every incident he'd shared with a woman once they were no longer lovers.

He stretched his muscles, inhaling the moist air, enjoying the burning of the steam as it filled his lungs and expanded his chest. He felt the sweat running out of his body. In his heart, Hawk was convinced that when he was finished with the sweat lodge his soul would be purer. The anger he felt toward Amanda and Red Wolf, along with the anger he felt toward himself for having allowed his weakness for women to distort his judgment, would be gone. He should have known from the very beginning that Amanda would bring nothing but trouble to his life.

But how could he have known she'd bring a passion that burned more brightly than he'd thought possible?

The instant the memories of their lovemaking began to fill his head, Hawk sighed and forced himself to begin thinking about his duties to the tribe, and where next he would hunt.

* * * *

Night Flower stood alone in the shadows, searching inside herself to find the courage to finish what she had started. Her knees were trembling, and her heart was racing with fear and anticipation. This was her sixteenth summer, and she felt it was time to find a warrior for herself. Other Sioux women her age were no longer maidens. They had accepted invitations to a courageous and proud warrior's tepee, and some of them were already mothers, raising the next generation of the tribe.

Night Flower knew she was attractive, and her spirit had drawn the attention of several warriors in the tribe. But none had measured up to the standards she'd set for herself. None of the braves who had smiled at her and wished to dance with her during the ceremonies were what she envisioned for herself.

But there *was* one brave in the tribe who measure up to Night Flower's standards of manhood—Hawk Two Feather. He alone was able to make Night Flower's heart accelerate by just smiling at her. When he was near Night Flower felt safe and secure, as though he alone was capable of defending the tribe from all its enemies.

Twice she had tried to let Hawk know that she was interested in him, and twice he had simply smiled at her, treating her kindly but giving no indication that he realized the depths of her desire for him. Tonight, Night Flower intended to make her intentions toward Hawk clear. There would be no possible misunderstanding...not when she walked into the sweat lodge, when she knew Hawk was inside, alone, and naked.

She looked around one more time, her mouth dry as she searched for spying eyes to witness her entrance into the sweat lodge. Seeing no one looking at her, she made her move quickly. She stepped out from her hiding place, then dashed across the small clearing and through the buffalo-hide flap of the sweat lodge.

He was spread out on his back, arms and legs outstretched, his glorious body completely naked and glistening from head to toe with perspiration. Night Flower, one step into the tepee, was transfixed in place, her eyes wide, her mouth slightly open as she looked down at the man who had been the object of her fantasies since she'd begun to have them.

He raised his head after a moment, clearly annoyed at having been disturbed from whatever thoughts had occupied his mind. Then, after blinking several times, he focused his gaze on Night Flower. He raised his right knee just enough to block his penis from her view, but other than that he didn't move.

A small eternity of time passed with neither of them speaking a word. Finally Hawk spoke, with a gentleness and understanding that surprised Night Flower.

"You have honored me, Night Flower," Hawk said softly, "but you should not have come here."

Night Flower tried to speak, but though she moved her lips, no words came forth. She cleared her throat, moistened her lips, and tried once more, determined to succeed now that she had come this far.

"I *had* to come here," she said, her voice a whisper of uncertainty. "I have tried to let you know that I want to be with you in your tepee. But when I have tried you have cast me aside like an old moccasin. Now I am here, alone with you in the sweat lodge, and you cannot cast me aside."

"No, I cannot," Hawk replied. "But you still should not have come here."

"I had to. You left me no choice."

Night Flower bent at the waist, reaching for the bottom of her buckskin dress, about to lift it up and over her head. But Hawk moved quickly, catching her wrist with his huge hand to stop her. Their eyes met, and after a moment Hawk shook his head.

"This is not the way it is to be for you," he said quietly, releasing Night Flower's wrist from his grasp.

Still standing, Night Flower looked down at Hawk, hating herself at that moment for having been foolish enough to intrude on a proud warrior's private sweat lodge ceremony. She had, she realized, made a terrible mistake, and she hoped that the rest of the tribe would never find out about what she had done. But she wasn't yet willing to give up on the plan. Hawk's reputation as an insatiable lover had been spread throughout the tribe, and Night Flower had received too many compliments in her young life for her to not know that she was a beautiful Sioux maiden.

"You are a mighty warrior, Hawk Two Feather," Night Flower said at last, thankful that she had finally found her voice, "but you do not know my future. This *is* the way it should be for me." She paused a moment. "And for you. I believe in my heart—" To emphasize the point, she placed her hand over her breast, and was pleased that Hawk's eyes followed her every move. "That you and I were meant to be together. I am the maiden the spirits wish you to mate with. The spirits have told me so."

Night Flower looked away for only a moment. Guilt caused her to look away, because the spirits had told her no such thing. But in her desperation she was willing to go to any length to get the man she desired. She wanted desperately for Hawk to be hers, from this night forward.

"There are other braves who look at me, and I can feel their hunger," Night Flower continued. "But you look on me differently. I know that you desire me. I have seen that desire in your eyes. But you do not look at me the way others do, and because you do not, my desire for you has grown."

Night Flower took a step closer to Hawk then got down on her knees at his hip. She could tell that he was very anxious in her presence, but she'd already gone too far with her plan to back away from it now. "Touch my breast, Hawk," she said softly, "and feel how I can feed the child we will create."

Hawk finally pulled up to a sitting position, folding his legs beneath him, casually placing the corner of the buffalo mat across his lap. He had known that Night Flower was interested in him. He would have had to have been blind not to have noticed, and Hawk had a notable ability to perceive interest from any woman instantly. Night Flower was a maiden, he knew, and much sought-after by the other braves in the tribe. Though she would surely make a magnificent wife, Hawk also knew that he must not touch her. She wasn't the woman for him, no matter how much his body desired the sexual release that she clearly was willing to give him.

"Can you feel how nurturing a mother I would be?" Night Flower asked, taking Hawk's hand and placing it on her breast.

Involuntarily, Hawk's fingers closed over Night Flower's breast, squeezing her through her dress. But rather than the instant burst of passionate interest he had expected to experience, he thought how she was not nearly as voluptuous as Amanda, and the comparison immediately destroyed whatever sensuality the moment might have possessed.

"Night Flower is beautiful and rare as her name suggests," Hawk said, easing his hand away from her, "but she is wrong to think that I am the only brave for her. Night Flower is very young and very kind. She must find for herself a warrior who is both strong and kind. But that warrior cannot be Hawk Two Feather."

It astonished Hawk to say such words. Could it really be that he, a man given to profligate excesses where women were concerned, was turning his back on a virgin? A young maiden not needing to be seduced, but rather needing only the attention she'd already shown she was desirous of?

For a moment Hawk closed his eyes, trying desperately to make some sense of his behavior. Was it Amanda who had caused him to be unreceptive to Night Flower's offer? Had Amanda somehow taken possession of his soul, causing him to behave so uncharacteristically?

"Tell me what you desire," Night Flower pressed, her voice a frightened whisper. "I will do anything you want. Teach me…and I will be yours forever."

Hawk took Night Flower's hands into his own and kissed them. He felt guilty that she desired him, as though he had encouraged her, though he could not say how. He looked into her eyes and saw the longing and the fear buried there.

"Night Flower is beautiful, but Night Flower must wait," Hawk replied. "There will be another forever for you. There will be a warrior who will teach you all that it is you do not know, but that warrior will not be Hawk Two Feather. Trust me. This is the truth that the visions have given me."

Though Hawk had never even thought of Night Flower in his vision, that lie didn't matter. What mattered was that he refuse her request without making her feel belittled. When he looked into Night Flower's eyes he saw a mixture of relief and sadness. She wanted him—or at least she thought she did—but he suspected she was mortally afraid of the reality of actually having a sexual relationship with him.

"There will come a time, in a year or two, when Night Flower will find the brave who will be her companion for life," Hawk continued, "but that time is not this time. Go, now, and be thankful that we both have listened to what the spirits have spoken."

* * * *

The mare was responding exactly as Amanda had hoped she would. Though new to the saddle and bridle, the horse was quick to learn the movements necessary to be a good cutting horse. Amanda's legs grasped securely around the animal's ribs, her entire body ready for the animal to move in any direction. Ahead of her, the year-old steer was trying to decide whether to run to the right or to the left, his frustration growing as the mare cut off his escape every time.

When the steer bolted to the left the mare moved in unison, and an instant later the steer was herded through the corral gate into the pen, where Amanda had wanted him.

"Good girl," Amanda purred, patting the horse's sleek, well-muscled neck. "You were perfect today. Every day you keep getting better and better."

Amanda had noticed that Billy, sitting on the top rail of the corral, had been watching her through the training.

"You've got yourself one fine horse there, Miss Amanda," Billy said as Amanda came closer.

"She is a good one," Amanda replied. "I don't think I've ever had a horse take to cutting quite as quickly as this one has."

"What's her name?" Billy asked.

Amanda shifted her weight in the saddle, uneasy with the question. Why didn't she have a name? Such a magnificent animal *should* have a name, she reasoned. But was it possible that she hadn't named the mare because of something Hawk had told her? He said the Sioux didn't believe in giving their horses names, only in giving their horses respect.

"Miss Amanda?" Billy asked, a bit more softly this time.

Amanda looked Billy straight in the eye and did her best to smile. "Billy, I'd be pleased if you'd name her for me," Amanda said. "She doesn't have a name because everything I think of just doesn't seem to fit. Maybe you can do better."

Billy's face broke into a broad smile. "I'd be right proud to do that for you, Miss Amanda. Right proud, indeed."

Amanda swung down from the saddle and handed Billy the reins. He would take care of the animal, seeing that she was brushed down, watered, and properly fed.

As Amanda started on the long walk from the training corral to the ranch house, she groaned softly. Her muscles felt stiff and sore from all the hours she'd put in lately, working to train the new cutting horses that would be sold in a month or two. In fact, the muscles in the back of her neck were always tense and tight these days, always knotted painfully. Even when she massaged her neck, the muscles relaxed only briefly before tightening up once again.

The hot bath she'd take would relieve her aching body temporarily. Her nightly baths in the large tub, the steaming water laced with scented soap, was the only extravagance she allowed herself — and they were something she began looking forward to earlier and earlier each day, it seemed.

Amanda knew why she was pushing herself so hard. It was Hawk, and the way he made her feel. No man had made her feel more precious, and no man had made her feel more cheap and tawdry. He'd brought her to the heights of ecstasy and the depths of abject humiliation. Amanda would drive his memory out of her mind with endless hours of hard labor.

Even most of the ranch hands, men not known for sophisticated perceptions, noticed something was driving her on other than training the cutting horses. They'd worked with her long enough to realize the difference in her behavior, though none of the men suspected the real reason for her abrupt change in work habits. No one would ever have connected the Indian's stay with their mistress's new mood.

How many times since Hawk had ridden away had she snapped at one of the ranch hands, castigating the poor man much more harshly than he deserved for an offense either real or imagined? Just off the top of her head, Amanda could think of three such incidents in which she had later apologized to a hired hand. And those were only the times when she had gone completely overboard in her response to an offense. Amanda was certain there were plenty of other things she'd said recently that she should have apologized for but was too emotionally distracted to be aware of.

Amanda sighed, hoping she hadn't caused any long-lasting hard feelings. She had always had a fine working relationship with the hands at the Circle S ranch, and she wanted it to stay that way.

* * * *

The dress had arrived that morning. Now, as Amanda looked at her reflection in her bedroom's full-length mirror, she wondered once again whether it was such a good idea to wear it for Travis Newton.

He deserves to have you dressed like a lady, not a saddle bum. Amanda felt angry with herself as she stared into the reflection of her own eyes. *Maybe if you had dressed like a lady for Hawk, he would have considered you a woman instead of a tramp.*

"I've got to stop thinking about him," Amanda whispered aloud, hoping that the sound of her own voice would somehow add emphasis to the order.

The eggshell white gown was modest and attractive, and the dressmaker's craftsmanship was beyond reproach. It was one of five gowns Amanda had ordered, impulsively deciding that if she made her wardrobe more feminine, her life might not feel so empty and barren without Hawk.

There was a soft knock on the door. "Amanda, Travis is here," Sonny called out.

Amanda inhaled deeply, closing her eyes. A silent, hopeful prayer passed through her mind that the evening would be entertaining, and that Travis would be the man to take her thoughts away from a Sioux warrior whose opinion of her was sorrowfully low.

Travis was waiting for her in the library, and the instant he saw Amanda in her new evening gown his jaw dropped. A handsome man several years older than Amanda, he came from a good family whom Amanda had known for several years. Even so, she'd never really considered allowing Travis to come courting before.

"Miss Amanda, you have never looked lovelier," Travis said, rushing forward, his face beaming with happiness. "Never, *ever* have you been more beautiful."

"It's just a dress, Travis," Amanda replied, suddenly unsure of what it was she wanted. She had chosen the dress so that Travis would be pleased with it, yet now that she had gotten exactly the response from him that she'd wanted, his pleasure rather annoyed her.

"But what a dress! I truly have never seen you look so much like...like—"

"Like a lady?"

"No, Amanda, that wasn't what I was going to say," Travis replied quickly. "That wasn't what I was going to say at all."

Amanda merely smiled at Travis. "You needn't be afraid, Travis. I'm fully aware that my usual attire is less than feminine. In fact, it's rather mannish, I should say."

"You would be lovely no matter what clothes you wore," Travis said, clearly relieved that Amanda wasn't really angry with him. He added, "I'll bet you'd be the prettiest girl in the whole territory even if you didn't have a stitch on."

The instant the words were out of his mouth, Travis Newton blushed crimson with embarrassment. Amanda laughed openly at the comment, realizing that Travis hadn't meant to insult her, and that his embarrassment was a thousand times worse than her own.

"Travis, why don't we step outside onto the porch?" Amanda suggested. "We can sit on the swing. I'm sure you could use a whiskey, and I'd like a glass of wine."

Travis nodded, then his eyes widened in surprise. "Miss Amanda, I didn't know you drank spirits."

"I'm only going to have a glass of wine, Travis. It isn't as if I'm breaking the law or anything."

"But do you think you should have it outside, where the hands might see you? They might not have such a high opinion of you if they found out you touch alcohol."

Amanda managed to keep her anger in check, though only because Travis was so genuinely concerned with what other people thought of her. "Why don't you let me worry about my own reputation? I'm sure we'll get along better that way."

"Whatever you want, Miss Amanda. My only concern is for you."

They sat on the front porch swing and discussed horses. Amanda was grateful for the topic, one that she could discuss at great length without having to feign interest. Even better, it was one Travis knew quite a bit about, though Amanda disagreed with him when it came to the best methods of training cutting horses, and on the use of spurs.

"I'm working with a mare that looks like she's got all the right instincts to be a first-class cutter," Amanda explained. In the back of her mind she wondered whether Billy had come up with a name for the mare.

"Will you be keeping her, or selling?"

"I think this one will have to stay at the Circle S," Amanda answered. "She's exactly the kind of horse that this ranch needs to rejuvenate its bloodlines."

Travis chuckled softly. "Doesn't seem to me the Circle S needs much rejuvenating, Miss Amanda. It's already the envy of every horseman for three hundred miles around."

Amanda playfully glanced sideways at Travis. "Just three hundred miles? I'd have thought our reputation goes farther than that."

"If you say it does, then it does, Miss Amanda," Travis replied agreeably.

Amanda knew that Travis was only trying to ingratiate himself with her, but she wished he could have stuck to his guns about the three hundred miles. Or, at least, that he could have teased her a little about her own boastfulness. Instead, he continued to go along with everything she said, subjugating his own honest feelings in an effort to have her like him. In the process, she lost some of her respect for him.

Travis bridged the narrow space that separated them on the swing, cautiously taking her hand in his. "It would give me the greatest pleasure if you could see it in your heart to let me hold your hand, Miss Amanda," Travis said softly, solemnly. "And when I leave here later tonight I want you to know that I'm not one of those men who'd go looking for a kiss goodnight. I respect you too much to ask that of you. You see, I'm a gentleman, and you're a lady, and that's the way I'll always treat you, Miss Amanda. Like a real lady, and nothing less."

"That's kind of you, Travis," Amanda said softly.

She didn't know what else to say. What would his opinion of her be if he knew the things that she'd done with Hawk? Would he think her so fragile if he knew the uninhibited behavior she'd exhibited in the arms of a half-breed Sioux warrior?

There was a certain comic quality to Travis being satisfied with simply holding Amanda's hand that not only touched her in a way, but also embarrassed her. Hawk wouldn't be satisfied with just holding her hand. Travis was too polite to even expect a kiss goodnight. And Hawk? Hawk's kisses were hotter than fire, touching her in ways she'd never imagined, kissing her in places she'd never dreamed of. There was simply no similarity between Hawk Two Feather and Travis Newton.

Finally the sun went down and Travis rose slowly from the swing. Still holding Amanda's hand, he gently pulled her to a standing position.

"Miss Amanda, it has been an honor to have this time with you," Travis said quietly, looking into Amanda's eyes. "I never thought I'd get the chance to be with you without other fellas around."

"You've been very sweet," Amanda replied honestly.

Travis Newton *was* a sweet man, kind and considerate, and he would make some woman a wonderful husband. But that woman wouldn't be Amanda. It wasn't that she didn't think he was suitable to be her husband. He was a wonderful man, but she knew that in time she would learn to hate him because she could control him, make him bend to her greater willpower. She needed a man who was as strong, as determined, as solid in his views as she was herself. She needed a man *like* Hawk, but not *Hawk*.

"Then you'll see me again?" he asked.

So filled with hope, Amanda thought sadly. She replied, "Someday. We'll see. You've been very kind, Travis. You're a perfect gentleman."

He left then, and Amanda watched him ride out through the arched gateway of the Circle S ranch. How could any man be so happy just to have held her hand? A gentleman could and would be happy just to hold the hand of a woman he was courting, Amanda thought.

She wasn't pleased with her thoughts. Travis was a kind and decent man, but she felt more protective than passionate toward him. Though he was older than her by several years, she felt herself to be the more worldly, the more experienced in life.

When she stepped into the house she saw a light glowing in the library. Sonny, casually dressed in a green robe, was reading a newspaper and having a whiskey.

"I'm going to bed now," Amanda said, standing in the doorway. "I've had a long day, and I've got a lot to do tomorrow."

Sonny looked up from his newspaper and smiled. "Why don't you sleep late tomorrow? The ranch can survive one day without you getting up at sunrise."

"No. There's too much to do for me to start getting lazy now."

"Lazy? Amanda, you're the hardest-working woman I've ever known in my life. Go ahead and take a morning off. It'll probably do you a world of good. You really have been pushing yourself too hard lately."

"Goodnight, Sonny," Amanda replied, turning away from her brother with a smile. "I'll see you in the morning."

"How was Travis?" Sonny called out.

"Fine. Just fine," Amanda replied, already heading down the hall.

She could hardly wait to get out of the gown, out of the corselet, out of the garters and stockings and all the other accoutrements of sophistication that she was unaccustomed to wearing. She wanted to crawl between the sheets of her bed and forget about every man in the world until morning. She hoped that with a goodnight's sleep her world wouldn't look quite so bleak and colorless.

Chapter Eighteen

He's more beautiful than ever.

This reaction didn't surprise Amanda, though it was disconcerting, coming so soon after promising herself to never become either physically or emotionally affected by Hawk's looks again. But here he came toward her, and while she knew she shouldn't be attracted to the man – his opinion of her was a matter of record, and the hours she had spent crying because of his words had not been forgotten – her body wasn't listening. In fact, her body had grown all jittery just at the sight of Hawk Two Feather.

He wore the leather garment she'd seen him in earlier, only now he was bare-chested and without the leggings. Only the loincloth and moccasins kept him from being completely naked. His broad, bronze-hued chest drew Amanda's eyes like a magnet, a magnet that wouldn't let go. She couldn't look away, not when the sheer perfection of his physique was there for her inspection. To make matters worse, there was an ebony fire in his eyes that told Amanda that his calm exterior hid an inferno in his soul.

"Say something," *Amanda said. Her voice sounded odd in her ears, trailing an echo, as if she were talking while standing inside a large empty grain bin. "Why have you come here?"*

It occurred to Amanda that she didn't know where here *was, though that hardly seemed to matter when Hawk was so near...and wearing so little.*

"What do you want from me, Hawk?" Her anger was surfacing now that he had chosen to re-enter her life, yet remain his typically silent, aloof self. "You can't keep doing this to me. It isn't fair. You know it isn't."

Hawk still said nothing, standing there like a statue, his feet spread to shoulders' width, his hands on his lean hips. She knew how fully aware he was of the impact his physical beauty had on women, that he counted on that impact to make up for whatever frazzled nervous and frayed tempers his idiosyncrasies elicited.

"Damn you, Hawk Two Feather," Amanda said, hating him then because he expected her to go to him. But she was just as furious with herself for being willing to do just that.

As she approached him slowly, everything seemed ethereal and disconnected to Amanda. His eyes were black as midnight, tempting as sin. He neither moved nor spoke, yet Amanda felt as though his thoughts and desires were somehow being transmitted directly into her being.

Then the strangest thing happened. Hawk's hands were on her, touching her in exactly the way he had taught her to enjoy, brushing the pads of his fingers over her enflamed nipples before pinching them with an artisan's precision. She heard herself sigh, a long, soft, warbling moan of contentment and passion, a sleepy sound of delight in the joy of living.

Yes, my darling. *Amanda rolled her head from side to side.* You're perfect. You do everything just right.

Then she suddenly realized that she was no longer standing but was instead in a bed with Hawk. Her eyes were closed and the room was engulfed in darkness. And even though Hawk had yet to speak even a single word,

Amanda felt his presence with her in the bed, recognized the familiarity of his touch, the surety and confidence of his skilled hands as his exquisite caresses sent her senses soaring.

"Yes, oh, my darling, yesss!" Amanda sighed, giving herself over completely to the feeling of the moment.

It didn't matter to her, then, whether or not Hawk respected her. It didn't matter that he had said cruel, vicious things to her the last time they were together. Nothing mattered but Hawk's touch, and the way she felt when he touched her.

I shouldn't let him. *Amanda parted her knees.*

It was a silly thought because she knew that she could deny Hawk nothing. Not this night. She had been denied the sweetness of his passion for too long. How had she become addicted to the ecstasy of his lovemaking with such frightening speed? She would give him everything, deny him nothing. When it was all over she might feel guilty — or maybe she wouldn't. Either way, she wouldn't stop now. There would be no barriers between them tonight.

Amanda arched her back with the slowly building tension and knew from experience what that meant. Soon Hawk would take her to that magical place where the pleasure was so intense that she had no choice but to explode, her body turning inside-out as her ecstasy reached its pinnacle. Closer and closer she felt herself being drawn.

"Yes, Hawk," Amanda purred, no longer hiding her pleasure.

She wanted to let Hawk know that she was willing to do anything, endure anything, provided he no longer deprive her of these feelings that she had become addicted to.

The moment of truth, that cataclysmic instant when the pleasure of Hawk's caresses couldn't become any more intense, was only seconds away. Amanda welcomed that approaching moment, knowing in her heart that afterward she would experience a blissful lassitude of mind and body that couldn't be achieved any other way.

When she was teetering at the edge of the chasm, about to fall into ecstasy and experience once more the glorious freefall of orgasmic culmination, she awoke.

For several seconds Amanda refused to believe that it had all been a dream, that Hawk hadn't really returned to her, and that the pleasures of the flesh that she'd experienced were a result of a dream-based imagination.

"What is happening to me?" she murmured aloud in the dark bedroom. She rubbed her eyes and blinked.

Suddenly, she was embarrassed at her state of arousal. Her body had responded to the fantasy of Hawk just as readily as it would have responded to the reality of his seduction. But now she lay alone in her own bed, trembling softly, her heart fluttering as she sought to calm the chaos within her.

She kicked off the light blankets and got out of bed. On the stand nearby stood a pitcher and a basin. She poured cool water into the basin, cupped her hands in the water then washed her face. She wished she could as easily wash away the stimulating dream.

More than anything, Amanda was shocked by the realization that there was now a face on the fantasy man of her dreams. Now, when erotic fantasies tormented her sleep, the faceless man of limitless seduction would have an identity and a name.

Was this knowledge a plague or a blessing?

Perhaps she would rest easier if she hadn't discovered that Hawk had become her dream lover.

Amanda went to the open window and breathed in the Dakota night air, unnaturally cool against her skin. She realized then how heated her body had become because of the erotic dream of Hawk.

"He's out of my life forever," Amanda determined.

She walked slowly back to the bed and crawled between the sheets. With some trepidation, she closed her eyes, hoping that sleep would bring her nothing but rest until morning.

* * * *

Walter Morrison was more than just a decent fellow, and Amanda knew it. Not yet forty, he owned the largest bank in Deadwood, and was partner in another bank somewhere in Minnesota. He had one child, who was in a private school in the East. His wife had died in a tragic carriage accident. Wealthy, rather handsome, profitably engaged in business matters, Walter Morrison was a man whom many of the young and not-so-young women in and around Deadwood hoped to 'hook' as a husband.

As Amanda rode in the carriage beside Walter, she wondered what kind of husband he would make. By all accounts he was a man who loved women, and that was good to know. Amanda had discovered that there were some men who coveted women sexually yet despised them in every other way. She couldn't tolerate the thought of living with a man who wanted her sexually, yet considered her inferior.

"This has been a wonderful evening, Amanda," Walter said as he guided his fine carriage through the arched gateway leading into the grounds of the Circle S ranch. "Do you feel the same way?"

Amanda almost said that she did, but then she wondered whether Walter had meant something more, so she simply nodded her head. When Walter repeated the question she made herself speak. "It was a fine evening. I've enjoyed myself."

"As have I. We should do this again sometime soon."

Out of the corner of her eye, Amanda looked at Walter and wondered why she didn't feel blessed. She could think of at least three women her age who would do anything to have spent an evening with Walter Morrison. He had behaved like a perfect gentleman, naturally, but Amanda knew that his experience with women was considerable. Since the death of his wife, and after a suitable period of mourning, Walter had been seen in the company of many of the more fashionable ladies of Deadwood, as well as Fargo. And, rumor had it, even St. Paul.

Amanda was impressed, but she simply wasn't interested. She had accepted Walter's offer of a carriage ride and dinner at a fashionable restaurant in Deadwood because she'd hoped that it would take her mind off Hawk. But instead, when Walter arrived in his carriage with the two matching horses, Amanda's first thought was about Hawk. Hawk Two Feather could never afford such a carriage, and even if he could, he would be so concerned with the needs of the tribe that he wouldn't spend the money on himself.

When the carriage came to a stop Walter quickly climbed down and rushed around the carriage to help Amanda out. His hands felt firm and confident as he placed them on her waist, even though Amanda had put out her hands, hoping he would take them instead.

Still, his touch on her was oddly disconcerting, and at first Amanda couldn't say why this was so. Clearly Walter hadn't been brutishly forward or even inappropriate in his attentions. Rather, he had touched her in a socially prescribed manner, in a way that

Amanda had been touched before by prospective suitors.

The instant her feet reached the ground, Amanda stepped straight back from Walter, though she didn't instantly turn away from him. She'd done that before with Hawk, and when she had her move unintentionally placed her breast into his hand. And that little mistake, however unintended, had led to caresses that were *not* unintentional, and led to lovemaking that was most certainly intentional, and satisfying to the nth degree.

"I'd like to thank you for this evening," Amanda said. "I've had a very entertaining time."

"Just entertaining?" Walter asked, following Amanda as she walked backward toward the front porch.

"Isn't entertaining enough?"

"It's good, but it isn't enough," Walter replied.

Amanda didn't like the tone he used. She couldn't say that he had been un-gentlemanly, but it was clear that he was hoping for something more from her than just a *thank you* for time and money spent.

Was that so much different than Hawk? Amanda asked herself.

Yes, Amanda amended a moment later. Perhaps she hadn't thought negatively at the time he was seducing her, but she did think nasty things of Hawk now that she was no longer under the influence of his erotic charm.

"What are you thinking of?" Walter asked, in step with Amanda as she turned around to reach the front porch.

"Nothing."

"Nothing?"

Amanda blushed slightly, wondering whether all men who had slept with several women had developed the ability to read the female mind. But she was making a terrible mistake by thinking about Hawk and Walter at the same time, by making any comparison of one to the other, she knew.

Give Walter a chance, Amanda decided. *He's a good man, and he's certain to treat you more respectfully than a certain Sioux warrior has.*

Amanda walked straight to the double front doors of the ranch house, then turned so that she faced Walter. She smiled up at him, a friendly smile that wasn't at all a come-on.

"Good evening, Walter," she said "I do want to thank you for this evening. I really have enjoyed myself."

"You have? I wouldn't have guessed," Walter said with a grin, placing his hands on Amanda's shoulders.

Amanda saw the kiss coming, and though her first instinct was to avoid it, her hope was that Walter—with his experience with women—would help her forget the Sioux warrior who'd been too much in her thoughts for too long.

She closed her eyes. When Walter's lips touched hers she waited for the quickening of her heart, for the rush of blood through her veins, for the heightened sensitivity to touch, to smell, to taste. She waited for all the things that had overwhelmed her with Hawk's kisses.

She waited…and waited…and waited.

And nothing happened.

The experience hadn't left her with a sense of revulsion, but though kissing Walter wasn't repulsive at all, it wasn't thrilling, either.

He pulled away finally and looked into Amanda's eyes. She didn't know what to say or do. She didn't want him to kiss her again, but she didn't want to shatter his hopes. More than anything, she wanted to get to her bedroom, get out of her dress and into her nightgown, and climb into her big, comfortable bed — the same bed she had wanted to share with Hawk, but hadn't because of circumstances that had been beyond her control.

"Amanda…" Walter began.

"Goodnight, Walter," Amanda said a bit apologetically, taking another step away from him.

Walter looked for a moment as though he were going to say something then went to his carriage. He didn't look back.

* * * *

Riding into Deadwood, Amanda got an eerie feeling, though she tried hard to dismiss it. This foreboding, she was convinced, could be attributed to the fact that the last time she'd come to Deadwood, she'd discovered Hawk jailed, beaten and utterly contemptuous of anyone who didn't have Sioux blood flowing in their veins.

For a moment she wondered whether Walter might have said anything bad about her after their evening together, but she dismissed this thought instantly. Walter was too much a gentleman to speak badly of a woman, and besides, even though the single kiss they'd shared hadn't started a fire, it wasn't as though Amanda had castigated him afterward for being a cur.

She did, however, feel the gaze of some of the people gathered along the boardwalk following her. Why were they watching her? This fear, as those before it, was put aside as Amanda realized people were gawking at what she was wearing — Levis, a man-cut cotton shirt, and a Colt strapped in a gun belt riding low around her hips. That was why the people were looking at her. It was the same reason they had for several years now.

Amanda rode more easily in the saddle after that. She'd long been the subject of discussion among the polite society of Deadwood because of her attire. Usually they spoke of her with some degree of sympathy, wondering why an attractive young woman, coming from a good family and with plenty of money behind her, would choose to dress and behave like a tomboy, when she could wear the finest gowns that money could buy.

By the time Amanda reached the sheriff's office she was feeling pretty good about herself. She might not have been appreciated by most of the citizens of Deadwood, but at least she was noticed by them. To Amanda's way of thinking, being scorned was infinitely better than being ignored.

She strolled through the front door of the sheriff's office and was surprised to see Darren Richards sitting behind his desk. His boots were up on the scarred desktop, and a cigarette dangled from his lips. He barely opened his eyes when Amanda first entered the room, though his lips did curl into a smile that made Amanda wary.

"You got my message." There was no courtesy in the sheriff's tone. "I like it when young gals do what they're told."

Amanda instantly felt her anger rising. "I got the message that the *deputy* wanted to see me. You may be the sheriff, but everybody knows the deputy is the only real law in this town," Amanda said. Then, when her gaze met the sheriff's, and she recalled Hawk's experience with him, she couldn't resist adding, "And now that I look real close, I see you aren't really much of a lawman, or even much of a man. Sheriff, I do believe you're not much of anything at all."

Sheriff Richards kicked his feet off the desk and bolted to his feet.

"You're in more trouble than you think," the sheriff warned.

"Trouble? I haven't done anything."

"So you say, but I've got a brother what's missing. He up and disappeared, and I've got a feeling that Injin I had locked up had something to do with it."

Amanda finally did step away from the sheriff. Would Hawk murder a man for no reason? She shook her head. "I don't know what your brother was doing, but if he picked a fight with Hawk, he made a big mistake. I've seen Hawk fight, Sheriff, and he isn't a man who loses."

"No stinkin' Injin could whip my brother and his drinkin' buddies in a fair fight!"

"How many of his friends did he bring along, Sheriff? Fair fight? Not likely. I'd say there wasn't anything fair about it at all, and still your brother ended up dead."

"Ain't nobody said he was dead. I said he was missing, that's all. Don't you go spreadin' rumors about my brother bein' dead."

Amanda heard the desperation and fear in Sheriff Richards' voice, but she could afford him no sympathy. Fair fight? He was the man who had beaten and kicked Hawk when his hands were cuffed behind his back. *That* was the kind of fair fight Sheriff Richards liked, and his brother was probably no different.

"I'm surprised you didn't go along with your brother." Amanda's lips curled with derision. "I've seen the way you fight, seen how brave you are when a man's hands are manacled behind his back. Were you afraid Hawk would come back for you? Did you *send* your brother after Hawk?"

Sheriff Richards's eyes became angry slits. He asked bitterly, "How well do you know that Injin? Sounds to me like you and he got yourselves *real* acquainted. That's what it sounds like, if you ask me."

"Well, I didn't ask you, Sheriff, and if you know what's good for you, you'll keep your damned opinions to yourself. If you start telling people lies about me, I swear I'll—"

"You'll what?" Sheriff Richards cut in, stepping forward so that he glared down at Amanda. "You're in big trouble, little lady. You had a criminal staying with you, and a judge might think you was aiding and abetting. That's against the law. Judge might even put you away for a couple of years for it."

Amanda's hand was also on her revolver. What angered her most was that the sheriff's insinuations were absolutely true. Amanda *was* closer to Hawk—or at least *had* been closer—than anyone knew, or that she would admit to.

"I think maybe you'd better start telling me everything you know about that redskin," Sheriff Richards said, his insolent gaze crawling over Amanda's bosom. "Maybe you're one of them girlies that likes the dark-skinned ones." He chuckled, then wiped saliva from his lips with the back of his hand. "Is that why you've always shied away from men at the dances and church socials? 'Cause they weren't the right color of skin?"

"You worthless pig," Amanda said in a softly venomous tone. She tried to make herself turn and walk out of the deputy's office. Why should she stand motionless and take the vicious man's insults? Still, inexplicably, she couldn't make her feet move. "You think the worst of everyone only because the worst is in you."

The sheriff laughed then, openly and scornfully. "Now I know you was spreadin' your legs for that Injin. Only a bitch that's spreadin' would—"

Amanda slapped him. Her right hand lashed out, as though it had a will of its own. When her palm connected with Sheriff Richards's cheek his head snapped around. When he looked at Amanda again his gun was in his hand and pointed at her chest.

"Assaulting an officer of the law's gonna put you in jail," he growled, thumbing back the hammer of his gun.

"Officer of the law? Hardly. You're just a criminal with a badge," Amanda replied.

But despite the brave front that she was showing the sheriff, there was fear in her heart. Whether he was a cretin or not, he was a duly appointed sheriff, whom she had assaulted. Amanda didn't doubt that her family connections could get her out of whatever trouble her temper had gotten her into, but she didn't need the trouble anyway.

"Git your hands up in the air." Sheriff Richards's eyes were bright with lust and hatred. "Git 'em up high 'cause I gotta search you for weapons before I lock you up."

The thought of Sheriff Darren Richards' hands on her body, touching and defiling her, jolted Amanda's senses. She turned on her heel and walked to the front door of the sheriff's office. Only after she had the door open, and she was standing where people out in the dusty street could see her, did she turn back toward the sheriff. She looked down the barrel of his revolver, knowing he wanted to shoot her, and that only the prospect of witnesses was stopping him.

"You want to arrest me, sheriff? Go ahead and try. But if you ever touch me, if you ever lay a finger on me, I swear I'll kill you."

Amanda was trembling with fear and rage as she climbed up into the saddle and turned Daisy back toward home. The threats that the sheriff had spoken rang in her mind, and though she tried to think of other things, she couldn't. The hatred, the foul lust, the twisted masculinity that Sheriff Darren Richards represented, made her want to rush to her bedroom, close and lock the door, and never come out.

Chapter Nineteen

Sonny — damn him straight to hell — is with his woman, whoever that happens to be.

Several things were absolutely clear to her at that moment. One was that all men were unworthy of her total trust. Another was that even a woman's brother, no matter how much he said he promised to be there for his sister, might be with his lover when his sister needed him. The third was that a horse was infinitely less likely than a man to disappoint a woman.

Even Amanda realized her line of thinking was convoluted.

Amanda paced through the long hallways of the ranch house, feeling restless, furious, and frustrated beyond anything she'd ever believed possible. The sheriff had enraged her. Most frightening of all was that Amanda realized that if she hadn't had the Wright name to back her up, if she hadn't the financial clout and a brother named Sonny who was willing to kill to protect her, she would have had to suffer through the despicable sheriff's mauling.

Suddenly Hawk's words, spoken long ago, came back to Amanda. Was it *really* so self-evident that her culture was vastly superior to his? Even though Hawk had the tendency to eat and love and live to excess when the opportunity was there, did that mean that his Sioux culture was vastly inferior to her own?

All that she'd been certain of was now subject to question.

Remembering her vision quest, Amanda went to her bedroom and, after pulling off her boots — what a hideous reminder of the constrictive society in which she lived — she sat in the middle of the bed, crossed her legs beneath her, and closed her eyes. Then she did something that she had never really done before.

Amanda let her thoughts travel aimlessly.

She simply thought, letting her mind move in whatever direction it wanted. Nothing more than that, no action taken whatsoever. All she did was sit alone in a perfectly dark room, close her eyes, and look inside herself for the answer to a question she didn't entirely understand and which she didn't completely comprehend.

Go to him.

The thought was so startling, was such a revelation, that Amanda's eyes snapped open.

Was she really to go to Hawk after all the things he had said to her, all the things she had said to him?

Go to him now.

For a moment Amanda wondered whether or not she was simply experiencing some after-effect of her vision quest, the one which had been only partially successful. Then Amanda realized that the direct influence of the quest had long since passed. Whatever thoughts going through her head now were a result of her own imagination.

Go to him, Amanda.

The voice sounded more clearly in her mind this time. What preparations would be necessary to go to Hawk? Two horses for riding, along with a packhorse. That would be the fastest method of getting to the Sioux camp.

She sat on the edge of her bed, tapping her toes lightly, nervously, against the floor. She wanted to go to Hawk. She knew that now, and accepted the reality of her desire. But did she dare go to him?

Sonny would be furious. Sonny liked Hawk, but not so much that he would turn a blind eye to an open affair. He would be angrier with her than with any of the other things that she'd done that had disappointed him in the past. And Vanessa would give her a lecture as well. Vanessa would tell Amanda how she was a Wright, and consequently was held up to standards that other people weren't, so she had to always bear that in mind before she acted impulsively.

If Amanda went to Hawk, she would disappoint her family, but if she stayed at the Circle S, she would disappoint herself. Which was more important?

As Amanda began changing her clothes, she decided that Daisy would be her primary riding horse. She'd leave the new cutting horse behind. Maybe Billy would have a name for her by the time she returned. And what food was on hand that she could take with her? The larder was always fully stocked.

Rushing around her room, gathering up some necessary travel items, Amanda asked herself, *If I ride as hard as possible, how long will it take me to reach the camp?*

* * * *

"You looked tired," Buttercup said, standing close to Amanda, a hand placed protectively on her shoulder.

"I am. Where's Hawk?" The words were out of Amanda's mouth without her thinking them through very carefully. She took a breath and said to Buttercup quietly, "I'm sorry. I don't mean to be abrupt. It's just that—"

"That you've ridden hard and fast from wherever you came to see Hawk, not me?" Buttercup patted Amanda's cheek lightly, a gesture more fitting coming from a grandmother than a girl still in her teens. "I understand. I'm just happy to see you again." Buttercup glanced away for a moment before looking back at Amanda. "Hawk's not here now. Since he came back from your home, he's had a difficult time. There have been accusations of disloyalty." Buttercup closed her eyes, clearly distressed with the lies that had been spoken about her brother. "It's all wrong, but the falsehoods hurt anyway. He's fasting now. Or perhaps he's already on his vision quest. He won't be back with us for a few days."

Amanda's shoulders suddenly sagged at the deflating news she'd received.

"He'll be back. I promise he will. Just give him a few days. And until he does, you'll have time to rest, get into clean clothes, make yourself pretty for him." Buttercup eased off Amanda's felt hat, giving her friend a smile of sympathy. "You love him, don't you? Only love could make a woman push herself as hard as you have."

In all the time Amanda had spent since leaving the Circle S in the dead of night, she'd never honestly asked herself that question. Now that Hawk's sister had put the question into words, she couldn't avoid it any longer, even if the answer frightened her.

"I don't really know," Amanda answered finally. "Sometimes I think I love him, but at other times I know for certain that I hate him. I know that doesn't make any sense but—"

"It makes perfect sense. Every woman hates the man she loves, at least a little bit, and at least some of the time."

Amanda's looked at Buttercup. After a long silence she said softly, "How did such a young woman become so wise?"

Buttercup shrugged her slender shoulders, her smile wide and guileless. "Would you like to try another vision quest?" she asked quietly. "You have far to go before you can completely understand the majesty of them."

Amanda nodded. "After I rest it would be good." Though the prospect of a vision quest was tantalizing, that wasn't the reason she'd ridden so hard to the Sioux camp.

* * * *

"Are you ready?" Buttercup asked.

Amanda looked down into the valley. She saw the camp, the children running and playing, and the women working. If she could see them, could they see her? *Ida Maka*, Mother Earth, wasn't ashamed of her nudity, Amanda reminded herself. Besides, from this distance she was little more than a pale speck against the foliage.

"If you don't want to go through with this, you don't have to," Buttercup said, kneeling on the buffalo hide where Amanda sat. She placed a protective hand on Amanda's shoulder. "A vision quest can be a frightening experience. The truth is not always pleasant."

Amanda shook her head as she patted the back of Buttercup's hand. "No, I'm not afraid of the vision. I just wish it wouldn't take so long."

Buttercup smiled. "Impatience is not a Sioux trait. Cross your legs now. Sit as I've told you. Close your eyes and then I will leave. I'll be back for you tomorrow."

Amanda angled her face toward the morning sun, closing her eyes. She crossed her legs and sighed, enjoying the warmth of the sun on her naked body. It didn't matter to her that neither Sonny nor Vanessa would ever understand what she was going through, or why. She hoped that the letter she'd written to Sonny before leaving the Circle S would give him some understanding of why it had been necessary for her to ride out in the dead of night to return to a people who were not her own.

She had not heard Buttercup walk away, but that didn't surprise her. Buttercup was very nearly as silent in her movements as Hawk was. Amanda wondered if she could ever learn to be so stealthy, and just how many traits of the Sioux she could adopt. Then she remembered that she wasn't supposed to be thinking at all, because conscious thoughts kept the visions from coming.

She inhaled deeply, feeling a sense of serenity pervading every pore in her body, touching and surrounding her with such bliss that her mouth curled into a smile. Blonde hair and pale skin be damned. She was becoming more and more of a Sioux all the time, she told herself.

* * * *

Red Wolf felt his anger rising. His hatred was so intense that he was on the verge of being nauseated. Despite the afternoon heat, he was alone in his tepee, his fists clenched into impotent weapons that lacked an object to strike out at, to beat down and punish.

Perspiration ran down from his forehead, stinging his eyes. He cursed, using foul, savage words, hating all gods and mortals alike. Surely everyone, even the gods, deserved to be punished for the cruel treatment that Red Wolf had received from Night Flower.

Two nights earlier, feeling his need for a woman continuously growing stronger, Red Wolf had sought out Night Flower. She was of an age now where she should choose a warrior, and her beauty made her a desirable Sioux maiden. Red Wolf knew in his heart that he alone was man enough to tame Night Flower's restless spirit.

On that night he had spotted her walking between several tepees, heading toward the perimeter of the camp. Sensing a sensual vulnerability on her part, Red Wolf followed her immediately. He asked himself how far he would go to convince the young woman to accept him, and even Red Wolf realized the answer depended upon whether anyone had witnessed him with Night Flower. If he got her alone in the darkness, far enough from camp so her screams would not be heard, then he would not have to stop, no matter how desperately she begged. And when he was finished, when his pent-up lust had poured forth, he would silence her forever. If the spirits were generous with him, the Cheyenne would be blamed for her death, or maybe the white man.

Night Flower had been walking purposefully. But when Red Wolf noticed her checking frequently behind herself, he realized she was doing something she shouldn't. His heart began to pound against his ribs in restless anticipation because he knew that if he caught the young woman doing something the tribal elders would not approve of, then he could demand the sexual satisfaction from her that he otherwise might have to take forcibly from her.

He'd been getting closer to Night Flower, moving farther away from the tribe's center of activity. Just seconds before Red Wolf was about to make his move, intending to rush forward and pounce upon her from behind, clamp a hand over her mouth, then carry her into the darkness, the worst possible thing happened. Night Flower stopped, looked around, and dashed into the sweat lodge. Red Wolf remembered Hawk was in the sweat lodge and so was certain that Night Flower knew that the sweat lodge was occupied, and by whom.

Standing alone in the darkness, his jaws clamped in rage, Red Wolf had stared at the sweat lodge, hatred blinding him to everything else. Why did Night Flower go to Hawk, when he already had so many other women wanting him?

Red Wolf's hand was clenched tightly around the handle of the long, deadly knife in the sheath at his hip. He thought of rushing into the sweat lodge and killing them both, but he worried that he might not be victorious even against an unarmed Hawk. Besides, he needed to disguise his crime of murder, not wanting to face the wrath of the elders. He determined it would be best to wait until Night Flower left the sweat lodge. He would force himself upon her, then kill her. He concocted a vague plan of blaming the girl's murder on Hawk. But as this general plan was forming in his mind, two braves walked by, pausing to look at him, their gaze questioning. At that point, Red Wolf knew that should anything bad happen to either Night Flower or Hawk as they came out of the sweat lodge, he would be suspected immediately.

Frustrated in both his desire for revenge and for brutal passion, he'd walked off into the night, vowing that the day would soon come when all his desires would be fulfilled, no matter how many people had to die.

Rising from his sitting position, shaking away thoughts of the recent past, Red Wolf now knew he had to leave his tepee. It was dreadfully hot, especially with the flap closed. His body glistened with sweat. When he stepped outside he squinted because of the brilliant sunlight. He waited several seconds for his eyes to adjust, then looked around at the camp.

To his left, working near their tepee, were two of Walking Elk's wives. When they saw him they snickered between themselves, making Red Wolf's anger grow just a little hotter, his desire for violence just a little more deadly.

What did they find so funny?

About to confront the women, Red Wolf felt a hand on his arm. He twisted sharply, shocked that anyone could walk up on him without being heard. Anger had blurred the sharp edge of his perceptions.

"Red Wolf acts like a guilty man," Dull Knife said, scrutinizing the young warrior. "Why is that? What have you done that makes you behave like a man whose guilt weighs heavily upon his shoulders?"

You pathetic old man.

"I think Dull Knife is mistaken," Red Wolf said finally, aware that the Sioux chieftain wouldn't leave until he'd received an answer.

"Perhaps. And perhaps Red Wolf knows that he has told lies about another warrior," Dull Knife countered, almost completely without emotion. "I have believed some of the tales you have told, and my belief is not to my honor. You spoke with such conviction. Such concern for your people rang in every word you spoke. But now I am wiser, and I see that you are perhaps more clever than I thought you to be. Are you a clever man, Red Wolf? Are you clever enough to destroy a man you hate with words when you cannot destroy him in battle?"

Red Wolf now was completely ill. Looking at Dull Knife, he saw the old man harbored more suspicions about him than just those he was willing to discuss. All of Red Wolf's lies, all the tawdry tales and veiled innuendo regarding Hawk's conduct and character, were now coming back to haunt him. He saw in Dull Knife's face the unraveling of his plan to destroy Hawk, which would have provided the opportunity for his own ascension in the tribe.

"Red Wolf is cunning to say nothing," the Sioux chieftain said. "It is words that have put his name in disfavor among the elders. Perhaps it will be silence that will make Red Wolf's name no longer sound like a curse."

Dull Knife walked away, having spoken his piece. Red Wolf stood frozen in place. How had the old man figured out that the stories he had told about Hawk weren't true? At first, when Red Wolf began telling them, the elders had listened carefully to everything he had said, and they had seemed to believe him. And now — this.

A brittle smile of contempt contorted Red Wolf's mouth. He knew that his desire to completely destroy

Hawk's reputation beyond salvage had caused him to tell stories that were beyond believability.

How long would it be before his own reputation was in rags? Red Wolf shuddered at the thought of no longer being feared by the young braves, no longer looked up to by the more gullible of the women in the tribe. Everything he had lived for was suddenly coming apart, and it was all because of Hawk and that golden-haired woman who had ridden into camp again just that morning, the one who looked at Red Wolf with such open scorn. If *she* had only given Red Wolf the passion due him, he wouldn't have had to destroy Hawk's reputation with lies.

Red Wolf walked without seeing where he was going. He was thinking about every insult, every scornful look he had ever received from a woman. All women are evil, he realized then. Every woman, white or Indian, was vile because she had the power to make a man crave her, then refuse to quench the desire she'd stoked.

They should all be punished, every single one, but the golden-haired woman and Night Flower would be the first to feel his wrath. They would receive the punishment they deserved for being women. And when Red Wolf was finished with them he'd move on to Buttercup.

She deserved punishment as well, though Red Wolf could not say exactly why.

Chapter Twenty

When Amanda was aware that she was no longer hungry or thirsty she felt certain her desire for a successful vision quest would be realized this time. As she lay naked on the buffalo mat beneath the stars, a sense of peace, of inner calm, came over her so slowly and completely that she wasn't at first aware of it.

It's happening. She recognized the words spoken inside her head, as clearly as if she'd spoken them aloud.

"Yes, it is happening. Welcome," an answering voice replied.

At first the sound of the voice startled Amanda, but she instantly saw the lovely doe of the earlier quest. There was little in her background that could prepare her for such an occurrence, but communicating with the doe now seemed as natural as eating or sleeping.

"I did not know if I would see you again."

"There is much you have to learn, much I have yet to teach you." The doe sent a sensation of love that filled Amanda's soul.

She asked, *"Will I ever learn everything?"*

The doe paused, her ears twitched, and her tail flicked. Amanda sensed that the animal was considering her answer. *"No,"* the doe finally answered. *"You will not learn everything, but no one ever does. When we have learned everything there is to learn then we will no longer have any need to be."*

"What can you teach me?" Amanda asked. The silence was intolerable now that she had finally made contact with the doe.

"Patience is one thing I will teach you," the doe replied. *"You must learn that before you can learn anything else."*

Amanda understood that she had been told that her impatience wasn't a good thing. She had promised herself a dozen times that she would learn to be more patient, though she'd never really meant to keep the promise. This time she suspected it would be different.

"What else must I learn?" Amanda inquired.

The doe raised her head swiftly, looking away. Amanda saw that the doe was always cautious—aware of her surroundings and the dangers that might be lurking just out of sight—yet she didn't seem continually edgy. How could she exhibit a perpetual awareness of the dangerous world she lived in but no intrinsic fear of that world? This, too, Amanda realized, was a lesson she would do well to learn.

"As important as learning is un-learning. You know in your heart what is right for you. Listen to your heart. That is where you will find the truth. But your truth will be tested often. Love will help you through those tests. Believe in yourself. Listen to your heart. But if you seek the truth, you must know that there is a cost."

Instantly, all of Amanda's fears came to the fore. She'd long believed that everything had a price, that nothing was truly free. She was profoundly disappointed to discover that this encounter, this vision quest, also had a price that she must pay.

She asked, *"What must I pay?"*

"You will learn that in time," the doe instructed. *"Listen to your heart. It is in your heart that you live, and it is a voice from the heart that will keep your love alive."*

There was a rustle in the bushes, and Amanda looked but couldn't see what had caused the noise. When she turned her mind's eye back to the doe all she saw was the animal's white tail as she leaped lightly between two trees and disappeared into the woods.

* * * *

Amanda came out of her meditation and sat up, crossing her arms over herself, instantly self-conscious of her nudity. But when she looked around the hillside she affirmed that she was alone and had been undisturbed throughout the night.

To the east, the first rays of morning sunlight were just showing pink and yellow on the horizon. Amanda pushed fingers through her hair, smoothing it away from her forehead. She rose slowly to her feet and stretched her arms over her head, working the tightness out of her muscles.

She had thought that if her vision quest had been successful, she would feel overjoyed, as though she wanted to celebrate. But now that she'd had her vision, she didn't feel overjoyed. That was too much of a surface emotion to truly express her feelings. Even now, as she looked far down into the valley at the Sioux encampment, she could remember everything that the doe had said to her, each little morsel of wisdom, along with the word puzzle that she'd left with Amanda.

"A voice from the heart will keep your love alive."

That could mean any number of things, Amanda realized. But she wasn't afraid. She refused to feel fear. Furthermore, the doe had given her words of wisdom that she would be foolish not to follow. She walked around slowly, enjoying the feeling of the grass beneath her bare feet. She didn't go without her boots often enough, she decided. Looking back at the camp, she saw several thin spirals of smoke coming from the morning campfires. The people moving about were just specks in the distance, but Amanda felt a little uneasy looking at them while she was naked.

I am with Ida Maka, she remembered, as all uneasiness vanished completely. She wiggled her bare toes into the grass and rolled her head slowly around her shoulders, turning to warm herself in the morning's pleasing sunlight. *There is no reason for me to hide or be ashamed when I am alone and at one with Mother Earth.*

Her clothes were hanging from a limb of a tree nearby, but Amanda felt no need to go to them. For a moment she considered returning to the camp instead of waiting for Buttercup, but she dismissed this as impatience. She would wait for Buttercup, and together they would return to the camp. Amanda considered that her first lesson in patience.

* * * *

When Hawk stumbled it took several steps before he completely regained his balance. His legs were weak, and exhaustion weighed upon him as though he carried a boulder on his shoulders.

He'd gone three days and two nights without food or water. After purging his soul in the sweat lodge he'd gone to speak with Dull Knife, who had suggested a vision quest. Hawk had walked alone into the hills, where he'd danced and chanted until he dropped exhausted to the ground. The visions came to him, one after another, each one more powerful and cryptic, more mysterious and enlightening, than the one before it.

He'd never before had visions so powerful, nor had he pushed himself so hard to receive them. His mouth was hideously dry, and even when he ran his tongue around his lips he couldn't moisten them. There was simply no more saliva left in him. And though he had always tended to be gaunt, his leanness was heightened greatly from his fasting, his ribs displayed the muscles in his stomach, shoulders and chest in stark relief. Only the inherited darkness of his skin kept the remainder of the bruises from being visible.

Hawk had hoped that the visions would bring him peace, would return to him the clarity of thought he'd known prior to Amanda's entrance into his life. But the visions hadn't brought him peace of mind, though they had given him understanding. For that reason, he was enormously grateful for Dull Knife's firm insistence that he go on a quest.

The understanding Hawk found was to put the memory of his mother, and the bitterness she had brought to them both, behind him. He had to bury the bitterness as a man would bury a deceased love one and, once buried, never speak of it again. Only then, by burying his anger, would he be able to look forward to the future with unclouded eyes. If he continued to cling to his anger, he'd never see the beauty of *Ida Maka* surrounding him, nor would he see the beauty in the people who populated his world. His past, he realized, was still painfully with him.

The visions had taught him something else. It was that Amanda wasn't to be blamed for what his mother had done. Amanda was white, wealthy, and rebellious, just as Hawk's mother had been. But that was where the similarities ended. For Hawk to blame Amanda for his mother's transgressions would be as irrational as Amanda blaming Hawk for her father's absence in her life.

Hawk made his way back to the tribe. So engrossed was he that he didn't notice Red Wolf striding purposefully to intercept him at the outer edge of the encampment.

"Why have you not run away like your coward friend Crow?" Red Wolf taunted aggressively.

Looking up, Hawk said nothing at first. It was obvious his old enemy was spoiling for a fight, and though Hawk might have welcomed the opportunity to give Red Wolf the beating he so richly deserved, he knew that he was now too weakened by hunger, thirst and sleep-deprivation to successfully battle Red Wolf.

"I am no coward, Red Wolf, and you know it," Hawk replied.

He spoke much more softly than his enemy. There were several young maidens nearby, and Hawk knew how impressionable they could be. He had no desire to make himself look weak in front of them, nor did he want to do anything that would make Red Wolf appear strong and manly.

"I am tired," Hawk continued. "Go away now. If you must talk to me, speak when I am not recently arrived from a vision quest."

Hawk started walking again, but Red Wolf moved to cut off his path. A dull ache began in Hawk's stomach, and he felt as he had when his hands had been manacled behind his back and Sheriff Darren Richards had been about to beat him.

"You have called me a liar," Red Wolf said, speaking louder than before.

The youngest of the maidens in camp, he had learned, were the most likely to be easily impressed with overt displays of strength. Hawk was a most formidable warrior, as everyone in the tribe knew, and to defeat him in front of young maidens would make Red Wolf appear virile, superior, manly.

"That is an offense that you must answer for. What have you to say for yourself?" Red Wolf demanded.

When Hawk looked into Red Wolf's eyes what he saw there frightened him. He'd always thought that Red Wolf was an evil man, but a man nevertheless. Now, when he looked into Red Wolf's eyes, he saw nothing at all, not even the slightest spark of humanity.

"You are an evil thing," Hawk whispered, shocked that he had not truly understood before how vile the man was.

Red Wolf nodded subtly so that only Hawk saw the movement. The slight curl to his lips was identical to that of a rabid hound who had taken to killing for pleasure. Though Red Wolf's one hand lay on the haft of his knife, the other hand ever so slightly motioned Hawk closer, daring him to try to return to the tribe.

"You are a very brave man," Hawk whispered sarcastically, calculating his odds of winning in a fight against Red Wolf.

He did not like his chances. He wore only a loincloth and moccasins, and he did not even have his knife with him. And, of course, he had been badly weakened by the vision quest. Red Wolf had none of these disadvantages. Even under the best of circumstances, Red Wolf was a formidable foe. Hawk doubted he had any chance at all of surviving a fight, especially not a knife fight.

"But you are only brave," Hawk noted, "when I am very weak. Isn't that so, you spawn of a maggot?"

Red Wolf chuckled hatefully. He knew who his parents were, even though he did not respect them.

"Brave talk for a bastard," he replied. "Do you even know who your father is? Your mother spread her legs with every warrior whose path she crossed."

The words bit into Hawk's heart, and their truth burned inside him. He glanced quickly at the young maidens standing nearby, wondering whether or not they thought Red Wolf was somehow heroic for what he was doing now. He wanted to lash out at Red Wolf, seeing him for the menace he represented to the tribe as a whole and to the women nearby who did not understand the extent of his immorality.

"Be a warrior," Hawk challenged, looking Red Wolf straight in the eyes. "Meet me in one day. Just the two of us. We'll settle our hatred with fists or with knives, whatever you choose."

Red Wolf shook his head slowly, and he took a step closer to Hawk. "What did you call me, bastard of a white whore?" he shouted, making sure that the maidens could hear.

A wave of revulsion swept over Hawk. Though he realized that Red Wolf required all his attention, he could not resist glancing over at the women tanning elk and deer hides. All they had heard was Red Wolf's incensed declaration that he had been insulted, and even though Red Wolf's reputation had already been besmirched throughout the tribe, the young women now regarded him as a brave man willing to stand up to a hero of the tribe to defend his own name and honor.

"Death would be too merciful for the likes of you," Hawk said under his breath.

Red Wolf attacked without warning, lashing out with his right fist then his left, striking Hawk rapidly in the jaw and cheek. Hawk staggered backward but did not drop to his knees, as he was certain Red Wolf had wanted. He braced himself for Red Wolf's next attack, but it did not come. Though hatred and rage begged for Hawk to rush his enemy, logic told him that he was too weak to fight effectively.

"You are a smart man," Red Wolf said loudly, turning and grinning triumphantly at the maidens who were watching in rapt attention. "You know when you are not man enough, and you shrink away like a gopher to his hole. Run away now, little man, or I will step on you."

"You vile maggot," Hawk replied. He no longer cared if he was defeated in battle. He could not listen to such insults without responding.

"You two disgrace the ground you walk on," Dull Knife interrupted, stepping forward, and even though he did not raise his voice, his words had the impact of gunshots.

Red Wolf walked away immediately. Hawk stood there, all but quivering with rage, forced to face the angry Sioux elder.

"Did you think he was worth your anger? Was Red Wolf sufficient to make you want to disgrace yourself?" Dull Knife asked, shaking his head slowly. "Do not allow such a warrior to force you into behaving as badly as he," the elder continued, his tone softening. "If you had fought and won, you would not have impressed anyone but those maidens, and they are too young to truly know anything at all. That is why we as elders do not allow them into a warrior's tepee."

"Yes, Dull Knife." Hawk's voice cracked with his disgrace. He was not angry with the elder, only with himself for allowing himself to be manipulated into precisely the disadvantageous position Red Wolf had wanted.

"The golden-haired maiden has returned," Dull Knife announced. When Hawk took a step toward camp the elder placed a firm hand on the young warrior's shoulder to stop his progress. "You are weak, hungry, thirsty. If you saw her now, you would impress her as little as you impressed Red Wolf. Think through your actions before you make them, Hawk, and you will be a leader among your people rather than just a lone hunter the squaws long to hold."

Hawk was shocked at the candor with which Dull Knife spoke. Did the old man know all of his secrets?

"Go now, and do not see the golden-haired maiden yet," the elder said sternly. "She has traveled far and fast to see you. Do you want her to see you as you are now?"

Hawk almost began to thank Dull Knife but then silenced himself. He knew that the older man didn't want to receive any compliments.

"I accept your wisdom, old one," Hawk replied finally, each word ringing with respect. "In time, if the spirits look kindly upon me, I will see *Ida Maka*, our people, and myself, as clearly as you do."

Though he wanted greatly to rush to Amanda, Hawk walked away, believing Dull Knife's wisdom was worth following.

Moving slowly toward his tepee, Hawk rubbed the side of his face, testing the swelling that Red Wolf's fists had caused. Despite this, a smile creased his mouth. Amanda had returned to him, and though Red Wolf had undoubtedly impressed several very young maidens, he had embarrassed himself in front of Dull Knife. The maidens would soon forget the incident. Dull Knife never would, and neither would Hawk.

There would come a day when Hawk would seek his revenge, and when that time came he would be as merciless as Red Wolf had shown himself to be.

* * * *

Amanda slowly dressed in her Levis and cotton shirt. She wished she had Buttercup's old dress, even though it was too small for her. Now that she was among the Sioux again, she wanted to be dressed like them.

Amanda was putting on her boots when she felt something in the breast pocket of her shirt. Straightening, she reached inside, and even before she saw what the pocket held she began to smile. Extracting an oblong quartz crystal, she then turned it over slowly in her hand, watching the way it reflected the early morning sunlight.

"My power stone." She closed her fingers gratefully around the crystal.

Closing her eyes, she uttered a small thanks to whatever powers had given her the stone. She still didn't know exactly what to believe about Sioux spirituality, but her mind had opened now. Nothing limited her thoughts, feelings, or perceptions.

"Good morning," Buttercup called, walking into the clearing, leading Daisy and another horse with her.

Beaming, Amanda waved at Buttercup, who returned a knowing smile.

"You had a vision!" Buttercup exclaimed. Amanda triumphantly held up the crystal between her forefinger and thumb. Suddenly, sunlight reflected through the crystal, causing a rainbow to form across her chest. "And there is your natural name," Buttercup said confidently. "Rainbow Heart is what you will be called among the Sioux."

"I like it," Amanda replied. She rolled the name over in her mind, listening to the music of the words. Rainbow Heart. Sonny would never understand it, and neither would Vanessa, but the truth of the name was so clear to Amanda that she wanted to sing it out to all the world.

"You'll be happy to know that Hawk has returned to camp from his own vision quest," Buttercup said. "He's sleeping now. Or maybe he's still eating. It was a very difficult quest for him. He's lost a great deal of weight. It will take some time for him to recover completely."

Amanda managed to contain her joy at the news. She was disturbed to hear that the vision quest had been so much more arduous for Hawk than for herself. "But he'll be all right soon?"

Buttercup nodded. "Better than ever, I should think. I didn't have much time to talk with him, but I could tell that he had learned much in the quest. He was going to speak with Dull Knife about it."

"Am I expected to speak with the elder?"

Buttercup shook her head.

"I'm famished." Amanda walked toward Daisy. "Will there be anything to eat when we return to camp?"

"Yes. And your belongings have been put into my tepee," Buttercup said. "Hawk will have to sleep elsewhere."

* * * *

Hawk brought the gourd to his lips and drank deeply. He felt strong and clean, inside and out. After sleeping for several hours he'd filled his stomach with venison stew. Each mouthful made him feel stronger.

The memory of what Red Wolf had said continued to haunt Hawk, though he was trying to push the incident aside. Since Red Wolf was more of an animal than a man, Hawk now realized, it was absurd for him to worry about anything the man said. Logic told him this, but his masculine pride had always sought to defend his name and honor. He wanted to seek out Red Wolf and give him a well-deserved thrashing.

Night Flower approached him. When Hawk's gaze met hers she smiled at him. "Did you enjoy the stew?" she inquired as, shyly, she knelt beside him. "I made it myself."

"You will make a proud brave fat if he is not careful," Hawk joked, and Night Flower's smile brightened.

"Someday," the young girl replied. "But I will wait until I am certain that I am ready to be a brave's wife." She took the empty bowl and gourd from Hawk, and though her fingers lingered briefly against his during the exchange, she was no longer trying to seduce him. "You are a kind man," she whispered, aware that there were many people near as she spoke. "What I did —"

"Shhh," Hawk replied. "You must not be embarrassed at what you did. I was flattered then, and I am flattered now. But you were not ready for a warrior then, and you are not now. When you are ready you will know it in your heart, and you will look into the eyes of a good and decent brave who will hunt often to see that you are never without food. He will teach your male children to be good braves."

"That will happen?" Night Flower's eyes were wide.

Hawk nodded, and Night Flower walked away with the empty wooden bowl and gourd. As he watched her go, he felt pleased with the way he'd handled her intrusion into his sweat lodge. He'd done the proper and manly thing, yet had not tarnished Night Flower's self-esteem as he denied her passionate request.

Hawk rose to his feet. It felt good to wear nothing but Sioux clothing, he decided. The moccasins, loincloth, and elk-hide vest did not constrict his movements. There would be no buckskin trousers for him while he was in camp, he decided, and no revolver in the holster, either. He would still carry the prized revolver with him only when he left the safety of the tribe.

Out of the corner of his eye he noticed Night Flower talking to Kahlia and Shining Lake. Shining Lake was a shy maiden a year older than Night Flower, and Kahlia, her older sister, was a widow. Hawk noticed Kahlia and Shining Lake look in his direction, then confer quietly between themselves. Hawk knew they were talking about him, and he wondered what it would be like to accept both sisters as wives. Neither woman was terribly attractive, though not hideous to look at, both would make wonderful mothers, and neither would cause disgrace to a warrior, or to his family.

A grin tugged at Hawk's sensual mouth as he considered the irony of going so long without taking a wife, then taking two of them at the same time. He heard soft laughter coming from the trio of women. Now he was certain they were talking about him.

Perhaps Night Flower had even confessed to her friends what she had done, and how Hawk had responded. Kahlia, whose husband had died in battle the previous winter, was experienced enough to give the younger women advice about warriors, and what a woman should expect from a brave. Where Shining Lake looked away the instant Hawk's gaze touched her, Kahlia looked back at him boldly, and the smile that touched her lips was a subtle invitation.

Hawk was happy to be thinking of a woman other than Amanda, and especially pleased to be thinking of women in the plural again. After Amanda had intruded into his life she'd taken over all his thoughts, been the center of all the romantic and libidinous urges that were so much a part of his nature.

As Hawk walked on, he fantasized about Kahlia and Shining Lake and the kind of life he could expect to have with them. The smile that had tickled his lips suddenly vanished. He couldn't make up for Amanda's loss with two women, or even three or four.

"Damn her," Hawk whispered, unconsciously slipping back into English when he thought of the blue-eyed vixen who had turned his thoughts, his life, even his sense of identity, upside down.

It was foolish to hold Amanda responsible, the rational part of Hawk's brain knew, for the life his own mother had led. This epiphany had made her seem less threatening. Nevertheless, he also had decided that only a Sioux woman should be his wife. A golden-haired woman bearing his children would carry the blame for seducing him from his lifelong goal: a tepee filled with Sioux children, who would bear Sioux grandchildren, with the stain of white blood eventually eradicated. To deviate from that goal now would be to allow his passions to control his life. Hawk wouldn't allow that to happen.

Though Amanda had been in camp for a day and a half, Hawk had not seen or talked to her. Now he was searching for her, though only a moment earlier he hadn't been completely aware of it. He walked purposefully, his head high, his shoulders squared, the confusion and doubt that had plagued him completely gone. He knew exactly what he expected of himself, and what the tribe expected of him. This certainty of purpose gave him confidence, and allowed him to seek out Amanda without fear that her physical attractiveness would melt his resolve.

First he would deal with the reason she'd returned to the tribe. He would handle her as gently and painlessly as he had Night Flower. He would explain why he and Amanda could never see each other again.

Once he'd finished with Amanda, he'd search out Red Wolf and beat him into unconsciousness. Hawk would suffer the punishment the tribe elders deemed necessary and appropriate for the aggressive offense, but Red Wolf *had* to answer for his insults. Hawk was strong and rested and had eaten well, now he demanded justice.

At last his mind and his body were in an accord he hadn't known since the first time he'd kissed Amanda.

He spotted Amanda standing beside Buttercup outside his tepee. She was wearing a Sioux dress that fit her perfectly. Her hair was a golden spray of color cascading over her shoulders, in beautiful disarray. Her legs were long and lovely, bare to above the knee, her feet encased in beaded moccasins.

When she noticed that Hawk had stopped dead in his tracks at the sight of her, she smiled at him. She did not rush into his arms, as he'd expected her to.

Any woman riding that far to see a man ought to at least run to him when she finally saw him, Hawk thought. The trouble was, Amanda wasn't just any woman. In fact, as he was continually surprised to discover, she wasn't like any woman he'd ever known in his life.

To Hawk's frustration she was, at that moment, more appealing than she'd ever been before. Her poise, combined with her own distinct beauty and enhanced by Sioux clothing, distorted his thoughts and conspired in the blink of an eye to make him forget his carefully planned speech—the one that would send Amanda on her way back home.

A thousand different things struck Hawk about Amanda at that moment, but most of all it was her serene smile and the blue of her eyes, brighter, more beguiling, than he had remembered. The sight of her caused the breath to catch in his chest, and even though he was a warrior too experienced in matters of the flesh to be rendered mute and breathless by the sight of a woman, that was precisely what had happened.

Damn. Damn.

"You're here," he said, glancing at his sister.

"Yes, I've come to see you," Amanda replied, looking up into Hawk's face with an expression unfamiliar to him.

She had changed, Hawk could tell, though he couldn't say how.

"Are you feeling better? I understand your vision quest was rather arduous," Amanda said. "You pushed yourself very hard…but then, you always do, don't you?"

Hawk didn't recognize Amanda's tone of voice. It was calm, confident, unusually mature, and definitely poised. Boyishly, he would much rather have had her giddy with excitement at seeing him. He tried to remember the vicious things she'd said to him at her ranch, but he couldn't think of a single cruel remark she'd ever made. Only the sound of her soft, passionate sighs as they made love came to mind. Then he remembered the scent of her hair as he held her head lightly on his shoulder, and that intoxicating look she would give him when she was eager to put an end to their love play, when nothing would satisfy her but Hawk's thrusting, all-consuming passion.

"Amanda went on a vision quest," Buttercup announced. "You can tell it was successful just by looking at her, can't you?"

"I can tell," Hawk agreed. Then, as a flicker of memory reminded him of his original resolve, he added, "Please, Buttercup, Amanda and I have to be alone now. There's much that we must discuss."

Buttercup pouted, turning her eyes toward Amanda for support. When she saw none forthcoming, she turned and walked slowly away.

"She's a lovely girl," Amanda said once Buttercup had gone. "It surprises me how mature she is, how much of life she understands at such an early age. I wish I could say as much for myself at that age."

Hawk still felt disoriented standing alone before Amanda.

He couldn't think of a single thing he'd intended to tell her. Again he was aware of being watched by the women, young and old, who were paying close attention now that Amanda had returned to the tribe.

"Yes, Buttercup is lovely, but she's also impulsive." Hawk searched for an appropriately stern tone. "She shouldn't have taught you about vision quests. Whose clothes are you wearing? They are not Buttercup's."

"No, they're not. I don't know who they belong to. Someone kind, I'm sure. I've met so many very kind people since I've been here."

"You must leave." Hawk forced the cold words out of his mouth. Amanda's calm implacability had become a threat to him, particularly since his own emotions were anything but calm. "I'm sorry if you've ridden all the way here from your ranch, but you've got to go, Amanda. You can't stay."

"And why is that?" When she looked him straight in the eye it was Hawk who turned away.

"Amanda, I must take a Sioux wife. I must. Just as you must find some rich white rancher to marry."

Amanda shook her head slowly, her eyes on Hawk. "No, I don't have to do that. In fact, I don't have to do anything I don't want to. That's more than you can say, isn't it, Hawk?"

"Don't try to make me angry, Amanda. My mind's made up. There are forces stronger than either of us that are at work here. We can't fight those forces and hope to win."

"You may be without hope, but I am not, Hawk. I've never given up on anything. Not on myself. Not on you...and not on us." She smiled, as though she knew something that Hawk could never truly understand. "You're afraid, Hawk. That's why you're saying these things. You're letting your fears make you behave stupidly."

Hawk tried to not scowl. No Sioux warrior who had repeatedly been in battle with armed enemies could listen to such words from a woman without reacting negatively. "Afraid? Was I afraid when I returned to the Cheyenne and stole their horses? Was I afraid when I went back to them a second time to take back your saddle from them?"

"You are brave and strong when your enemy is a man who wants to kill you, but when you are confronted by a woman who only wants to love you, then you *are* afraid, my darling. There is no other word for it."

Hawk looked skyward and muttered, "Buttercup never should have taken this blue eyes to my *Hookah*. It has twisted her mind."

Amanda sputtered with anger. "*Hookah?* That's a sacred space, Hawk. You thought I didn't know, but I do. Buttercup taught me. I even had my vision quest—the first one, anyway—where you had your first one. I've got a natural name now, and there's nothing you can say that will change that. I've been to your *Hookah*. I've experienced it as my own sacred space, and even your stubbornness cannot take that away from me."

Amanda stepped closer to Hawk. He felt the gazes of the people nearby upon him, and it wasn't a comfortable feeling.

"I will learn your language, Hawk," she said, "just as you have learned mine. And I will learn the ways of the Sioux, just as you have learned the ways of the white man."

"Perhaps," Hawk said, "but I *am* both Sioux and white. The blood of both flows in my veins. You cannot say the same."

"You hate the blood that flows in your veins, Hawk Two Feather," Amanda replied. "You dishonor it by wishing the white blood was not a part of you. Isn't that true, Hawk? How can a man have peace in his heart when he hates what is a part of himself?"

"I don't have to listen to this," Hawk snapped, furious now that Amanda wasn't flustered.

He'd spent much of his adolescent, and all of his adult life, able to charm women, able to control conversations with them so that the discussions went wherever he wanted them to go, centered on the topics that he desired. With Amanda he could do neither.

"Such a *brave* man," Amanda whispered, drawing out the damning word.

"If you were a warrior…" Hawk countered, his huge hands balled into fists that would have frightened anyone but Amanda.

"If I were a warrior," Amanda replied, an incendiary emotion flaring in her blue eyes, "you wouldn't be so helplessly in love with me."

Chapter Twenty-One

Hawk was walking, and walking fast. He'd begun moving away from Amanda when he didn't know what to reply to her utterly infuriating statement.

He couldn't really love her, could he? What madness it was that she'd spoken such words.

His eyes were cast down as he walked, and he did not respond when he heard a brave call his name. He did not want to speak to anyone until he could determine whether Amanda was the most tempting liar ever to walk *Ida Maka*, or whether she spoke a truth that he could not bear to hear.

Hawk wanted to talk with Crow. His trusted friend was well versed in the ways of women and, in addition, was very wise. But Crow was still in Fargo. Hawk's mental agitation couldn't wait until Crow returned to the camp. He needed to discuss his problems with someone else, only the venerable Dull Knife was available to provide wisdom and guidance.

He found the Sioux chieftain sitting with several other elders, nibbling on sweet berries, sharing stories of better times for the tribe, when the buffalo herds were vast and roamed far.

"May I speak with you, Dull Knife?" Hawk asked. "I seek your wisdom."

The elder's wizened face creased into a proud, knowing smile. "You do not seek my wisdom, you seek your own. What you want is for me to make wisdom easy for you to find."

Though Hawk grinned, he was still not in a good mood.

"As usual, you are more than correct," he said. He knew that if he did not tell the whole truth to Dull Knife, he would be lying to himself as much as to the elder. The two men walked far enough to find privacy for their discussion. Then Hawk said, "The golden-haired woman is troubling me, and I cannot say exactly why. When I went on my vision quest I saw many things, had many questions answered. I saw in my visions that I must stop troubling myself with thoughts of Amanda, that I must forget her."

"*Forget* her, or stop *troubling* yourself with her?"

"I do not understand."

The old man smiled. "That is why you are here. Now think about my question. Think about your vision. Are you to stop troubling yourself with her, or to forget her?"

"The two would be the same, wouldn't they?"

"Hawk, I know that your life has been a difficult one. You have searched for a people you could call your own, and I do not know if you have completely accepted the Sioux as your people."

When Hawk started to defend his loyalty to the tribe he was silenced by an upraised hand.

"In some ways our people have been as unkind to you as the blue-eyes have," Dull Knife continued. "You think you can become of pure blood if you have a wife whose skin is dark, and who will give you children who are darker than yourself." The old man smiled at Hawk's expression. "Do not look so surprised. We have talked of you often at the council of elders. We have seen you grow into a worthy warrior, and we know when you are invited into a woman's tepee. The council of elders has not always been proud of you, Hawk. You are strong and handsome, and the words you say please the maidens…but you have not taken a wife, have you?"

Hawk looked away for a moment, wondering if he'd made a mistake by speaking with the Sioux leader. He had not really been seeking advice, he now realized. Rather, he'd hoped Dull Knife would agree with him when he said that any lingering involvement with Amanda would be a mistake.

"No, I have not taken a wife," Hawk admitted. "I have not found the right woman, I suppose."

The old man rarely smiled, but his lips curled at the corners. "If that is true, it is not because you have not *tried.* How many women *have* you enjoyed?"

Hawk gave Dull Knife a look of incredulity. He would not answer this question, and he was shocked that he was even asked it. Then he saw the expression on the old man's face, and discovered, much to his surprise, that the elderly man possessed a sense of humor and was enjoying himself at Hawk's expense. Then, even Hawk couldn't resist smiling, actually enjoying being on the receiving end of a friendly joke.

"When a man searches and searches and cannot find, then he is either not searching honestly, or he is searching where what he seeks cannot be found." Putting his hand on Hawk's shoulder, Dull Knife looked up into his eyes. "You have not had an easy life, young one. You seldom choose the easy path to follow. Perhaps the spirits have chosen a difficult path for you, perhaps you have chosen that difficult path yourself. It matters not. What matters is that you live in harmony with *Ida Maka* and with yourself. The golden-haired girl, you think, will bring disgrace to you because her skin is white. But her blood is red, the same as yours and mine," Dull Knife explained. "From what I have heard, the vision quest she experienced was as though the blood of the Sioux flowed in her veins. Do not, yourself, be so much like the white man that you blind yourself. Will hating her make you a more powerful warrior? Answer that question for yourself, and then you will know the path that you must follow."

"Yes, Dull Knife, I will do as you suggest," Hawk said.

But he was not content, his heart and soul not at ease. The words that he'd heard were ones he hadn't wished to hear. He had expected Dull Knife, who had fought many wars against the white man, to warn that Amanda was tempting but dangerous, both for himself and for the tribe. Instead, the wise elder had suggested that Hawk let his heart guide him, rather than his lifelong prejudice.

Confused, yet wanting desperately to be considered an honorable Sioux warrior, Hawk thanked Dull Knife once again for his time and his wisdom and walked away. Never was a proud and noble warrior, he thought, so adrift between two cultures, neither of which accepted him completely. For once in his life, not only was Hawk Two Feather unsure of what was expected of him by his tribe, he no longer had any real certainty of what he expected of himself.

* * * *

Hawk sat alone, leaning back against the base of a tree, looking at the tepees in the valley below. He chewed on a piece of pemmican and sipped from a skin of cool water. Though his eyes were open, he saw nothing at all. His mind had traveled back to the recent vision quest, and to the strange and tantalizing scenes that had unfolded before him.

What had they meant? There had been an eagle in a hawk's nest, and he'd seen the eagle and hawk together in other places several times during the course of his visions. But what did it mean?

Hawk considered how angry he'd become when Dull Knife had chosen to be cryptic rather than enlightening. Or perhaps Dull Knife was just trying to be annoying by not giving Hawk the answers he sought.

No, Dull Knife is not cruel just to be cruel. He speaks, and when he speaks, he teaches. Whether I learn from his teaching is up to me. I must find the answer that cannot be given to me.

Since Dull Knife's intention had not been to make Hawk angry, it had to have been to teach him something...but what?

Never before in his life had Hawk felt as though he was being attacked from all sides by an enemy he couldn't see or understand. Red Wolf had challenged and insulted him in front of the maidens when Hawk had been physically incapable of defending himself. Later, he had been thoroughly prepared to tell Amanda that he had no room in his life for her. Rather than the histrionics for which Hawk had prepared himself, Amanda had calmly and confidently called him a coward and said he didn't know what he was talking about. And lastly, when he sought out sage advice from Dull Knife, certain that the Sioux chieftain would proclaim that only a Sioux maiden would truly be worthy of a warrior, Hawk had been given a totally different view of the problem.

An eagle in a hawk's nest. But there was something else in the vision. What was it? During the vision something that had seemed perfectly natural at the time had appeared to Hawk, but now he realized it as something meant to teach him. But what had it been?

After he'd relaxed for a while the image came back to him. As it unfolded, it struck him as being profoundly odd. Was his memory of it accurate? An eagle in a hawk's nest. And there, just peeking up over the rim of the nest, was a young dove…

What did the vision mean?

Instinctively, Hawk began moving away from the base of the tree, twisting sharply on his knees, all his senses knife-blade keen even before he realized why he had moved at all.

Red Wolf, who had been approaching him from the high side of the hill, stopped short.

"Attacking from behind?" Hawk spit the words out with venom. "I expected no less from you."

Having already risen to his feet, Hawk wished he had his revolver with him. How he wanted to shoot Red Wolf down like a rabid animal! Hawk flexed his arms and legs, testing his strength, hoping he had regained enough to withstand this formidable foe. Without even a knife, he felt naked.

Red Wolf approached slowly, gauging how much strength had actually returned to the warrior who'd been his enemy for too many summers, too many winters.

"I came here to be with *Ida Maka*." Hawk watched Red Wolf's every movement. "Why are you here?"

"You scurried away from me before, when I could not follow you," Red Wolf taunted, inching forward.

As he walked, he put his hand on the haft of his long, deadly knife. He smiled.

"I don't intend to kill you, Hawk. That wouldn't accomplish what I desire." He laughed softly for a moment. "I want to crush you, to batter that beautiful face with my fists until it is no longer beautiful. Then I want to show the women your ugliness." He inhaled deeply, the let his breath out with a long, slow sigh. "I will show the women my supremacy. They will finally know how inferior you are to me."

"Do you expect me to run?" Hawk asked.

"No, Hawk," Red Wolf finally answered. "I expect you to bleed."

Hawk had known that Red Wolf would attack and wasn't surprised by his brutality. With a rabid-sounding growl, Red Wolf rushed forward, flaying wildly with his fists. Hawk easily blocked the initial blows intended for his head and, pivoting on the toes of his right foot, he aimed a short, chopping punch to Red Wolf's kidneys.

As Hawk almost landed a crushing strike to his body, Red Wolf spun sharply, swinging in a wide arc with a huge right fist. Targeted for Hawk's temple, if the blow had connected it would have sent Hawk into unconsciousness instantly. Instead, Red Wolf's knuckles slammed into the side of Hawk's jaw, snapping his head around, causing his knees to buckle momentarily. Brilliant lights exploded in his head, and Hawk very nearly went down, but a voice warned him that if he did, Red Wolf would show him no mercy. So he rose up again, adopting a defensive posture to protect himself against the onslaught that he was certain would follow immediately.

Once he'd hurt Hawk, Red Wolf became impetuous. He rushed forward, hands outstretched, going for Hawk's throat. Hawk was certain that if he got a stranglehold on him, he could choke the life out of him. Hawk knew his enemy was trying to kill now, no longer willing to simply maim and torture.

Hawk ducked as Red Wolf attacked. He brought his left fist sharply sideways, batting aside Red Wolf's clutching hands. Stepping close, Hawk threw a short, chopping punch to Red Wolf's stomach. The breath gushed from Red Wolf's lungs, and before he had a chance to inhale, Hawk followed up the first strike with a left fist to the solar plexus.

Hawk stepped back. Still dazed from the blow to his jaw, Hawk could see that Red Wolf was also badly hurt, perhaps even more than he was himself.

"When the elders say that you must be killed, I will ask to kill you myself." Hawk blinked his eyes, hoping his vision would clear soon, hoping, too, that Red Wolf would not realize how dazed he was. "You are like a dog who eats the poison berries. You attack those who would defend you, so it will be an act of mercy to put you out of your misery."

Hawk had seen what happened to any animal who'd eaten the purple, poisonous berries that grew in the Badlands. The animal first went mad, attacking whatever was near him. In a day or two, after the poison had worked thoroughly through its system, the animal writhed in hideous pain, dying a slow, painful death.

In his heart Hawk felt that Red Wolf, the vile warrior who loved to kill, was afflicted with a similar poison. Hawk wanted to believe that *something* was responsible for Red Wolf being the way he was, rather than him simply being evil from birth.

"The elders...are weak...they are old men," Red Wolf gasped, slightly bent over. His expression was strained with hatred and pain. "They...would not dare...banish me. None have the courage to give the order to send me to the spirits. They hate me, but they fear me...and it's their fear I've wanted all along!"

The two combatants began circling each other slowly.

"I had intended to beat you down...then spit on you," Red Wolf said, circling slowly. "You have become strong again." He pulled out the long, deadly knife from the sheath at his hip, the one he was never without. "And because you are not weak, I will have to kill you here and now. The coyotes will have eaten your carcass before anyone finds you."

Hawk's mind raced as he watched Red Wolf slowly twisting the knife in his hand. Without a weapon of his own, Hawk realized that he was in grave danger. But even as he stared at the knife, he still found it hard to believe that he actually needed to raise a weapon against a member of his own tribe.

As he circled Hawk, Red Wolf's confidence grew. He had made a mistake in his fight against his lifelong enemy, but the error had cost him nothing more than a little breath and some pain. In the process, he had learned much about Hawk and what it was he must do now. He *did* want to beat Hawk. Ruining his face for the fawning squaws would bring only half the satisfaction.

This scenario could be played out only provided Hawk posed no serious threat to Red Wolf in personal combat. Red Wolf had come to realize that Hawk was a legitimate threat, which reinforced the course of action that would satisfy Red Wolf. He would kill Hawk, and hope the coyotes and wolves ate the corpse, here on the hills, before it was found by the tribe.

Hawk had made many legitimate and dangerous enemies during his lifetime, so no individual would automatically be assumed to be the culprit.

Red Wolf watched Hawk, looking for a defensive weakness, but found nothing.

"How was it with Night Flower?" Red Wolf decided on a new tactic. "Did she bleed when you took her?"

Hawk tried to block the words from his mind, understanding that if Red Wolf made him lose his temper, he would become a less formidable foe. Warfare was best waged with cool detachment, not with anger. Just the same, Hawk couldn't help wondering how Red Wolf knew that Night Flower had come to him seeking passion.

"Was she good, Hawk? Or did she lay there like dead flesh?"

Hawk clenched his teeth. Red Wolf wasn't worthy of speaking the name of such a gentle and loving maiden.

"You speak the words of a fool," Hawk said, balancing lightly on the balls of his feet. He kept himself ready to spring upon his enemy if the opportunity presented itself, or leap away if Red Wolf attacked with the knife.

"Do I? I saw her go into the sweat lodge." Red Wolf's dark eyes glittered with hatred. "Everyone knows you'll lay with any squaw."

Hawk felt a small sense of relief at Red Wolf's answer. All Red Wolf had seen was Night Flower going into the sweat lodge. Everything beyond that was speculation from him, and faulty speculation at that.

"Tell me about the golden-haired girl." Red Wolf smiled maliciously. "Is she like so many of the blue-eyes? I've had many of them, and they are all alike. Little lambs wanting to be slaughtered by a forbidden blade." He smiled. "Have you turned the heifer into a cow yet?"

"You maggot."

It took all of Hawk's willpower to keep from rushing Red Wolf. Only the big, deadly knife in Red Wolf's hand kept Hawk back. Some of the Sioux men had adopted the white man's language in ways that were insulting to the white man. They spoke, thus, of white women in terms of cattle, with 'heifers' being white women who had not yet borne a child, and 'cows' those who had. It was a vile insult used mostly by braves who visited brothels filled with white women.

"What does she like? Tell me, Hawk. Does the golden-haired whore drop to her knees for you? Does she like to suck dark cock?"

Hawk couldn't listen to Red Wolf demeaning Amanda any longer.

Rushing forward just as Red Wolf lashed out with his knife, Hawk dodged, enabling him to catch Red Wolf's wrist. They wrestled to the ground, and Hawk grabbed Red Wolf by the throat. Instantly he began pummeling his foe, smashing his fist time after time into Red Wolf's mouth, nose, and chin until his enemy dropped his knife. Once the knife was out of the contest, Hawk used both fists. Though Red Wolf delivered a few bruising punches, the early damage he had received could not be overcome. Then, when Hawk suddenly landed a bone-crushing punch to Red

Wolf's nose, his head snapped to the side, his eyes rolled back in his head, and the brave lapsed into unconsciousness.

Gasping for breath, Hawk stood up on shaky legs and looked down at his vanquished, unconscious enemy.

I should kill him. If Red Wolf won, he would have slit my throat. Sooner or later, he'll cause great pain and suffering for the tribe. It would be better for everyone if I kill him now. Then the women will be safe.

Hawk looked on the ground at the knife, which would have been used to kill him had he not been just a little quicker, a little stronger, than Red Wolf. Hawk picked it up, slowly turning over the weapon in his hands, wondering how many times Red Wolf had used it against a helpless enemy. How many women had died from this knife? The question itself sent a shudder through Hawk. He looked down at Red Wolf and saw the blood flowing from both nostrils. Hawk had broken his nose, smashing its broad bridge. Red Wolf would never again be thought of by any squaw as a handsome brave. He would always carry the smashed and flattened nose as a reminder of the fight he'd had with Hawk.

I should kill him now. Now, while I have the chance. I'll regret it if don't.

But he couldn't do it—not like this, anyway. Red Wolf's life had been an insult to all the Sioux, but Hawk could not make the decision to end it. That decree, should it be made, would come from the Council of Elders.

Turning, Hawk then tossed the knife deep into the trees, then slowly headed back toward the encampment. He had to speak with Amanda. He did not know exactly what he would say once he found her, but he knew he had to speak to her.

* * * *

The great, body-wrenching sobs had finally ended. Amanda sat with her legs folded beneath her, her face in her hands, trying to even her breathing. She had no more tears left to shed.

She had never truly considered the possibility that Hawk wouldn't want her back, that he wouldn't be happy to see her. She simply assumed that he would see the world as she saw it. It was so logical. They were *meant* to be together. Why couldn't Hawk accept that simple, unalterable truth?

She looked around the tepee, which suddenly seemed so foreign to her. *Of course it looks foreign. You don't belong here.*

Amanda wiped the tears from her eyes, determined to get her spirits back and her thoughts in order. The question she had to ask herself next was one she didn't want to answer—what to do now?

Amanda had to think about it. She had, after all, ridden away from the Circle S ranch in the dead of night. The note she'd left probably prompted more questions than answers. Next, she'd ridden at full gallop through the countryside to the Sioux encampment, where she'd recently discovered she was not welcome. At least not welcome by the man who'd made her act so foolishly.

But when exactly did this foolishness begin? Clearly, when Hawk entered her life, her rock-solid willpower became a negotiable thing. Ironically, after Hawk had rescued her, he himself had ensnared her, showing Amanda Wright that she wasn't as impervious to the charms of men as she'd always believed.

She stopped her pacing for a moment and looked herself over. The dress she wore, made of leather — she could not say with any confidence whether elk hide or deerskin — fit her perfectly. She'd truly enjoyed wearing it until only moments earlier, when she decided that she was in unfriendly territory.

"To hell with him." The tone of her voice in the tepee sounded in her ears. For hours now the only sound to reach her was that caused from her own weeping. Now, a second time, more forcefully than the first, she said, "To *hell* with him."

Amanda felt better saying the words. How unfair that Hawk should have such power over her life, that he could — with a simple wave of his hand — dismiss her completely, relegating her to nothing more than a passing memory. He might *think* that he had the power to simply snap his fingers and make her leave, but that was just...

"Just what?" Amanda asked herself aloud.

She didn't have any rights in the tribe, and she knew it. She would be allowed to stay, but only as long as they wanted her to. All her wealth, the social connections that the Wright name provided, meant nothing at all. Here she had to stand, wearing a borrowed leather dress unadorned with even a single strand of beadwork anywhere on it, upon her own merits. But her own merits, which she'd thought sufficient for Hawk, were, quite simply and bluntly, insufficient. At least he felt they were.

For an instant Amanda thought the tears would return, but she held them back. Tears were for weak women, and she wasn't weak. A huge, empty, aching hole had been cut into her heart by the man she'd been silly enough to fall in love with. But that didn't mean she was weak. Foolish? To be sure. Unwise?

Undoubtedly. Naive? Naturally. Weak? Not in ten thousand years.

Amanda felt her confidence returning, which was a good sign, she decided. Just a moment earlier it had seemed as though everything she had ever accomplished had been rendered worthless because Hawk Two Feather had said she couldn't stay in camp, that he didn't want her to be a part of his life. Embracing her anger, she clenched her fists and pounded them against her thighs as she paced back and forth in Buttercup's tepee.

"To hell with Hawk Two Feather." Amanda's voice grew louder still. "He's a damn fool if he doesn't know a good woman when he sees one."

Amanda paced faster and faster, as if marching into the future, refusing to let any man—even Hawk Two Feather—dominate her life, her thoughts, her emotions. She had problems, she knew, but she could overcome them.

What would the people think?

She sighed, knowing her reputation was ruined. They would never forgive her for the behavior she had exhibited the last time she and Hawk were in town. Though she didn't much care what the people thought, she was concerned that her behavior might reflect badly on her family. However far outside the boundaries of decency she had stepped, Amanda didn't want her brother and sister to suffer.

"To hell with everyone." Amanda longed to tell the fine people of Deadwood exactly what they could do with their opinions. Now she had the perfect excuse to write them all off forever.

From outside the tepee came a voice. Amanda stopped her pacing and asked, "Yes?"

"Amanda, Hawk's here." The nervous tension in Buttercup's voice could not be missed. "I think you'd better come out here."

"No!" Hawk said loudly, forcefully. "I'll go in there!"

Amanda's heart stopped in her chest.

Chapter Twenty-Two

Hawk put a hand on his sister's shoulder and pushed her aside. Still charged with the adrenaline that had been produced by his fight with Red Wolf, he was behaving rashly, and he knew it.

"I don't want to be disturbed," Hawk told Buttercup.

"Don't send her away." Buttercup implored. "You're frightening me. I've never seen you so—"

"Silence," Hawk said, without raising his voice. He stepped into the tepee, pausing at the sight of Amanda, and announced, "I have come to talk."

"Good. Just be prepared to listen."

Her reply took him aback, and he moved farther into the tepee. Looking into Amanda's eyes, he saw not only that anger glittered in their blue depths, but that they were also slightly red-rimmed from crying.

"Perhaps you would like to talk first," he offered.

Putting her hands on her hips, Amanda glared at him. After several seconds of silence, she shook her head.

"You've come to me." The tone of her voice indicated that she'd backed down all she could, cried as many tears as her eyes held. "You talk first. When you're finished, I'll talk. When I'm finished we'll be finished talking. That seems fair enough, doesn't it?"

Hawk opened his mouth, but no sound came out. Fair? Indian braves never negotiated with women. It was clear that she already had her mind made up, and that nothing he could say or do would change the way she felt.

"I fought Red Wolf." The words were hardly out of his mouth when he realized they had nothing to do with what he wanted to say.

"Why? Not to impress me, I hope," Amanda replied. "I've always found violence abhorrent."

"Actually, it did have something to do with you, in a way," Hawk replied. "He was talking about you, saying things about you."

Amanda looked at Hawk. "There was a time when I needed you to be violent. That time has come and gone, Hawk."

Hawk felt his anger growing and didn't have a clue as to whom he was really angry with. Himself? He accepted that. He'd made enough mistakes in the last weeks to fill a lifetime.

"You shouldn't have come here," he said. Once again, the instant the words were out of his mouth he wished he hadn't said them.

"You've already told me that."

Hawk looked at her, half-expecting her to say something more, perhaps toss out an insult or try once more to make him see that he should keep her in his life. She didn't do any of those things, and because she didn't, he felt disoriented.

"Yes, I have," he said finally, not knowing what else to say. He rubbed his jaw, which was slightly swollen from the fight.

"Yes, you have. So what else have you got to say for yourself? It's clear by looking at you that you've got yourself in a state. It's safe to assume that there's a reason for it. Perhaps you'd be kind enough—for a change—to let me in on it?"

"I didn't come here to listen to your sarcastic comments."

"I'm sure you didn't."

"Are you going to keep them up?"

"Only as long as you haven't got anything worthwhile to tell me."

Hawk looked Amanda in the eyes and for the first time wondered if she was worth all the trouble she'd caused him. From the first moment she'd entered his life, when he'd ridden into the clearing to save her life from the white outlaws, she had been nothing but trouble to him.

The problem was, she was also something more. And she wasn't a Sioux. Worse than that, she was white. Amanda Wright was what the tribe had always thought of as the enemy, what Hawk had both publicly and privately considered a demon. She was everything he found tempting, everything he despised.

"I suppose you'll have to leave," Hawk said.

Amanda continued to stare straight into his eyes, but again Hawk broke the connection.

"Marry me." Hawk stopped, and for a moment peered around, wondering who had spoken such nonsense. A second later he understood he was the only person talking.

Amanda studied him quizzically. "What did you say?" she asked finally.

Hawk closed his eyes for a moment. *Is that what I want?*

"Marry me."

He looked into Amanda's beautiful blue eyes, taking her small hands into his. Suddenly the enormity of his words struck him. But as he stared deep into her eyes, he knew that if he didn't make her his wife, he would regret it for the rest of his life. She had vexed, tantalized, and tormented him, but she had made him feel more alive and filled with joy than anyone else. He couldn't let her ride out of his life a second time. He'd left her once before, and he'd never again let that happen.

"Marry me, Amanda. I don't care how or where, just marry me. I want you to be my wife."

"What did you say?" she asked, a slight tremulous quality to her voice. "Are you under a spell of some sort?"

"I said I want you to be my wife." Hawk squeezed her hands tighter. He hadn't expected to ask Amanda to marry him, but now that he had, her hesitancy in giving him an answer was most unsettling.

"You want me to be your wife. That isn't exactly the same as wanting to be a husband." Amanda tried to pull her hands out of Hawk's but he held them too tightly.

"Of course it is."

"No, it's not. Some men want wives, but they don't want to be husbands." She inhaled deeply. "I won't sit idly by while you share your passion indiscriminately."

"I want you to be my wife, Amanda. I want to be your husband." Hawk, aware that in his nervous tension he was squeezing Amanda's hands too tightly, relaxed his grip. He raised his hands slowly to cup her face, his palms and fingertips touching her. "Say you will marry me, Amanda. Make me the happiest man in the world."

"In a church?" Amanda ears were ringing, and she felt as though she was in a daze. This was what she had always wanted, she now realized, yet now that the moment was here she could hardly make her mouth form the words.

"In any church you want," Hawk replied.

And that was all that Amanda really needed to know. As long as she could have a church wedding, then surely his sentiments had to be sincere. She stepped closer to Hawk, twisting her arms around his middle, pressing her cheek against his chest. "I don't care about the differences between us," she said. "I know our life together is going to be difficult, and that many people won't approve of what we're doing. But I don't care. I want to be with you, Hawk. Not just for a little while, but for always, and that's all that matters to me."

Feeling his hand stroking her hair, hearing the soft murmur of his love words, Amanda knew she had made the right decision. She had chosen love. She had fought that love, and so had Hawk, and still the love remained.

Whatever anyone else thought of her marriage to a Sioux warrior was immaterial, she had followed the guidance of her heart, and her heart wouldn't lead her astray.

* * * *

Throughout the ride from the Sioux encampment to the Circle S Ranch, Hawk had been planning what it was he would say to Sonny. Once Amanda realized that Hawk intended to ask Sonny's permission to marry her, Amanda's fury began to boil. She believed her marriage was nobody's business but her own. But Hawk, distinctly aware of the many transgressions he was committing by simply *wanting* Amanda to marry him, insisted that at least some semblance of protocol and decorum should be maintained.

Now that the two men were sitting face-to-face, brandy snifters in hand, Hawk had serious doubts about whether Amanda's brother could be made to see reason. The cold look in Sonny's eyes suggested he could not.

"Once more?" Sonny asked. He sipped his brandy.

"I said, I would like to marry your sister, and I'd like your blessing."

"And if I say no?" Sonny asked

"Then Amanda and I will get married anyway." Hawk's tone was like granite. Polite enough to ask Sonny for his blessings, he would not be so polite as to allow for an unwanted answer. "Don't be mistaken, Sonny, I'm not really *asking*. I'm actually warning you. Amanda and I *are* going to be married. Nothing and no one can change that. I'm just trying to be as polite as I can about this." He hesitated a moment, then added, "Under the circumstances."

It was common knowledge that nobody talked to Sonny Wright that way.

Nobody, except Hawk Two Feather.

"You're determined to marry her, aren't you?"

Hawk nodded his head, his gaze never leaving Sonny's.

"Do you know what I'd do to anyone who came in here and talked to me that way?" Sonny asked.

"I can make a pretty good guess what you would try to do," Hawk replied, letting Sonny know that he didn't back down from threats.

"I suppose that's got to make you a pretty brave man. But then, a man would have to be brave to want to marry Amanda." It suddenly became obvious that Sonny realized the unintended double entendre, and a twinkle came to his eyes. He sipped his brandy. "Does Amanda want to marry you?"

"You can ask her that for yourself," Hawk answered, seeing the new brightness in Sonny's eyes and sensing his acceptance, but not willing to believe it entirely until he heard the words. "But I think she does. She says she does. I know she can be impulsive, and sometimes she says things that she doesn't completely mean, but she loves me and I love her, and that's what is most important."

Sonny sighed. A long, weary sigh. Though his shoulders sagged, there was a smile on his lips and a brightness in his eyes.

"I've been protecting Amanda for so long, it's difficult to relinquish my hold." He inhaled deeply through his nostrils, then exhaled very slowly. "If ever there was a man who could keep my sister safe from harm, I guess that man's you." He sighed wearily. "It's a strange world we live in, isn't it, Hawk?"

"Yes." Hawk wanted to smile, but he wouldn't allow himself to do so until he received Sonny's answer.

"I don't suppose there's a damn thing I can say or do that will stop the two of you from getting married?"

Hawk shook his head slowly, his lips curled downward at the corners. He'd been concerned that Sonny might try to bribe him into leaving Amanda. And though he didn't seem about to do that, Hawk still couldn't be sure.

"Then as long as there isn't a damn thing I can do about it anyway, I don't suppose I have any choice but to give my blessing," Sonny said. Now that the words were finally out of his mouth he smiled broadly. "You know, I'm going to have a hell of a time finding a priest who'll marry the two of you." Sonny rose from his chair and crossed the room to where the brandy decanter sat on the liquor cart. Unstopping the bottle, he then brought it over to Hawk and poured a hefty measure into his snifter. Then, filling his own snifter, he said, "What the hell! I've never had a drink with a future brother-in-law before. Why don't we have a few too many drinks and a couple of good cigars, and find out what we're both made of, eh?"

Hawk looked at the brandy in the snifter. It was a lot of liquor, and though he suspected that Sonny might just be trying to get him drunk so he'd let his defenses down, he decided to meet the challenge.

The cigar was as good as Sonny had promised, and by the time Sonny had refilled Hawk's snifter again, they were talking and laughing like lifelong friends.

* * * *

Amanda was mad enough to kill. Maybe not kill, exactly, but certainly mad enough to knock her brother's and her lover's heads together.

Standing outside the library, she heard the raucous laughter coming from inside. The telltale signs of alcohol consumption were unmistakable, as was the smell of cigar smoke. An hour earlier, when Amanda had knocked, she had been told that she wasn't allowed in. Her brother had broken into a peal of laughter, accompanied by, if Amanda was not mistaken, Hawk's muffled laugh. Amanda had returned to her bedroom to fume about the situation.

In the first place, she'd told Hawk not to ask for Sonny's blessing for their wedding. Amanda felt she was old enough to make her own decisions. But instead of following her wishes, Hawk had barricaded himself with Sonny in the library, where they had been for almost three hours now.

Able to contain her fury no longer, she returned to the library and pounded on the door. "Damn it all, open the door this instant." When there was no response Amanda impulsively lashed out with a kick. Since she was barefooted, her agonized gasp created more noise than her toe had on the wood. Sonny opened the door, his eyes a bit glassy from brandy, a smirk on his lips as Amanda danced around on one foot, holding her throbbing toe in her hands.

"I hope you're satisfied," she snapped, her fury now reaching a fevered pitch.

"Why blame me? I'm not the one who started kicking."

"You're the one who locked it," Amanda said in a tone that growled. As she limped past her brother into the library, she delivered a sharp elbow to his ribs.

Hawk was seated on the sofa, his long legs stretched out and crossed at the ankle. He wore his buckskin trousers and leather-fringed shirt. For an instant, Amanda was stunned at how perfectly natural he looked in the library, with a brandy snifter in one hand and a cigar in the other.

"I suppose you think this is all very funny, don't you?" she asked, still limping up to the sofa, looming over Hawk.

"I admit, there are elements of humor that have not completely missed me," Hawk replied quietly, a smile curling the edges of his mouth. Amanda had never before seen Hawk having had too much to drink, but she could tell from the look in his eyes that the brandy was affecting him...and that he was feeling romantic. This observation did absolutely nothing to lessen Amanda's combative mood.

"I'd like to talk privately with you." Amanda clenched her teeth. That the men weren't taking her anger seriously only fueled her fury.

Sonny wobbled somewhat as he crossed the room and set his snifter down on the liquor cart. "You're on your own, my friend." His words were a little slurred. "You might just as well get used to this now. My sister has a hellish temper when she gets her feathers ruffled."

A deadly look from Amanda hastened Sonny's retreat from the library. When she turned back to Hawk he was getting to his feet. The penetrating look in his ebony eyes suggested familiar pleasures...which Amanda, this time, had no intention of experiencing.

"You think it's funny to sit here with my brother, the two of you men discussing my life, deciding what it is you will and won't let me do." Amanda waggled a finger under Hawk's nose. "Well, I've got some news for you, Hawk—news you're not going to want to hear."

"Then let it wait until later." The smooth texture of Hawk's tone made Amanda wonder exactly how powerful her conviction was. "Why waste the remainder of this perfectly fine evening discussing that which, as you've already pointed out, I do not want to hear?"

Casually, he reached for Amanda, but she slipped away. She knew her own weaknesses, how difficult and sometimes impossible it was for her to remain angry whenever Hawk touched her. But this time would be different.

"No more loving, mister," Amanda warned. She glanced away from Hawk to the door, and noticed that her brother had closed it behind him. She didn't want her brother to hear what she was about to say.

"What?" Hawk looked skeptically at Amanda. "Isn't it a little late for taking vows of celibacy?"

"I said no more loving. Not one little bit. Not until we're husband and wife."

Hawk stopped his slow advance. He pushed his eyebrows together, and he turned his face slightly to the side, peering suspiciously at Amanda.

"You can't mean that." He cleared his throat. "You...um...you don't really mean that...do you?"

"I *can*, and I *do!*" Amanda answered, and now she was the one who was smiling. "Want to make my decisions for me? Fine! Go ahead! You and Sonny can sit in here and decide my whole life for me if you want to, and drink until your eyeballs fall out for all I care! But here's a little something for you to think about...you're not touching me, not kissing me, not even being alone in the same room with me until you and I are legally wed."

Amanda turned then, striding purposefully to the door. She couldn't let Hawk talk to her for long because if she did, she knew that soon he would be touching her, and then there would be kisses and more, and then her speech will have meant nothing at all.

"You can't mean that," Hawk said again when Amanda had reached the library door.

"Oh, lover, I most certainly do." She smiled triumphantly—and a bit wickedly—at him, sensing that she had won an enormous victory, and that from this point forward he would pay closer attention to her wishes. "Sleep well. I'll see you in the morning." She tossed her head back, laughed heartily, and left the library.

As Hawk made his way to his bedroom, he pondered the possible problems caused by his being a Sioux warrior wanting to marry a white woman. A priest had taught Hawk how to read and write. Would another priest be open-minded enough to officiate at a wedding ceremony? And just exactly how determined *was* Amanda to keep Hawk at arm's length until they were married?

* * * *

Red Wolf eyed the council, not intimidated by the suspicions of the elders who thought him a troublemaker. For every elder who disliked him and refused to believe his words, there was one on his side, listening carefully to everything Red Wolf said, nodding occasionally in agreement.

"We mustn't allow ourselves to become weak, dull, diluted." Red Wolf, speaking slowly and clearly to the old men, looked around the large tepee, feeling his confidence growing. "We have suffered greatly in the past, suffered from the white man and his ways. And what does Hawk do? He takes a white wife. Is he here now, teaching her our ways so that she can act as a young woman should? No, he is not. He is with the white man. Does he hunt to feed his own people? He does not. He rides in and out of camp without so much as a word to anyone."

"That isn't true," Dull Knife interrupted. "Hawk talked with me before he left camp with the golden-haired one. He explained that she has ways that he must follow."

"Yes, she has ways. But what of *our* ways? Does he think of that? No, I think not. Does he care that there are women and children here who must be cared for, who need food in their bellies and tepees that are warm and safe?"

"He has given us much money," the elder reminded, a tightness in his words indicating his roiling emotions. "With that money blankets can be bought. Much good can come of it."

Red Wolf sneered, as though the thought of accepting money from the white man was, under any circumstance, abhorrent. Only Dull Knife, who had long ago realized the avaricious heart that beat in Red Wolf's chest, was fully cognizant of the warrior's hypocrisy.

"Why do you come here, Red Wolf? Why do you say these things about one of your own?" Dull Knife asked quietly. "What do you seek by saying such things to us?"

"I seek a stronger people," Red Wolf replied without a moment's hesitation. Prepared for the question, he was enormously pleased with the affirming response he saw on the faces of many of the elders. "I seek strength. Can you call strong a warrior who takes a white woman as his wife? We have been fighting the white man for years, and now Hawk sleeps in the bed of a white woman. What warrior can know this and not be ashamed for Hawk? What warrior can know his shame and not turn his eyes downward in disgust?"

The elders were nodding. Most of them were, anyway, and that was enough for Red Wolf to consider himself victorious.

"I do not doubt that you seek strength, Red Wolf. I do not doubt that you seek power." Dull Knife truly studied the warrior, as though seeing him for the first time. "I do not know for whom you seek the power — for your people, or for yourself?"

Spreading his hands, Red Wolf smiled. He knew there was no need to answer aloud. The expressions he received from most of the elders told him they found his concerns about Hawk's loyalty valid.

* * * *

An hour had passed since Red Wolf had spoken with the elders. In that time he'd felt the heat rising in his blood. He had discredited Hawk, at least partially, and soon his revenge would be complete. Hawk had bested him in combat, and for that offense he would suffer greatly. Hawk would be a man without friends, without a people, without a home. But even if all that happened, it still wouldn't be punishment enough to satisfy Red Wolf's thirst for vengeance. There must be something more, a greater price still, that Hawk must pay.

Red Wolf hadn't really planned in advance how great a price he intended for Hawk to pay. It wasn't until he had noticed Buttercup heading away from camp, moving toward the hillside where the berries grew fat and sweet, that he fully understood the penalty Hawk must pay for besting him at every turn.

Now, from a safe distance, Red Wolf followed Buttercup. With each step he took, he could feel his heart beating just a little faster, feel the heat in his blood become just a little hotter. Buttercup's smooth flesh would be the perfect balm to satisfy Red Wolf's fury. She was young and beautiful, her mixed-blood heritage making her skin lighter than other maidens in the tribe. And now she was headed away from camp, walking in her usual carefree, exuberant stride.

As Red Wolf followed her, he glanced around, making certain that no one else was watching him. The spirits had at last chosen to be generous, for they were directing Buttercup to the hills, where she would be alone. Red Wolf would feast upon her tender flesh and make her pay dearly for his misfortunes.

But once Buttercup was out of camp, and Red Wolf about to follow her, a voice called out to him. Startled, Red Wolf wheeled toward the voice, his hand instinctively moving to his hip, where his knife used to be. But his hand remained empty, he had been unable to find his knife after being knocked unconscious in his fight with Hawk. His heart was pounding fast with excitement and guilt, which he tried to keep from showing in his expression as the old man who had called out to him approached.

One of the elders was following him, seeking further explanation regarding Hawk's danger to the tribe. Though Red Wolf was not in a mood to continue the discussion, he had little choice in the matter, especially since the old man was clearly an ally against Hawk.

Though Red Wolf answered the old man's questions, it took all of his willpower not to glance in the direction in which Buttercup had gone. When the curious old man had finally heard as much as he wanted, Red Wolf discovered that Buttercup had completely disappeared into the trees.

He felt himself smile, and fought to keep the emotion from showing on his face. Still, his lips curled at what had just happened. So she had disappeared! He would hunt her down as he would any other animal that he intended to devour to sustain his life.

He would prove his superiority over Buttercup—and over her brother—by tracking her down, by taking his pleasure with her, and by silencing her voice for all time.

Chapter Twenty-Three

Dull Knife could not say why he felt the need to follow Red Wolf. The warrior had merely left camp to go to the hillside. But there was something different in Red Wolf's step, in the way he moved and held his shoulders that gave Dull Knife a feeling of unease.

Red Wolf was far away, almost at the lower edge of the tree line, before Dull Knife had gathered his horse and headed out of camp. He was an old man but still nimble and sure when riding a well-trained Sioux pony, and he covered the distance to Red Wolf quickly.

The elder could not be sure that Red Wolf was up to no good until, at the sound of a horse, he spun around quickly to face the approaching rider. The expression on Red Wolf's face clearly indicated guilt, though of what Dull Knife could not say.

"What are you doing?" Dull Knife asked.

Red Wolf walked another dozen feet, moving deeper into the trees.

"What do you think I am doing?" Red Wolf replied, looking up at the old man, who remained astride his pinto.

Dull Knife was shocked at Red Wolf's undisguised lack of respect. "A warrior does not answer a question with a question. He does not speak that way to an elder."

Red Wolf stepped a little closer, looking up at the old man.

"Why have you come out here? Why have you followed me?" Red Wolf asked. "What makes a tired old man do that?" He leaned closer. "What makes a tired old man do something like that? So exhausting, isn't it, for an old man like you to try to keep up with a powerful warrior like me?"

Not even Dull Knife's extraordinary discipline could keep the revulsion he felt from showing in his expression. No warrior had ever spoken to him in such a manner, with such complete lack of respect.

"You have done all that you could to turn the council against Hawk," Dull Knife said after a moment. "You have even succeeded...for now. But in the end you will not succeed. I do not know what you plan, but I believe you will fail. You are evil, and evil will always fail eventually. The spirits will have it no other way. Now tell me, why have you come out here?"

Red Wolf moved another step closer to Dull Knife. He looked into the old man's eyes and said, "I've followed Buttercup out here. She's somewhere around, picking berries. I don't think anyone knows she's out here. I don't think anyone knows you're out here either. I know that nobody knows I'm out here."

The words, with their underlying meaning, made Dull Knife feel ill. He had seen men who killed for pleasure, men who were evil through and through, but he hadn't thought that any brave of his tribe was one of them. Instinctively, even though he had not actually fought in years, he reached for the knife at his hip, his fingers gripping the handle of the weapon.

"Where is your knife, Red Wolf?" the elder asked. No warrior would be without his knife, which was both a weapon and a tool. Red Wolf had a reputation for being skilled in knife fighting.

It was that question that solidified whatever doubts might have been in Red Wolf's mind about the action he was about to take. Had Hawk spoken with Dull Knife, telling the old man about the fight, and that Hawk had taken Red Wolf's cherished weapon? Red Wolf could picture the two warriors, one old and frail and the other young and strong, laughing between themselves about Red Wolf's failure.

"Old man," Red Wolf said, taking one step closer, "you ask too many questions."

Red Wolf moved quickly, decisively. His reflexes were swift, his strength overwhelming. He leaped forward, catching Dull Knife's wrist with one hand, preventing the old man from drawing his knife. With his other hand he pulled Dull Knife off the pinto's back and tossed him to the ground.

Red Wolf did not taunt his victim. He did not toy with him as a cat does with a mouse before the final deadly defeat. Red Wolf used the elder's own knife against him, and when he was done, when he stood triumphant over the corpse of the old man, the laughter that bubbled up out of his chest revealed such sublime joy that tears welled up in his eyes and rolled down his cheeks.

Red Wolf felt the sweat running down his chest. He was gulping air, with a fury burning in his soul and making him clench his teeth so hard his jaws ached from the strain.

After the ecstasy of killing Dull Knife, Red Wolf realized that he could not let the elder's pinto live. The animal would surely walk back to the camp, which would prompt an immediate search for Dull Knife. Red Wolf couldn't afford that, with the elder's own knife he dispatched the horse as well.

Then, on foot, he set out, searching for Buttercup. By his reasoning, she could not be far away.

But that had been two hours earlier, and the sun was almost down now. Within minutes he would be plunged into darkness. Somehow, some way, Buttercup had eluded him, without even trying. Her aimless wandering in search of berries had taken her to areas Red Wolf had not found. By now, with the sun nearly beneath the horizon, she was back at the camp, sharing with the tribe the berries she had gathered, eating and chatting with others before going to her tepee for the night.

Red Wolf cursed the spirits for allowing Buttercup to escape the punishment he felt she deserved. He wanted to scream at the heavens, but doing that would accomplish nothing. For several minutes he stood at the tree line and watched numerous campfires come to life in the valley below. Buttercup would be alone in her tepee, now that Hawk had left camp with the golden-haired woman.

Did he dare sneak inside the tepee in the dead of night? Could he get away with entering her tepee with so many others surrounding him? If she made even a single sound of alarm, Red Wolf would be overwhelmed by countless warriors who would swarm over him in defense of the maiden Buttercup.

How had it all gone so thoroughly and horribly wrong? If only he had found Buttercup in the woods, away from the prying eyes of the camp! Had he found her there, his revenge would have been at least partially satisfied. Buttercup's body would have been discovered by searchers, along with that of Dull Knife. As a member of the search party, Red Wolf's feigned shock and horror at 'finding' the slain bodies of the tribal elder and the young maiden would have confirmed his innocence.

It would have been so perfectly easy, if only Buttercup had cooperated and allowed Red Wolf to catch her.

Though Red Wolf felt futile hatred welling up in him, he also felt the early stages of a slowly building panic. Dull Knife was no longer a young man who might somehow be excused if he was not in his tepee on a particular night without explaining his whereabouts. As a wise and respected tribal elder, Dull Knife was continually being sought out for advice on all sorts of subjects. His absence might already have been missed. Red Wolf closed his eyes for a moment, giving himself time to consider what he had done. It was not really such an offense, he reasoned, to kill Dull Knife. The old man had lived a long life — too long, with his continual open contempt for Red Wolf's behavior. That had to be a serious enough offense for which to die, wasn't it?

He started back toward the encampment, feeling a little more confident about the future than he had. Dull Knife had paid his penalty and in time Buttercup, too, would pay for her offenses against Red Wolf. When that was done there would be the golden-haired girl to think about.

* * * *

"Come on, Darren, don't let it spoil the whole night," Beth Ann said as she sat on the bed behind the sheriff and began rubbing his neck and shoulders.

Beth Ann was the sheriff's favorite prostitute at the Arone Saloon. He saw her almost every other week, when he had the money to spend. She knew that he had enough money in his pocket right now for her, but his mood seemed more inclined toward heavy drinking than toward sexual satisfaction. But Beth Ann was confident that she could turn his attitude around.

"That lousy bitch," Darren Richards said, slurring his words slightly. He brought the whiskey bottle to his lips and took a swig, grimacing as the cheap liquor burned its way down his throat. "She's gonna get herself hitched to that stinkin', murderin' redskin!"

"Don't let that worry you none, darlin'," Beth Ann purred. She leaned closer, pressing her breasts against the sheriff's back. Her goal was to turn his thoughts away from Amanda Wright's upcoming wedding and toward herself, the willing woman currently in bed with him. "What about you and me just havin' ourselves a gay ol' time? One of those bounce-off-the-walls great ol' times?"

Sheriff Richards mumbled something beneath his breath, completely ignoring Beth Ann even as she played her hands over his shoulders and chest. She leaned away from him, looking at him from behind, doubting now that she really wanted to be with him.

Though the sheriff was one of her regulars, he was a brutish man, often harshly physical to the point of being violent when they were together in bed. On two occasions he'd demanded her professional services, then refused to pay her. Since he wore the town sheriff's badge on his chest, there wasn't much she could do to stop him, and there was no one to complain to, either.

If it hadn't been for her sister's pressing financial concern — the second one this year — caused by Gerald, her improvident husband, Beth Ann wouldn't have urged the sheriff on. But she needed the money, and business had been slow for the past couple of days.

Yes, Sheriff Richards was a repellent customer, but he was one that Beth Ann knew and understood, and he generally presented no problems she couldn't tolerate.

"Forget about her. She's not worth it," Beth Ann purred.

"You talk too much." The sheriff took another swig.

Beth Ann recoiled from the comment. It wasn't that she was insulted, in the past she'd been spoken to much more insultingly by the sheriff and hadn't taken offense. What scared her was that the last time the sheriff had said something like that, he had followed it up with a backhand across the mouth that sent her spinning to the floor. She'd been left with a fat, bloody lip that curtailed business considerably for the better part of a week.

Beth Ann almost spoke back to the sheriff. He carried a badge and a gun, but that didn't mean he was better than she was, she reasoned. Furthermore, it was her firm conviction that she was no worse than the men who rented her passion, and they had no right to look down their sanctimonious noses at her.

Speaking out against the sheriff, however, was not an idea that lasted long in Beth Ann's mind. She had learned that, as often as not, it was best to let sleeping dogs lie, and the sheriff was a dog if ever there was one.

"You're right, as usual," Beth Ann said, with just the right amount of solicitous regard for Darren Richards's delicate sensibilities. "Instead of me doin' all the talkin', why don't you jus' tell me every little thing that's on your mind? Jus' unburden yourself to Beth Ann, an' let her share your troubles."

Sheriff Richards looked over his shoulder, confusion showing in his eyes.

"Why is it you're such a curious little bug all a-sudden like?"

Beth Ann smiled, batted her lashes, glanced away briefly, then back to the sheriff. "I just don't like to see you upset," she said, monumentally pleased with her performance. For the first time in her life she began to seriously wonder if she could make more money with her mind and her ability to manipulate men's emotions than she could using her body and satisfying their lusts.

"Is that a fact?" the sheriff asked, smiling. "Truth is, I don't know as I can remember anyone actually liking me for who I am." He pulled loose several buttons on his shirt as Beth Ann began kneading the muscles in his back and shoulders. "It's that Wright girl that's causin' all the trouble. She's gettin' married to a redskin. I know the fella. Stinkin' redskin is what he is."

"They're all stinking if they're redskins, if you asks me," Beth Ann added, getting into the spirit of the conversation.

"Isn't that a fact," the sheriff said, grinning, obviously pleased with Beth Ann's attitude. "Anyway, I know for a fact that it was that redskin who kilt my brother."

"You do? Then why don't you go an' arrest him?"

"Well, I know I should, but I don't know what I can tell the judge. You see, when you're a sheriff and a sworn officer of the law, you gotta do things jus' so. It ain't jus' anybody that can do it, you know."

"Don't I know it?" Beth Ann exclaimed, moving close enough to the sheriff once again so that he could feel her breasts against his back. "Tell me more. I want to know it all."

"It's the Injin that's got me all outta whack," Sheriff Richards continued. "I jus' know he kilt my brother, and now he's gonna marry himself all that money, and he's going to be a rich man. It jus' don't seem right to me that there should ever be such a thing as a rich redskin, 'specially not a *really* rich redskin." The sheriff twisted suddenly, his eyes dark and dangerous. He grabbed Beth Ann's upper arm so hard that she knew instantly she'd have bruises. "You ain't never let a redskin touch you, have you? I jus' couldn't live if I knew I'd done it with a whore that done it with a redskin."

"No, of course not, Darren," Beth Ann said, managing to smile weakly. "What kind of lady do you think I am?"

After a moment the sheriff turned around, and only then did Beth Ann breathe a sigh of relief. She had, in fact, rented her body to several Indian men. Her priorities ran more toward the color of a man's money, rather than the color of his skin. But she knew that when Sheriff Richards said he couldn't live with himself, what he really meant was that he would kill her if he discovered she'd had sex with an Indian.

The vitriol continued, with Sheriff Richards vowing an assortment of violent acts upon Amanda Wright, the Indian she was about to marry, and several of the more respectable residents of Deadwood. Beth Ann listened carefully and talked little, and only occasionally asked questions.

She carefully monitored the level of whiskey in the bottle from which the sheriff swigged. Shortly after it was completely empty, and just before the sheriff was snoring loudly in her bed—and thereby preventing her from bringing anyone else from the saloon up to her room—Beth Ann was told the real reason the sheriff was so furious about the upcoming wedding of Amanda Wright and some Indian.

Apparently Sheriff Richards had beaten the man and now was concerned that the Indian, with the Wright wealth behind him, would come looking for revenge. Yes, Sheriff Richards was concerned about the disappearance of his brother, and he held the Indian responsible, but the truth was that he'd never really thought that much of his brother, and the more the sheriff drank, the more the truth had spilled out.

Beth Ann sat in her corset and stockings on the window ledge looking out over the street below, smoking a cigarette and listening to the sheriff snore as she watched the men walking from saloon to saloon in Deadwood.

Tonight she had learned that Sheriff Richards had, for no reason at all, severely beaten an Indian. That Indian had, apparently, killed the sheriff's brother, though from the facts Beth Ann had been able to glean, it appeared that nobody other than the sheriff knew that the Indian had killed the men missing from Deadwood. She figured there had to be a way to make a profit from knowing what she had learned.

From the bodice of her corset, Beth Ann pulled out four dollar bills. That was all the sheriff had on him. She'd expected him to have much more than that, and she'd been disappointed at the results of her theft. In the morning, when the sheriff discovered his money missing, Beth Ann would complain that he'd been such a stallion that she wouldn't be able to work for a week. After that comment Sheriff Richards would smile sheepishly, pretend he actually did remember the night-long sexual marathon to which Beth Ann alluded, then gingerly put his sweat-stained felt hat back on his throbbing head and leave her room.

Beth Ann sighed wearily as the sound of the sheriff's snoring became deeper, stronger, the alcohol settling into his system. She hoped that one of the other prostitutes would let her sleep in her room so she wouldn't have to listen to the sheriff all night.

As she tossed the remains of her cigarette out the window, Beth Ann wondered if she should tell Amanda Wright that the sheriff of Deadwood was planning to kill her fiancé.

By the time Beth Ann reached the door she decided that the best thing she could do was mind her own business.

* * * *

"You look so beautiful," Vanessa said, standing back so she could get a better look at her handiwork with Amanda's hair. The string of tiny pearls that Vanessa had carefully woven into Amanda's coiffure was the final touch. That accomplished, she was certain that Amanda was, beyond doubt, the most beautiful bride ever to walk the face of the earth. She'd been saying as much for the past twenty minutes.

"Do you really think so?" Amanda implored.

Had it been any woman other than Amanda, Vanessa would have been convinced that the question was an appeal for compliments. But Vanessa understood her sister and so did not casually dismiss the anxiety behind the question.

"Amanda, you are a very beautiful g—" Vanessa caught herself before uttering the word *girl,* briefly pretending to be choked with emotion, then continued, "Beautiful woman. There isn't going to be a man or woman in this church who won't realize that the instant they see you."

"I don't care what anyone else thinks," Amanda said, "so long as Hawk thinks I'm beautiful."

Vanessa kissed her younger sister on the cheek. "He will," she whispered. "Now I'm going to leave you alone for a bit, as the priest asked me to. He wants you to think about what you're about to do."

Amanda clutched her older sister's hand, not wanting to be left alone. Then, almost immediately, she released Vanessa. "Go," she insisted. "I'll be fine."

Amanda wasn't afraid of becoming Hawk Two Feather's wife. Actually, quite the opposite was true. She believed with all her heart that her marriage to Hawk was the perfect thing to do. Though Amanda had not yet completely inculcated the spirituality of the Sioux, she believed in her heart that her marriage to Hawk was preordained, decreed by the spirits.

It wasn't what *she* thought about the marriage that worried her—it was what everyone else thought about it, and how those feelings and prejudices would affect the running of the Circle S Ranch. Amanda herself was perfectly willing to face whatever excoriating hatred the people of Deadwood might feel toward her for falling in love with a Sioux warrior, but she didn't want her family to suffer for what she had done.

Alone in the back room of the church, Amanda sat in the high-backed, hard wooden chair and closed her eyes. She thought about the doe that had come to her in her vision quest, and about Hawk, and the kind of life they would have together. She thought about Buttercup, and how important it was to completely empty the mind of all thoughts and emotions so that only the truth remained, so that only the truth was left to enter the mind and heal the soul.

* * * *

As Vanessa left Amanda's room, Sonny Wright walked out of a small back room on the opposite side of the church, leaving Hawk Two Feather, resplendent in his wedding finery, the beauty of which completely sent several of the more racist members of the community into fits of apoplexy considering the absurdly that man wearing such finery was, in fact, a half-breed. Hawk was in no mood to contemplate the future, nor to ponder the possible reactions of others to his marriage. As much as anything else, he wondered how long he could stand to wear the infernal black shoes that Sonny had absolutely demanded be worn during the wedding ceremony.

With a conscious effort to control his rising anger, Hawk stopped pacing the small room, closed his eyes and forced himself to take several long, deep breaths.

With a rueful acceptance of a wealth Hawk could hardly imagine, he quickly had come to realize that between Sonny and Vanessa, absolutely no expense would be spared on the wedding.

With no small effort, Hawk forced himself to sit in the only chair in the room. Immediately feeling uncomfortable, he moved to the floor, crossed his legs beneath him and willed himself to forget the stiff new shoes and the necktie that threatened to choke off his breath at any moment. He asked himself a single question—why was he so angry?

The answer came to him quickly—every little thing was bothering him now because Amanda, more than a week ago, had vowed to deprive him of her sensual charms until they were legally husband and wife. As the week had worn on and Hawk found himself being rebuffed at every turn, he realized she wasn't simply mouthing empty threats. And worse, she hadn't merely deprived him of her sensuality—she hadn't even allowed him the pleasure of a kiss.

Celibacy had been avoided by Hawk, for most of his life, with approximately the same zeal that other men avoid small rabid animals.

In less than an hour the way of life Hawk had always known would be gone forever. He would be—against all odds and earlier predictions—a married man.

He felt peculiar. It wasn't that he didn't want Amanda to be his bride, or that he didn't want all the world to know that he was her husband. What Hawk wanted at that moment was one last reckless, impulsive adventure before his days and nights as a single man were gone forever. When Amanda had entered his life, he had discovered her to be his equal in adventurous spirit. Though she had lacked sexual experience, she was an apt pupil, and on more than one occasion she had proven herself to be not merely a student in the art of sensuality, but a teacher as well.

Hawk was on his feet in an instant, positioning a chair beneath the attic grate in the ceiling. The grate lifted with little resistance, and not nearly enough noise to draw the attention of the men and women in the main area of the church.

His heart pounding and a grin on his lips, Hawk mentally prepared himself. Leaping high, he then got a good handhold on the attic lumber, which creaked in protest at his weight. Always agile, Hawk soon pulled himself completely through the square opening in the ceiling to crouch in the dusty attic.

How much noise had he made?

He did not wait for his eyes to adjust to the darkness of the attic. He didn't have time for that. From his jacket pocket he extracted a small box of matches, removed one, and lit it. Hawk could see that the attic had at one time been used as a storage area but had not seen any use recently. A thick layer of dust covered the various boxes and packages jammed against the walls.

Before the match had burned to Hawk's fingers, he determined the direction to the room in which Amanda waited. He didn't bother with a second match. The low ceiling made it impossible for him to stand, so he duck-walked across the width of the church.

Part of him wondered what the priest would do if he heard noises overhead, and part of him wondered how long it would take Amanda to forgive him for what he was about to do.

Reaching the ceiling grate above her room, he looked down through it without alerting Amanda to his presence. Sitting in her lovely white gown she was nervously chewing on a knuckle.

For an instant Hawk was stopped by her extraordinary beauty. The woman he'd seen dressed so often in denim trousers and a flannel man-cut shirt wore a gown that had cost more than many ranchers earned in a year. Her long blonde hair had been swept up in an intricate coiffure laced with a long strand of small pearls. Had Hawk not already witnessed the incredible polarity of her personality, he would not have believed that this angelic woman sitting nervously in a church back room was the rough-and-tumble Amanda Wright he'd come to love.

When Hawk lifted the grate Amanda jumped so high and fast that she practically levitated out of her chair.

"Be quiet," he said, carefully setting the grate aside. He placed his hands on either side of the opening, let his legs dangle down into the room, then lowered himself as far as he possibly could before dropping to the floor.

Absolute incredulity filled Amanda's expression. Looking as though she wanted to scream the church down, she seemed afraid of making even a single sound for fear that the priest would hear and come to investigate.

"I couldn't wait to see you," Hawk whispered. Now in a room that was filled with light, he could see how dusty his black suit had gotten in the attic. He brushed off his trousers quickly and, as he batted away the dust on the elbows of his jacket, began advancing on Amanda.

"You shouldn't have come here," Amanda said a bit weakly, her head spinning and her thoughts in utter disarray. Why was he walking toward her with a smile on his lips? She knew only too well what that meant. "This is a mistake."

Hawk was still smiling as he advanced. He said, "I recall saying something very much the same to you not long ago when you had come to me. It turns out I was wrong to try to push you away, and you were right to come to me. If it was right then, it must be right now."

Amanda retreated until she felt the wall against her shoulders. The days she'd spent without tasting Hawk's kisses had been difficult for her, but she hadn't backed down from her promise to refuse Hawk so much as a kiss in the days before their marriage.

The separation, however, had caused her passionate dreams to reappear nightly, and with a vengeance. Each morning Amanda awoke convinced she was even more exhausted than she had been when she'd gone to sleep. And the memory of her dreams — and it was always Hawk in her dreams, working his erotic magic on her — never failed to color her cheeks. This embarrassing condition delayed her appearance at breakfast with her sister and brother each morning.

To see Hawk standing before her now, looking deliciously sophisticated, yet earthy and wild with his long ebony hair and his burnished skin, sent shivers of alarm racing through her. *Never* had Hawk looked so enticing to Amanda, not even when all he wore was his loincloth and moccasins.

"What are you doing here?" Amanda whispered, recognizing only too well the gleam in Hawk's eyes. "Can't you wait just a few more hours?"

Hawk shook his head slowly, then reached for Amanda.

She twisted nimbly to the side, moving out of his reach. His grin broadened.

"I can't wait, Amanda, and I suspect you can't either."

Amanda put her hands on her hips and stamped her slippered foot. "I can control myself very well, thank you very much. That's why I'm *not* giving in to this foolish little whim of yours."

"Trust me," Hawk said, moving so that he had Amanda trapped in a corner of the room. "This is neither foolish nor a whim."

Amanda wanted to be angry with him. Looking up into his eyes, she could see the humor bubbling from his soul, the seductive sense of mischievous adventure she found absolutely impossible to resist. She wished that she could have known Hawk as a boy, before the things that now made him angry had become ingrained in him, before he'd begun to learn about prejudice and injustice, hunger and unending hard work.

"Please, Hawk," she whispered, her thoughts spinning dizzily in every direction. He put his hands lightly on her hips. "Everyone is just outside. Soon we'll be married. I promise, it won't change between us. I'll always want you."

"Then want me now."

Hawk's voice was husky with passion. He brought his hands up Amanda's sides, very nearly touching her breasts, and a shiver went through her. She put her hands on his chest, trying to push him away.

"Soon we'll be husband and wife," Hawk continued. "Just another married couple like so many other married couples."

Amanda laughed softly. "There's not going to be anything about us that's like anyone else, Hawk, I assure you." She didn't mention Hawk's mixed blood, or her own wealth, though those characteristics wouldn't be forgotten by anyone else who knew them.

"We weren't meant to be like the others," Hawk agreed, spreading his fingers, sliding his hands slightly higher up Amanda's sides, using his thumbs to graze the outermost curve of her breasts. She brought her hands from his chest down to his wrists, about to push him away. "Remember when the Cheyenne were so close, and still I couldn't stay away from you? I couldn't keep from kissing you, touching you, even though we were in so much danger. The danger added to the excitement, Amanda."

Even through the material of her wedding gown, Amanda could feel the heat of Hawk's hands upon her. In her heart she knew that what he said was absolutely true, their passion *was* different. It blazed like a comet streaking across the sky, white hot against the ebony darkness. It had never been, and would never be, commonplace, or for the faint of heart.

Amanda closed her eyes for an instant, inhaling deeply, needing to compose her thoughts. The scandal of marrying a Sioux warrior would be nothing compared to the stories that would circulate if she were to give in now to Hawk's passion. If her weakness was discovered...

"Just wait," she whispered, her eyes still closed. The warmth of Hawk's touch was a temptation she was still incapable of resisting. "I promise, just as soon as we're married and alone, I'll—"

Amanda's words were cut off, her breath sucked in, when Hawk's hands moved to brush the tips of her breasts with his thumbs. An instant later his lips touched her in a soft kiss promising further enticements. When Amanda tilted her head back the kiss became firmer. She felt dizzy. Rather than push Hawk away, her curled her fingers around the lapels of his jacket.

"I can't wait that long." Hawk's lips were moist and warm against Amanda's as he spoke. "And I don't think you can, either. This is our last chance to be truly wicked and scandalous."

Amanda turned her face away from Hawk. His thumbs, brushing lightly across her breasts, had caused her nipples to become almost painfully taut, making them hard and infinitely capable of feeling even the gentlest caress. She felt him kiss her cheek, her temple, then trace the shell of her ear with the tip of his tongue, carefully avoiding the dangling diamond earbob.

He spread his fingers, encompassing her breasts, squeezing them firmly through the stiff, lacy bodice of her gown as he kissed her temple.

"I don't want to be scandalous," Amanda whispered, the quiver in her voice caused by suppressed excitement. "I just want to be your wife."

"You can't have one without the other," Hawk replied.

She turned then and looked at him, knowing that he was right, and that her marriage to Hawk was against every criterion imposed upon her by white, upper-class society. With a slight tug against his lapels, Amanda closed her eyes and Hawk kissed her once again, fiercely and deeply. He invaded her mouth with his tongue, adding to the heated excitement that Amanda had tried so hard to deny.

Very much aware of the people just outside the door, Hawk moved Amanda's body sideways as he continued kissing her, until her shoulders rested against the outside wall of the room.

He wanted to pull the pins from her hair to let the blonde tresses cascade down around her shoulders in the manner that he found most attractive. He wanted to feel her hair's silken extravagance against his palms as he feasted on her mouth, but he couldn't. In mere minutes she would be standing at the altar in front of a priest and all her friends, and there would be no way of explaining a disheveled coiffure. Besides, he knew that she and Vanessa had tried countless variations on the style of her hair in the past few days, and it would be a shame to undo their handiwork before the guests had a chance to see it.

He leaned into Amanda, feeling the voluptuous curves of her body molding to his. He heard the soft intake of breath when she became aware of the fierceness of his cock, still trapped inside his trousers and already fully erect. He kissed her hungrily, pressing her against the paneled wall, reaching down to grab the skirt of her gown, pulling it up her legs.

"Hurry, Hawk," Amanda whispered, bringing her hands up his chest, wishing she could feel his skin instead of the crisp white shirt. She laced her fingers together behind his neck. Unsure of exactly how Hawk intended to consummate their passion, she felt certain that if she did not feel him thrusting deep inside her soon, she would surely lose her mind.

"Hurry," Amanda gasped, clutching Hawk, her passion heightened by the danger of the moment.

His touch scorched her flesh when at last he brought his hand around to touch her intimately through her drawers. Amanda gasped and raised up on her tiptoes, her legs quivering with excitement.

As he fumbled with the drawstring of the drawers, she couldn't help him, fearing she would fall to the floor if she didn't continue holding onto his powerful shoulders. She felt his fingers curl into the waistband, then heard the tear as her impatient husband-to-be ripped the satin undergarment from her.

"Hurry, my darling," Amanda whispered, raising her right knee and sliding her leg along the outside of

Hawk's as he opened his trousers to free his rampant arousal.

She was balanced precariously on one foot, and wrapped her right leg around Hawk's thigh. She wanted to tell Hawk how much he excited her, and that he always would. She wanted to tell him a thousand things, but just as she was about to speak Hawk bent his knees and his cock entered her in a single, breath-taking thrust. Amanda felt her hips strike the wall behind her, and heard the soft *thump!* of her head hitting it as well, but she couldn't concern herself with what noises were made, or who might hear them. Not when Hawk was filling her so completely and she could feel every magnificent inch of his rock-hard flesh sliding deep inside her.

There was nothing gentle about Hawk's lovemaking. He cupped the cheeks of Amanda's bottom and squeezed tightly, pulling her hips toward him as he thrust into her with such strength that he very nearly picked her completely off the floor. She wanted to kiss him, but he was too tall, and her breath was too labored.

"Yes, Hawk," Amanda gasped, each fierce thrust slamming her against the wall, sending her soaring closer to the chasm of ecstasy. In a choked whisper, she said, "Oh, *yesss!*"

In an oddly distanced way, Amanda was aware of all that was happening to her, yet detached from it. Now she was two distinct people—one a woman of wealth and privilege, both rational and sane—the other a daring sexual adventurer mad with desire for the man she loved. She heard the crackling sound of her dress, bunched up at her stomach and trapped between her body and Hawk's, being crushed by his thrashing movements, and wondered whether the fabric would be so wrinkled that everyone in church would realize instantly how the garment had been bruised. She was distinctly aware of the strength of Hawk's hands on her ass, pulling her toward him to meet his impaling thrusts. She had no choice but to meet the forceful thrusts that sent her backward against the wall, and she wanted it no other way.

She was aware of the heat and strength of Hawk as he lanced into her, filled her, possessing her so thoroughly and completely that she knew with certainty that she would always want to make love with him. The dichotomy of his nature had never been more apparent than at this moment, as they made wild, dangerous love.

Amanda felt the rapid tightening of the muscles in her stomach and knew she was going to reach the summit of ecstasy with frightening speed and force. She squeezed her eyes shut, her hands grasping frantically at Hawk's shoulders, holding on tightly as he thrust into her time and again. She felt utterly possessed by Hawk's extraordinary strength and virility, and completely protected by it.

She opened her mouth wide as she felt the scream of ecstasy about to explode in her throat. To prevent a sound from escaping, she caught the lapel of Hawk's jacket between her teeth and bit down with all her might.

The climax hit her forcefully, almost painfully in its intensity. Four inner contractions were followed by three more of lesser force. As the last of her spasms subsided, Amanda heard a mighty rumble erupt from Hawk's great chest, then he thrust into her harder and deeper than ever before, raising her to her tiptoes as his surging passion erupted. For the first time ever, he allowed himself the privilege of climaxing inside her.

Amanda was gulping in air as though she'd run a dozen miles. How long had it been since Hawk had first entered this room? Three minutes? Five at most? Was it possible that their passion could burn that hot, that fast?

The low hum of a voice caught Amanda's attention. She blinked her eyes, not yet fully back to earth from the heights to which her passion had taken her. Hawk was still within her, leaning into her, trapping her between himself and the wall. She put her right foot down on the floor but continued to hold onto Hawk because her legs were weak and wobbly.

"Someone's talking to you," Hawk whispered.

Amanda looked at Hawk, pleased that he appeared nearly as disheveled as she felt. What difference could it possibly make if someone was talking to her? She was with Hawk, and that was all that counted.

"Amanda, are you all right in there?" Vanessa asked softly through the closed door.

Amanda opened her eyes wide, and the afterglow in which she had been reveling vanished instantly. She pushed against Hawk's chest, forcing him to take a step backward. She felt warm and wet inside, and disquietingly empty.

"Answer her or she'll come in," Hawk said, struggling to rearrange his own clothing.

"Amanda?" Vanessa asked.

As Amanda saw the knob turn, she made a dash for the door.

Chapter Twenty-Four

The door opened just an inch before Amanda hit it with her shoulder. She heard Vanessa gasp on the other side of the door, but she couldn't apologize, nor could she give any reason for her peculiar behavior.

"Amanda, are you all right?" Vanessa asked again, louder this time.

Amanda leaned against the door, frantically looking for a lock, horrified to discover that there wasn't one. She looked over her shoulder just in time to see Hawk step up onto the chair, then leap high to reach inside the attic grate. For a few seconds he seemed to dangle in midair in the center of the room, and then his brightly polished boots disappeared through the square opening in the ceiling. Only then did Amanda stop pushing hard against the door.

The moment she released her pressure on the door, Vanessa forced her way into the room. There was a worried look in her eyes as she took in Amanda's appearance.

"What happened? Your dress is all wrinkled, and look at your hair! Amanda, what on earth were you doing in here?" Vanessa asked, already attempting to tuck a lock of blonde hair back where it belonged.

"I was just pacing, I guess," Amanda said, struggling desperately for a lie that might sound plausible. "I tripped and fell over, and I was cursing under my breath, I guess, when you knocked on the door."

Amanda studied Vanessa's face as her sister worked on her hair. Vanessa was as preoccupied with the wedding as Amanda was, it seemed, because she didn't question the story which, even on the face of it, lacked a great deal of credibility.

"I was worried about you," Vanessa said, taking Amanda by the shoulders and turning her to work on the hair that had formerly been secured with pins near the back of Amanda's head. "I've been working on this wedding, day and night, and it's going to go off just as your brother and I have planned. That's all there is to it."

"Don't worry, Vanessa, it'll be just as you planned," Amanda said comfortingly, a smile on her lips. This was one of the very few times in her life she'd seen her learned sister, the tough lawyer willing to fight anyone in a court of law, appear thoroughly nervous. "Shouldn't we put on my veil now?"

The instant the words were out of Amanda's mouth, something on the floor caught her attention. There, near the chair, were her drawers, destroyed by Hawk's powerful hands when he'd ripped them from her body.

"Someone's at the door," Amanda said quickly, almost pushing Vanessa in that direction.

"I didn't hear anything."

"Check, won't you?"

While Vanessa opened the door a crack, Amanda moved to the chair so that her drawers were hidden beneath her now-wrinkled gown.

"I guess I'm just a little nervous," Amanda explained when Vanessa returned to her with another questioning look in her eyes.

"I guess you've got a right to be nervous," Vanessa said as she picked up the white lace veil and began to pin it into place.

* * * *

Father Patrick O'Rourke had his misgivings about this wedding. He wasn't a man to look kindly on marriages between white women and Indians, but Sonny Wright had made an enormous donation to the church, as well as a sizable offering to the priest's personal finances. Father O'Rourke told himself that he could do much good for his flock if he simply accepted the money and performed the ceremony.

He looked out over the congregation and thought that if he could draw this many people on a Sunday, he wouldn't have need of Sonny Wright's bribe. This bitterness was short-lived, however. A pragmatic man, the priest knew that rules sometimes had to be bent if a greater good was to be realized. There were times when saving souls required money as well as faith.

He turned away from the congregation and went to the side room where the heathen, Hawk Two Feather, was waiting. An instant before the father's knuckles rapped on the door, he heard a *thump!* of boots striking the floorboards. Without bothering to knock, he opened the door wide and stepped inside.

"What was that noise?" the priest asked sternly. Hawk spun to face the intruder. "I'll only ask you one more time. What were you were doing?"

"I'm not used to wearing shoes like these," Hawk explained. "They're pinching my feet. I can't wait to get out of them and back into my moccasins."

Father O'Rourke was about to scold the redskin, but then he saw the dust on the knees of Hawk's trousers. A slow smile spread across the priest's lips.

"Try to be calm," Father O'Rourke said, stepping forward to pat the tall Sioux warrior's shoulder comfortingly. "At a time like this everyone tends to be a little nervous, but there's really no need for it. Just listen to my instructions, and I'll guide you and Amanda through the service. Oh, and one more thing, brush the dust off your knees. They got dusty when you were kneeling to pray." He smiled. "Have I found a convert?"

* * * *

Amanda made sure the wedding celebration was the most lavish party anyone in Deadwood could remember, and nearly everyone was invited— everyone, except Sheriff Darren Richards, and the whole town knew why he had been excluded. By the time of the wedding, Amanda had found out that the rumor mill had succeeded in informing all of Deadwood, and almost everyone in the territory, that the sheriff had beaten Hawk after arresting him on trumped-up charges. Later, Richards's brother and other men, known more for working with guns than with their hands, had decided they would even the score with Hawk.

She had heard a dozen different explanations of what happened next—including two eyewitness reports bearing no similarity to each other—with only one common thread of truth: Some men had ridden out of Deadwood intending to do Hawk bodily harm, and that was the last anyone had seen of them.

To prove that he made his own decisions, Sheriff Richards had gone to the wedding. He stood at the outer ring of bonfire light, watching as the line dancers moved in unison to the music of a six-piece band. The sheriff was thinking about the undetermined fate of his brother, and how unjust it was that Hawk should now be married to a beautiful and wealthy woman. A redskin shouldn't have that much luck working for him, plain and simple, and the sheriff figured he was just the man to right the wrong.

Hanging loose in his left hand was the bottle of whiskey he'd taken from one of the long tables set up just outside the Circle S ranch house. Some of the tables were laden with food, some with drink. There was enough for all the guests to immoderately partake in food and drink.

The ranch hand at the table had volunteered to pour a whiskey for Sheriff Richards, but the sheriff wanted the entire bottle. When the man said that wasn't the way the shindig was supposed to be, Darren Richards pointed to the badge pinned to his leather vest, then calmly withdrew his revolver and threatened to arrest the man. The sheriff got a full bottle of liquor, all for himself, with no more questions asked.

This fine whiskey rattled the sheriff's nerves. All that good liquor was being given away? The cost of the shindig, complete with a steer on the spit and delicacies of every variety, was something the sheriff could hardly stand to think about. Why was it that he, a hard-working man, couldn't afford to throw such a party, and yet a redskin could? It wasn't right. Something had to be very wrong in the world for something like this to happen.

He took another swig from the bottle and felt the delicious burn of the liquor going down his throat and into his stomach. The line dancers had stopped and the band had started a romantic ballad, sung by a fiddle-playing, sweet-voiced boy barely in his teens. Couples paired off quickly and began swaying under the stars to the slow, melodic music. Sheriff Richards saw this as the right time to show some of the unattached ladies of Deadwood just what they had passed up thus far.

Her name was Susan Quist—Suzie, to her friends, though she now believed that at seventeen she was too old for such a childish moniker—and she'd never looked twice at the sheriff. He decided, with a quarter of the contents of the bottle now in his stomach, that it was time to change her opinion of him.

"Evenin', Miss Quist," the sheriff said, finally coming closer to Suzie, who stood near the dancers. "Let's you an' me dance." He reached for her hand, but she pulled away from him as if he were poison. The sheriff grinned, but it was tight and forced. "I think it's time you and me got better acquainted. Now let's dance."

The three girls Suzie had been standing with seemed like they all wanted to run for their lives, though none was willing to abandon a friend. Huddling together, their eyes were wide and filled with both caution and contempt.

Ernest Quist, Suzie's father, stepped forward. "Walk away, Sheriff," Ernest said, his eyes hard as diamonds. His right hand held a mug of beer so tightly his knuckles were turning white. His opinion of Sheriff Richards, evident in his expression, indicated that he wouldn't tolerate the sheriff even speaking to his daughter.

"Are you telling me what to do?" Sheriff Richards asked with a sneer. He still held the bottle in his left hand, but his right hand was free for his revolver.

"That's right, I am." Ernest smiled and patted his stomach. "Got just enough beer in me to see you for exactly what you are." He chuckled. "And that ain't much."

"Maybe I oughta arrest you for that."

Darren Richards waited to see the fear in Ernest's eyes, but it never came. Looking around, the sheriff discovered nearly fifty men and women, their activities stopped, surrounding him. And even though none were armed, all appeared ready to take up weapons against him.

"This ain't no place for you, Sheriff," Ernest said. "Any place my daughter is ain't no place for you. In fact, any place *any* decent woman is ain't no place for you."

A smattering of laughter from the guests tore into Darren Richards's insides. Then someone from the crowd shouted, "That's telling him, Ernest! I wouldn't let the skunk near my daughter. No how, no way." Someone else shouted, "He's just a bum with a badge, Ernest. We're on your side."

It was bad enough to have the men laughing at him. It had happened to Sheriff Richards on several occasions. What he couldn't tolerate was looking over at Suzie and finding the girl and her friends laughing at him.

Sheriff Richards wanted to gun them all down. Every one of them. And he might have done just that if he hadn't been so certain that the most he could do was kill six of the people now. The instant his revolver was empty they would pounce on him and hang him from the nearest tree.

He took a drink from his bottle and pulled his Colt half out of his holster as a threat. Then he let the weapon fall back into place. He'd seen an instant fear in the eyes of some of the women when he'd feigned drawing his weapon, and that sign of fear was all he'd really wanted. He tossed his head back and laughed, then sauntered away, pretending not to care that the laughter he heard was at him, that the hatred directed toward him was so thick he could practically taste it in the air.

* * * *

Hawk sensed that something was wrong, though he couldn't say what. He'd seen several ranch hands glancing in his direction. They didn't seem angry with him for marrying Amanda. But something was wrong. The ranch hands were looking for leadership, and they weren't yet comfortable looking to him for it.

"What is it, Billy?" Hawk asked, approaching the young ranch hand whom he knew Amanda thought a great deal of.

Billy avoided Hawk's eyes for a moment. When Hawk placed a large hand on the boy's shoulder Billy's lips pursed into a thin line. "I'm really sorry to have to say this, but Sheriff Richards is here, an' it looks like he's fixin' for a fight."

"Thank you for telling me, Billy," Hawk said, squeezing the boy's shoulder and, after a moment, issuing the smallest of smiles, even though he was furious with the sheriff for disturbing his wedding reception. "You've done the right thing."

"The sheriff was over near where we're all dancin', last I heard."

"I want you to keep an eye on Amanda. I don't want this celebration disturbed for her. I don't want her made unhappy for any reason."

"I understand, sir," Billy replied.

Hawk turned away from the young man, searching for Darren Richards. Hawk believed in natural justice, the justice understood by the animals in the forest and on the grassy plains. He didn't have any faith, nor take any comfort, in the justice found in courts. Crow believed that wrongs could be righted working through the legal system, and that guilty men could be made both to see the error of their ways and to face an appropriate penalty for what they'd done.

Hawk believed men held justice in their own hands.

With each step Hawk took, his feet still uncomfortable in the stiff black shoes, he felt his anger rising. His senses were becoming more sharp-edged as he realized that he should have sought out the sheriff long before this moment. Had he gone after Sheriff Richards earlier, when Amanda was safely tucked away at the Sioux encampment, the foul lawman wouldn't be here now, trying to spoil the party. Hawk held himself responsible for this lack of foresight, but he intended to make up for his mistake, once and for all.

* * * *

Sheriff Richards had moved away from the musicians, realizing that there wasn't a female at the shindig who would dance with him. What bothered him most was the lack of respect in the eyes of the people who looked at him. Never before had the sheriff seen so little fear in the people he passed.

He'd long known that there were those men and women in Deadwood who didn't like him, and others who loathed him. But those people had always been careful to keep their feelings hidden from him as best they could. They didn't dare face his wrath, it had seemed.

But now all that had changed. Never before had the sheriff felt so isolated and outnumbered. And though his impulse was to leave, his pride refused to let him do so. If the rest of Deadwood was invited to the shindig, then he should have been, too. He was just as good as anyone in town, and better than most. There wasn't a man alive in any position to tell him what he could or couldn't do.

He passed a long table where a dozen fried chickens had been laid out for guests to feast upon at their leisure. As he drew nearer the table, the people who had been picking at the delicious chicken, chatting with each other as they ate and sipped beer, spotted the sheriff. They moved away, wrinkling their noses as though they suddenly smelled something foul.

Contemptuously, Sheriff Richards ripped the leg off a chicken, took one bite from it, then tossed the uneaten food to the ground. He wiped his fingers on the white linen tablecloth. A dozen people saw the disgusting gesture, and none of them hid their displeasure.

"You're leaving now."

The commanding male voice came through the crowd, which parted quickly to make way for the tall man's angry, long-legged form. When Hawk stepped into the clearing, his necktie pulled loose and his jacket and the top two buttons of his starched white shirt unfastened, his hands were already balled into huge fists.

"Are you talkin' to me, Injin'?" Darren Richards flipped the half-empty whiskey bottle aside and placed his right hand on the butt of his gun. His gaze went over Hawk, taking instant notice of his lack of a weapon. The right side of his mouth pulled upward. "You better watch your tongue, boy. I gave you one beatin', and if you're not real careful, I'll give you another."

"No, you won't." Hawk approached slowly. A hush had fallen over the crowd, and the musicians had stopped playing to watch the scene in the clearing. "The only thing you're going to do is leave. Leave now and never come back...if you know what's good for you."

The sheriff made a snorting sound of contempt, but he took a step backward just the same. He was aware of all the eyes upon him, and how the buzz of activity had stopped at Hawk's entrance. Though at first the sheriff might have felt fear, he had just enough whiskey in his blood to want to prove himself in front of all the people who had never truly given him the respect he'd always deserved.

"Boy, you'd better learn to watch your tongue." Sheriff Richards took a big step toward Hawk. "I suppose you think you're something special now that you married yourself into all this money, don't you? Well, I've got some news for you, redskin. As far as I'm concerned, you're just another murderin' Injin'. That's all you'll ever be. An' right now I'm takin' you into town for questioning."

"No, you're not," Hawk replied, his voice a breath above a whisper.

Someone from the crowd said, "Good Lord, Sheriff, the man just got married. Can't your questioning wait until tomorrow?"

Darren Richards shook his head slowly, never taking his eyes off Hawk. The more he thought about it, the more he liked how it would look to take Hawk away from his own shindig. Once the sheriff had done that, nobody would ever again question his authority.

"I'm takin' you back to the jail, redskin, and while we're there I'm going to ask you a few questions about my brother. He's disappeared real sudden like, and I'll bet if I ask you in just the right way, you'll give me the answers I've been lookin' for."

Hawk said quietly, "Your brother was as big a fool and a bushwacking coward as you are."

"Let's go, boy," the sheriff said, taking another step closer to Hawk. Barely five feet separated the men. "Don't make me have to hurt you."

From the crowd, the sheriff heard someone say quietly, "Don't trust him, Mr Hawk. The sheriff's got mean blood in him."

Sheriff Richards grinned, liking what he heard. "The boy knows the truth, redskin," he said, almost in a whisper, standing just outside arm's reach. "You bes' just come along or I'll put a bullet in you right here, right now...and there ain't a damn thing you can do about it."

Darren Richards had seen it before—the anger, the futile rage of a man not wanting to give ground, yet knowing in his heart that he had to. It was one of the things about the job that he never failed to appreciate. The only thing that bothered him was the look in the tall Indian's eyes. There wasn't a shred of fear, not even the slightest glimmer. But that didn't completely disconcert the sheriff. He figured that after he'd tapped Hawk half a dozen times on the head with the butt of his revolver, then introduced his ribs to the toes of his boots once more, he'd see fear in the half-breed's eyes.

"Let's walk, boy," the sheriff said slowly taking the gun from his holster. The crowd gasped in unison at the sight of the weapon. "Either you walk or I'm taking you back to Deadwood tossed over a saddle." He chuckled. "And then we'll see what answers the undertaker can get from you."

The sheriff reached for Hawk, but his hand didn't quite go far enough. Something in Hawk's stance warned Sheriff Richards, and he stopped himself, then took a step backward and thumbed back the hammer of his revolver.

"I told you to walk."

"You'll never get away with it. Not this time, Sheriff. To you I'm just another Indian, which means you think you can do to me whatever you like, and there's nothing that anyone else will do or say about it. But this time there's money behind the Indian. Money and power, and those are two things you don't have, isn't that so, boy?"

The notion of an Indian calling him *boy* was more than the sheriff could tolerate. He raised his gun, pointed it at Hawk's head, and squeezed the trigger.

Even before he was able to pull the trigger and send a bullet smashing into the Indian's face, Hawk lashed upward to grab the barrel of the gun. The sheriff's bullet went harmlessly into the night sky.

Sheriff Richards swung hard with his left fist, red-hot rage boiling in his veins. Though Hawk held the barrel of his revolver, Darren was still in control of the handle and trigger, and he fired again as he struggled with Hawk, this time sending a bullet ricocheting off the ground and hitting the leg of a table, splintering the wood and causing it to buckle under the weight of the feast.

Sheriff Richards again thumbed back the hammer, determined this time to put a bullet in the Indian's stomach so he could watch him die writhing on the ground. The sheriff had spent his life teaching men just like Hawk that they weren't worth the dirt beneath his feet, and he wasn't about to stop giving those lessons now — even if the redskin had managed to marry himself into the richest family in the territory. With a grin on his lips, Darren Richards squeezed the trigger of his revolver.

He felt the bullet slam into his own stomach because Hawk had twisted the weapon in his hand.

It was like being kicked by a horse, and the sheriff staggered backward three steps, releasing his hold on his revolver.

"You stinkin' redskin. When we get back to jail I'm going to kick your guts out for this," Darren Richards said, falling to his knees.

The sheriff could no longer keep his legs beneath him. And when he landed on his face in the dirt his last thought was that he was *really* going to make Hawk suffer this time.

Hawk wasn't surprised by the commotion that followed. However, the words of encouragement and support given to him by people whose names he didn't even know astonished him.

"I saw the whole thing," one elderly woman was saying, tugging at Hawk's sleeve to get his attention. "The sheriff was insane. Mad in the head — loco. He didn't give you no choice, and I'll tell the whole world in court, if you want me to."

Another man was telling Hawk that he'd done Deadwood a favor by killing Sheriff Richards, and if Hawk hadn't done it, someone else would have sooner or later.

Sonny came rushing forward, pushing people aside, a grim expression on his face.

"I'll explain later," Hawk said, placing a hand on his brother-in-law's broad shoulder. "Right now, I just want to make sure Amanda doesn't see any of this. I don't want the evening ruined for her."

"I'm afraid that's already happened," Sonny commented sternly. "Go to the library. I'll meet you there, with Vanessa and Amanda. We'll discuss what must be done now."

* * * *

Fifteen minutes later, Hawk was pacing the library while Sonny smoked a cigarette furiously, and Vanessa comforted Amanda.

"I've got twenty people as witnesses," Hawk said. He took a sip of brandy, then set the glass aside. Circumstances had taken the flavor out of the liquor for him. "He wasn't invited, and everyone saw him spoiling for a fight."

"There's nothing for you to worry about," Sonny said.

"It's self-defense, to be sure, but it's also a situation where an Indian man killed a white sheriff. Times have changed. We can't just pretend this didn't happen, as so often happened in the old days. Hawk's going to spend time in jail until we can clear his name."

The word 'jail' put an end to Hawk's pacing. He'd lived his life too free, too unencumbered, to ever consider spending another minute locked up like an animal. Holding his words in check, he looked at Vanessa. Maybe she had something else to tell him.

"Would you both mind leaving Deadwood for a while?" Vanessa asked, looking first at Hawk and then at Amanda. "I don't know for how long. At least a couple of weeks. Maybe through the winter, and then you can return in the summer. Would it be too much to stay with Hawk's people?"

Amanda shook her head vigorously. "Not at all," she answered.

"We can leave tonight, if that would be best," Hawk said, relieved at Vanessa's solution. He stepped forward, reaching down for Amanda's hands. When he held them tenderly in his, he got down on one knee before her, kissing her fingers lightly. "I'm sorry, Amanda, that you won't have the comforts of your home—"

"Don't apologize," Amanda said quickly, her eyes glistening with tears. "I'll be more than happy to live with your people. They're my people too, now, in a way. I don't care where I live, or how, so long as it's with you."

"Then we'll leave tonight."

Vanessa said, "We won't tell a soul where you've gone. By spring, I'll have pulled enough strings with territory authorities and judges to make it a guarantee that Hawk won't even have to make a statement."

Chapter Twenty-Five

The trip to the Sioux encampment was leisurely. Hawk paid even more attention to Amanda than usual. He suspected that she was secretly disappointed at not being able to stay at the Circle S to enjoy all the comforts of life that were there for her, but was hiding her innermost feelings from him. They rode slowly, stopping regularly to frolic in a stream that they came across, to make love often, sometimes in the sunlight with only *Ida Maka* to witness their happiness, and sometimes under the moon and stars, sharing their bliss with the night.

Amanda's appetite seemed to have increased somewhat, Hawk noted. He hoped she was pregnant, now that he was her husband. Having been born a bastard, he understood all too well the almost insurmountable difficulties a child faced not having a father, not having a name. Once he teased Amanda, suggesting she might be pregnant, but she dismissed the joke quickly, insisting she'd be the first to know if she was going to become a mother.

Hawk was disappointed as they approached the camp. He hadn't had enough of Amanda yet, hadn't gotten tired of monopolizing her time and attention. Her bright and sunny smile was just as heart-warming to him now as it had been the first time they had touched. And when she opened her arms to hold him, the fire that burned within him was just as intense as it ever had been.

"Don't be surprised if the children touch your hair," Hawk said as they walked their horses into camp. "Now that you're with me, they'll probably take a few liberties."

"Why would they want to touch my hair?" Amanda asked, thinking this very odd behavior.

"How many blonde Sioux have you seen? When you were a guest they kept their distance somewhat. They didn't want to be disrespectful. But now you're here with me, and they'll want to know if your skin feels different from theirs, your hair different."

Amanda looked to her left, where children had stopped playing and simply stared as she and Hawk rode into camp. "I think we're going to surprise a few people with our return."

It was Hawk who first sensed something was wrong. It wasn't just the children's behavior—he expected such bluntness from children—but women and braves also stared as they passed.

"What is it?" Amanda whispered.

"Red Wolf," Hawk answered, keeping his voice down so only Amanda could hear him.

"What's he done?"

"I don't know yet, but I'll find out."

Crow approached them first, with Buttercup running to catch up with them all.

"We've got to talk," Crow said, taking the reins of Hawk's stallion. He turned to Buttercup and said, "Will you take care of the horses?"

"No, I want to—"

"Buttercup!" Hawk spoke the single word sharply, and it silenced the girl. "Do as Crow says. There will be time later for you to learn what has been said."

Buttercup was clearly unhappy about being excluded, however temporarily, but she did as her brother instructed.

They went directly to Crow's tepee. If Hawk hadn't known better, he'd say that some of the braves in camp actually walked away from him to avoid acknowledging his return to camp. Though Hawk had been treated with disrespect as a child, once he'd reached his full height and learned to hunt and fight for himself and his tribe, few braves openly scorned his presence, and none directly to his face.

"What has happened here?" Hawk asked the instant the tepee flap fell back into place behind Crow.

"Dull Knife is dead."

Hawk grimaced in physical pain at the news. Crow placed his hand on Hawk's shoulder. Both men had liked the elder chieftain, but the loss was especially hard for Hawk, who had placed such value in the man's advice.

"He was murdered about the time that you and Amanda left for Deadwood. That's what people here are guessing, anyway."

"Who killed him?"

"We don't know. He was found up in the hills. The wolves have—" Crow stopped.

"You don't have to worry about me," Amanda said. "I don't need to be coddled. I just want to know the truth."

"There are stories going around the campfires, Hawk," Crow continued. "Some braves have had their suspicions about you for a long time. Not everyone thinks you're as charming as the ladies do." Crow glanced at Amanda again. "And there's the missing money. Almost half of the two thousand you gave to the elders is gone."

"Let me guess," Hawk said bitter. "The money disappeared about the same time that I left camp, right?"

"Naturally."

"What kind of logic does that make?" Hawk snapped. "Why would I give money to the tribe only to steal it back? That would be like stealing from myself. Isn't there anyone who understands that? And if I was in such need of money, why would I give it to the council in the first place? Nobody knew I had the money."

"That's what I've been telling everyone who will listen. Unfortunately, not many on the council have been interested in what I have to say." Crow shrugged his shoulders. "It's not like in a white man's court where I get to give my side of the story to the jury and they have to listen to me."

"I'm gone a little over two weeks and all this happens?" Hawk asked incredulously. "What more could they have against me?"

"Your wife, I should think," Amanda said, stepping forward.

"We're not that way," Hawk informed her.

"Yes, we are," Crow replied. "I'm sorry, but it's true. You marrying a white woman has not endeared you to many in the tribe. It's just one more thing that casts you in a suspicious light."

"And it has been Red Wolf who has spoken out most against me, hasn't it?"

Buttercup came inside the tepee then, doing the almost unthinkable by entering without being invited. She went straight to Hawk and put her arms around him. He stroked her hair lightly and said, "None of what you've heard is true. It's all lies."

"I knew they were lies," Buttercup said quietly. "But it's good to hear you say so."

Never before had Amanda felt quite so much like an outsider as she did at that moment. She understood so little of what was expected of Sioux men and women. She watched as her husband, her sister-in-law, and her husband's best friend talked. But now the words flowed over Amanda, not really touching her, not registering in her brain. Though all three—with their dark hair, eyes, and skin—looked reasonably the same, she looked completely different. How it pained her that Hawk, under suspicion for a crime he did not commit, was more deeply incriminated because he'd fallen in love with an outsider and had taken her for his wife.

A single question kept going through her mind: How much would the man she loved suffer because he'd married her?

Hawk, Crow, and Buttercup were already sitting in a tight triangle, their knees touching. Amanda, on the outside, quietly stepped behind Hawk, then knelt and placed her hands lightly on his shoulders. She leaned forward to put her cheek against his back. Closing her eyes, she issued a silent prayer of hope, then listened to what was being said.

Crow said, "We've got to face our accusers. It's the only way we'll ever gain any credibility."

"It's not *our* accusers," Hawk said. "You're not the one they're blaming for the murder of Dull Knife."

"We're in this together," Crow said with quiet conviction.

Hawk placed his hand over Crow's, squeezed his friend's hand a moment, then nodded. They'd been through many battles together, and an attack upon one was an attack upon both.

"Then we'll face our accusers standing shoulder to shoulder," Hawk said. "I say we find Red Wolf now and take him before the elders. Then we'll hear what he has to say when we are there to defend ourselves from his lies."

"But first there is something we must do," Crow said.

Hawk gave him a quizzical look.

"Amanda is the target of anger and suspicion," Crow continued. "Why not remove her from danger, at least until we can explain to the elders that we're not responsible for Dull Knife's death, or the missing money."

"The cave? You haven't told anyone else about it?" Hawk asked.

Crow looked at him and smiled. "Never. We made a promise to each other."

The cave was tucked away, completely isolated from the camp, high in the hills. Hawk had discovered it as a young man when he'd first begun to hunt on his own for food for the tribe. There he could sit quietly with his friend and talk without fear of being overheard. Both men were loners, and when the crowded camp became too cloying for them, they'd often spent a day or two at the cave by themselves.

Whenever the tribe was in the territory, Hawk had visited the cave to enjoy some solitude.

"Buttercup can take Amanda there," Hawk continued, liking the idea more as time passed. "I've brought plenty of food here with me. We can give them enough to last three or four days. That should be all the time we need to remove the stain from our names."

* * * *

"We're going to catch hell for that," Hawk commented quietly as he watched Amanda and Buttercup ride away from camp, leading a packhorse laden with supplies and food. "The elders are going to wonder why I've sent Amanda away so soon after arriving, and they'll want to know why Buttercup went with her. They'll be furious at not being consulted first."

"Don't worry about their questions," Crow replied, patting his friend on the back. "At least you know now that your wife and sister are safe."

When Hawk turned around, facing the inner circle of the camp, he could feel the gaze of braves and squaws upon him. How many of them believed that he was responsible for the murder of Dull Knife?

The sun was high overhead, and Hawk was thankful. He didn't want Amanda and Buttercup traveling at night. The rocky terrain surrounding the cave held countless natural dangers. Who could be sure that a horse wouldn't be spooked and stumble off the trail, sending horse and rider plummeting over a steep, craggy cliff?

Though the huge tepee loomed before them, Hawk was surprised at how little trepidation he felt. When he was younger a meeting with the elders had always troubled him. Now, with his wife and sister safely out of camp, he welcomed the chance to challenge his accuser. Face-to-face, he would confront Red Wolf before the elders, and when he was done he would not only have cleared the name of Hawk Two Feather, but he would have more credibility with the elders than ever before.

They had almost reached their destination when Red Wolf stepped out from behind a tepee, leading his horse by the bridle. He seemed shocked to suddenly find himself facing Hawk, though neither victory nor anger showed in his expression.

"Running away, Red Wolf?" Hawk asked, his lips twisted in a scowl. "Afraid to end what you have started?"

"Not at all," Red Wolf replied quickly. "I welcome the chance to teach you once and for all that a bastard is, first and last, always just a bastard." He turned away.

When Hawk moved toward Red Wolf, Crow intervened, stepping between the two braves.

"Don't start a fight. It's just what he wants you to do." Crow seemed determined not to let Hawk's fiery nature work against himself. "You'll only look bad before the council if you attack him now."

Hawk gritted his teeth, knowing in his heart that the words Crow spoke were wise ones. But it was impossible to look at Red Wolf's evil face and not want to attack him, not want to strike out at him for being the foul man that he was.

"We'll see how you smile when the council hears what I have to say," Hawk said, looking over Crow's shoulder at his enemy. "Then we will see who has courage, won't we?"

"Run away, you fatherless maggot," Red Wolf replied, but even as he spoke he was already moving away from Hawk and Crow.

As Red Wolf retreated, Hawk at first felt he'd achieved some kind of victory because he had stood his ground and his enemy had retreated. Then he wasn't so sure. He didn't understand Red Wolf's behavior — at first surprised to be confronted by Hawk, then strangely unwilling to engage in a more forceful confrontation.

"Ignore him." Crow nudged Hawk toward the giant tepee once more. "Red Wolf has already built a funeral pyre for himself. It's only a matter of time before he lights the flame himself."

"You're right, of course." Hawk couldn't shake the feeling that somehow, some way, he had once again been manipulated by Red Wolf.

* * * *

Crow spoke slowly, choosing his words for the emotional impact his information would have upon the stony-faced tribal elders. He spoke for an hour, detailing the exploits of Hawk Two Feather and the heroism and selflessness he'd shown toward the tribe throughout his life. Crow chronicled major events, including the time when, in the dead of winter, Hawk had tracked a small herd of mule deer for several days. With bow and arrow he had killed four of the deer. With the meat those deer provided for the tribe, Hawk had eased the hunger that had gripped the tribe for weeks.

And Crow spoke of the bravery Hawk had shown in battles against the Cheyenne and Blackfeet. Yes, Crow said, Hawk's ancestry was suspect. But to hold him accountable for the misdeeds of others? Hawk's loyalty to the Sioux was limitless and unwavering. Hawk should be judged by his actions, Crow argued, not by the words of a man who had, throughout his life, shown little interest in the welfare of the tribe.

Reaching this part of his speech, Crow glanced sideways at Hawk, as though to let his friend know that now he was going to change tactics. He had first established Hawk as an honorable warrior for the Sioux, now he was going to call into question the motives and honor of Red Wolf.

But Hawk was hardly listening. Looking into the faces of the old men judging him, he tried but failed to anticipate the verdict. Instead, his thoughts were distracted by the confrontation he'd had with Red Wolf. What was it about those brief moments that should mean something to him?

"I see that Red Wolf is not here." Crow's voice rose slightly. "That doesn't surprise me. Why should a liar stand before his elders and be proven to be just exactly that?"

"Red Wolf was told to be here," one of the elders said. It was the first time any of them had spoken since Crow had begun, and the sound of his voice caught Hawk by surprise.

"Red Wolf is supposed to be here?" Hawk asked.

The eyes of the council turned to Hawk. Not having been asked to speak, he showed either a lack of understanding of the ways of the Sioux or a disrespect for their customs to do so. Crow turned to look at Hawk and, without words, warned Hawk with his eyes not to speak again unless asked.

Hawk couldn't be bothered with the customs he might be violating or the propriety he was offending. Instinctively, he knew that Red Wolf was up to something, that he had some devious plot in mind and perhaps was even now putting it into motion. What could be so vital that Red Wolf would miss this? He had, with his lies, turned Hawk's reputation into a shambles. Now he could be finishing Hawk's destruction, before the elders, by voicing his "concern" for the safety and integrity of the tribe. Instead, he was allowing Hawk to clear his own name without rebuttal. Why? What could be so compelling?

Reactions circulating through the group in the tepee flowed over Hawk, and though the significance for his future could not be overestimated, he didn't listen to a single word.

Hawk asked himself, *What does Red Wolf want most in this world?* He answered himself with, *To destroy me.* Then he asked himself, *What would destroy me?* At first he thought of the obvious — murder. But then another thought came to mind, and it was so blood-chilling that Hawk, though he was a courageous man who had faced mortal danger without blinking, shivered. What would destroy him, sentence him to a living hell, was not the loss of his own life…but the loss of Amanda's.

"I have to leave." Hawk jumped to his feet, addressing Crow, who immediately caught Hawk's wrist. "I *have* to leave," Hawk repeated, more quietly this time.

Crow's eyes were dark as midnight. "You *will not leave!* Not now. If you leave now, you'll make yourself look guiltier to these men by your actions than by anything Red Wolf has said."

Hawk looked around at the faces of the tribal elders. He could not tell how many understood English well enough to follow Crow's words. All Hawk was certain of was that he did not care. He didn't care if the elders thought he was guilty of every crime known to the

Sioux, or even the white man. All that mattered and motivated him was the fact that Red Wolf wasn't in the tepee when he should have been.

Hawk shook his arm free from Crow's grip. "I'm sorry," he said, leaving his friend in a terrible position with the elders, yet seeing no other course of action open to him. "I'm sorry, but I *have* to go. I think Amanda's in danger."

"How?"

"Where's Red Wolf?" Hawk asked. "Keep the elders here as long as you can." Hawk garbled his speech just enough to make his words impossible to understand unless a listener spoke English fluently. "I'll look guilty by leaving, so you've got to convince them that I had to go get something and that I'll be back. Make up any story you think is convincing. I'm going after Amanda. I think that's where Red Wolf is headed right now."

"He's more than an hour ahead of you," Crow said.

In the next instant Hawk was out of the tepee, pausing to hear the beginning of Crow's' eloquent, though rambling, explanation of why Hawk Two Feather, esteemed hunter and loyal warrior for the Sioux, would leave the presence of the tribal elders without asking permission. Hawk smiled grimly to himself, wondering what kind of lie Crow was about to give, then began jogging to his tepee. First, he would get his weapons, then his stallion, and then, if he was lucky, he would ride to the cave where Amanda and Buttercup were hiding and discover that his fears were groundless.

But as a Sioux, for whom a feeling was as good as a fact, he knew in his soul that Amanda was in danger, and that Red Wolf was the cause of it.

* * * *

"Someone's following us," Amanda said. The words had simply entered her head, and it was only later, after she'd heard what she'd said, that she felt fear.

Buttercup reined in her pinto, turning the animal around to align it with Amanda's Daisy. "Where?" she asked, "My eyes do not see what yours do."

Amanda apologized. She had always been a woman who spoke first and decided later whether it might have been better to remain silent. She looked back into the foothills, searching for the source of her concern.

"I don't see anything either," Amanda concluded. She was about to turn Daisy around and continue on her way toward the cave, but Buttercup stopped her.

"Perhaps you are looking with your eyes instead of your mind," Buttercup said, still staring intently into the foothills. "Your soul can see that which your eyes cannot."

Amanda tried to dismiss her worries as unfounded, but the sense of unease would not leave her. She wished that Hawk was with her. When he was near, even if the enemy was many and mighty, she felt confident, sure that Hawk would think of some brilliant strategy with which to either defeat or elude them.

"How far do you think we are from the cave?" Amanda wasn't disguising her concern.

Buttercup pulled the crudely drawn map from her *parafleche* and unfolded it. "At least two hours, provided…"

"Provided we don't get lost?" Amanda asked. "Don't worry, we won't get lost," She assured her, tapping her heels to Daisy's ribs. "You shouldn't let imaginary worries play on your mind. Soon enough, you'll have a man in your life. That's when you'll *really* have something to worry about."

Resisting every urge to glance over her shoulder, Amanda forced herself to pretend that she felt no fear. It was bad enough that she was worried. She didn't want to incite Buttercup's fears as well. So, though she did not feel at all light-hearted, Amanda kept up a continuous stream of stories for Buttercup regarding the wedding, and how handsome a figure Hawk had cut in the immaculate suit he had complained about constantly.

"It didn't bother you that the ladies were all looking at him?"

"At first it did, I guess," Amanda admitted, "but then I realized that it didn't matter how many women were looking at Hawk so long as he was only looking at me."

Buttercup laughed softly. As Amanda twisted in the saddle to glance back at her, a movement caught her eye, far off in the foothills. Studying the area where the motion had come from, she again saw nothing unusual. The movement could have been caused by anything from a mule deer or a coyote to dried brush tossed about by the wind.

"Was my brother really nervous before the wedding?" Buttercup asked, mischief in her voice.

"Incredibly so," Amanda said as she repeated the fabrication of only a few minutes before.

Chapter Twenty-Six

Hawk's great stallion—lathered, with its enormous chest heaving and its nostrils flaring, as powerful muscles propelled horse and rider ever higher up the hillside—had to be making ground on Red Wolf. Without any actual proof that the renegade Sioux warrior was after Amanda and Buttercup, Hawk knew it in his heart.

Around his hips hung his holstered revolver. The heavy-caliber Colt was the only weapon he had grabbed before rushing out of the camp. What weapons did Red Wolf have with him? Hawk clenched his teeth as he thought of Red Wolf's suspicious behavior and his unwillingness to fight just before the meeting with the elders.

As he was cursing himself for what he could not possibly have known, Hawk's stallion made an odd, almost sideways movement. Years of riding experience kept Hawk in the saddle, but the stallion's stride had changed just enough for Hawk to know that something was wrong.

"Come on, boy," Hawk urged, leaning low over the stallion's neck and imploring the spirits to banish the hitch in the animal's gait.

He waited five more strides, and when the slight hitch in the stallion's stride became a limp he could no longer pretend to not know what had happened. He reined the horse to a stop, though the stallion at first resisted him.

Hawk dismounted, then raised the stallion's front left hoof to look at the underside. There, near the soft inner circle, was the stone bruise, already beginning to swell and discolor. Hawk cursed, squeezing his eyes shut for only an instant as the consequences of the minor injury washed over him like a tidal wave.

Hawk was now on foot. Even if he had been cruel enough to continue riding the stallion, pushing the animal onward, it would have been only a matter of time—and very little time at that—before the hoof's swelling would cause the stallion to be in constant, ever-increasing pain. Before long, not even the stallion's great will to run would be enough to keep him pushing onward. The only remedy for a stone bruise was time and rest.

"Go on, boy," Hawk ordered.

The stallion pranced a few steps to the side but did not leave. He turned huge brown eyes on his master.

"Go on, I said." Hawk slapped the animal's rump hard, and this time the stallion headed back toward camp.

Hawk turned uphill and tried to calculate how much time he had before sundown. Once the sun went down, his dangers—and the dangers for Amanda and Buttercup—would become increasingly ominous. Ahead was the woman he loved enough to make her his wife. Also ahead was the only man in the world Hawk wished he had killed when he'd the chance.

* * * *

Red Wolf knelt to inspect the tracks more closely. The rocky ground made it difficult to trail riders, though the task was made slightly easier because Amanda's mare was shod. Horseshoes tended to leave marks on the rocks that unshod hooves would not.

How far ahead were Amanda and Buttercup? Where were the two women headed? Near the dry bluffs? That was a possibility to which Red Wolf didn't give much consideration. The dry bluffs weren't fit for man or beast. But there was the high cave? Red Wolf had once tracked Crow to find out where he went when he left camp. Though he'd lost Crow several days later, Red Wolf had discovered a cave, looking as though it had held a recent occupant. If Crow knew about the place, then so did Hawk, Red Wolf reasoned. Perhaps that's where the women were going.

If that was the case, then Red Wolf knew a shortcut, making it possible for him to beat the women to their destination. The thought sent an emotion though him that was like an electrical charge.

Red Wolf climbed back onto his pinto. The lies he'd been telling about Hawk would soon come completely unraveled. Red Wolf knew and understood this, accepting it as fact. Once Crow got to talking, using skills he'd learned in the white man's schools and courts of law, the inconsistencies in Red Wolf's stories would become increasingly obvious until, at last, the elders would have no choice but to eventually come to the conclusion that Red Wolf was the liar. He would be seen as the threat to the tribe, the one worthy of being tossed out of the camp, naked, without weapons to defend himself, clothes to warm himself, a horse to carry him.

But the elders would come to this conclusion too late. By the time the old men had discussed his fate, after a long and painful deliberation, Red Wolf would already have ridden many, many miles to the south. He would abandon the tribe before the tribe cast him out. But he would leave them with something to remember him by. He would exact his revenge upon Hawk, and the rest of the tribe, by attacking Amanda and Buttercup.

Now the spirits were conspiring together with him to make his vicious dreams come true, Red Wolf thought. Though Amanda and Buttercup had a sizable lead on him, Red Wolf believed he knew where they were headed, and his confidence was soaring. Now that they had ridden away from camp without either Hawk or Crow to escort them, the spirits were telling him that he was justified in taking his revenge upon Hawk's two women.

Red Wolf kicked his pony with his heels, urging the animal on. It was all perfectly fitting, he thought. He was riding a pony stolen by Hawk. In time, he would capture Hawk's sister and wife. And with them under his power, he would prove he was many times the warrior that Hawk was. And once he'd convinced them of his superiority, and his lust was sated, he would kill.

That accomplished, he would ride hard and fast, with the thousand dollars he'd stolen from Dull Knife's tepee to help him forget that he was a warrior without a tribe, a man whose name was a curse, his existence a blight.

He pushed up the foothills, his eyes searching for the women. In a corner of his mind he pondered a single question: Would he force Amanda to satisfy his desires first, or would he first take Buttercup's virginity?

* * * *

Amanda looked up at the rock formation and smiled. It was exactly as Hawk had described it—two large boulders standing with a flat boulder lying atop both, creating a natural archway.

"There it is," Amanda breathed softly, pointing to the archway. "Hawk's hiding place. We're safe at last." Trying to sound confident.

"I knew Hawk wouldn't let us down," Buttercup replied. She rushed forward to inspect the cave.

Amanda peered around, still not certain that the cave was such a secret. There was no source of water, and if the wind blew strong and cold from the north, the cave itself would be unbearable. But taking those factors into account and planning for them, one could use the cave as a safe haven of warmth and security.

She looked to the west and smiled. In only a few minutes the sun would settle beneath the horizon, then the narrow arroyo where Hawk's cave was hidden would be plunged into darkness. Then she and Buttercup could pass the time sharing stories while Hawk at last put an end to all the damaging rumors that had been spread about him.

"Take the water in first," Amanda said, dismounting. "Once we take care of the horses for the night we can finally relax."

Amanda studied the arroyo one more time before starting to remove Daisy's saddle. She still felt something disconcerting...but what? She was confident that she hadn't allowed anyone to follow them.

She heard a sound from inside the cave, and Amanda's heart skipped a beat. Then she recognized the sound, and sighed. Buttercup had dropped the water pouch. Amanda wondered what problems the inaccessibility of water would cause, but dismissed the matter from her immediate concern. Whatever was necessary would have to wait until the morning.

"Buttercup, are you all right in there?" Amanda called out after a moment.

There was no answer. Amanda glanced into the black entrance of the cave, and frowned. Then she removed the saddle from Daisy.

"Buttercup?"

Still no answer.

Amanda felt a coldness in her stomach and a tightness in her throat. She dropped the saddle to the ground and took a single step toward the cave. Then Buttercup stepped out, with Red Wolf directly behind her, his arm around her throat and a huge knife in his right hand, the point of the blade held against her ribs.

"Damn you!" Amanda spat, frozen in midstride.

"He wanted me to tell you to come into the cave, but I wouldn't," Buttercup said, her eyes wild with fear.

Red Wolf shook Buttercup so that her entire body quivered, her toes barely touching the ground. Both her hands clutched the forearm, thick with muscle, that pressed against her throat.

"Don't hurt her," Amanda said, her voice deceptively calm. She raised her hands toward Red Wolf, fingers spread to show that she held no weapons. "She's only a child."

The grin Red Wolf showed Amanda was pure evil. "She is old enough for me," he said softly, malevolently, tightening his arm around Buttercup's throat. "When I am finished, she will feel like an *old* woman. A thoroughly fucked old woman."

He laughed then, and Amanda knew deep in her heart that Red Wolf was insane. She had heard about men like him, men who possessed no sense of right and wrong, and standing face to face with such evil made her shiver.

"My horse is over that rise," Red Wolf said, nodding to the left, where more boulders had been piled by nature. "Get him and bring him to me. If you don't hurry, I will cut her pretty face to the bone. You know I will."

"Don't do it, Amanda," Buttercup warned. "Run while you have the chance."

Red Wolf shook Buttercup again, and pressed the point of his knife more firmly against her ribs, causing her to gasp softly.

"Hurry, I say," Red Wolf said, his eyes brilliant, demonic. "She would not be the first squaw I have put my knife through."

Amanda knew that Red Wolf was telling the truth. Gazing into his eyes she saw a man who enjoyed inflicting pain, especially when there was no chance that he would be hurt himself. She ran to the rise and saw the horse. The animal was nervous, sensing danger, as Amanda brought it back to the entrance of the cave.

"I've done what you've asked." Amanda approached Red Wolf and Buttercup slowly. There was a rifle in a scabbard affixed to the horse's saddle, but she made no effort to remove it.

"Your rifle is still where you put it. I can't hurt you...so why don't you let her go?"

"Inside," Red Wolf said, his grin even broader and more wicked as his victory seemed imminent. "You will soon learn what it is to be with a real warrior."

Amanda's glance went from Red Wolf to Buttercup. The girl was terrified, her young body rigid with fear. She looked to Amanda as though for salvation.

"Let her go," Amanda said with quiet authority. She knew there was a chance her tone would anger Red Wolf, but she had to risk it to save Buttercup. "She's not the one you want. It's me you want, because you hate Hawk. Isn't that so?"

Red Wolf was half hidden in the shadows at the mouth of the cave, and his teeth shined eerily white in the darkness as he smiled. "You are wise for a white squaw."

"Yes, I am wise. I know how to please a man," Amanda replied, and the flirtatious sound and meaning of her words made her sick to her stomach. Already she felt violated, even though she hadn't been touched. "Why waste your time with a girl who knows nothing when you can be with a woman who knows everything?"

"Hawk has taught you well?" Red Wolf asked, the tone of his voice curious, envious.

"Hawk has taught me *everything*," Amanda replied. She took several steps forward, letting the reins of Red Wolf's pinto fall from her fingertips. She exaggerated the sway of her hips as she walked, and hated herself just a little for the seductive way she gazed at Red Wolf and moistened her lips. "And I've liked what I've learned, and you will, too."

They were words no beautiful woman had ever spoken to Red Wolf. Not even the prostitutes he'd bought had been able to say such words so convincingly—even though he'd demanded it of them. With Amanda almost within arm's reach of him, he could hardly wait to touch her, to feel her voluptuous body crushed beneath his. He had dreamed that he would teach her what it was like to be with a real warrior, but now he wondered whether she would be the one to teach him what pleasures of the flesh were possible.

"Just let the girl go," Amanda said, her voice still a seductive whisper. "She means nothing to either of us. She'll only get in the way, don't you see?"

Red Wolf needed a free hand and he had none. He had chosen to use the knife because it was his favorite weapon, so deadly, so personal. And it was especially gratifying to know that it was Dull Knife's weapon that he now held in his hand. Though he felt the warmth of Buttercup's young body, her back against his chest, suddenly she was not as desirable as she had once seemed.

"Go inside," Red Wolf demanded of Amanda, his eyes wide with a feral light.

"Let her go first," Amanda replied in a sultry purr, keeping just out of arm's reach from Red Wolf. "She'll only get in the way of what we want to do."

She could see that the arm around Buttercup's throat wasn't as tight as it had been, and though Red Wolf continued to hold the large-bladed knife in his hand, the deadly point was no longer touching Buttercup's ribs.

"I cannot be tricked by a white woman," Red Wolf said viciously, his eyes practically glowing like the embers of a campfire. "Go into the cave."

He reached for Amanda, attempting to hold the heavy knife in one hand as he tried to catch the sleeve of her shirt in the fingers of the other hand. Amanda didn't hesitate to make her move. She lashed out at Red Wolf's wrist, hitting it with all her might. The knife twirled out of his grasp.

"Run, Buttercup!" Amanda shouted, lunging at Red Wolf, her fingers curled as she clawed at his eyes.

Amanda felt the soft tissue of Red Wolf's face tear beneath her fingernails, then felt the warrior's fist slam into her stomach, knocking the breath from her lungs. Her knees buckled beneath her, but she still managed to shout for Buttercup to run one more time as she continued her struggle with the renegade Sioux.

She wasn't entirely certain what happened next because Red Wolf's fist struck a glancing blow against the top of her head. But an instant later it was she who had her back to Red Wolf, his forearm tight across her throat. He'd recovered his knife and was brandishing it against her cheek. Through blurred vision, she watched as Buttercup disappeared out of the cave.

"Run!" she cried triumphantly.

Red Wolf was hissing into Amanda's ear, words she didn't understand, although their meaning was clear—he was going to punish her for freeing Buttercup. Amanda had done what she had to do, what her sense of honor and her heart had dictated, and if she had to pay a price for her actions now, then so be it.

When Buttercup had almost disappeared into the darkness outside she stopped and looked back into the cave. Amanda could see the fear in her eyes. She didn't want to leave.

"Go!" Amanda shouted, and for her defiance, Red Wolf shook her, the arm around her throat tightening so that she could hardly breathe.

"Come back or I will cut her!" Red Wolf shouted.

Buttercup turned away and disappeared into the night, and Amanda felt an almost overpowering sense of accomplishment, of victory over evil.

"You still have me," Amanda said after a moment, though Red Wolf continued cursing in a language she did not understand. Now that Buttercup was safe, Amanda was already thinking of a way to free herself. "She's gone," Amanda said quietly, feeling the razor-sharp blade against her cheek. "There's nothing you can do about that now. But you've still got me, Red Wolf."

"You will suffer. When I am done Hawk will vomit at the sight of you."

Amanda had no doubt that Red Wolf had made others suffer so. He pushed her toward his pinto, which had been spooked when Buttercup had bolted from the cave.

Hawk appeared out of the shadows, like the embodiment of vengeance. He held his revolver in his hand, though it was not pointed at Red Wolf.

Red Wolf spotted Hawk a moment after Amanda did. He flinched and bent his knees so that he was partially hidden behind Amanda's body. He brought the knife around, touching the point to her back.

"Let her go, Red Wolf," Hawk said. "Let her go now and I will not kill you."

Red Wolf moved his right hand, showing Hawk that he held a knife to Amanda's body. As she looked helplessly at Hawk, Red Wolf's chin was nearly touching her shoulder. "Drop the gun," Red Wolf said. "Drop the gun or I'll cut her right now. You cannot stop me. Do as I command."

Hawk didn't drop his gun, though he did holster the weapon. He saw that Red Wolf had Dull Knife's knife in his hand, and in an instant he realized who had killed the wise chieftain. Hawk felt his heart tighten at the thought of Dull Knife's senseless death.

"Toss the gun away." Red Wolf said sharply, bringing the deadly edge of his blade once more to Amanda's cheek. "Do it or you'll watch her bleed."

Hawk shook his head slowly. He had delayed long enough so that he wasn't quite so winded. His breathing was now almost normal. His gaze locked with Red Wolf's as he slowly walked forward, his hands hanging limp at his sides, his posture indicating a man at ease.

"Let her go." Hawk spoke a little louder than he had before. "I'll kill you if you spill a single drop of her blood. You know that is the truth."

"She will die before your eyes if you take another step." Red Wolf spoke in a flat, level tone, equal to Hawk's. "Now take the gun from your holster and drop it. Do it before I cut her just to hear the music of her screams in my ears."

Amanda expected Hawk to do as he had been commanded. She knew he loved her, and that he would do anything to see to it that she was safe. But instead of tossing the Colt to the ground, Hawk simply stood there, shaking his head slowly, his gaze boring into Red Wolf's.

For an instant Amanda squeezed her eyes shut. Why wasn't Hawk doing as he'd been told? Did he want to see her hurt?

"Let her go," Hawk said, taking yet another step closer to Red Wolf and Amanda. "Do it now and I give you my word of honor that I will not harm you."

"Your word? What good is your word?"

"You know what it is," Hawk shot back quickly, stepping closer to reduce the distance between them to less than twenty feet. "It is my life. You cannot say as much. Your honor is without value. You are no more trusted than a white man."

"Can you make it?" Red Wolf asked after a moment, his voice tight and strained, a twisted smile curling his lips. "Can you make the shot, Hawk? It is what you are thinking. Do not tell me you are not asking yourself whether your skill is enough to save your life and end mine."

At first Amanda didn't understand what the men were talking about. Make the shot? Hawk had no shot to make, she thought. Red Wolf was completely hidden behind her, with the exception of his head. He was using her as a shield, his cheek pressed against her ear—too close to her, surely, for Hawk to risk firing his revolver. Or was it?

Amanda had become a pawn in a gigantic, all-too-real chess game, with life and death stakes. She wanted to close her eyes to shut out the horror, but she didn't dare. She wanted to scream, but her throat had tightened with fear as to make breathing difficult and speech impossible.

Hawk was standing with his feet spread slightly apart, his hands held away from his hips, the handle of his revolver inches from his grasp.

"Are you that good, Hawk?" Red Wolf asked, then chuckled. "If you miss, you will shoot your wife. I have killed women before. Have you?"

Amanda had heard enough. Red Wolf was beyond pure evil. If she allowed him to live, if she did anything that would make it possible for him to go on in his villainy, she knew she could never forgive herself.

"Do it," she said to Hawk.

A doe sprinted out of the shadows. Red Wolf's attention was diverted for only an instant

One second Red Wolf had his face pressed up tightly against hers, his big, lethal knife ready to take her life with just a flick of his wrist. But Hawk moved so swiftly his action was just a blur, then there was an enormous roar as his revolver fired a single deadly bullet. Red Wolf's head snapped back on his shoulders.

Amanda waited, afraid to turn around, fearful that somehow Red Wolf would still be alive, his deadly knife still in his hand.

"It's over," Hawk assured her, holstering his weapon as he rushed forward to take Amanda into his arms. "It's all over, Amanda."

Amanda was too frightened and too relieved to cry. The doe, as promised in the vision quest, had saved her life because she'd trusted her love. She buried her face in Hawk's neck and held on to him tightly, her arms encircling his waist. When she could hear Buttercup to her right, crying softly, she reached out a hand for the girl.

"We're together now," Amanda whispered, not taking her face away from Hawk's neck even to speak. "Nobody can separate us again. Promise me that."

"I promise," Hawk whispered, his arms so tight around Amanda that they nearly crushed her. "Together for always."

Epilogue

It was the first snow of the winter, and Amanda was oddly pleased to watch the heavy white flakes drifting to the ground. When she had lived near Deadwood, in her big, comfortable ranch house, she had hated the coming of winter. The long days with nothing much to keep her occupied had lay ahead. Boredom and the sense of being cooped up, more than the cold and the snow, was her enemy.

But it would be different this winter. She was at work stitching together a heavy elk hide cape that would keep her warm, and Buttercup had already made her a pair of oversized moccasins that, when properly insulated with prairie grass, would be considerably warmer than any boots Amanda had ever owned. Buttercup had promised it. The cape would keep her warm in the strongest winter winds, and was large enough to allow for her expanding waistline.

Amanda patted her belly, a faint smile curling her lips. Hawk's vision quest had come true, she realized. He'd had the vision of an eagle in a hawk's nest, with a small dove just peeking its head over the rim of the nest. Amanda believed that she represented the eagle in Hawk's nest, and the dove—the Dove of Peace—was the child now growing within her. That child, Amanda believed, would bring peace to the Sioux, would be a bridge between the two cultures that all too often had been at war with each other.

The sound of a horse drawing near Amanda's attention, and she looked up to see Hawk approaching. A smile curved his lips, though concern darkened his eyes as he dismounted.

"You should put on something warmer," he said, taking long strides to where she was kneeling just outside the tepee they shared. "There is a chill in the air."

From inside the tepee Buttercup began to laugh. "You are sounding more like a father all the time," she teased her half-brother.

Amanda made no effort to suppress her grin. "She's right, you know. There's no need to worry so much about me."

Hawk got down on one knee beside his wife. He placed a hand gently on her slightly rounded stomach. "I only worry because you have never spent a winter in a tepee. You don't know how difficult it can be, especially carrying a child."

Amanda pressed her palm against her husband's cheek. Since he had discovered that he was going to be a father, he'd become monumentally concerned with her happiness and comfort, and for that she was eternally grateful.

"I keep telling you that I've never been so happy in my life. I wish you'd believe me. In the spring, after the baby is born, maybe we can return to the Circle S, if that's what you really want to do. But I'm perfectly content here. In fact, I've never felt so happy." When she passed the pad of her thumb across Hawk's lips, he kissed it. "Truly. I have never been so happy."

Hawk bent to kiss his wife.

"Are you two kissing again?" Buttercup teased.

Hawk shot his sister a comically stern look and replied, "There's going to come a day when I'll disturb you every time you try to kiss the person you love, then we'll see how funny you think it is."

"Enough now, both of you," Amanda interrupted, enjoying the almost continual banter between brother and sister.

They were her family now, and soon there would be another addition, a beautiful child who would bring peace to the land that had known little peace in many years.

About the Author

Robin Gideon is the author of numerous novels and novellas. Now an exclusive Totally Bound author, she will soon be writing a contemporary ménage series taking place in London, and is also releasing 100k+ word historicals. She was born in North Dakota (USA) and now lives, with her husband and daughter, on the Canadian border in Minnesota (USA).

Robin Gideon loves to hear from readers. You can find her contact information, website details and author profile page at http://www.totallybound.com.

Totally Bound Publishing

Home of Erotic Romance